Italian Fantasies by Israel Zangwill

Israel Zangwill was born in London on 21st January 1864, to a family of Jewish immigrants from the Russian Empire.

Zangwill was initially educated in Plymouth and Bristol. At age 9 he was enrolled in the Jews' Free School in Spitalfields in east London. Zangwill excelled here. He began to teach part-time at the school and eventually full time. Whilst teaching he also studied with the University of London and by 1884 had earned his BA with triple honours in philosophy, history, and the sciences.

His writing earned him the sobriquet "the Dickens of the Ghetto" primarily based on his much lauded novel 'Children of the Ghetto: A Study of a Peculiar People' in 1892 and its glimpse of the poverty-stricken life in London's Jewish quarter.

As a writer he was keen to reflect on his political and social outlooks. His simulation of Yiddish sentence structure in English aroused great interest. His mystery work, 'The Big Bow Mystery' (1892) was the first locked room mystery novel.

Zangwill was also involved with narrowly focused Jewish issues as an assimilationist, an early Zionist, and later a territorialist. In the early 1890s he had joined the Lovers of Zion movement in England. In 1897 he joined Theodor Herzl (considered the father of modern political Zionism) in founding the World Zionist Organization.

Zangwill quit the established philosophy of Zionism when his plan for a homeland in Uganda was rejected and founded his own organisation; the Jewish Territorialist Organization. Its stated goal was to create a Jewish homeland in whatever territory in the world could be found for them.

Amongst the challenges in his life he found time to write poetry. He had translated a medieval Jewish poet in 1903 and his volume 'Blind Children' in 1908 shows his promise in this new endeavour.

'The Melting Pot' in 1909 made Zangwill's name as an admired playwright. When the play opened in Washington D.C., former President Theodore Roosevelt leaned over the edge of his box and shouted, "That's a great play, Mr. Zangwill, that's a great play."

Israel Zangwill died on 1st August 1926 in Midhurst, West Sussex.

Index of Contents

OF BEAUTY, FAITH, AND DEATH: A RHAPSODY BY WAY OF PRELUDE

I too have crossed the Alps, and Hannibal himself had no such baggage of dreams and memories, such fife-and-drum of lyrics, such horns of ivory, such emblazoned standards and streamered gonfalons, flying and fluttering, such phalanxes of heroes, such visions of cities to spoil and riches to rifle—palace and temple, bust and picture, tapestry and mosaic. My elephants too matched his; my herds of mediæval histories, grotesque as his gargoyled beasts. Nor without fire and vinegar have I pierced my passage to these green pastures. "Ave Italia, regina terrarum!" I cried, as I kissed the hem of thy blue robe, starred with white cities.

There are who approach Italy by other portals, but these be the true gates of heaven, these purple peaks snow-flashing as they touch the stainless sky; scarred and riven with ancient fires, and young with jets of living water. Nature's greatness prepares the heart for man's glory.

I too have crossed the Rubicon, and Cæsar gathered no such booty. Gold and marble and sardonyx, lapis-lazuli, agate and alabaster, porphyry, jasper and bronze, these were the least of my spoils. I plucked at the mystery of the storied land and fulfilled my eyes of its loveliness and colour. I have seen the radiant raggedness of Naples as I squeezed in the squirming, wriggling ant-heap; at Paestum I have companied the lizard in the forsaken Temple of Poseidon. (O the soaring Pagan pillars, divinely Doric!) I have stood by the Leaning Tower in Bologna that gave a simile to Dante; and by the long low wall of Padua's university, whence Portia borrowed her learned plumes, I have stayed to scan a placarded sonnet to a Doctor of Philology; I have walked along that delectable Riviera di Levante and left a footprint on those wind-swept sands where Shelley's mortal elements found their fit resolution in flame. I have lain under Boccaccio's olives, and caressed with my eye the curve of the distant Duomo and the winding silver of the Arno. Florence has shown me supreme earth-beauty, Venice supreme water-beauty, and I have worshipped Capri and Amalfi, offspring of the love-marriage of earth and water.

O sacredness of sky and sun! Receive me, ye priests of Apollo. I am for lustrations and white robes, that I may kneel in the dawn to the Sun-God. Let me wind in the procession through the olive groves. For what choking Christian cities have we exchanged the lucid Pagan hill-towns? Behold the idolatrous smoke rising to Mammon from the factory altars of Christendom. We have sacrificed our glad sense of the world-miracle to worldly miracles of loaves and fishes. Grasping after the unseen, we have lost the divinity of the seen. Ah me! shall we ever recapture that first lyric rapture?

O consecration of the purifying dawn, O flame on the eastern altar, what cathedral rose-window can replace thee? O trill of the lark, soaring sunward, O swaying of May boughs and opening of flower chalices, what tinkling of bells and swinging of censers can bring us nearer the divine mystery? What are our liturgies but borrowed emotions, grown cold in the passing and staled by use—an anthology for apes!

But I wrong the ape. Did not an Afric explorer—with more insight than most, albeit a woman—tell me how even an ape in the great virgin forests will express by solemn capers some sense of the glory and freshness of the morning, his glimmering reason struggling towards spiritual consciousness, and moving him to dance his wonder and adoration? Even so the Greek danced his way to religion and the drama. Alas for the ape's degenerate cousin, the townsman shot to business through a tube!

I grant him that the shortest distance between two points is a straight line, yet 'tis with the curve that beauty commences. Your crow is the scientific flier, and a dismal bird it is. Who would demand an austere, unbending route 'twixt Sorrento and Amalfi instead of the white road that winds and winds round that great amphitheatre of hills, doubling on itself as in a mountain duet, and circumvoluting again and yet again, till the intertangled melody of peaks becomes a great choral burst, and all the hills sing as in the Psalmist, crag answering crag! Do you grow impatient when chines yawn at your feet and to skirt them the road turns inland half a mile, bringing you back on the other side of the chasm, as to your mere starting-point? Do you crave for an iron-trestled American bridge to span the gap? Nay; science is the shortest distance between two points, but beauty, like art, is long.

What is this haste to arrive? Give me to walk and walk those high paths hung 'twixt mountain and sea: the green wild grass, with its dots of daisy and dandelion; cactus and asphodel overhanging from the mountain-side, figs, olives, vines, sloping in terraced patches to the sea, which through bronze leafy tunnels shows blue and sparkling at the base of contorted cliffs. A woman's singing comes up from the green and grey tangle of gnarled trunks, and mingles with the sweet piping of the birds. A brown man moves amid the furrows. A sybil issues from a pass, leaning on her staff, driving a pair of goats, her head swathed in a great white handkerchief. I see that the Italian painters have copied their native landscape as well as their fellow men and women, though they pictured Palestine or Hellas or the land of faery. Not from inner fancy did Dosso Dossi create that glamorous background for his Circe. That sunny enchantment, that redolence of mediæval romaunt, exhales from many a haunting spot in these castled crags. Not from mere technical ingenuity did the artists of the Annunciation and other sacred indoor subjects introduce in their composition the spaces of the outer world shining through doors or windows or marble porticoes, vistas of earthly loveliness fusing with the holy beauty. Geology is here the handmaiden of Art and Theology. The painters found these effects to hand, springing from the structure of cities set upon ridges, as in a humble smithy of Siena whose entrance is in a street, but whose back, giving upon a sheer precipice, admits the wide purpureal landscape; or in that church in Perugia, dominating the Umbrian valley, where the gloom of the Old Masters in the dim chapel is suddenly broken by the sunlit spaciousness of an older Master, framed in a little window. Do you wonder that the

Perugian Pintoricchio would not let his St. Jerome preach to a mere crowded interior, or that the Umbrian school is from the first alive to the spirit of space? Such pictures Italy makes for us not only from interiors, but from wayside peep-holes, from clefts in the rock or gaps in the greenery. The country, dark with cypresses or gleaming with domes and campaniles, everywhere composes itself into a beautiful harmony; one needs not eye-points of vantage. The peep-hole simply fixes one's point of view, frames the scene in one's horizon of vision, and suggests by its enhancement of Nature the true task of Art in unifying a sprawling chaos of phenomena. And if to disengage the charm of space, Raphael and Perugino and Francia and even Mariotto Albertinelli make such noble use of the arch, was it not that its lovely limitation and definition of the landscape had from early Roman antiquity been revealed by Architecture? Arches and perspectives of arches, cloisters and colonnades, were weaving a rhythm of space round the artists in their daily walks. Where Nature was beautiful and Art was second Nature, the poets in paint were made as well as born.

Paradox-mongers have exalted Art above Nature, yet what pen or brush could reproduce Amalfi—that vibrant atmosphere, that shimmer and flicker of clouds, sunshine, and water; the ruined tower on the spit, the low white town, the crescent hills beyond, the blue sky bending over all as over a great glimmering cup? Beethoven, who wrote always with visual images in his mind, might have rendered it in another art, transposing it into the key of music; for is not beauty as mutable as energy, and what were the music of the spheres but the translation of their shining infinitude?

Truer indeed such translation into singing sound than into the cacophonies of speech, particularly of scientific speech.

I saw a great angel's wing floating over Rimini, its swan-like feathers spread with airy grace across the blue—but I must call it cirrus clouds, forsooth—ruffling themselves on a firmament of illusion. We name a thing and lo! its wonder flies, as in those profound myths where all goes well till scientific curiosity comes to mar happiness. Psyche turns the light on Cupid, Elsa must know Lohengrin's name. With what subtle instinct the Hebrew refused to pronounce the name of his deity! A name persuades that the unseizable is seized, that leviathan is drawn out with a hook. "Who is this that darkeneth counsel by words without knowledge?" Primitive man projected his soul into trees and stones—animism the wise it call—but we would project into man the soullessness of stones and trees. Finding no soul in Nature, we would rob even man of his, desperately disintegrating it back to mechanic atoms. The savage lifted Nature up to himself; we would degrade ourselves to Nature. For scientific examination read unscientific ex-animation. And now 'tis the rare poet and artist for whom river and tree incarnate themselves in nymphs and dryads. Your Böcklin painfully designs the figures once created by the painless mythopoiesis of the race; your Kipling strives to breathe back life into ships and engines. As philosophy is but common sense by a more circuitous route, so may Art be self-conscious savagery. And herein lies perhaps the true inwardness of the Psyche legend. The soul exchanges the joys of naïveté for the travails of self-consciousness, but in the end wins back its simple happiness, more stably founded. Yet, so read, the myth needs the supplement of an even earlier phase—it might well have occupied a spandrel at least in those delicious decorations for the ceiling of the Villa Farnesina that Raphael drew from the fable of Apuleius—in which Psyche, innocent of the corporeal Cupid, should dream of Amor. For me at least the ecstasy of vision has never equalled the enchantment of the visionary. O palm and citron, piously waved and rustled by my father at the Feast of Tabernacles, you brought to my grey garret the whisper and aroma of the sun-land. (Prate not of your Europes and Asias; these be no true geographic cuts; there is but a sun-life and an ice-life, and the grey life of the neutral zones.) But the solidities cannot vie with the airy fantasies. Where is the magic morning-freshness that lay upon the dream-city? Dawn cannot bring it, though it lay its consecrating gold upon the still lagoons of a sea-city, or upon the flower-stones of a

Doge's palace. Poets who have sung best of soils and women have not always known them: the pine has dreamed of the palm, and the palm of the pine.

"Heard melodies are sweet, but those unheard . . ." Ah, those unheard! Were it not better done—as poets use—never to sport with Beatrice in the shade, nor with the tangles of loved Laura's hair? Shall Don Quixote learn that Dulcinea del Toboso is but a good, likely country lass? I would not marry the sea with a ring, no, not for all the gold and purple of the Bucentaur. What should a Doge of dreams be doing in that galley? To wed the sea—and know its mystery but petulance, its unfathomed caves only the haunt of crude polypi; no mermaids, no wild witchery, and pearls but a disease of the oyster!

Mayhap I had been wiser to keep my Italian castles in Spain than to render myself obnoxious to the penalties of the actual. Rapacity, beggary, superstition, hover over the loveliness of the land like the harpies and evil embodiments in Ambrogio Lorenzetti's homely Allegory of Bad Government in the Sala della Pace of Siena. To-day that fourteenth-century cartoonist would have found many a new episode for his frescoed morality-play, whereof the ground-plot would run: how, to be a Great Power with martial pride of place, Italy sacrifices the substance. Incalculably rich in art, her every village church bursting with masterpieces beyond the means of millionaires, she hugs her treasures to her ragged bosom with one skinny hand, the other extended for alms. Adorable Brother Francis of Assisi, with thy preachment of "holy poverty," didst thou never suspect there could be an unholy poverty? 'Tis parlous, this beatitude of beggary. More bandits bask at thy shrine than at almost any other spot in Christendom. Where the pilgrims are, there the paupers are gathered together; there must be rich prey in those frenzied devotees who crawl up thy chapel, licking its rough stones smooth. Thou hadst no need of food: if two small loaves were provided for thy forty days' Lent in that island in the Lake of Perugia, one and a half remained uneaten; and even if half a loaf seemed better to thee than no bread, 'twas merely because the few mouthfuls chased far from thee the venom of a vainglorious copy of thy Master. Perchance 'tis from some such humility the beggars of Assisi abstain from a too emulous copy of thee. Thou didst convert thy brother, the fierce wolf of Agobio, and give the countryside peace, but what of this pack of wolves thou hast loosed—in sheep's clothing! With what joy did I see in a church at Verona an old barefoot, naked-kneed beggar, who was crouching against a pillar, turn into marble!

Or shall we figure Italia's beggars as her mosquitos, inevitable accompaniment of her beauties? The mosquito-mendicant, come he as cripple or cicerone, buzzes ever in one's ears, foe to meditation and enkindlement. Figure me seeking refuge in a Palazzo of once imperial Genoa; treading pensively the chambers of Youth and Life, the Arts, and the Four Seasons, through which duchesses and marchese had trailed silken skirts. With gaze uplifted at the painted ceilings, I ponder on that magnificence of the world and the flesh which the Church could not wither—nay, which found consummate expression in the Pope's own church in St. Peter's, where the baldachino of twinkling lights supplies the one touch of religious poetry. I pass into the quiet library and am received by the venerable custodian, a Dr. Faustus in black skull-cap and white beard. He does the honours of his learned office, brings me precious Aldines. Behold this tome of antique poetry, silver-typed—a "limited edition," twenty-four copies made for the great families. He gloats with me over Ovid's "Metamorphoses"; over the fantasy of the title-page, the vignettes of nymphs and flowers, the spacious folio pages. Here is Homer in eight languages. My heart goes out to the scholarly figure as we bend over the parallel columns, bookworms both. I envy the gentle Friar of Letters his seclusion and his treasures. He lugs out a mediæval French manuscript, a poem on summer—"Saison aussi utile que belle," he adds unexpectedly. We discourse on manuscripts: of the third-century Virgil at Florence and its one missing leaf in the Vatican; how French manuscripts may be found as early as the tenth century, while the Italian scarcely precede Dante, and demonstrate his creation of the language. We laud the Benedictines for their loving labour in multiplying texts—he is wrought up to produce the apple of his eye, an illuminated manuscript that had belonged to a princess. It is bound in parchment, with golden clasps. "Figures de la Bible" I seem to remember on its ornate title-page. I bend lovingly over the quaint letters, I see the princess's white hand turning the polychrome pages, her lace sleeve ruffled exquisitely as in a Bronzino portrait. Suddenly Dr. Faustus ejaculates in English: "Give me a drink!"

My princess fled almost with a shriek, and I came back to the sordid Italy of to-day. Of to-day? Is not yesterday's glamour equally illusionary? But perhaps Genoa with her commercial genius is no typical daughter of Italia. Did not Dante and the Tuscan proverb alike denounce her? Does not to-day's proverb say that it takes ten Jews to make one Genoese? And yet it was Genoa that produced Mazzini and sped Garibaldi.

Would you wipe out this bookish memory by a better? Then picture the library of a monastery, that looks out on the cypressed hills, whose cloisters Sodoma and Signorelli frescoed with naïve legends of St. Benedict and Satan. See under the long low ceiling, propped on the cool white pillars, those niched rows of vellum bindings guarding the leisurely Latin lore of the Fathers. Behold me meditating the missals and pontificals, pageants in manuscript, broidered and illuminated, all glorious with gold initials and ultramarine and vermilion miniatures; or those folio processions of sacred music, each note pranked in its bravery and stepping statelily amid garlands of blue and gold and the hovering faces of angels; dreaming myself into that mystic peace of the Church, till the vesper bell calls to paternosters and genuflexions, and the great organ rolls out to drown this restless, anchorless century. Now am I for nones and primes, for vigils and sackcloth, for breviaries and holy obedience. In shady cloisters, mid faded frescoes, round sleepy rose-gardens, I will pace to papal measures, while the serene sun-dial registers the movement of the sun round the earth. Who speaks of a religion as though it were dependent upon its theology? Dogmas are but its outward show; inwardly and subtly it lives by its beauty, its atmosphere, its inracination in life, and its creed is but a poor attempt to put into words a thought too large for syllables, too elusive for phrases. Language is a net that catches the fish and lets the ocean stream through. Again that fallacy of the Name.

Beautiful I will call that service I saw at Bologna on Whitsun Sunday, though you must dive deep to find the beauty. Not in S. Petronio itself will you find it, in those bulbous pillars swathed in crimson damask, though there is a touch of it in the vastness, the far altar, the remote choir and surpliced priests on high, the great wax candle under the big baldachino, the congregation lost in space. Nor will you easily recognise it in the universal disorder, in that sense of a church parade within the church, in the brouhaha that drowns the precentor's voice, in the penny chairs planted or stacked as the worshippers ebb or flow, in the working men and their families sprawling over the altar-steps, in the old women coifed in coloured handkerchiefs, with baskets that hold bottles as well as prayer-books; not even in the pretty women in Parisian hats, or the olive-skinned girls in snoods, least of all in the child's red balloon, soaring to the roof at the very moment of the elevation of the Host, and followed with heavenward eyes by half the congregation. And yet there is no blasphemy even in the balloon; the child's innocent pleasure in its toy is mixed with its sense of holy festivity. There is no sharp contrast of sacred and secular. The church does not end with its portals; it extends into the great piazza. Nor do the crowds squatting on its steps in the sun, and seething in the square it dominates, feel themselves outside the service. The very pigeons seem to flutter with a sense of sacred holiday, as though they had just listened to the sermon of their big brother, St. Francis. The Church, like the radiant blue sky, is over all. And this is the genius of Catholicism.

Not without significance are those thirteenth-century legends in which even the birds and the fishes were brought into the fold universal, as into a spiritual Noah's Ark, all equally in need of salvation. Some of the Apostles themselves were mere fishers, spreading no metaphoric net. What an evolution to St. Antony, who wins the finny tribes to reverence and dismisses them with the divine blessing! Even the horses are blessed in Rome on St. Antony's Day, or in his name at Siena before the great race for the Palio, each runner sprinkled in the church of its ward.

To think that missionaries go forth to preach verbal propositions violently torn from the life and the historic enchainment and the art and the atmosphere! If they would but stay at home and reform the words, which must ever change, so as to preserve the beauty, which must never die! For words must change, if only to counterbalance their own mutations and colourings, their declines and falls. They are no secure envelope for immortal truths: I would as lief embody my fortunes in a paper currency. Let the religion of the future be writ only in music—Palestrina's or Allegri's, Bach's or Wagner's, as you will—so that no heresies can spring from verbal juggles, distorted texts, or legal quibbles. And yet—would the harmony be unbroken? What quarrels over misprinted sharps and naturals! How the doctors of music would disagree on the tempo and the phrasing and burn and excommunicate for a dotted semibreve! What Church Councils—the pianissimo party versus the fortissimo, legato legions and staccato squadrons, the Holy Wars of Harmony—all Christian history da capo!

I like that gracious tolerance of humanism you find in some Renaissance pictures, those composite portraits of ideas, in which Pagan and Christian types and periods mingle in the higher synthesis of conception—or perhaps even in a happy inconsistence of dual belief. Raphael could not represent the conflagration in the Borgo that was extinguished by papal miracle without consecrating a corner of his work to the piety of Æneas, carrying Anchises on his back in a parallel moment of peril. Raphael's work is, in fact, almost a series of illustrations of the Sposalizio of Hebraism and Hellenism. That library of Julius II in the Vatican may stand as the scene of their union. Beyond the true Catholicism of its immortal frescoes humanism cannot go. If the Theology is mainly confined to Biblical concepts and figures, it is supplemented by Perino del Vaga's picture of the Cumæan Sybil showing the Madonna to Augustus, which is at least a dovetailing of the divided worlds and eras. And if to explain the parity of Sybils with prophets in the designs of Michelangelo you call in those Fathers of the Church who found Christology in the old Sybilline leaves and have coupled David and the Sybil in the Catholic funeral service, you must admit a less dubious largeness in Raphael's cartoons for the dome mosaics in the Cappella Chigi of Santa Maria del Popolo; for to group the gods of Hellas round the Creator and His angels, even by an astronomic device involving their names for the planets, shows a mood very far removed from that of the Christians who went to the lions in this very Rome. (The consistent Christian mood is seen in the Quaker's avoidance of the heathen names of our days and months, mere bald numeration replacing the Norse and Roman divinities.) Moreover, Raphael's Parnassus is almost wholly to the glory of ancient Greece and Rome. It is Dante and Petrarch who are honoured by neighbouring Homer and Virgil. It is the violin that is glorified by Apollo's playing upon it. Anachronism if you will. But Art may choose to see history sub specie æternitatis, and surely in Plato's heaven rests the archetypal violin, to which your Stradivarius or Guarnerius is a banjo.

Nor has antiquity ever received a nobler tribute than in The School of Athens, that congregation of Pagan philosophers to which the Dukes of Urbino and Mantua repair, to which Raphael himself brings his teacher, while Bramante, builder of St. Peter's, is proud to adorn the train of Aristotle. See, too, under the ceiling-painting of Justice, how Moses bringing the tables of the Law to the Israelites is supplemented by Justinian giving the Pandects to Tritonian. Thus is Justice more subtly illustrated than perhaps the painter consciously designed. How finely—if even more paradoxically—this temper repeats itself later in the English Puritan and Italian sonneteer, Milton, whose "Lycidas" vibrates 'twixt the Classic and the Christian, and whose very epic of Hebraism is saturated with catholic allusiveness, and embraces that stately panegyric of

"Athens, the eye of Greece, mother of arts
And eloquence."

Why, indeed, quarrel over religions when all men agree; all men, that is, at the same grade of intellect! The learned busy themselves classifying religions—there are reviews at Paris and Tübingen—but in the crude working world religion depends less on the belief than on the believer. All the simplest minds believe alike, be they Confucians or Christians, Jews or Fantees. The elemental human heart will have its thaumaturgic saints, its mapped hells, its processional priests, its prompt answers to prayer, and if deprived of them will be found subtly to reintroduce them. Mohammed and the Koran forbade the worship of saints, yet the miracles and mediations of the walis and the pilgrimages to their tombs—with Mohammed himself as arch-wali—are inseparable from Islam. The Buddha who came to teach a holy atheism was made a god, the proclaimer of natural law a miracle-monger, his revolution turned into a revolution of prayer-wheels and his religion into the High Church Romanism of Lamaism. The Hebrew Torah which cried anathema on idols became itself an idol, swathed in purple, adorned with golden bells, and borne round like a Madonna for reverent kisses. The Madonna herself, overgrown with the roses of a wayside shrine, perpetuates the worship of Flora. On the very gates of St. Peter's, Europa, Ganymede, and Leda show their brazen faces. Not Confucius nor Christ can really expel devils. What grosser idolatry than the worship of those dressed wax dolls which make many an Italian church like a theological Madame Tussaud's! The Church has its Chamber of Horrors too, its blood and nails and saintly skulls; the worship of Moloch was not more essentially morbid. At the base of the intellectual mountain flourishes rank and gorgeous vegetation, a tropic luxuriance; higher up, in the zone of mediocrity, there are cultivated temperate slopes and pruned gardens, pleasant pastures and ordered bowers; at the snowy summits, in the rarefied æther, flash white the glacial impersonal truths, barely a tuft of moss or lichen. Hark! peak is crying unto peak: "Thy will be done."

But what is this new voice—comes it from the mole-hills?—"Our will be done." See—in the mask of the highest Christianity and science—the old thaumaturgy creeping in, though now every man is his own saint, healing his own diseases, denying death with a Podsnappian wave o' the hand. O my friends, get ye to the Eternal City—that canvas for the flying panorama of races and creeds—and peep into a coffin in the Capitoline Museum, and see the skeleton of the Etruscan girl, with rings glittering on her bony fingers, and bracelets on her fleshless wrists, and her doll at her side, in ironic preservation, its blooming cheeks and sparkling eyes mocking the eyeless occiput of its mistress. Even so shall your hugged treatises and your glittering gospels show among your bones. Do you not know that death is the very condition of life—bound up with it as darkness with light? How trivial the thought that sees death but in the cemetery! 'Tis not only the grave that parts us from our comrades and lovers; we lose them on the way. Lose them not only by quarrel and estrangement, but by evolution and retrogression. They broaden or narrow away from us, and we from them; they are changed, other, transformed, dead and risen again. Woe for the orphans of living parents, the widowers of undeceased wives! Our early Ego dies by inches, till, like the perpetually darned sock, it retains nothing but the original mould and shaping. Let us read the verse more profoundly: "In the midst of life we are in death." Whoever dies in the full tilt of his ambitions is buried alive, and whoever survives his hopes and fears is dead, unburied. Death for us is all we have missed, all the periods and planets we have not lived in, all the countries we have not visited, all the books we have not read, all the emotions and experiences we have not had, all the prayers we have not prayed, all the battles we have not fought. Every restriction, every negation, is a piece of death. Not wholly has popular idiom ignored this truth. "Dead to higher things," it says; but we may be dead too to the higher mathematics. Death for the individual is the whole universe outside his consciousness, and life but the tiny blinking light of consciousness. But between the light and the dark is perpetual interplay, and we turn dark to light and let light subside to dark as our thoughts and feelings veer this way or that.

And since 'tis complexity of consciousness that counts, and the death of the amœba or the unborn babe is less a decomposition than the death of a man, so is the death of a philosopher vaster than the death of a peasant. We have but one word for the drying up of an ocean and the drying up of a pool. And the sediment, the clay that we bury, wherefore do we still label it with the living name? As if Cæsar might truly stop a bung-hole! Mark Antony might come to praise Cæsar; he could not bury him.

Here lies Mazzini forsooth! As if that spirit of white fire could rest even on the farthest verge of thee, O abominable Campo Santo of Genoa, with thy central rotunda pillared with black marble, thy spires and Grecian buildings, thy Oriental magnificence, redeemed only by the natural hills in which thou nestlest. Are our ashes indeed so grandiose and spectacular a thing? Or art thou a new terror added to death? From thy haughty terrace—whereon Death himself in black marble fights with a desperate woman—I have gazed down upon thy four parallelograms, bounded by cypresses and starred with great daisies, that seen nearer are white crosses, and a simple contadina lighting the lamp for her beloved dead alone softens the scene. O the endless statuary of the gallery, the arcades of slabs and reliefs, the faded wreaths, or those drearier beads that never fade!—I could pray to the Madonna whose blue and gold halo shines over thy dead to send a baby earthquake to swallow thee up.

Away with these cemeteries of stone, this frigid pomp of death, that clings on to life even while spouting texts of resignation! Who cares for these parish chronicles, these parallelograms of good people that lived and fell on sleep, these worthy citizens and fond spouses. Horrid is that clasp of intertwined hands. I could chop at those fingers with an axe. 'Tis indecent, this graveyard flirtation. Respect your privacy, good skeletons! Ye too, couples of the Etruscan catacombs, who dash our spirits from your urns, to what end your graven images outside your incinerated relics? Not in marmoreal mausolea, nor in railed-off tombs, with knights and dames couchant, not in Medici chapels nor in the florid monuments of Venetian Doges, not in the columbaria of the Via Appia nor in the Gothic street-tombs of the Scaliger princes, resides death's true dignity—they are the vain apery of life—but in some stoneless, flowerless grave where only the humped earth tells that here lies the husk of one gathered into the vastness of oblivion.

There are times when one grows impatient for death. There is a sweetness in being gathered to one's fathers. The very phrase is restful. Dying sounds more active; it recalls doing, and one is so tired of doing. But to be culled softly, to be sucked up—the very vapour of the Apostle—how balmily passive: to be wafted into the quiet Past, which robs even fame of its sting, and wherein lie marshalled and sorted and ticketed and dated, in stately dictionaries and monumental encyclopædias, all those noisy poets, painters, warriors, all neatly classified and silent. And the sweet silence of the grave allures even after the bitter silence of life; after the silent endurance that is our one reply to the insolence of facts. And in these delicate, seductive moments, half longing, half acquiescence, the air is tremulous with tender, crooning phrases, with gentle, wistful melodies, the hush-a-bye of the earth-mother drawing us softly to her breast.

But an you will not acquiesce in simple earth-to-earth, I commend you to the Greek sarcophagi you may see in the Naples Museum. There you will find no smirking sentiment, no skull and cross-bones—ensign of Pirate Death—but the very joy of life, ay, even a Bacchanalian gladness. I recall a radiant procession,

Not without significance are those thirteenth-century legends in which even the birds and the fishes were brought into the fold universal, as into a spiritual Noah's Ark, all equally in need of salvation. Some of the Apostles themselves were mere fishers, spreading no metaphoric net. What an evolution to St. Antony, who wins the finny tribes to reverence and dismisses them with the divine blessing! Even the horses are blessed in Rome on St. Antony's Day, or in his name at Siena before the great race for the Palio, each runner sprinkled in the church of its ward.

To think that missionaries go forth to preach verbal propositions violently torn from the life and the historic enchainment and the art and the atmosphere! If they would but stay at home and reform the words, which must ever change, so as to preserve the beauty, which must never die! For words must change, if only to counterbalance their own mutations and colourings, their declines and falls. They are no secure envelope for immortal truths: I would as lief embody my fortunes in a paper currency. Let the religion of the future be writ only in music—Palestrina's or Allegri's, Bach's or Wagner's, as you will—so that no heresies can spring from verbal juggles, distorted texts, or legal quibbles. And yet—would the harmony be unbroken? What quarrels over misprinted sharps and naturals! How the doctors of music would disagree on the tempo and the phrasing and burn and excommunicate for a dotted semibreve! What Church Councils—the pianissimo party versus the fortissimo, legato legions and staccato squadrons, the Holy Wars of Harmony—all Christian history da capo!

I like that gracious tolerance of humanism you find in some Renaissance pictures, those composite portraits of ideas, in which Pagan and Christian types and periods mingle in the higher synthesis of conception—or perhaps even in a happy inconsistence of dual belief. Raphael could not represent the conflagration in the Borgo that was extinguished by papal miracle without consecrating a corner of his work to the piety of Æneas, carrying Anchises on his back in a parallel moment of peril. Raphael's work is, in fact, almost a series of illustrations of the Sposalizio of Hebraism and Hellenism. That library of Julius II in the Vatican may stand as the scene of their union. Beyond the true Catholicism of its immortal frescoes humanism cannot go. If the Theology is mainly confined to Biblical concepts and figures, it is supplemented by Perino del Vaga's picture of the Cumæan Sybil showing the Madonna to Augustus, which is at least a dovetailing of the divided worlds and eras. And if to explain the parity of Sybils with prophets in the designs of Michelangelo you call in those Fathers of the Church who found Christology in the old Sybilline leaves and have coupled David and the Sybil in the Catholic funeral service, you must admit a less dubious largeness in Raphael's cartoons for the dome mosaics in the Cappella Chigi of Santa Maria del Popolo; for to group the gods of Hellas round the Creator and His angels, even by an astronomic device involving their names for the planets, shows a mood very far removed from that of the Christians who went to the lions in this very Rome. (The consistent Christian mood is seen in the Quaker's avoidance of the heathen names of our days and months, mere bald numeration replacing the Norse and Roman divinities.) Moreover, Raphael's Parnassus is almost wholly to the glory of ancient Greece and Rome. It is Dante and Petrarch who are honoured by neighbouring Homer and Virgil. It is the violin that is glorified by Apollo's playing upon it. Anachronism if you will. But Art may choose to see history sub specie æternitatis, and surely in Plato's heaven rests the archetypal violin, to which your Stradivarius or Guarnerius is a banjo.

Nor has antiquity ever received a nobler tribute than in The School of Athens, that congregation of Pagan philosophers to which the Dukes of Urbino and Mantua repair, to which Raphael himself brings his teacher, while Bramante, builder of St. Peter's, is proud to adorn the train of Aristotle. See, too, under the ceiling-painting of Justice, how Moses bringing the tables of the Law to the Israelites is supplemented by Justinian giving the Pandects to Tritonian. Thus is Justice more subtly illustrated than perhaps the painter consciously designed. How finely—if even more paradoxically—this temper repeats itself later in the English Puritan and Italian sonneteer, Milton, whose "Lycidas" vibrates 'twixt the Classic and the Christian, and whose very epic of Hebraism is saturated with catholic allusiveness, and embraces that stately panegyric of

"Athens, the eye of Greece, mother of arts
And eloquence."

Why, indeed, quarrel over religions when all men agree; all men, that is, at the same grade of intellect! The learned busy themselves classifying religions—there are reviews at Paris and Tübingen—but in the crude working world religion depends less on the belief than on the believer. All the simplest minds believe alike, be they Confucians or Christians, Jews or Fantees. The elemental human heart will have its thaumaturgic saints, its mapped hells, its processional priests, its prompt answers to prayer, and if deprived of them will be found subtly to reintroduce them. Mohammed and the Koran forbade the worship of saints, yet the miracles and mediations of the walis and the pilgrimages to their tombs—with Mohammed himself as arch-wali—are inseparable from Islam. The Buddha who came to teach a holy atheism was made a god, the proclaimer of natural law a miracle-monger, his revolution turned into a revolution of prayer-wheels and his religion into the High Church Romanism of Lamaism. The Hebrew Torah which cried anathema on idols became itself an idol, swathed in purple, adorned with golden bells, and borne round like a Madonna for reverent kisses. The Madonna herself, overgrown with the roses of a wayside shrine, perpetuates the worship of Flora. On the very gates of St. Peter's, Europa, Ganymede, and Leda show their brazen faces. Not Confucius nor Christ can really expel devils. What grosser idolatry than the worship of those dressed wax dolls which make many an Italian church like a theological Madame Tussaud's! The Church has its Chamber of Horrors too, its blood and nails and saintly skulls; the worship of Moloch was not more essentially morbid. At the base of the intellectual mountain flourishes rank and gorgeous vegetation, a tropic luxuriance; higher up, in the zone of mediocrity, there are cultivated temperate slopes and pruned gardens, pleasant pastures and ordered bowers; at the snowy summits, in the rarefied æther, flash white the glacial impersonal truths, barely a tuft of moss or lichen. Hark! peak is crying unto peak: "Thy will be done."

But what is this new voice—comes it from the mole-hills?—"Our will be done." See—in the mask of the highest Christianity and science—the old thaumaturgy creeping in, though now every man is his own saint, healing his own diseases, denying death with a Podsnappian wave o' the hand. O my friends, get ye to the Eternal City—that canvas for the flying panorama of races and creeds—and peep into a coffin in the Capitoline Museum, and see the skeleton of the Etruscan girl, with rings glittering on her bony fingers, and bracelets on her fleshless wrists, and her doll at her side, in ironic preservation, its blooming cheeks and sparkling eyes mocking the eyeless occiput of its mistress. Even so shall your hugged treatises and your glittering gospels show among your bones. Do you not know that death is the very condition of life—bound up with it as darkness with light? How trivial the thought that sees death but in the cemetery! 'Tis not only the grave that parts us from our comrades and lovers; we lose them on the way. Lose them not only by quarrel and estrangement, but by evolution and retrogression. They broaden or narrow away from us, and we from them; they are changed, other, transformed, dead and risen again. Woe for the orphans of living parents, the widowers of undeceased wives! Our early Ego dies by inches, till, like the perpetually darned sock, it retains nothing but the original mould and shaping. Let us read the verse more profoundly: "In the midst of life we are in death." Whoever dies in the full tilt of his ambitions is buried alive, and whoever survives his hopes and fears is dead, unburied. Death for us is all we have missed, all the periods and planets we have not lived in, all the countries we have not visited, all the books we have not read, all the emotions and experiences we have not had, all the prayers we have not prayed, all the battles we have not fought. Every restriction, every negation, is touch swallowed up in the mouldering ruggedness, the houses at the base merely burrowed, the abodes of cave-dwellers.

II

I saw the sea-serpent at Naples, though not in the Aquarium. Its colossal bulk was humped sinuously along the bay. 'Twas the Vesuvius range, stretching mistily. Mariners have perchance constructed the monster from such hazy glimpses of distant reefs. Still, no dragon has wrought more havoc than this mountain, which smokes imperturbably while the generations rise and fall. Beautiful the smoke, too, when it grows golden in the setting sun, and the monstrous mass turns a marvellous purple. We wonder men should still build on Vesuvius—betwixt the devil and the deep sea—yet the chances of eruption are no greater than the chances of epidemic in less salubrious places, as the plague-churches of Italy testify.

But should a new eruption overwhelm Pompeii, and its first record be lost, there were a strange puzzle for the antiquarians of the fiftieth century exhuming its cosmopolitan population; blonde German savages in white pot-hats, ancient Britons in tweeds, extinct American cycle-centaurs; incongruously resident amid the narrow streets and wide public buildings of a prehistoric Roman civilisation.

Pompeii is buried some twenty feet deep. The Middle Ages walked over these entombed streets and temples and suspected nothing. But all towns are built on their dead past, for earth's crust renews itself as incessantly as our own skin. We walk over our ancestors. There are twenty-seven layers of human life at Rome.

It needs no earth-convulsions, no miracles of lava. One generation of cities succeeds another. Nature, a pious Andromache, covers up their remains as softly as the snow falls or the grass grows. When man uncovers them again, he finds stratum below stratum, city below city, as though the whole were some quaint American structure of many storeys which the earth had swallowed at a single gulp, and not with her stately deglutition. At Gezer in Palestine Macalister has been dissecting a tumulus which holds layers of human history as the rocks hold layers of earth-history. Scratch the mound and you find the traces of an Arab city, slice deeper and 'tis a Crusaders' city; an undercut brings you to the Roman city whence— by another short cut—you descend to the Old Testament; to the city that was dowered to Solomon's Egyptian Queen, to the Philistine city, and so to the Canaanite city. But even here Gezer is but at its prime. You have sunk through all the Christian era, through all the Jewish era, but fifteen centuries still await your descent. Down you delve—through the city captured by Thotmes III, through the city of the early Semites, till at last your pick strikes the Hivites and the Amorites, the cave-men of the primitive Gezer. Infinitely solemn such a tumulus in its imperturbable chronicling, with its scarabs and altars, its spear-heads and its gods, the bones of its foundation-sacrifices yet undecayed. The Judgment Books need no celestial clerks, no recording angels; earth keeps them as she rolls. In our eyes, too, as we gaze upon this ant-heap of our breed, a thousand years are but as a day—nay, as a dream that passeth in the night. We are such stuff as dreams are made on, and our little life is rounded with a mound. Beside Gezer, Pompeii and Herculaneum are theatrical, flamboyant, the creatures of a day, the parvenus of the underworld.

Mentally, too, strange ancestral strata lie in our deeps, even as the remains of an alimentary canal run through our spine and a primitive eye lies in the middle of our brain—that pineal gland in which Descartes located the soul. Sometimes we stumble over an old prejudice or a primitive emotion, prick ourselves with an arrow of ancestral conscience, and tremble with an ancient fear. Mayhap in slumber we descend to these regions, exploring below our consciousness and delving in the catacombs of antiquity.

The destruction of Pompeii was effected, however, not by Vesuvius, but by the antiquarian. He it was to whom Pompeii fell as a spoil, he who turned Pompeii from a piece of life to a piece of learning, by transporting most of its treasures to a museum. The word is surely short for mausoleum. For objects in a museum are dead, their relations with life ended. Objects partake of the lives of their possessors, and when cut off are as dead as finger-nails. A vase dominating the court of a Pompeian house and a vase in the Naples Museum are as a creature to its skeleton. What a stimulation in the one or two houses left with their living reality—their frescoes and their furniture, their kitchens and middens! 'Tis statues that suffer most from their arrangement in ghostly rows. A statue is an æsthetic climax, the crown of a summit, the close of a vista. See that sunlit statue of Meleager in the grounds of the Villa Medici, at the end of a green avenue, with pillar and architrave for background, and red and white roses climbing around it, and imagine how its glory would be shorn in a gallery. The French have remembered to put the Venus of Milo at the end of a long Louvre corridor, which she fills with her far-seen radiance. These collections of Capolavori—these Apollos and Jupiters, and Venuses and Muses, dumped as close as cemetery monuments—are indeed petrified. The fancy must resurrect them into their living relations with halls and courtyards, temples and piazzas, shrines and loggias. The learned begin to suspect that the polytheism of Greece and Rome is due to the analogous aggregation of local gods, each a self-sufficing and all-powerful divinity in its own district. When there were so many deities, their functions had to be differentiated, as we give a different shade of meaning to two words for the same thing. Were one to collect the many Madonnas in Italy, one might imagine Christianity as polytheistic as Paganism.

But the most perfect visualising of a god's statue in its local setting will not annul that half-death which sets in with the statue's loss of worship. These fair visions of Pallas and Juno, shall they ever touch us as they touched the pious Pagan? Nay, not all our sense of lovely line and spiritual grace can replace that departed touch of divinity.

The past has indeed its glamour for us, which serves perhaps as compensation for what we lose of the hot reality, but an inevitable impiety clings to our inquisitive regard, to our anxious exhumation of its secrets. Unless we go to it with our emotions as well as our intellect, prepared to extract its spiritual significance and to warm ourselves at the fire of its life and pour a libation to the gods of its hearth, a wilderness of archæological lore will profit us little. A man is other than his garments and a people than its outworn shell.

There is perhaps more method than appears at first sight in the madness of the Turk, who reluctantly permits the scientific explorer to dig up the past but insists that once he has unearthed his historic treasure, his buried streets and temples, ay, of old Jerusalem itself, he shall cover them up again. The dead past is to bury its dead. Death, whether in citizens or their cities, is sacred. Cursed be he who turns up their bones to the sun. And who will not sigh over the mummies, doomed to be served up in museums after five thousand years of dignified death? Princesses and potentates were they in their lives; how could they dream, as they were borne in their purpureal litters through the streets of the Pharaohs, that they would make a spectacle for barbarians on wet half-holidays? And thou, Timhotpu, prefect of the very Necropolis of Thebes in the eighteenth dynasty, how couldst thou suspect that even thy gilded sarcophagus would be violated, thy golden earrings wrenched off, thy mortuary furniture stolen, and thy fine figure exhibited to me in the Turin Museum, turned into a grey char under thy winding-sheet! The very eggs placed in the tombs of thy cemetery have kept their colour better: one feels that under heat they might still hatch a hieroglyphic chicken. But thou art for evermore desiccated and done with.

Saddest of all is the fate of the immortals: goddesses of the hearth and gods of the heaven are alike swept into the museum-limbo. They are shrunk to mythology, they who once charioted the constellations. For mythology dogs all theologies, and one god after another is put on the bookshelf.

All roads lead to the museum. Thither go our old clothes, our old coins, our old creeds, and we wonder that men should ever have worn steel armour or cast-iron dogmas. Gazing at the Pompeian man, that "cunning cast in clay," whose clutch at his money-bags survives his bodily investiture, who does not feel as one from another planet surveying an earth pygmy? What strange limited thoughts were thine, O Pompeian of the first century! I warrant thou hadst not even heard of the Man of Nazareth: how small thine atlas of the world, not to say thy chart of the heavens! Poor ignoramus—so unacquainted with all that hath happened since thy death! How wise and weighty thou wast at thy table, recumbent amidst thy roses, surrounded by those gay frescoes of Cupids and Venuses; with what self-satisfaction thou didst lay down the Roman law, garlanded as to thy narrow forehead!

But if 'tis easy to play the Superman with this fusty provincial, 'tis not hard to smell the museum must in our own living world. Too many people and things do not know they are essentially of the museum: have the arrogance to imagine they are contemporary. How full of life seems the cannon as it belches death! Yet 'tis but an uncouth, noisy creature, long since outgrown and outmoded among the humanised citizens of the planet; some day it will be hunted out like the wolf and the boar, with a price upon its mouth.

'Tis to the stage that extinct human types betake themselves by way of after-life—the theatre serving as the anthropological museum—but there are some that linger unconscionably on this side of the footlights. Bigots, for example, have an air of antediluvian bipeds, monstrous wildfowl that flap and shriek. I even gaze curiously at Gold Sticks and pages of the Presence. They are become spectacular, and to be spectacular is to be well on the way to the museum. Mistrust the spasmodic splendour—leap of the dying flame. Where traditions must be pored over, and performers rehearsed, it has become a play; is propped on precedent instead of uplifted by sap. The passion for ritual is one of the master-passions of humanity. Yet stage properties can never return to the world of reality. The profession will tell you that they are sold off to inferior theatres, never to the real world outside. What passes into the museum can never repass the janitor.

On the leaders of life lies in each generation the duty of establishing the museum-point. The museum-point in thought, art, morals. No matter that obsolete modes prevail in the vulgar world: do the ladies allow the mob to dictate their fashions? Hath a bonnet existence because it survives in Seven Dials or the Bowery? Is a creed alive because it flourishes in Little Bethel? Man is one vast being, and the thought of his higher nerve-centres alone counts: generation hands the torch to generation. Doubtless the lower ganglia are not always ready for the new conception. But such considerations belong to Politics, not to Truth. At the worst the map must be made while the march is preparing.

III

No object in the Naples Museum fascinates the philosophic mind more than Salpion's vase. Who was Salpion? I know not, though his once living hand signed his work, in bold sprawling letters,

ΣΑΛΠΙΩΝ ΑΘΗΝΑΙΟΣ ΕΠΟΙΗΣΕ

An Athenian made you, then, I muse, gazing upon its beautiful marble impassivity, and studying the alto-relievo of Mercury with his dancing train giving over the infant Bacchus to a seated nymph of Nysa. He who conceived you made you for sacrifices to Bacchus, lived among those white temples which the Greeks built for the adoration of their gods, but which remain for our adoration. He mounted that hill agleam with the marble pillars of immortal shrines, he passed the Areopagus, and the altar "to the unknown God"; he entered the Propylæa and gazed through the columns of the Acropolis upon the blue Ægean. He sat in that marmoreal amphitheatre and saw the mimes in sock and buskin take the proscenium to the sound of lyres and flutes. Perchance 'twas while seeing the Mercury fable treated in a choric dance in the sanded orchestra that he composed this grouping. Perhaps he but copied it from some play lost to us, for the Greek theatre, with its long declamations, had more analogy with sculpture than with our agitated drama of to-day. The legend itself is in Lucian and Apollonius. But Salpion is not the beginning of this vase's story. For the artist himself belonged to the Renaissance, the scholars say; not our Renaissance, but a neo-Attic. Salpion did but deftly reproduce the archaic traditions of the first great period of Greek sculpture. Even in those days men's thoughts turned yearningly to a nobler past, and the young prix de Rome who should find inspiration in Salpion would be but imitating an imitation. Nor is Athenian all the history this fair Attic shape has held. Much more we know, yet much is dim. In what palace or private atrium did it pass its first years? How did it travel to Italy? Was it exported thither by a Greek merchant to adorn the house of some rich provincial, or—more probably—the country seat of a noble Roman? For the ruins of Formiæ were the place of its discovery, and mayhap Cicero himself—the baths of whose villa some think to trace in the grounds of the Villa Caposele—was its whilom proprietor.

But, once recovered from the wrack of the antique world, it falls into indignity, more grievous than its long inhumation through the rise and fall of the mediæval world. It drifts, across fields of asphodel, to the neighbouring Gaeta—the Gibraltar of Italy, the ancient Portus Caeta, itself a town-republic of as many mutations and glories—and there, stuck in the harbour mud, performs the function of a post to which boats are fastened. Stalwart fishermen, wearing gold earrings, push off from it with swarthy hands; bronzed women, with silver bodkins pinning in their black hair with long coils of many-coloured linen, throw their ropes over its pedestal. Year after year it lies in its ooze while the sun rises and sets in glory on the promontory of Gaeta: it reeks of tar and the smell of fishing-nets; brine encrusts its high-reliefs. The clatter of the port drowns the hollow cry of memory that comes when it is struck by an oar: there is the noise of shipping bales; the crews of forth-faring argosies heave anchor with their ancient chant; the sails of the galleons flap; the windlasses creak. Perchance a galley-slave, flayed and fretted by chain and lash, draws up with grappled boat-hook, and his blood flows over into Salpion's vase.

And then a tide of happier fortune—perhaps the same that bore the Sardinians to the conquest of Gaeta and the end of the war for Italian independence—washes the vase from its harbour mud and deposits it in the cathedral of Gaeta. The altar of Bacchus returns to sacerdotal uses: only now it is a font, and brown Italian babies are soused in it, while nurses in gilt coronets with trailing orange ribbons stand by, radiant. Doubtless the priests and the simple alike read an angel into Mercury, the infant Jesus into the child of Jupiter and Semele, and into the nymph of Nysa the Madonna whose Immaculate Conception Pio Nono proclaimed from this very Gaeta.

Its Bacchantes are now joyous saints, divinely uplifted. And why not? Is not the Church of Santa Costanza at Rome the very Temple of Bacchus, its Bacchic processions in mosaic and fresco unchanged?

Did not the early Church make the Bacchic rites symbolic of the vineyard of the faith, and turn to angels the sportive genii? Assuredly Salpion's vase is as Christian as the toe of Jupiter in St. Peter's, as the Roman basilicæ where altars have usurped the ancient judgment-seat, as the Pantheon wrested from the gods by the saints. Nay, its Bacchic relief might have been the very design of a Cinquecento artist for a papal patron, the figures serving for saints, even as the Venetian ladies in all their debonair beauty supplied Tintoretto and Titian with martyrs and holy virgins, or as the beautiful, solemn-robed, venerable-bearded Bacchus on another ancient vase, which stands in the Campo Santo of Pisa, served Niccolo Pisano for the High Priest of his pulpit reliefs.

Outside Or San Michele in Florence you may admire the Four Holy Craftsmen, early Roman Christians martyred for refusing to make Pagan deities. They had not yet learned to baptize them by other names.

And now Salpion's vase has reached the Museum, that cynosure of wandering tourists. But it belongs not truly to the world of glass cases: it has not yet reached museum-point. It is of the Exhibition: not of the Museum proper, which should be a collection of antiquities. Other adventures await it, dignified or sordid. For museums themselves die and are broken up. Proteus had to change his shape; Salpion's vase has no need of external transformations. Will it fume with incense to some yet unknown divinity in the United States of Africa, or serve as a spittoon for the Fifth President of the Third World-Republic?

O the passing, the mutations, the lapse, the decay and fall, and the tears of things! Yet Salpion's vase remains as beautiful for baptism as for Pagan ritual; symbol of art which persists, stable and sure as the sky, while thoughts and faiths pass and re-form, like clouds on the blue.

And out of this flux man has dared to make a legend of changelessness, when at most he may one day determine the law of the flux.

Everything changes but change. Yet man's heart demands perfections—I had almost said petrifactions—perfect laws, perfect truths, dogmas beyond obsolescence, flawless leaders, unsullied saints, knights without fear or reproach; throws over its idols for the least speck of clay, and loses all sense of sanctity in a truth whose absoluteness for all time and place is surrendered.

Yet is there something touching and significant in this clinging of man to Platonic ideals: the ruder and simpler he, the more indefectible his blessed vision, the more shining his imaged grail. And so in this shifting world of eternal flux his greatest emotions and cravings have gathered round that ideal of eternal persistence that is named God.

IV

There are two torrents that amaze me to consider—the one is Niagara, and the other the stream of prayer falling perpetually in the Roman Catholic Church. What with masses and the circulating exposition of the Host, there is no day nor moment of the day in which the praises of God are not being sung somewhere: in noble churches, in dim crypts and underground chapels, in cells and oratories. I have been in a great cathedral, sole congregant, and, lo! the tall wax candles were lit, the carven stalls were full of robed choristers, the organ rolled out its sonorous phrases, the priests chaunted, marching and bowing, the censer swung its incense, the bell tinkled. Niagara is indifferent to spectators, and so the ever-falling stream of prayer. As steadfastly and unremittingly as God sustains the universe, so steadfastly and unremittingly is He acknowledged, the human antiphony answering the divine strophe.

There be those who cannot bear that Niagara should fall and thunder in mere sublimity, but only to such will this falling thunder of prayer seem waste.

Yet as I go through these innumerable dark churches of Italy, these heavy, airless glooms, heavier with the sense of faded frescoes and worm-eaten pictures, and vaults and crypts, and mouldering frippery and mildewed relics, and saintly bones mocked by jewelled shroudings, and dim-burning oil-lamps—the blue sky of Italy shut out as in a pious perversity—and more, when I see the subjects of the paintings and gravings, these Crucifixions and Entombments and Descents from the Cross, varied by the mimetic martyrdoms of the first believers, it is borne in on me depressingly how the secret of Jesus has been darkened, and a doctrine of life—"Walk while ye have the light . . . that ye may be the children of light"—has been turned to a doctrine of death. St. Sebastian with his arrows, St. Lawrence with his gridiron, are, no doubt, sublime spectacles; but had not the martyr's life been noble, and had he not died for the right to live it, his death would have been merely ignominious. The death of Socrates owes its value to the life of Socrates. Many a murderer dies as staunchly, not to speak of the noble experimenters with Röntgen rays, or the explorers who perish in polar wastes, recording with freezing fingers the latitude of their death.

Painting half obeyed, half fostered this concentration on the Passion, with its strong lights and shadows. Indeed, the artistic strength of the mere story is so tremendous that it has wiped out the message of the Master and thrown Christianity quite out of perspective. Tintoretto's frescoes in San Rocco—indeed, most sacred pictures—are like a picture-book for the primitive. (Picturæ sunt idiotarum libri.) The anecdotal Christ alone survives. And the painters were the journalists, the diffusers and interpreters of ideas.

The true Christ was crucified afresh in the interests of romance and the pictorial nude. Crivelli painted with unction the fine wood and the decorative nails of the Cross; even the winding-sheet is treated by Giulio Clovio for its decorative value. Where in all these galleries and legends shall we find the living Christ, the Christ of the parables and the paradoxes, the caustic satirist, the prophet of righteousness, the lover of little children? The living Christ was overcast by the livid light of the tomb. He was buried in the Latin of the Church, while every chapel and cloister taught in glaring colour the superficial dramatic elements, and Calvaries were built to accentuate it, and men fought for the Cross and swore by the Holy Rood, and collected the sacred nails and fragments of the wood and thorns of the crown.

The Sacro Catino of Genoa Cathedral once held drops of the blood; a chapel of marble and gold at Turin still preserves in the glow of ever-burning lamps the Santo Sudario, or Holy Winding-sheet. Strange mementoes of the plein air Prophet who drew his parables and metaphors from the vineyard and the sheepfold! The Santo Volto for which pilgrims stream to Lucca is not the holy face of loving righteousness, but a crucifix miraculously migrated from the Holy Land and preserved in a toy tempietto. Of the fifteen mysteries of the Roman Catholic Rosary, five are of Birth, five of Death, five of Glory. But none are of Life. There are also the rosaries of the Five Wounds and the Seven Dolors.

No doubt the majestic and sombre symbolism of the Cross owed its power over gross minds to its very repudiation of the joy of life, but the soul cannot healthily concentrate on death, nor can "Holy Dying" replace "Holy Living." Those early purple and gold mosaics of the Master with His hand on the Book of Life, placed over altars—as in the cathedral of Pisa—taught, for all their naïveté, the deeper lesson: "Ego sum lux mundi." The rude stone sculptures on the portals of Parma Baptistery depict a Christ grotesque in a skull-cap, yet active in works and words of love, and Duccio's panels on that reredos in Siena in the dawn of Italian art equally emphasise the life of Christ, and not its mere ending. In fact, the earlier the art the less the insistence on darkness and death. The Christians of the Catacombs, for whom death and darkness were daily realities, turned all their thoughts to light and life. They enjoyed their crypts more than the Christians of to-day enjoy their cathedrals. "The Acts of the Apostles," says Renan in his St. Paul, "are a book of joy." It was the later ages, which found the battle won, that took an artistic and morbid pleasure in depicting martyrdoms and created those pictorial concepts that tend to caricature Christianity. It is worth remarking that Tempesta, who brought pictorial martyrology to its disgusting climax in S. Stefano Rotondo at Rome, came so late that he lived to see the eighteenth century in. A pity that temporary necessities of martyrdom among the early Christians lent colour to the misconception of Christianity as a religion of death. Toleration or triumph robbed the saint of his stake, and left to him a subtler and severer imitatío Christi. Buried so long beneath his own Cross, the true Christ will rise again—to the cry of "Ecce Homo!"

On that day the teaching of Arius as to the originate nature of Christ, or the modal trinitarianism of Sabellius by which the same God manifested Himself as Father, Son, and Holy Ghost, may cease to be a heresy, or Joachim of Flora's expectation of a Super-Gospel of the Spirit may find transformed fulfilment. For if Christianity has a future, that future belongs, not to its dogmas, but to its heresies, the thought of the great souls who, instead of receiving it passively, wrestled for themselves with its metaphysical and spiritual problems, and passed through the white fires and deep waters of the cosmic mystery. There is scarcely a heresy but will better repay study than the acrid certainties of St. Bernard or the word-spinnings of Athanasius triumphant contra mundum.

Art is, indeed, not sparing of the resurrected Christ who rules in glory, such as He whose majestic figure dominates and pervades St. Mark's; but this Christ who presides in so many pictures at the Last Judgment, His foot on the earth-ball, His angel-legions round Him, and who, indeed, in some is actually represented as creating Adam or giving Moses the Law; this Christ who—by a paradoxical reversion to the Pagan need for a human God—has superseded His Father with even retrospective rights, is still further removed than the crucified Christ from the Christ of life.

This apotheosis, how inferior in grandeur to his true presidence over the centuries that followed his death! And this death, how infinitely more tragic than the conventional theory of it! Naught that man has suffered or man imagined, no Dantesque torture nor Promethean agony, can equal the blackness of that ninth hour when "Jesus cried with a loud voice, saying, Eli, Eli, lama sabachthani?" Where be the twelve legions of angels, where the seat for the Son of Man at the right hand of power? Why this mockery, this excruciation?

Purblind must be the dry-as-dust who can read this passage and doubt that Jesus was an historical person. As if, despite Psalm xxii, the writers of Matthew and Mark could have invented so wonderful a touch, or would, had they understood its full import, have inserted so flagrant a contradiction of the Christian concept—a contradiction that can only be counteracted by an elaborate theory of kenosis. The dying cry of Jesus stamps him with authenticity, as the complaints of the Israelites against their leader guarantee Moses and the Exodus.

What a colossal theme—Ormuzd broken by Ahriman, the incarnation of light and love agonising beneath the heel of the powers of darkness and goaded into the supreme cry: "My God, my God, why hast Thou forsaken me?" I have seen only one Crucifixion that adequately renders this dreadful moment—the supreme loneliness, the unrayed blackness—for most Crucifixions are populated and bustling, like Tintoretto's or Altichieri's or Foppa's or Spinello Aretino's, or that congested canvas of the brothers San Severino, when they are not also like Michele da Verona's, a translation of the tragedy into a Carpaccio romance of trumpeters and horsemen and dogs and lovely towered cities and mountain bridges, not to mention the arms of the magnificent Conte di Pitigliano. But what painter it is who has caught the true essence and quiddity of the Crucifixion I cannot remember, nor haply if I saw his picture in Spain and not in Italy, nor even if I dreamed it.

Lucas Van der Leyden and Van Dyck give us the lonely figure, but in Italian art before our own day I can only recall it in an obscure picture of the Parmese school, and in a small painting of the eighteenth-century Venetian, Piazzetta. Tura's impressive, sombre study is only a fragment of a stigmata picture. Guido Reni suggests the loneliness, but he leaves the head haloed and melodramatic, besides sketching in shadowy accessories. A nineteenth-century Italian, Giocondo Viglioli, places the lonely Christ against the shadowy background of the roofs and towers of Jerusalem. But the picture I have in my mind is Rembrandtesque, the blacks heaviest at the figure in the centre, who, unillumined even by a halo, uncompanioned even of thieves, hangs nailed upon a lonely cross in a vast deserted landscape. For Jesus at this tremendous moment is alone—however vast the crowd—alone against the universe, and this universe has turned into a darkness that can be felt; felt as a torment of body as well as a shattering of the spirit.

When I looked upon the myth of Psyche in the Villa Farnesina at Rome as designed by Raphael, it was borne in on me how the primitive Greek, penetrated by the certainty and beauty of his body, had made the world and the gods in its image. But the race of Jesus, evolved to a higher thought, had demanded that the universe should answer to its soul. "Shall not the Judge of all the earth do right?" asks Abraham severely of God in another epochal passage of the Bible. And now here is a scion of Abraham who has staked his all upon the innermost nature of things being one with his own, upon a universe aflame with love and righteousness and pity, and lo! in this awful hour it seems to reveal itself as a universe full of mocking forces, grim, imperturbable, alien. It is an epic moment—the tragedy not only of Jesus, but of man soaring upwards from the slime—

"Such splendid purpose in his eyes"

—and finding in the cosmos no correspondence with his vision. Nor could Jesus, who had outgrown the notion of a heavenly despot, even find the satisfaction of the Prometheus of Æschylus:

"You see me fettered here, a god ill-starred,
The enemy of Zeus, abhorred of all
That tread the courts of his omnipotence,
Because of mine exceeding love for men."

Yet in a sense the despair of Jesus was unwarranted. The universe had not forsaken him; it contained, on the contrary, the media for his eternal influence. On the physical plane, indeed, it could do nothing for him; crucifixion must kill or the cosmos must change to chaos. But on the spiritual plane he could neither be killed nor forsaken. Infinitely less tragic his death than that of Napoleon, of whom we might say, in the words of Sannazaro,

"Omnia vincebas, superabas omnia Cæsar,
Omnia deficiunt, incipis esse nihil."

It was Moses who more voluntarily than Jesus offered his life that the equilibrium of this righteous universe should not be shaken. "Ye have sinned a great sin; and now I will go up unto the Lord;

peradventure I shall make an atonement for your sin." And the atonement offered ran: "Blot me, I pray Thee, out of Thy book which Thou hast written." Here, then, in the Old Testament, and not in the New, first appears the notion of vicarious atonement. But the Old Testament sternly rejects it; "Whoever hath sinned against Me, him will I blot out of My book." Beside which trenchant repudiation the Christian reading of the Old Testament as a mere prolegomenon to the Crucifixion, an avenue to Calvary strewn with textual finger-posts, appears a more than usually futile word-play of the theological mind. One might, indeed, more easily discover the germ of the atonement idea in Iphigenia. And that the Greek mind had spiritualised itself—even before it contributed the logos to Christianity—is obvious not only from its literature and its Orphic and Eleusinian mysteries, but from its art. For the Hellenic art of Raphael was, after all, only the Renaissance view of Hellas, and the Greek myths in his hands were merely a charming Pagan poetry, no truer to the Hellenism of the great period than was the "Endymion" or "Hyperion" of Keats. How can I look at the statue of Apollo in this same Museum of Naples and not see that the very type of Christ had been pre-figured? I mean the Christ with the haunting eyes and the long ringlets, for this Apollo is a nobler figure by far than the Christ of the Byzantine mosaics. And I am not the first to remember that Apollo is the Son of Zeus the Father.

It is very strange. The Greeks, beginning with a Nature-religion, come in the course of the centuries to find it inadequate and to yearn for something beyond—

"Tendebantque manus ulterioris ripæ amore."

The Nature-religion, therefore, gradually replaces itself by a Jewish heresy, expounded in Greek, largely influenced by Greek Alexandrian philosophy, and organised by a Greek-speaking tent-maker of Jerusalem named Saul or Paul, who, shutting out infinity with a tent, after the fashion of his craft, left a Church where he had found a Christ. Some fourteen centuries later old Greek thought is rediscovered, and operates as the great liberator of the mind from the constriction of this Church which has obscured and overgloomed Nature. But only subconscious of itself, this movement back to Nature, this renewed joie de vivre, finds its expression in the adornment of altars for the worship of sorrow, and under the ribs of death a new soul of loveliness is created that can vie with the art of the Greeks. And finally this new Nature-worship grows conscious again of its inadequacy to the soul of man, there is a Reformation and a Counter-Reformation, and then both are outgrown and humanity stands to-day where the old Greeks stood at the dawn of Christianity. The wheel has come full circle. And meantime the original Mosaic cult stands unmoved by these two millenniums of heresy, unbroken by the persecution, still patiently awaiting the day when "God shall be One and His Name One." What are the fantasies of literature to the freaks and paradoxes of the World-Spirit?

V

It is as the Bambino that Christ chiefly lives in Art, and at this extreme, too, we miss his true inwardness. Yet the tenderness of the conception of the Christ-babe makes atonement. What can be more touching than Gentile da Fabriano's enchanting altar-piece of the Adoration of the Magi, in which—even as the glamorous procession of the Three Kings resteeps the earth in the freshness and dew of the morning— the dominance of holy innocence seems to bathe the tired world in a wistful tenderness that links the naïve ox and ass with the human soul and all the great chain of divine life.

The Christ-child, held in his mother's arms, lays his hand upon the kneeling Magi's head, yet not as with conscious divinity: 'tis merely the errant touch of baby fingers groping out towards the feel of things. No lesson could be more emollient to rude ages, none could better serve to break the pride and harshness of the lords of the earth. "A slave might be elder, priest, or bishop while his master was catechumen," says Hausrath of the early days of Christianity. Yet this delicious and yearning vision of a sanctified and unified cosmos remains a dream; futile as a Christmas carol that breaks sweetly on the ear and dies away, leaving the cry of the world's pain undispossessed. It was precisely in Christian Rome that slavery endured after all the other Great Powers of Europe had abolished it.

Nay, were the dream fulfilled it could not undo the centuries of harsh reality. Here in Naples, under the providence of a kindly English society, the wretched breed of horses, whose backs were full of sores, whose ribs were numerable, have been replaced by a sleek stock, themselves perhaps soon to be replaced by the unsentient motor. But what Motor Millennium can wipe out the ages of equine agony?

And despite the Christ-child and the Christ crucified, nowhere does the triumph of life run higher than in this sunny land of religious gloom, Mantegna's conversion of the babe into a young Cæsar being a true if unconscious symbol of what happened to the infant. Flourishing the forged Donation of Constantine to prove its claim to the things that were Cæsar's, it grew up into that "Terrible Pontiff" whose bronze effigy by Michelangelo was so aptly cast into a cannon, and whose Christian countenance you may see in the Doria Gallery at Rome; or into that Borgian monster who was to bombard a fortress on Christmas Day, and who, crying joyfully, "We are Pope and Vicar of Christ," hastened to don the habit of white taffeta, the embroidered crimson stola, the shoes of ermine and crimson velvet. God might choose to be born in the poorest and worst-dressed circles of the most unpopular People, but the lesson was lost. His worshippers insisted on thrusting Magnificence back upon Him. Or perhaps it was their own Magnificence that they were protecting against His insidious teaching. Consider their cathedrals, built less in humility than in urban emulation—the Duomo of Florence to be worthy of the greatness, not of God, but of the Florentines; S. Petronio to eclipse it to the greater glory of Bologna; Milan Cathedral to surpass all the churches in Christendom, as Giangaleazzo's palace surpassed all its princely dwellings. In whose honour did the Pisans encircle their cathedral with a silver girdle, or the Venetians offer ten thousand ducats for the seamless coat? Poor Babe, vainly didst thou preach to Italy's great families, when in humble adoration of thee they had themselves painted in thy blessed society, the Medici even posing to Botticelli as the Three Magi, and thrusting their magnificence into thy very manger.

And in our own northern land the ox, companion of the manger, for whose fattening at Christmastide St. Francis said he would beg for an imperial edict, is fattened indeed, but merely for the Christmas market, stands with the same pathetic eye outside the butcher's shop, labelled "Choose your Christmas joint," and the clown and pantaloon come tumbling on to crown the sacred birthday.

Alas! history knows no miracles of transformation. Evolution, not revolution, is the law of human life. In Santa Claus's stocking what you shall truly find is traces of earlier feasts. The Christian festival took over, if it transformed to higher import, the Saturnalia of earlier religions and natural celebrations of the winter solstice. Holly does not grow in Palestine; the snowy landscapes of our Christmas cards are scarcely known of Nazareth or Bethlehem; mince-pie was not on the menu of the Magian kings; and the Christmas tree has its roots in Teutonic soil. But even as the painters of each race conceived Christ in their own image, so does each nation unthinkingly figure his activities in its own climatic setting. And perhaps in thus universalising the Master the peoples obeyed a true instinct, for no race is able to receive lessons from "foreigners." The message, as well as the man, must be translated into native terms—a psychological fact which missionaries should understand.

for mermaid or Lorelei, naiad or nymph, there is no reason in Nature why all that poets feigned should not come into being. The water-babe might have been as easily evolved as the earth-man, the hegemony of creation might have been won by an aquatic creature with an accidental spurt of grey matter, and the history of civilisation might have been writ in water. The merman is a mere amphibian, not arrived. The gryphon and the centaur are hybrids unborn. 'Tis just a fluke that these particular patterns of the kaleidoscope have not been thrown. We may safely await evolutions. The winged genius of the Romans, frequent enough on Pompeian frescoes, may even be developed on this side of the skies, and we may fly with sprouted wings and not merely with detachable. Puck and Ariel perchance already frisk in some Patagonian forest, Caliban may be basking in forgotten mud. Therefore, poets, trust yourself to life and the fulness thereof. Whether you follow Nature's combinations or precede them, you may create fearlessly. From the imitatio Naturæ you cannot escape, whether you steal her combinations or her elements.

Shelley sings of "Death and his brother Sleep," but gazing at this mystic marine underworld of the Naples Aquarium, I would sing of Life and his brother Sleep. For here are shown the strange beginnings of things, half sleep, half waking: organisms rooted at one point like flowers, yet groping out with tendrils towards life and consciousness—the not missing link between animal and vegetable life. What feeling comes to trouble this mystic doze, stir this comatose consciousness? The jelly-fish that seems a mere embodied pulse—a single note replacing the quadruple chord of life—is yet a complex organism compared with some that flit and flitter half invisibly in this green universe of theirs: threads, insubstantialities, smoke spirals, shadowy filaments on the threshold of existence, ghostly fibres, flashing films, visible only by the beating of their white corpuscles. 'Tis reading the Book of Genesis, verse by verse. And then suddenly a hitherto unseen entity, the octopus, looses its sinuous suckers from the rock to which its hue protectively assimilates—a Darwinian observation Lucian anticipated in his "Dialogue of Proteus"—and unfolding itself in all its manifold horror, steals upon its prey with swift, melodramatic strides.

From the phantasmal polyzoa to these creatures of violent volition how great the jump! Natura non facit saltum, forsooth! She is a veritable kangaroo. From the unconscious to the conscious, from the conscious to the self-conscious, from the self-conscious to the over-conscious, there's a jump at every stage, as between ice and water, water and steam. Continuous as are her phases, a mysteriously new set of conditions emerges with every crossed Rubicon. Dante, in making the human embryo pass through the earlier genetic stages ("Purgatory," Canto XXV), seems curiously in harmony with modern thought, though he was but reproducing Averroes.

But mankind has never forgotten its long siesta as a vegetable. Still linked with the world of sleep through the mechanic processes of nutrition, respiration, circulation, consciously alive only in his higher centres, man tends ever to drowse back to the primal somnolence. Moving along the lines of least resistance and largest comfort, he steeps himself in the poppies of custom, drinks the mandragora of ready-made morals, and sips the drowsy syrups of domesticity, till he has nigh lapsed back to the automaton. But ever and anon through the sluggish doze stirs the elemental dream, leaps the primeval fire, and man is awake and astir and athrill for crusades, wars, martyrdoms, revolutions, reformations, and back in his true biological genus.

Not only in man appears this contest of life and sleep: it runs through the cosmos. There is a drag-back: the ebb of the flowing tide. How soon the forsaken town returns to forest! Near the Roman Ghetto you may note how the brickwork of the wall of the ancient Theatre of Marcellus has relapsed to rock; man's

Prometheus is also Man the Proteus. Dante praised Nature for having ceased to frame monsters, save the whale and the elephant; he did not remark that Man had continued her work on a substratum of himself.

The forms of the typewriters are even more clearly conditioned by the struggle for life. The early patents are the creatures in possession, and to develop a new type without infringing on their pastures, and risking their claws, a machine is driven into ever-odder contrivances, like creatures that can only exist in an over-crowded milieu by wriggling into some curious shape and filling some forgotten niche. The lust of life that runs through Nature transforms the very dust to a creeping palpitation, fills every leaf and drop of water with pullulating populations. 'Tis an eternal exuberance, a riotous extravagance, an ecstasy of creation. Great is Diana of the Ephesians, for this Diana, as you may see her figured in the Naples Museum, black but comely, is a goddess of many breasts, a teeming mother of generations, the swart, sun-kissed Natura Nutrix, who ranges recklessly from man to the guinea-pig, from the earwig to the giraffe, from the ostrich to the tortoise, from the butterfly to the lizard, from the glued barnacle timidly extending its tentacles when the tide washes food towards its rock, to the ravenous shark darting fiercely through the waters and seizing even man in its iron jaws. Yet they are at best mere variations on the primal theme of heart, brain, lungs, and stomach, now with enchanting grace as in the gazelle, now with barbaric splendour as in the peacock, now with a touch of grotesque genius as in the porcupine. And directly or indirectly all of them pass into one another—in the most literal of senses—as they range the mutual larder of the globe.

'Tis well to remember sometimes that this globe is not obviously constructed for man, since only one-fourth of it is even land, and that in a census of the planet, which nobody has ever thought of taking, man's poor thousand millions would be out-numbered by the mere ant-hills. And since the preponderating interests numerically of this sphere of ours are piscine, and in a truly democratic world a Fish President would reign, elected by the vast majority of voters, and we should all be bowing down to Dagon, the Aquarium acquires an added dignity, and I gaze with fresh eyes at the lustrous emerald tanks.

Ah, here is indeed a Fish President, the shell-fish that presided over the world's destinies; the little murex that was the source of the greatness of Tyre, and the weaver of its purpureal robes of empire. Hence the Phœnician commerce, Carthage, the Punic Wars, and the alphabet in which I write.

Not only is colour softened by a sea change, but in this cool, glooming, and glittering world the earth-creatures seem to have been sucked down and transformed into water-creatures. There are flowers and twigs and green waving grass that seem earth-flowers and twigs and grass transposed into the key of water.

Only, these flowers and grasses are animal, these coralline twigs are conscious; as if water, emulous of the creations of earth and air, strove after their loveliness of curve and line, or as if the mermaidens coveted them for their gardens. And there are gemmed fishes, as though the mines of Ind had their counterpart in the forces producing these living jewels. And there are bird-like fishes with feathery forms, that one might expect to sing as they cleave the firmament of water: some song less troubling than the Lorelei's, with liquid gurgles and notes of bubbling joy. And the sea, not content to be imitative, has added—over and above its invention of the fish—to the great palpitation of life; priestly forms, robed and cowled, silver-dusty pillars, half-shut parasols. Even the common crab is an original; a homely grotesque with no terraceous or aerial analogue, particularly as it floats in a happy colour-harmony with a brown or red sponge on its back, a parasite literally sponging upon it. But though you may look in vain

Although the Pilgrims' Way is a shady arcade, yet the ascent from Vicenza was steep enough to be something of a penance that sultry spring evening, and I was weary of the unending pillars and the modern yet already fading New Testament frescoes between them. But I was interested to see which parish or family had paid for each successive section, and what new name for the Madonna would be left to inscribe upon it. For even the Litany of Loreto seemed exhausted, and still the epithets poured out—"Lumen Confessorum," "Consolatrix Viduarum," "Radix Jesse," "Stella Matutina," "Fons Lachrymarum," "Clypeus Oppressorum"—a very torrent of love and longing.

At last as I neared the summit of the Way, a fresco flashed upon me the meaning of it all—an "Apparitio B.M.V. in Monte Berico, 1428," representing the Virgin in all her radiant beauty appearing to an old peasant-woman. So this it was that had raised this long religious road to the Church of Our Lady of the Mountain! I remembered the inscription in S. Rocco, telling how 30,000 men had pilgrimed here in 1875—"spectaculum mirum visu."

But where was the church that had been built over the spot of the Madonna's appearance? I looked up and sighed wearily. I was only half-way up, I saw, for the road turned sharply to the right, and a new set of names began, and a new set of frescoes—still cruder, for I caught sight of nails driven into the Cross through the writhing frame of the Christ. But even my curiosity in the cornucopia of epithets was worn out. The corner had a picturesque outlook, and on the hill-side a bench stood waiting. Vicenza stretched below me, I could see the Palladian palaces admired of Goethe, the Greek theatre, the Colonnades, the Palace of Reason with its long turtle-back roof; and, beyond the spires and campaniles, the gleam of the Venetian Alps. A church-bell from below sounded for "Ave Maria." I sat down upon the bench and abandoned myself to reverie. Why should not the Madonna appear to me? I thought. Why this preference for the illiterate? And then I remembered that this very Pilgrims' Way had served as a battle-ground for the Austrians and the poor Italians of '48. How these Christians love one another! I mused. And so my mind's eye flitted from point to point, seeing again things seen or read—in that inconsequent phantasmagoria of reverie—to the pleasant droning of the vesper bell. Presently, telling myself it was getting late, I arose and continued my ascent to the Church of Our Lady of the Mountain.

But I looked in vain, as I came up the hill, for the inscriptions and the frescoes. The sun was lower in the west, but the sunshine had grown even sultrier, the sky even bluer, the road even steeper and rougher, and it was leading me on to a gay-flowering plain lying in a ring of green hills amid the singing of larks and the cooing of turtle-doves. And on this plain I saw arising, not the church of my quest, but a far-scattered village, whose small square, primitive houses would have seemed ugly had their roofs not been picturesque with storks and pigeons and their walls embowered in their own vines and fig-trees and absorbed into the pervasive suggestion of threshing-floors and wine-presses and rural felicity. By a central fountain I could perceive a group of barefoot maidens, each waiting her turn with her water-jar. They seemed gaily but lightly clad, in blue and red robes, with bracelets gleaming at their wrists and strings of coins shining from their faces.

Anxious to learn my whereabouts, yet shy of intruding upon this girlish group, I steered my footsteps towards one who, her urn on her shoulder, seemed making her way by a side-track towards a somewhat lonely house on the outskirts, overbrooded by the brow of a hill. She was brown-skinned, I saw as I came near, very young, but of no great beauty save for her girlish grace and the large lambent eyes under the arched black eyebrows.

"Di grazia?" I began inquiringly.

Nor is it in the Palestine of to-day that the true environment of the Gospels can best be recovered, for, though one may still meet the shepherd leading his flock, the merchant dangling sideways from his ass, or Rebeccah carrying her pitcher on her shoulder, that is not the Palestine of the Apostolic period, but the Palestine of the patriarchs, reproduced by decay and desolation. The Palestine through which the Galilæan peasant wandered was a developed kingdom of thriving cities and opulent citizens, of Roman roads and Roman pomp. Upon those bleak hill-sides, where to-day only the terraces survive—the funereal monuments of fertility—the tangled branchery of olive groves lent magic to the air. That sea of Galilee, down which I have sailed in one of the only two smacks, was alive with a fleet of fishing vessels. Yes, in the palimpsest of Palestine 'tis an earlier writing than the Christian that has been revealed by the fading of the later inscriptions of her civilisation. And even where, in some mountain village, the rainbow-hued crowd may still preserve for us the chronology of Christ, a bazaar of mother-o'-pearl mementoes will jerk us rudely back into our own era. But—saddest of all!—the hands of Philistine piety have raised churches over all the spots of sacred story. Even Jacob's well is roofed over with ecclesiastic plaster; incongruous images of camels getting through church porches to drink confuse the historic imagination. Churches are after all a way of shutting out the heavens, and the great open-air story of the Gospels seems rather to suffer asphyxiation, overlaid by these countless chapels and convents. Is it, perhaps, allegorical of the perversion of the Christ-teaching?

The humanitarian turn given to Yuletide by the genius of Dickens was at bottom a return from the caricature to the true concept. Dickens converted Christmas to Christianity. But over large stretches of the planet and of history it is Christianity that has been converted to Paganism, as the condition of its existence. Russia was baptized a thousand years ago, but she seems to have a duck's back for holy water. And even in the rest of Europe upon what parlous terms the Church still holds its tenure of nominal power! What parson dares speak out in a crisis, what bishop dares flourish the logia of Christ in the face of a heathen world? The old gods still govern—if they do not rule. Thor and Odin, Mars and Venus—who knows that they do not dream of a return to their ancient thrones, if, indeed, they are aware of their exile. Their shrines still await them in the forests and glades; every rock still holds an altar. And do they demand their human temples, lo! the Pantheon stands stable in Rome, the Temple of Minerva in Assisi, Paestum holds the Temples of Ceres and Minerva, and on the hill of Athens the Parthenon shines in immortal marble. Their statues are still in adoration, and how should a poor outmoded deity understand that we worship him as art, not as divinity? It does but add to his confusion that now and anon prayers ascend to him as of yore, for can a poor Olympian, whose toe has been faith-bitten, comprehend that he has been catalogued as pope or saint? Perchance some drowsing Druid god, as he perceives our scrupulous ritual of holly and fir-branch, imagines his worship unchanged, and glads to see the vestal led under the mistletoe by his officiating priest. Perchance in the blaze of snapdragon some purblind deity beholds his old fire-offerings, and the savour of turkey mounts as incense to his Norse nostrils. Shall we rudely arouse him from his dream of dominion, shall we tell him that he and his gross ideas were banished two millenniums ago, and that the world is now under the sway of gentleness and love? Nay, let him dream his happy dream; let sleeping gods lie. For who knows how vigorously his old lustfulness and blood-thirst might revive; who knows what new victims he might claim at his pyres, were he clearly to behold his power still unusurped, his empire still the kingdom of the world?

THE CARPENTER'S WIFE: A CAPRICCIO

"Habent sua fata—feminæ."

Her brow wrinkled thoughtfully. "Doubtless Yeshua is possessed of a demon," she said. "One of our sisters, Deborah, was likewise a Sabbath-breaker, but now that she is old, having nineteen years and three strong sons, she is grown more pious than even our uncle Yehoshuah the Pharisee."

"Lives she here?"

"Ay, yonder, near my mother's sister, the wife of Halphaï."

She pointed towards a battlemented roof, but my eyes were more concerned with her own house, at which we were just arriving. It was a one-storey house, square and ugly like the others, redeemed by its little garden with its hedge of prickly pear, though even this garden was littered with new-made wheels and stools and an olive-wood table.

"Halphaï is gone up for the Passover," she added. She stopped abruptly. The tinkle of mule-bells was borne to us from a steep track that came to join our slower pathway.

"Lo, my mother!" she cried joyfully; and placing her urn upon the ground, she hastened down the narrow track. I moved delicately, yet not without curiosity, to the flank of the hedge, and presently a little caravan appeared, ambling gently, with the girl walking and chattering happily by the side of her mother, who rode upon an ass. I noticed that the woman, who was small and spare, listened but little to her daughter's eager talk, and seemed deaf to the home-coming laughter of her four curly-headed sons, who rode their mules sideways, with their legs dangling down like the fringes of their garments. Her shoulders were sunk in bitter brooding, and when a sudden stumbling of her ass made her raise her head mechanically to pull him up, I saw the shimmer of tears in her large olive-tinted eyes. Certainly I should not have called her made in the image of her daughter, I thought at that moment, for the face was sorely lined, and under the cheap black head-shawl I saw the greying hair that was still raven on her arched eyebrows. But doubtless the burden of much child-bearing had worn her out, after the sad fashion of Eastern women.

These reflections were, however, dissipated as soon as born, for a little cry of dismay from the girl brought to my perception that it was the forgotten water-jar that had caused the ass's stumble, and that the urn now lay overturned, if not shattered, amid a fast-vanishing pool.

The little mishap made her brothers smile. "Courage!" cried the eldest. "Yeshua will fill it with wine instead." At this all the four rustics broke into a roar of merriment. The youngest, a mere beardless youth, added in his vulgar Aramaic, "What one ass hath destroyed another will make good."

The little woman turned on him passionately. "Hold thy peace, Yehudah. Who knows but that he did change the water into wine?"

"Let him come and do it here," retorted the eldest. "Thou hast not forgotten what befell when he essayed his marvels in Nazara. No mighty works could he do here, albeit Shimeon and Yosé, inclining their ears to Zebedee's foolish wife, were ready to sit on his right and left hand in the Kingdom."

The two young men who had not yet spoken looked somewhat foolish.

"He laid his hand upon sick folk and healed them," one said in apology.

"Aleikhem shalôm," tripped off her tongue in heedless answer. Then, as if grown conscious I had said something strange, she paused and looked at me, and I instinctively became aware she was a Hebrew maiden. Yet I had still the feeling that I must get back to Vicenza.

"How far is thy servant from the city?" I asked in my best Hebrew.

"From Yerushalaim?" she asked in surprise. "But it is many parasangs. Impossible that thou shouldst arrive at Yerushalaim before the Passover, even borne upon eagles' wings. Behold the sun—the Sabbath-Passover is nigh upon us."

Ere she ended I had divined by her mispronunciation of the gutturals and by the Aramaic flavour of her phrases that she was a provincial and that I was come into the land of Canaan.

"What is this place?" I inquired, no less astonished than she.

"This is Nazara."

"Nazara? Then am I in Galila?"

"Assuredly. Doubtless thou comest from the great wedding at Cana. But thou shouldst have returned by way of Mount Tabor and the town of Endor. Didst thou perchance see my mother at Cana?"

"Nay; how should I know thy mother?" I replied evasively.

She smiled. "Am I not made in her image? But overlong, meseems, have ye all feasted, for it is two days since we expect my mother and brothers."

"Shall thy servant not carry thine urn?" I answered uneasily.

"Nay, I thank thee. It is not a bowshot to my door. And," she added with a gentle smile, "my brothers do not carry my burdens; why should a stranger?"

"And how many brothers hast thou?" I asked.

"Some are dead—peace be upon them. But there are four yet left alive—nay," she hesitated, "five. But our eldest hath left us."

"Ah, he hath married a wife."

She flushed. "Nay, but we speak not of him."

"There must ever be one black sheep in a flock," I murmured consolingly.

She brightened up. "So my brother Yakob always says."

"And Yakob should speak with authority on the colour of sheep, and not as the scribes." I laughed with forced levity.

"How many?" queried young Yehudah scornfully. "And how many are alive to-day? Nay, Shimeon, if he be Messhiach let him heal us of these Roman tyrants—not go about with their tax-farmers!"

"Peace, Yehudah!" The little mother looked round nervously, and a fresh terror came into those tragic eyes. There was something to me deeply moving in the sight of that shrinking little peasant-woman surrounded by these strong, tall rustics whom she had borne and suckled.

"Let Yeshua hold his peace!" answered the lad angrily, "and not prate about rendering unto Cæsar the things that are Cæsar's. But, God be thanked, a greater Yeshua hath arisen—Ben Abbas—a true patriot, who one day—"

"Aha! Behold my flock at last!" Startled by this sudden new angry voice, I glanced over the hedge, and saw standing on the doorstep cut in the rock, with a hammer in his horny hand, a big red-bearded peasant with bushy eyebrows. "These two days, Miriam, have I awaited thee."

The little woman slid meekly off her ass. "But, Yussef," she said mildly, "thou saidst thou wouldst go up for the Paschal sacrifice!"

"And how could I go up to the Holy City with all this work to finish, and not one of my four sons to carry my work to Sepphoris before the Sabbath!" He glared at them as they began to lead their beasts behind the garden. "Halphaï was sorely vexed that I did not company him and join in his lamb-group. And the house is not even ready for Passover at home; I shall be liable to the penalty of stripes."

"I baked the mazzoth ere I departed," his wife protested, "and Sarah hath purged the house of leaven." She patted her daughter's head.

"Sarah?" he growled, reminded of a fresh grievance. "Sarah should have had a husband of her own. But with these idle sons of mine, feasting and merrymaking while I saw and plane, I cannot even save fifty zuzim for her dowry."

Sarah blushed and hastened to pick up her urn and carry it back to the fountain.

"Nay, but we have tarried at Kephar Nahum," said Yakob defensively, as he disappeared.

The carpenter turned on his wife, his eyes blazing almost like his beard. His hammer struck the table in the garden, denting it. "'Twas to see thy loveling thou leftest home!"

The little mother went red and white by turns. "As my soul liveth, Yussef, I knew not he would be at the wedding."

"He was at the wedding?" he asked, softened by his surprise.

"Ay, he and his disciples."

"Disciples!" The carpenter sniffed wrathfully. "A pack of fishers and women, and that yellow-veiled Miriam from Magdala."

"The Magdala woman was not there!" she murmured, with lowered eyes.

"She knew thy kinsman would not suffer her pollution. Ah, Miriam, what a son thou hast brought into the world!"

Her eyes filled with tears. "Thou must not pay such heed to the Sanhedrim messengers. In their circuit to announce the time of the New Moon they gather up all the evil rumours of Galila. This Magdala woman is repentant; her seven devils are cast out."

"Miriam defends Miriam," he said sarcastically. "But thou canst not say I trained him not up in the way he should go. Learning could we not afford to give him, but did not thine own brother, Jehoshuah ben Perachyah, teach him Torah, and did I not teach him his trade? His ploughs and yokes were the best in all Galila."

"And now his followers say his homilies are the best," urged the poor mother.

"Homilies?" he roared. "Blasphemies! But were his Midraschim Holy Writ itself, I agree with Ben Sameos (his memory for a blessing!) greater is the merit of industry than of idle piety."

"But why should he work?" cried Yakob, who with Yehudah now reappeared from the stable. "Would that the wife of Herod's steward followed me!"

"Or even that Susannah ministered to us with her substance!" added Yehudah. "Then I too would teach, take no thought for the morrow!" And he laughed derisively.

"He never took thought for anything save himself," said Yussef, shaking his head. "Dost thou not remember, Miriam, those three dreadful days when he was lost, as we were returning from his Bar-Mitzvah in Yerushalaim! God of Abraham, shall I ever forget thy heart-sickness! And what was it he answered when we at length found him in the Temple with the doctors? He was about his father's business! He was assuredly not about my business."

"The Sabbath and Passover are drawing nigh," she murmured, and slipped past her sons into the house.

"And what did he answer thee at Kephar Nahum?" her husband called after her. "'Who is my mother?' The godless scoffer! The Jeroboam ben Nebat! I thank the Lord I did not try to bring him back home. He might have asked, 'Who is my father?'"

There was no reply, but I heard the nervous bustling of a broom. The carpenter turned to Yakob.

"And what said he at Cana?"

"He demanded wine, he and his disciples!"

"Methought he was an Ebionite or an Essene!"

"Nay, as thou saidst, Yeshua was ever a law unto himself. But there was no wine."

"No wine?" cried Yussef. "So great a wedding company and no wine? Methought the Chosan was rich enough to plant wine-booths all the way from Cana to Nazara, like the Parnass of Sepphoris, and had as many gold and silver vessels as the priests in the Temple."

"True, my father, but Yeshua had brought with him that vile tax-farmer Levi, who grinds the faces both of rich and poor, and, seeing the spying publican, the bridegroom straightway bade the servants hide the precious flagons and goblets, lest more taxes be squeezed out for the Romans."

Yussef grinned knowingly. "And so poor Yeshua must go athirst."

"Nay, but hear. When he clamoured for wine the servants wist not what to do, and my mother said gently to him, 'They have no wine.' But Yeshua turned upon her like a lion of Mount Yehudah upon a lamb, and he roared, 'Woman, what have I to do with thee? My hour is not yet come to be a Nazarite.'"

The carpenter chuckled. "Now she will know to stay at home. 'Woman, what have I to do with thee?'" he repeated with unction.

"Howbeit, my mother feared that his demon again possessed him, and she besought the servants to do whatsoever he said unto them. But they still held back. Then Yeshua, understanding what it was they feared, said, 'Bring the water-pots.' So they went out and brought the earthen pots wherewith we had washed our hands for the meal—albeit Yeshua would not wash his—and lo! they were full of wine."

The carpenter repeated his knowing grin. "And Levi the publican—what said he?"

"He was the first to cry 'A miracle!'" laughed Yakob, "and Shimeon-bar-Yonah held up his hands and cried, 'Master of the Universe! Now is Thy glory manifest!'"

Yussef joined in his son's laugh. "Is not Shimeon the lake fisherman?"

"Yea, my father; him whom Yeshua calls the Rock."

"The Rock, in sooth!" broke in fiery young Yehudah. "Say rather, the Shifting Sand. It was from Shimeon I learned to be a Zealot, and now this recreant Maccabæan is bosom friend of Roman tax-gatherers and babbles of the keys of Heaven."

"Babble not thyself, little one," the father rebuked him. He turned to Yakob. "And what said Yeshua after the wine?"

"When he beheld his disciples had drunk new faith in him, he too was flown, and prophesied darkly that he would appear on the right hand of power, with clouds of glory and twelve legions of angels, whereat my mother feared that his madness was come upon him as of yore, and she made us follow in his train as far as his lodging in Kephar Nahum. And we spake privily to Yudas that he should watch over him till his unclean spirit was exorcised."

"Yudas!" cried Yussef. "What doth an honest Israelite like Yudas in such company? But did I not foretell what would come of all these baptizings of Rabbi Jochanan, all these new foolish sects with their white garments and paddles and ablutions? Canaan is full of wandering madmen. The Torah I had from my father, Eli—peace be upon him!—is holy enough for me, and may God forgive me that I have not gone up to kill the Paschal lamb."

Yakob lowered his voice. "Thou wouldst have met the madman."

"What! Yeshua is gone to Yerushalaim?"

"Sh! My mother knoweth naught. We spake him secretly as though converted, saying, 'Lo! we have seen this day how thou workest miracles. But if thou do these things, show thyself to the world. Depart hence and go into Yudæa, that men may see the works that thou doest.' For there is no man that doeth anything in secret, and he himself seeketh to be known openly. So he is gone up to Yerushalaim!"

The malicious glee on Yakob's face was reflected in his father's. "Now shall the mocker be mocked! Even thy learned uncle, Ben Perachyah, they scoff at for his accent, nor will they let him read the prayers. How much less, then, will they listen to Yeshua!"

"And the Pharisees hate him," said Yakob, "because he hath called them vipers, and the Shammaites for profaning the Sabbath; even the Essenes for not washing his hands before meals."

"And all the Zealots hold him a traitor!" cried Yehudah with flashing eyes.

"Nor will the Sadducees or the Bœthusians listen to a carpenter's son," added Yakob laughingly.

"Shame on thee, Yakob, for fouling thine own well!" And Sarah, returning with her pitcher on her shoulder, went angrily within.

Yakob grew red. "And dost thou think the nobles of Yerushalaim who eat off gold and silver will follow him like fishers?" he called after her. "Say they not already, 'Can anything good come out of Nazara?'"

"Yeshua is gone to Yerushalaim?" The little mother had dashed to the door, her eyes wide with terror. The urn she had just taken from her daughter fell from her trembling hand and shattered itself on the rocky doorstep, splashing husband and son.

"Woman!" cried the carpenter angrily, "have more care of my substance!"

"Yeshua is gone to Yerushalaim!" she repeated frenziedly.

"Ay, like a good son of Israel. He hath gone up for the Paschal sacrifice. Mayhap," he added with his chuckle, "he will do wonders with the blood of the lamb. Come, Miriam, let us change our garments and anoint ourselves for the festival."

He pushed the woman gently within the room, but she stood there as one turned into a pillar of salt, and with an Eastern shrug he went in.

Presently Sarah came and wiped the steps with a clout and gathered up the shards, and then, with a new pitcher on her shoulder, she bent her steps towards the fountain.

I skirted round to meet her on her return, not a little to her amazement; but this time she surrendered her burden to my entreaty, though the ungainly manner in which I poised the pitcher lightened her clouded brow with inner laughter.

"This wandering brother of thine," I ventured to ask at length, "dost thou think harm will befall him in Yerushalaim?"

Her brow puckered thoughtfully. "Perchance these strangers will believe on him, not knowing as we do that he hath a demon. Yeshua was wroth with us when he came, crying out that a man's foes are those of his own household, and a prophet is nowhere without honour save in his own country. But how should Yeshua be able to work miracles more than Yakob or Yehudah? When he stood up in our synagogue on the Shabbos to read and expound the prophet Yeshaiah, his lips were touched with the same burning coal—almost he persuaded me to be a heretic—but inasmuch as he could do no miracles, all they in the synagogue were filled with wrath, and rose up and thrust him out of the city." She pointed to the brow of the hill hanging over us. "Up there they led him, that they might cast him down headlong. But out of compassion for my mother, who had followed with the crowd, they let him go, and he returned to Kephar Nahum and continued to make yokes and wheels for his livelihood."

"And he still works there?"

"Nay, he neglected his craft to preach in the great synagogue built by the centurion—indeed, it is a hot place for work down there by the lake, neither is it so healthy as here in Nazara. Also he had free lodging with the family of Shimeon-bar-Yonah whom they call Petros, while Shalome, the wife of Zebedee, and other women tended him and mended his garments. But his fever took him and he began to wander about all Galila, teaching in the synagogues and preaching his strange gospel?"

"What gospel?"

"How should a girl know? Some heresy anent the Kingdom. And there went out a fame of him through all the region round about, and some said he healed all manner of sickness, so that there followed him great multitudes of people. But many came to us and said, 'Alas! he is beside himself.' And the Messengers of the New Moon told us many strange tales, so that my mother was nigh distraught, and when it was bruited that he had said Kephar Nahum shall be thrust down to hell, she journeyed thither, she and my brothers, to bring him home and watch over his affliction. But lo! they could not lay hold of him, for he was surrounded by such a press of people that they could not even come nigh unto him. So she sent a message that his mother and brothers desired to have speech of him. And he answered, 'Who is my mother? Who are my brothers?' and he stretched forth his hand towards his disciples and said, 'Behold my mother and my brothers.' So she returned home sorely stricken, and put on mourning garments, and even the birth of her grandchildren gave her no joy. But when came the marriage of her rich kinsman in Cana my father would have her go, being weary of her weeping and thinking to cheer her heart; but lo! her last state is worse than her first, inasmuch as—" She broke off abruptly as we reached the hedge of prickly pear. "But why have I told all this to a stranger?"

"Because I have none else with whom to eat the Passover," I answered boldly.

She turned and looked at me. Then, taking her pitcher from me with a word of thanks, "I will tell my father," she answered gravely.

I waited in the little garden, watching a patriarchal tortoise. Presently the carpenter reappeared on the doorstep, a new man in festal garment and mien, his head anointed with oil.

"Baruch Habaa!" he cried cordially. "Since I cannot go up to Yerushalaim, Yerushalaim comes up to me."

I followed him into the house, duly kissing the mezuzah as I went through the door. The room was small and dark, with bare walls built of little liver-coloured blocks of cemented stone, and the matted floor seemed to hold less furniture than that which littered the garden. The carpenter's bench had been covered with cushions, and I could see that the divan was used for a bed. Very humble was the house-gear, these earthenware dishes and metal drinking-cups and brass candlesticks on the Passover table, and I saw no ornaments save a few terra-cotta vases, a Hebrew scroll or two, and a rudely painted coffer. The housewife, busy at the hearth with the roasted egg and bone of the ritual, greeted me with wistful eyes and lips that vainly tried to murmur or smile a welcome, and I watched her deft mechanic movements as I sat lightly gossiping with the males over the exegesis of the seventh chapter of Yeshaiah. I told them that the Septuagint translator had darkened the fourteenth verse by loosely rendering עלמה as παρθένος, or "virgin," instead of "maiden," but this did not interest them, as they knew no Greek. The room took a more cheerful air when the mother lit the Sabbath candles with a blessing almost as inaudible as her welcome to me, and soon my host began the Haggadah service by holding his hands over the wine-goblet. But Yehudah asked the ritual question, "Why does this night differ from all other nights?" with a touch of sarcasm, and interrupted himself to cry passionately: "How can we celebrate our deliverance from Egypt when the Roman Eagle hangs at the very door of our Temple?" At this the little mother turned yet paler, and every eye glanced uneasily towards the stranger.

"Nay, I am no friend of the Romans," I said reassuringly.

Yehudah continued the formula sullenly. It was as I had always heard it, save for the question, "Why is the meat all roasted and none sodden or boiled?" But the father had scarcely begun his ritual reply when we heard a loud knocking on the door, the latch was lifted, and in another instant we saw a burly man panting on the threshold, and behind him, more vaguely in the dusk, an agitated woman under a head-shawl.

"O Reb Yussef!" breathed the newcomer.

"Halphaï!" cried the carpenter in amaze. "Art not in Yerushalaim?"

The little mother had sprung to her feet.

"They have killed my Yeshua!" she shrieked.

"Sit down, woman!" said the carpenter sternly.

But she gestured to the figure in the rear: "Speak, my sister, speak."

"Nay, I will speak," grumbled her sister's husband. "Why else did I take horse from the Holy City without hearing the Levites sing or the trumpets blow for the blood-sprinkling? Thy Yeshua came up through the Fountain Gate riding on an ass, and as one flown with new wine."

"Yea, the wine of the water-pots!" laughed Yakob.

"And a very great multitude spread their garments in the way; others cut down branches from the trees and strewed them in the way. And the multitudes that went before and that followed cried, 'Hosanna to the son of David!'" He paused for breath, leaving this picture suspended, and I saw a new light leap into the mother's tragic eyes, a strange exaltation as of a secret hope incredulously confirmed.

"In Yerushalaim?" she breathed. "They cry Hosanna in Yerushalaim?"

"Yea," said her sister. "And Halphaï told me, even the little children cried, 'Hosanna to the son of David!'"

The carpenter was crumbling a mazzo with nervous fingers; an angry vein swelled on his forehead. "And Pilatus permitted this?" he cried.

"Patience, Reb Yussef!" said Halphaï. "There is more to come. For, growing yet more swollen in his presumption, Yeshua went to the Holy Temple, and, entering the Court of the Gentiles, where sit those who sell the sheep and the oxen and doves, instead of purchasing a sacrifice for his sins, he drove them all out with a scourge of small cords and poured out the changers' money!"

Horror held the household dumb. I saw Halphaï look round complacently, as though compensated for his hot ride to Nazara. "And ye know what profit Hanan makes out of his bazaars," he added significantly.

The mother was wringing her hands. "Hanan will never forgive him," she cried. "They will kill him as they killed Jochanan the Baptizer."

"Peace, woman," said Yussef impatiently. "The High Priest and the Elders will but drive him from the city."

"Nay, nay," said Halphaï. "They hold him captive. And his disciples are fled. All save Yudas, who led a multitude with swords and staves to find him. And Shimeon-bar-Yonah too is taken, merely because his speech betrayeth him as a Galilæan. How then should I dare stay, who have the ill-hap to be married to his mother's sister!"

The little mother was moving towards the door. Her husband stopped her. "Whither goest thou?"

"To saddle the ass. I must to Yerushalaim!"

"Thou!"

"Who else? Shall that yellow-veiled woman of Magdala give him comfort?"

"And will he take comfort from thee? Doth he not teach his followers to hate their father and their mother? And doth he not scoff at the womb that bare him?"

"Not he, but his demon," she answered obstinately, and pressed forward again.

His brow grew black. "But it is the Sabbath!"

"It is my first-born."

"Thou speakest more foolishly than Job's wife. Now we see whence Yeshua sucked his blasphemies."

"It is my first-born!" she repeated more frenziedly.

"Thy first-born! But did he keep to-day the Fast of the First-born?"

"Let her go, Yussef," pleaded Halphaï. "As Rabbi Hillel taught (his memory for a blessing), the Sabbath was handed to man, not man to the Sabbath!"

"And the wife to the husband," retorted Yussef, "not the husband to the wife. I forbid thee, Miriam, to disturb the Passover peace. Go—and I put thee away publicly!"

She blenched and sank back on the divan. "Peace?" she moaned. "Thou callest this peace!"

"Obey thy lord, Miriam! I will go." And Halphaï's wife stooped and kissed her.

Miriam burst into loud sobs. She caught her sister to her breast, and the two women mingled their tears.

The carpenter shrugged his shoulders. "Blessed art Thou, O Lord, who hast not made me a woman," he said drily.

The walls of the little room seemed higher, the light stronger, the prayer devouter, the company more numerous. Instead of the two little Sabbath candles and the earthenware dishes, I saw a barbaric blaze of gold and rich stuffs and jewels, and my eyes blinked before the flames of tall candles shining in gold candlesticks on a magnificent altar, in the niche of which stood a black cedar-wood idol, crowned and holding a crowned doll, and wrapped in a marvellous ornate vestment widening out like a bell. Over my head around the rough, liver-coloured stone walls hung lamps and bronzes and candles held by Cupids, and gilded busts, and medallions and hearts and bronze reliefs and pictures, and even a cannon-ball, and at my feet surged the white head-shawls of prostrate worshippers, like a great wave breaking on the crimson steps of the altar.

And gradually I became aware that the room had now doors on the right and the left, and these of bronze and wondrously wrought after the fashion of the Renaissance, through which a stream of worshippers poured, kissing the bronze as they passed in and out. And following one stream and vaguely looking for Miriam and her husband and the Passover table, I was borne back into the room, through another door, and now found myself in a narrow and still more crowded space at the back of the altar, where the gorgeous jewelled black idol with her doll stood in her niche in the gleam of ever-burning silver lamps, and I saw a golden eagle in a yellow sun flying over her head, and over the eagle two gilded angels holding a glittering wreath, and still higher, through a hole in the roof, as riding on clouds, a blue-mantled Mother and Child among a soaring escort of angels, while near the floor I beheld a large metal box with a yawning slit, into which a kneeling, weeping press of people rained money.

"Il Santo Camino, signore!" said an ingratiating voice, and looking up I perceived at my side a beadle with a wand.

"The holy kitchen?" I repeated in amaze.

"Si, signore. Here is the hearth at which the Madonna cooked for the Holy Family."

He pointed to the money-box, and I now indeed recognised the fireplace whence Miriam had taken the roasted bone and egg. But it had moved to another side of the living-room, unless I was confused by the altar planted in the place of the Passover table.

"Then this is the house of Nazara?" I said in a whisper, for, dazed as I was, I feared to disturb the worshippers.

"Sicuro!" He smiled reassuringly. "La Santa Casa! Here the Holy Family abode in the peace and love of the Holy Ghost. And here there is Plenary Indulgence every day in the year. Ecco! One of their pots!" And he produced a terra-cotta vessel, not unlike one I had seen the little olive-eyed woman wiping, save that it was lined with gold and adorned with bas-reliefs of the Manger and the Annunciation.

"That must have cost money," I murmured feebly.

"Già," he assented complacently. "And behold the Madonna Nera, carved by St. Luke. Her attire is worth 1,800,000 lire."

"Come?" I gasped.

He spurned a sobbing peasant-woman with his foot and cleared a space with his staff that he might plant me at the centre of the money-box.

"Passi," he said pleasantly, seeing I hesitated to displace these passionate souls. "Regard the jewels and precious stones of her robe, the diamonds, emeralds, and pearls in her crown, the collars of Oriental pearl, the rings, the crosses of topaz and diamonds, the Bambino's diamond necklace, the ring on his finger, the medallion with the great diamonds given by the King of Saxony—" He trolled off the glittering catalogue, on and on, in a joyous, dominant voice, to which the sighs and groans of the worshippers made an undertone. Countesses and Cardinals, Popes and Marchese had vied in dressing the idol, and decorating the kitchen. "And you must see the Treasury," he wound up. "Gifts from all the royal houses of Europe to Our Lady of Loreto!"

"Loreto?" I repeated dully.

He looked at me sharply, as at a scoffer.

"But how did the Holy House get to Loreto?" I added hastily.

"It was carried by angels," he answered simply.

"But when?"

"On the night of the tenth of December in the year 1294 from the bearing of the Virgin."

"Who saw it carried?"

"You are an Englishman," he answered briefly. "You shall see it in English."

He made a path through the praying crowd, and I followed him without, and my breath failed me as I became aware that the Holy House was inclosed in a precious outer casing of marble, carved with beautiful reliefs of the life and death of the Virgin, holding all round its four lofty walls niches with statues of prophets and sybils and other gleaming altars, each with its surf of worshippers, and that this marvellous screen, so rich in the work of the Masters, was itself engirdled by a vast high-domed church with rich-dyed windows, gilded like a Venetian palace and full of arches and pillars and altars and chapels and mosaics and statues and busts and thick-populated frescoes, while from the centre of the choir windows a haloed Lady in a blue mantle gazed down upon her white-hooded ghostly worshippers filling the nave. And all around her from the interlacing of the arches and from the painted walls haloes gleamed like a firmament of crescent moons.

"Behold there!" said the beadle, pointing with his staff, and I saw that round the projecting base of the marble walls ran two deep parallel furrows. "Worn in the stone by the knees of six centuries of pilgrims," he said pleasantly. "Of course there are not many to-day, being an ordinary Sunday, but in the year there are a hundred thousand, and in the season of the pilgrimages, or on the Feast of the Assumption—" An expressive gesture wound up the sentence.

We passed along the aisles, just peeping into the copious chapels, all pervaded by the ubiquitous Maria in picture or mosaic, in statue or bas-relief—Maria Immaculate, Maria the Virgin, Maria the Mother of God, Maria the Compassionate, Maria the Mediatress, Maria Crowned; and the marriage of Maria, and her death, and the visit to Elizabeth, and the Annunciation, and her family tree, and the disputes of the Sorbonne over the dogmas concerning her. And as we walked the organ began pealing, and priests and choristers chanted.

"Ecco!" cried the beadle, as he stopped in the left aisle and pointed to a great black-framed slate between two altars. "In your own English!"

I looked and read the headline of white letters:

"The Wondrous Flitting of the Kirk of our Blest Ledy of Lavreto."

Underneath ran in parallel columns these two sentences:

"By decree of the Meikle Werthy Monsignor Vincent Casal of Bolonia Ruler of This Helly Place Vnder the protection of the Mest Werthy Cardinal Moroni."

"I Robert Corbington Priest of the Companie of Jesvs in the Zeir MDCXXXV Heve Trvlie translated the premisses of the Latin Storie Hangged vp in the seyd Kirk."

And underneath these parallel statements were the words, "To the Praise and Glorie of the Mest Pvre and Immaculate Virgin."

Then began the story proper:

"The Kirk of Lavreto was a caumber of the hovse of the blest Virgin near Jerusalem in the towne of Nazaret in which she was borne and treined vp and greeted of the angel and hairin also Conceaved and norisht har sonne Jesvs."

My eye ran impatiently over these known details and lighted at a lower point of the great dimly lit slate.

"Pavl de Sylva an eremyt of micle godliness, wha woned in a cell near by this Kirk whair daily he went to mattins, seyd that for ten zeirs, one the eight of September, twelve hovrs before day, he saw a light descend frem heaven vpon it, whilk he said was by the bu weathair shawed har selfe [sic] one the feest of har birth. In proof of all whilk twa verteous men of the seyd towne of Recanah many times avowed to me Rvler of Terreman and Govenor of the forseyd Kirk as followeth. Ane of them, nemmed Pavle Renallvci, affirmed that his grandsyres grandsyre sawe when the angels broght it over sea setting it in the forseyd wood and hed oft frequented it thair, the other nemmed Francis Prior sicklik seyd that his Grandsyre, being a hunder and twaintie zeirs awd hed also meikle havnted it in the same place and for a mere svr testimony that it had beine thair he reported that his grandsyres grandsyre hed a hovse beside it wharin he dwelled and that in his dayes it was beared by the angels frae thence to the hill of they tweye brothers whar they set it as seyd. . . ."

"The angels seem to have carried it about more than once," I interrupted.

"Già," said the beadle. "At first they placed it on the hill of Picino, in a grove of laurels which bowed before it and remained in adoration. But so many thieves and assassins took cover under them to plunder the pious pilgrims of their offerings that the laurels raised their heads again, and after a stay of only eight months the Holy House moved."

"And came here?"

"Not yet. It moved first to a pleasant hill belonging to the brothers Artici, ancestors of Leopardi."

"Ah, the hill of they tweye brothers," I murmured.

"But the treasure heaped upon it dazzled them. They might have fought over it like Cain and Abel. So the house moved on."

"And yet even Leopardi chanted the Madonna," I said.

"Lo credo," said the beadle, unastonished. "And there is still an inscription on the hill, but it does not console the neighbourhood any more than the chapel at Ravinizza."

"The chapel at Ravinizza?"

"Did I not say? That was where it stopped first—near Dalmatia."

"Quite a wandering Jew-house," I murmured.

"That was in 1291, when the Holy Land fell into the power of the Infidel"

"Ah, that was why it left Palestine!"

"Naturally. And you may imagine the agony of the Dalmatians when they returned from the Crusades to find the Holy House no longer in Ravinizza. Even to-day the pilgrims sail out in little boats singing, 'Return to us, Maria, with thy house!' But how could it return to Dalmatia, seeing that seventy-five years before it left Palestine the blessed St. Francis had foretold its coming here by his word Picenum, which is a region on our side of the Adriatic, and being, moreover, interpreted by Latin scholars is a prophetic acrostic?"

"It seems a pity the house did not come straight to Loreto," I ventured.

"We are fortunate it did not go straight back to Nazareth after the battle of Lepanto," he said simply. "It was after our Lady's victory over the Turks that this marble screen was placed around it. Here is the Treasury." And thrusting roughly through the press of congregants, he opened a door and ushered me into a palatial room where under the ceiling-frescoes of Pomerancio of Pesaro I saw what seemed a vast bazaar of every precious article known to humanity.

"The New Treasury," he said apologetically. "The old treasure was seized by Napoleon. It was worth 96,000,000 lire." He looked sad.

"And how much is this worth?"

"Only 4,000,000." And the unctuous catalogue recommenced. "A Genoese family had given this case of jewellery; it was worth 100,000 lire. These were the copes and vestments of Pio Nono (150,000 lire). This was the diadem of Maria, Queen of Spain, wife of Carlo IV—behold the amethysts, the brilliants, the rubies. These Oriental pearls were from the Princess of Würtemberg. Each pearl cost 150,000 lire and there were forty-three pearls—the signore could calculate for himself. This diamond tiara with an Oriental pearl in the centre was given by Maria Louisa, Duchessa di Parma. It was worth 420,000 lire."

"Restoring some of her first husband's plunder," I interrupted.

"Già. And the Madonna Nera was given back too. And this pearl and gold covering for her is from Maria Theresa, Archduchess of Austria. It is worth 12,000 lire. And Giuseppe Napoleon's wife gave us this monstrance. And this cup is from Prince Maximilian of Austria, and these regalia—"

The list went on, and I studied a coral model of the Santa Casa with the Mother and Son riding on the roof, while from the church came a boy's voice soaring heavenward.

"And do you refuse offerings from those who are not royal?" I broke in at last.

"Ah, no," he said seriously. "See! In that glass case are a thousand rings from a thousand pilgrims, and this standard is from a pilgrim of Budapest, and this little wooden ship—the Maria—was given by a sailor, and this pearl showing the Madonna and her Son was found inside a fish by a fisherman, and these ornaments painted with the juice of grass are the work of priests, and this beautiful bronze candelabrum was given by the Guild of Blacksmiths of Bologna. A Capuchin father from South America brought us these great bouquets of flowers made of the wings of Brazilian birds, and a Roumanian noble this little Byzantine brass Madonna, and Prince Carraciolo of Naples—"

"Basta!" I cried hurriedly, for he was back in the "Almanach de Gotha," and, slipping a large piece of silver with a royal portrait on it into his hand, I moved towards the door.

His face shone. "But you have not seen the cups in the Santa Casa from which the Holy Family drank. And their little bells, and—"

"I have seen enough," I said.

"And the cannon-ball," he went on in undiminished gratitude. "The cannon-ball which shattered the pavilion of Pope Julius II when he was besieging a city, but which by the grace of the Blessed Virgin left him un—"

I escaped into the crowd of snooded peasant women and worked my way along the aisle till I stood outside the portal under a gigantic Madonna and Child.

But the beadle was beside me.

"Go and look at the Fontana della Santa Casa." And he pointed in parting gratitude to the centre of the piazza. "Bellissima!"

I did not go, but I looked at the great marble fountain with its grotesque beasts and Cupids and basins, and remembering the humble village fountain at which the carpenter's daughter had filled her urn, I turned sharply to the right and found myself descending a long sordid street of shops and stalls, all doing a busy trade—despite the Sunday—in crosses, rosaries, crucifixes, chaplets, picture-postcards, medals, and all the knick-knacks of holiness. Sometimes through open windows of the ugly one-storey houses I caught sight of the landscape below—the path descending to the sea, bordered with buttercups and a-flutter with birds, the rolling olive-plains, the strip of blue sea, the wonderful headland. Never had I seen a lovelier view shut out by meaner buildings. With its patches of refuse and its dreary shops and booths it seemed the ugliest street in all Italy, bearing on its face the mark of its bastard origin—a city grown up not from natural healthy human life, but for the exploitation of a miracle.

And this it was that drew gold like water from the crowned heads of Europe. And this it was that had drawn hither even Descartes, the first Apostle of Philosophic Doubt. Surely "Non cogito, ergo sum," is the motto of Faith, I thought.

I stood in a vast ancient market-place among canvas-covered stalls, by a lovely fountain with a smiling little Bacchus that faced an old cathedral, and I gazed like ten thousand others at a lovely open-air pulpit that rose in the shadow of a tall campanile. From a bronze capital it rose, girdled with beautiful marble reliefs of dancing children by Donatello and protected from the sun by a charming circular roof, and in this delectable coign of vantage stood a priest holding something that fevered the perspiring mob.

"La sacra cintola! La sacra cintola!"

I knew what the Virgin's girdle would be like, for had I not seen her handing it to St. Thomas in Lippo Lippi's picture in this same town of Prato, as she flew up to heaven in the radiance of her youth and beauty, standing on cherubs' heads and escorted by angels? But now so far as I could see this tasselled belt, it seemed to correspond ill with the waist measurement of the little mother of Nazara.

Some white pigeons fluttered round the priest's head and settled on the pulpit, and a great sigh of ecstasy went up from the people.

I looked round at the little Bacchus. But he was still smiling.

I stood before an altar in a little church, but this time a sweet-faced woman in a wimple stood beside me.

"The wall is behind the altar," she said. "And once a year the miraculous image of the Madonna of the Bed is shown to the people of Pistoja and the pilgrims, exactly as Our Lady of the Graces impressed it on this piece of wall here when she appeared to the sick girl. Very beautiful is she in her crown and mantle, clasping to her arms the crowned Bambino as she flies upwards."

"And where is the bed?"

"The bed was removed from this sanctuary, which it blocked up disproportionately. A separate little chapel was built for it."

We passed to the bed-chapel by way of the old cloisters of the Ospedale, and saw in a small room a heavy brownish wooden bed with a red quilt, made as for an occupant. A Madonna and Child was painted on the headpiece, and a Madonna and Child at the foot, and a Madonna and Child hung on the wall.

"And when was the miracle wrought?" I asked.

"In 1336."

The very year of the death of Cino, the poet of Pistoja and the friend of Dante, I remembered. And Dante and Cino had receded into the dim centuries while this bed with its prosaic quilt and pillows stood stolid, inscribed at head and foot with inscriptions dated 1336 and 1334, begging me to pray for the souls of Condoso Giovanni and Fra Ducchio.

"Here," explained the sweet-faced sister, "the poor girl had lain many long years, incurable, when one day the Virgin appeared in dazzling beauty, holding the Child, and told two little boys who happened to be in the hospital to fetch brother Jacopo della Cappa. The venerable brother, being busy confessing, refused to be disturbed, whereupon the Virgin sent a second message bidding him come at once, for she desired him to predict a pestilence in Pistoja, of which he would die in a month. So he came forthwith, but he had scarcely entered the room when the dazzling apparition disappeared. But she left the invalid girl in perfect health, and her holy image on the wall."

"And did Fra Jacopo duly die?"

"To the day. And so great was the plague that there was scarcely any one left to administer the last office."

"As disproportionate as the bed to the church," I thought, "to kill off all Pistoja and save one bedridden girl." But how utter such a thought to this sweet-faced sister?

"Since then the bed and the image on the wall have wrought many miracles," she said. "The blind have had their sight, the deaf their hearing, the paralysed their limbs. That was why the name was changed from Our Lady of the Bed to Our Lady of the Graces. And countless were the pilgrims that came. But in 1780 the wicked Scipione Ricci, who was a secret Jansenist, was made our bishop, and he tried to destroy the faith in our sanctuary and in the Girdle of Prato. But our neighbours of Prato rose against him, rushed into the cathedral, smashed his episcopal chair, and sacked his palace. He had to resign his bishopric, and so our faith was purged of the heretic, and Maria was avenged. Ah, that jubilee of her Immaculate Conception in 1904! It was a day of Paradise."

Again a haze disturbs my vision. For a moment I see the little olive-eyed Jewess of Nazara, racked between husband and son, wringing her impotent hands; then my vision clears, and I am reading a printed Italian prayer before a chapel of the Madonna in a mighty fane.

"TO THE HOLY IMMACULATE VIRGIN OF HOPE VENERATED IN THE BASILICA OF S. FREDIANO

"Kneeling before you, Immaculate Virgin, Mother of God, consoler of the afflicted, refuge of sinners, we pray you to turn upon us your looks full of goodness, compassion, and love. You see all our spiritual and temporal needs. Obtain from your divine Son sincere contrition for sin, light to know the truth, force to conquer temptations, help to believe and act as true Christians, patience in tribulations, peace of heart, holy perseverance to the end. Obtain for us that there may remain far from us disease, pestilence, hunger, war, earthquakes, fires, drought, flood, sudden death. Take this City under your particular protection, preserve it, defend it, cause ever to reign therein the spirit of religion and of concord, and in private families mutual charity, domestic content, and good morals. . . . Whoever will devoutly recite this will acquire forty days' Indulgence already conceded by His Most Reverend Excellence Monsignore the Archbishop Filippo Santi.

"Lucca, 1848."

I seemed to be back in Asia on a burning June day fifteen hundred years before this prayer was written, much pushed about by the crowd that surged round a church.

"Is it the Whitsuntide service?" I asked a priest at last in the Greek I heard on all sides.

"Nay; art a barbarian or a worshipper of the Temple of Diana that thou knowest not the Church of the Theotokos, and the great Imperial Council of Bishops that is sitting there to avenge the insults of Nestorius to the Virgin?"

"What insults?" I murmured.

"Surely thou hast snored in the cave in the Pion Hill with our Seven Sleepers! This blasphemous Patriarch of Constantinople denies our Lady the title Theotokos, would argue that she is not Mother of God, but that the Christ born through her was only the human part of Him, not the Eternal Logos." His voice trembled, his beady eyes flamed with passion. "And he dares come defend his thesis here—in Ephesus, where the Holy Virgin lies buried! But our saintly Cyril of Alexandria hath drawn up twelve anathemas and will stamp him out as he stamped out that minx Hypatia."

"Is Cyril here too, then?"

"Ay, and what an ambrosial homily he preached! 'Hail, Mary, Mother of God, spotless dove! Hail, Mary, perpetual lamp at which was kindled the Sun of Justice! Hail, Mary! Thanks to Thee, the archangels rejoice and sing; thanks to Thee, the Magi followed the star; thanks to Thee the college of Apostles was established. . . .'" His voice died away in reminiscent ecstasy.

"Then Cyril and Nestorius are now in debate?"

"Nay, the heretic shrinks from appearing—he pretexts that all the bishops are not arrived, and he induced the Emperor's commissioner to protest against the sitting. But as thou seest, the Council is going on—hath been going on from early morn—there are two hundred bishops."

"There are only a hundred and fifty," put in a voice. "It is scandalous."

"Ay," assented another voice. "Where is the Patriarch of Antioch?"

The priest turned on the Nestorians. "It is beasts like you with whom Paul fought here," he said.

"Beast thyself," retorted a physician in a long robe, "to suggest that God could be contained in the womb." It was the beginning of a scuffle that grew to a bloody battle between the Nestorian minority and the orthodox. Daggers and scimitars gleamed in the air. I saw a group of Nestorians take refuge in a church, but fly from it again, leaving a trail of bleeding corpses along the aisle. The survivors made for the harbour, hoping doubtless for safety in the multitude of boats and ships.

And ever thicker grew the crowd surging round the Council-chamber, till at last as the long summer day closed, a rumbling as of distant thunder was heard from within—"Anathema! Anathema!" And the cry passed to the crowd—"Anathema! Anathema!"—till the whole firmament seemed to crash and rock with it and men cheered and danced and tossed their weapons in air. And as the venerable figures began to troop out and the word came that Nestorius was deposed, a thousand torches leapt as by magic into flame, and men escorted the Bishops to their lodgings, leaping and singing, and lo! round the whole city blazed illuminations and bonfires.

And my eyes, piercing through the future, beheld Italian bottegas with immortal Masters and Pupils, turning out through the centuries portraits of the Madonna and Child, to be blazoned henceforward inseparable, a symbol of the true faith: delectable, innumerable, filling the whole earth with their glory.

The close smell of the studios gave way again to the odour of crowded humanity and I was in the arena of Seville. But never, not even at Easter, had I seen the populace so joyous, the ladies shrouded in such rich mantillas or flirting such precious fans, the picadors so gaily caparisoned, the toreadors so daring, the bulls maddened with so many banderillas or disembowelling so many horses. It was the mutual ecstasy of slaughter. And from all parts of the city penetrated the chiming of bells, while the thunder of festive cannon sometimes drowned even the roar of the ring. And at every thrilling stroke or perilous charge there came from parted lips, "Ave Maria purissima" or "Viva nuestra Señora," and from all around rose the instinctive reply: "Sin peccado concebida."

Gradually, as I listened to the conversation in the intervals of the bull fights, I became aware of the sense of the Fiesta. All this overflow of religious rapture sprang not from the bulls but the Bull—Regis

Pacifici—which after centuries of passionate controversy had at last been launched by Paul V in this sixteen hundred and seventeenth year from the bearing of the Virgin, forbidding the opponents of Immaculate Conception to sustain their doctrine in public. Maria had been conceived without sin. The last flaw had been removed from her perfection.

"Heaven rewards us for expelling the last of the Moors," cried a lovely Señora with a dazzling flash of eyes and teeth. "And now that we have purged Spain and placed her and her mighty possessions under the protection of the Immaculate Conception, her future shall be even more glorious than her past."

But my reply was drowned by the roar of the ring as the dead bull was trailed off at a gallop.

"Ave Maria purissima!"

"Sin peccado concebida!"

I am still in Spain, watching Señor Bartholomé Estéban Murillo polish off his Madonnas for country fairs or South American convents. Presently under the guidance of Señor Pacheco, Holy Inquisitor of pictures, he paints the popular dogma of the day, in the shape of little angels floating below a lovely lady in a blue mantle standing with clasped hands on the earth-ball, and the scene shifts to France where two centuries later the picture is purchased at a fabulous price by the Louvre, just before Pio Nono from his refuge at Gaeta publishes the Bull Ineffabilis, definitely declaring that the freedom of the Virgin from original sin is a divine revelation. Cheap coloured pictures of the "Immaculate Conception" multiply, and Bernadette, a pious young shepherdess in the French Pyrenees, beholds in a grotto by a spring a White Lady, veiled from head to foot, with a cerulean floating scarf, a chaplet with golden links, and two golden roses on her naked feet, who announces herself as "The Immaculate Conception" and demands a Procession to her shrine.

And before my eyes unrolls the long panorama, painted in immortal colours by the epical brush of Zola: the mushroom Lourdes of hotels and holy shops replacing the rude village, the Hospital of our Lady of Sorrows, the crowned statue of our Lady of Salvation, the Fathers of the Grotto, the Blue Sisters, the Church of the Rosary, the Basilica swathed in splendid banners, glittering with golden hearts innumerable, and jewels and marbles and marvellous lamps; the unending masses and litanies, the three hundred thousand pilgrims a year, the thaumaturgic bathing pools, unclean, abominable, the White Train rolling through the night with its hideous agglomeration of human agonies, amid ecstatic canticles to the Madonna, the thirty thousand tapers winding round in leagues of flame to the rhythm of interminable invocations, the perpetual thunder of supplication breaking frenziedly on the figure of the Madonna framed in the ever-blazing Grotto.

The thunder continued but it was again the roar of an arena, though by the towered old palaces round the great semi-circle of cobbled piazza and by the fountain with the bas-reliefs of Christian virtues I knew I was back in Italy, in my beloved Siena. But what was this smoky flame that shot skyward and what was this tree near the Christian fountain that they were breaking up to throw on the bonfire? What was this dreadful sport that had replaced the Palio?

In a vast pyre burnt a great huddle of writhing figures, whose shrieks were drowned by the fiendish roar of the drunken mob.

"Viva Maria! Viva Maria!"

And I remembered that Siena had peculiarly dedicated itself to the Holy Mother, was the civitas Virginis, and that the Madonna was its feudal suzerain, formally presented with the keys of its gates. Visions from the old chronicles floated before me—the dedication of 1260, the weeping Syndic in his shirt, a rope round his neck, prostrate with the Bishop before the altar of the Virgin, or walking behind her as she was carried in the great barefoot procession to the chanting of Ave Marias; and the victory over Florence that duly followed, when, throwing her white mantle of mist over her city, she enabled her faithful feudatories to slay ten thousand Florentines "as a butcher slays animals in a slaughter house," so that the Malena ran bank-high with blood, and the region, polluted by the carcases of eighteen thousand horses, was abandoned to the wild beasts, and coins were struck in her honour; and the renewed dedications whenever the Commune was in peril, the gorgeous processions and "Te Deums," the great silk standard showing the Madonna rising into heaven over the city, the Cardinal, the Prior, the Captain of the People, the Signoria in violet and cloaked as on Good Friday, the trumpeters trumpeting in the striped Duomo, the feudal keys in a silver basin, the fifty poor damsels in white, dowered annually so long as the Virgin did her duty as suzerain—

But the shrieks from the bonfire brought me back to the moment.

"Whom are they burning?" I cried in horror.

"Only Jews," replied my neighbour reassuringly, and indeed, I could now distinguish the Hebrew death-cries of the victims.

"Hear, O Israel, the Lord Our God, the Lord is One."

"We burn them and the Tree of Liberty together!" my neighbour chuckled. "No godless French Republic for us!" A fierce yell from the crowd underlined his remark. He craned forward, beaming, exalted.

"They have found another! O Blessed Virgin of Comfort, they have found another!"

And I perceived, dragged along towards the pyre by her greying hair, a little olive-eyed Jewish mother, whose worn face I seemed to recognise under her dishevelled head-shawl.

"Viva Maria! Viva Maria! Viva la Madre di Dio!"

The spectacle was too horrible. With a convulsive shudder I shook off these visions and rose, cramped, to my feet. The sun was dipping beyond the mountains of Vicenza, the peaceful bell from below was still tolling, the air was cool and delicious. Now I could continue my climb to the church of Our Lady of the Mountain. And the loving epithets recommenced—"Debellatrix Incredulorum," "Janua Coeli," "Turris Davidica," without pause, without end. And as I walked, other of her countless names began crowding upon me, from "Our Lady of Snows" to "Our Lady of Sorrows," from "Our Lady of the Porringer" to "The Queen of the Angels," and all the symbols of her, from the Pomegranate to the Sealed Book, from the Dove to the Porta Clausa; and all the myriads of churches and altars that had been dedicated to her from Rome to Ecuador—from Milan Cathedral with its hundred spires to the humblest wayside shrine of Sicily or Mexico—and all the feasts, all the "Months of Maria," all the Pilgrimages, with all the medals and missals, all the effigies in wood or wax or bronze, all the marbles and mosaics, from the crude little black sacrosanct Byzantine figures to the exquisitely tender marble Pietà of Michelangelo, and all the convents and orders she had created, all the Enfants de Marie, and Serviti di Maria, and Sisters of the

Immaculate Conception, and all the hymns, antiphons, litanies, lections, carols, canticles. The air was full of organ sounds and the melody of soaring voices. "Ave Maris Stella" they sang, and "Salve Regina" and "Stabat Mater," and then in an infinite incantation, sounding and resounding from all the spaces of the world: "Sancta Maria, ora pro nobis! Sancta Maria, ora pro nobis!" And her figure floated before me, pure, radiant, loving, as it has floated before millions of households for hundreds of years, consoling, blessing, vitalising.

And I thought of her long adventure to reach this marvellous apotheosis: in what a strange little source this mighty river had begun; how that looseness of the Septuagint translator in rendering the Hebrew for "maiden" by "virgin" in an utterly irrelevant passage of Isaiah had led to Mary's virginity; how she had remained a virgin through all the vicissitudes of her married life, Joseph turning into a man of eighty with children by his former wife, or even remaining virgin himself, the brothers of Jesus changing into his cousins; how her son had been born as a ray of light or even as an illusive appearance; how, with the growth of theology and Mariolatry and nunneries and monasteries, she had grown holier and holier, immaculate, impeccable, a model to men and maidens, the Queen of Heaven, mighty beyond all the saints, giving four feast-days to the Church, entering into the liturgy, redeeming souls from purgatory on Assumption Day, and even sustaining the saintly with her milk; how her final purification from the taint of original sin had been a stumbling block for the more rigid theologians, St. Bernard opposing the festival, Aquinas and the Dominicans denying the dogma against Duns Scotus and the Franciscans; but how the "intellectuals"—so serviceable to the mob when their logic found contorted reasons for the popular faith—were sooner or later swept aside, the harsh definers of heresy themselves left heretics, when they ran counter to the popular emotion, the popular festivals, the popular instinct for an ideal of purity and perfection. What a curious play and interplay of schoolman-logic and living emotion, working ceaselessly through the centuries, combining or competing to re-shape and sublimate the carpenter's wife till she was wrought to the mould of the popular need, her very parents, unknown to the Gospels, becoming, as Joachim and Anna, the centre of a fresh cycle of legends, pictures, Church festivals. And what uncountable volumes of monumental learning and jejune controversy, from Augustus and Anselm and the venerable Bede to the two thousand and twelve pages of Carlo Passaglia of Lucca, the respondent to Renan!

And my thoughts turned from the theologians to the poets and painters, to the Vergine Bella e di sol vestita—the beautiful Apocalyptic Virgin, clothed with the sun—of Petrarch, and the weeping Virgin of Tasso, and the Vergine Madre Figlia del tuo Figlio of Dante, and the images in all these forms created by the artists, for whom the Madonna sufficed to open all the mansions of art; who could cluster all the poetry of the world round her glory or her grief, were it rural loveliness or the beauty of lilies, or lofty architecture, or space-rhythm, or begemmed and brocaded attire, or the sculptural nude; who set her rich-carved throne, adorned with arabesques or hued in strange green and gold, amid palatial pillars under diapered ceilings or within glamorous landscapes, or in the bowers of roses or under the shadow of lemon-trees; who even crowned her with the Papal tiara.

But none of these images would stay with me: for not even the triple crown, surmounted by the golden globe and cross, not even this symbol of temporal, spiritual, and purgatorial authority, could banish the worn face of the carpenter's wife under the cheap head-shawl, the little olive-eyed mother in Israel, in whose ears sounded and resounded the terrible words: "Woman, what have I to do with thee?"

From the swinging of the bronze lamp in the nave of Pisa Cathedral Galileo caught the idea of measuring Time by the pendulum; by the telescope he made at Padua he mapped Space. Within a decade of the burning of Giordano Bruno the heavens were opened up to show the infinity of worlds, and the heliocentric teaching of Copernicus was confirmed by the revelation of Jupiter's satellites. What the Sidereus Nuncius of Galileo announced was the end of an era. By this terrible book and his terrible telescope the poor little earth was pushed out of the centre of the stage. The moon—no longer teres atque rotunda—lost her beautiful spheric smoothness, her very light was a loan—unrepaid. Great Sol, himself, the old lord of creation, gradually sank to the obscure coryphæus of some choric dance veering towards and around some ineffable pivot in a measureless choragium. The ninefold vault engirdling Dante's universe was shrivelled up. The cosy cosmos was replaced by a maze of solar systems, glory beyond glory, of milky ways that were but clouds of worlds, thick as a haze of summer insects or a whirl of sand in the Sahara. The poor human brain reeled in this simoom of stars, and to complete its confusion, the philosophers hastened to assure it that with the universe no longer geocentric, man could no longer flatter himself to be its central interest.

"So many nobler bodies to create,
Greater, so manifold, to this one use,"

appeared disproportionate to Milton's Adam. Homo could not be the Master-Builder's main concern—the great human tragedy was a by-product. A sad conclusion, and possibly a true—but a conclusion utterly unwarranted by these premises. More sanely did the beneficent and facile Raphael remind the doubting Adam,

"Whether heaven moves or earth
Imports not."

The noble astronomic questionings in the eighth book of "Paradise Lost" testify to the ferment among the first inhabitants of the new cosmos—Milton was born in the same year as the telescope and met Galileo at Florence—but despite the poet's half-hearted protests, man has swallowed too humbly the doctrine that our earth is not the centre of the universe. Pray do not confound me with those pious pundits whose proofs of the flatness of the earth are still the hope of a lingering sect, and a witness to the immortality of human stupidity. I am no Muggletonian whose sun is four miles from the earth. I have no lance to tilt against the mathematicians and their tubes. But I fail to see how the mere broadening out of our universe can displace Terra from the centre. Till we have the final and all-inclusive chart of the heavens—and worlds immeasurable are still beyond our ken, worlds whose light speeding to us at eleven million miles or so a minute is still on its way—how can any one assert conclusively that our earth is not in the exact centre of all the systems? That it goes round the sun—instead of being the centre of the sun's revolution—is nothing against its supremacy or central status. The fire exists for the meat, though the spit revolves and not the fire.

And if the earth be not in the centre of the systems, it assuredly remains at the centre of Space. For by that old definition of Hermes Trismegistus to which Pascal gave currency, every point of an infinite area is really its centre, even as no point is its circumference. And in a psychological sense too, wherever a spectator stands is the centre of the universe.

But grant the earth be not the centre of Space or the systems! What then? How does it lose its lofty estate? Is London at the globe's kernel? Did the axis pass through Rome? Kepler wasted much precious time under the current philosophic obsession that the orbits of the planets must be circular—since any figure less perfect than a circle were incompatible with their dignity. Hence the cumbrous hypotheses to explain their apparent deviation from perfection, hence was the sphere girt

"With centric and eccentric scribbled o'er,
Cycle and epicycle, orb in orb."

The same fallacy of symmetry surely underlies the notion that the earth is dethroned from its hegemony of the stellar system merely because the lines drawn to it from every ultima Thule of the universe are unequal. 'Tis a confusion of geometric centre with centre of forces. It may be that just this asymmetric station was necessary for the evolution of the universe's crowning race.

For if the Universe has not its aim and centre in man, pray to what other end all this planetary pother? If man is but a by-product of the cosmic laboratory, what is the staple? Till this question is answered, we may safely continue anthropocentric.

Man abased forsooth by this whirl of mammoth worlds! Nay, 'tis our grandeur that stands exalted, our modesty that stands corrected. We did not dream that our facture required such colossal machinery, that to engender us a billion billion planets must be in experimental effervescence. A fig upon their size! Do we rank Milton inferior to the megatherium? Can a man take thought by adding a cubit to his stature? The ant is wiser than the alligator, and the sprawling saurians of the primal slime may have their analogue in the huge weltering worlds that have never evolved a human brain. And had the earth swollen herself to the gross amplitude of the sun, her case were no better: she would still be—in the infinite wash of Space—a pebble, even as a pebble is a stellar system in miniature. There lies the paradox of infinity. Nothing in it is large enough to be important—if quantity is the criterion of importance. To be in one spot of Space is as dignified or undignified as to be in another. Why, I wonder, has position in Time escaped this invidious criticism. As well assert that nothing important can happen or nothing that happens can be important, because everything must happen at a mere point of Time, which is not even Time's central point. It was a truer sense of values that made Christendom and Islam boldly place their foundation at Time's central point, up to which or back to which all the ages lead. The year One begins with Christ's birth, with Mohammed's Hegira. In the same spirit, though with a more literal belief, did the old cartographers draw their world round Jerusalem as a centre. Position in Time or Space is not the measure of importance, but importance is the measure of position in Time or Space. Where the highest life is being lived, there is the centre of the world, and unless a higher life is lived elsewhere, the centre of the universe. Not, where are we in Space, but are we on the central lines of cosmic evolution? That is the question.

Theology, then, stands where it did, wherever Terra stands. Not the mythical theology of sacred books, but the scientific theology of sacred facts. The expansion of the universe from a mapped parish to a half-uncharted wilderness of worlds cannot shake religion—a Deity is more suitably lodged in infinity than on a roof-garden—but it did shake the Church, so recklessly committed to a disprovable cosmogony. And the Church burnt books and men with its habitual consuming zeal, denying the motion of the earth as it had denied the Antipodes, clinging to an earth surrounded by menial planets, as it had clung to the flat plane of "Christian Topography."

But is there nothing to be said for the Churchmen? Were they mere venomous obscurantists? Nay, they were patriots fighting for their father-world, for the cosmos of their ancestors, pro aris et focis. They saw their little universe threatened by the rise of a great stellar empire. They saw themselves about to be swallowed up and lost in its measureless magnificence. And so in a frenzy of chauvinism they gagged Galileo and burned Giordano Bruno, those traitors in the camp, in league with Reason, emperor of the stars.

But despite the Church's defeat, our little globe still maintains a sturdy independence. And until you bring me evidence of a superior genus, I shall continue to regard our good red earth as the centre of creation, and man as the focus of inter-celestial planetary forces.

Millions of spiritual creatures may walk the earth unseen, as Milton asserts, and millions more may be invisible in Mars and the remoter seats of the merry-go-round, but de non apparentibus et de non existentibus eadem est ratio. It is William James who of all philosophers in the world would argue our fates regulated by superior beings with whom we co-exist as with us our cats and dogs. The analogy has not even one leg to stand on. The cat and the dog have solid proof of our existence, they see and hear us, and we share with them a large segment of existence. Our anatomy and theirs are much of a muchness. They divide with us our food and our drink and bask at the same fire, nay, it requires a vast conceit to look them in the face and deny our kinship. But who save Gulliver hath beheld a bodily Superman or partaken of his meals? Even with our spiritual superiors, with our Shakespeares and Beethovens, we have a substantial basis of identity. The range of thought which circumscribes ours must at the same time partially coincide with it, and though our thoughts be not wholly their thoughts, their thoughts must needs be partially ours.

God may be infinitely more than man, but He is not finitely less. Even a God without humour would be—to that extent—man's inferior. Matthew Arnold's gibe of the "magnified non-natural man" is groundless. I do not become a magnified non-natural dog because I have attributes in common with my terrier. The God of theology is already divested of man's matter; deflate Him likewise of man's spirit, and what remains? In robbing their Deity of all human traits the de-anthropomorphic philosophers have overshot the mark and reduced Him to a transcendental nullity who can neither be comprehended by His creatures nor comprehend them.

Or if they allow Him ideas and passions, they neutralise and sterilise them in a frenzy of scholastic paradox. "Amas, nec æstuas," cries St. Augustine, "zelas et securus es; pænitet te et non doles; irasceris et tranquillus es." God repents, but without regret; He is angry but perfectly tranquil. To evade the limitations of any attribute we endow Him at the same time with its opposite, as who should say a white negro. But such violent assaults upon the unthinkable yield no prize either of understanding or of satisfaction.

If "the love that moves the sun and the other stars" be not that same love which a noble man may feel for his fellow-creatures of every order of being, if it be a love that is at the same time indifference, or even hate, then it may equally be expressed as "the hate which moves the sun and the other stars" (and which is at the same time love). Or it may find far honester expression as the agnostic's unknowable—the X that moves the sun and the other stars. If God's justice be not man's justice, then it is no justice. It must be our justice—if it is justice at all—our justice, only occupied and obscured by innumerable pros and cons to us unknown, and extending over times and spaces beyond our ken, so that were we placed in possession of all the evidence we should applaud the verdict. The philosophers do but narrow their God under illusion of broadening Him—or rather they broaden Him so tenuously that He becomes an infinite impalpability, whose accidental evaporation would scarcely be noted. It was a more consistent mystic who said: "God may not improperly be styled nothing."

So that our circumnavigation of the infinite brings us back to our noble selves and our own door-step. The sun is still there to give us light by day, and the moon and stars still shine to give us light by night. Nor is it less their function to nourish us with beauty and with mystery.

"When Science from Creation's face
Enchantment's veil withdraws,
What lovely visions yield their place
To cold material laws!"

Campbell, who thus complained, was no profound poet. The laws are neither cold nor material, nor do the lovely visions yield their place. Their loveliness is as abiding as the laws which produce them. 'Tis true that at first Galileo seemed to have profaned Cynthia, the "goddess excellently bright." The moon, the beautiful moon of poets and lovers, lay betrayed—a dead planet, a scarred desolation, seamed with arid ravines and pitted with a pox of craters. Is then the moon of the poets a delusion which science bids us put away like a childish toy? No, by her own heavens, no. A more scientific science restores the glamour. The moon has all the beauty she appears to have. The loveliest woman's face, viewed through a magnifying glass, appears equally scarred and seamed and pitted. But here 'tis the lens that is accused of falsification, 'tis the ugliness that is pronounced the delusion—a face was meant to be seen at a certain distance and with the natural eye. Even so—and the moon chose her distance with admirable discretion.

The synthesis of everyday reality is always man's central verity. The peering unnatural scientific vision of the moon has the lesser truth, is but a spectral rim of the whole-orbed reality. 'Tis the poet's moon that is the full moon. But the poet were as foolish as the astronomer if he in his turn imagined himself dealing with absolutes, if he forgot that in logic as in landscape all views depend on the point at which you place yourself. It is only from the true point of view that the earth remains the centre of the universe.

OF AUTOCOSMS WITHOUT FACTS: OR THE EMPTINESS OF RELIGIONS

And what is the invasion of our consciousness by the extended stellar system to its invasion by the intensive infinities of our own globular parish? The endless galaxy of the centuries and the civilisations has opened out before our telescopic thought. We are no longer at the centre of our cosmos—we can no longer snuggle in a cosy conceptual world, Classical or Christian, nor can we make the best of both these worlds, like Raphael or Milton. The dim populations have become lurid. Japan pours her art upon us, and her equal claim to hold a chosen people—"pursuing," as its Emperor's oath declares, "a policy co-extensive with the heavens and the earth." Egypt unrolls the teeming scroll of her immemorial dynasties. The four hundred millions of China lie on our imaginations like a nightmare in yellow, and we perceive that the maker of man hath a predilection for pigtails. India opens out her duskily magnificent infinities and we are grown familiar with Brahma and Vishnu, with Vedas and Buddha-Jâtakas. Persia reveals to us in the Zend Avesta of Zoroaster a strangely modern gospel, glimmering through grotesque images of space and time. Mohammed is no longer an Infidel, and we recognise the subtlety alike of the Motekallamin and the Arabic Aristotelians. We respect the Norse Gods and the great Tree Yggdrasil. The Teutonic divinities have reappeared in every part of the civilised earth and their operatic voice is heard with more reverence than any other god's. Even the old Peruvian civilisation solicits us, that successful social order of the Incas. The stellar swirl of worlds is a crude puzzle in quantity beside these mental worlds which the peoples have spun for themselves like cocoons.

But not only the peoples. Each creature that has ever lived, from the spider to Shakespeare, has spun for itself its own cosmos. Microcosm we cannot call this cosmos, since that implies the macrocosm drawn to smaller scale, and this—like all creations—is a mere selection from the universe, excluding and including after its own idiosyncrasy. Autocosm is the word we need for it—a new word, but a phenomenon as old as the first created consciousness, and a phenomenon that has never perfectly repeated itself since that day. For no two autocosms have ever been precisely alike. In the lower orders of being the autocosm may be substantially identical throughout all the individuals of the species, but as we mount in the grade of organisation, the autocosm becomes more and more individual. And even the large generic autocosms, how variously compounded—the scent-world of dogs, the eye-world of birds, the uncanny touch-world of bats, the earth-world of worms, the water-world of fishes, the gyroscopic world of dancing-mice, the flesh-world of parasites, the microscopic world of microbes. These worlds do not need untrammelled orbits, they intersect one another inextricably in an infinite interlacing. Yet each is a symmetric sphere of being, a rounded whole, and to its denizens the sole and self-sufficient cosmos. One creature's poison is another creature's meat, one creature's offal is another creature's paradise, and our cemetery is a nursery aswarm with creeping mites. If on the one hand Nature seems a wasteful housekeeper, scattering a thousand seeds that one may bear, on the other hand she appears ineffably ingenious in economising every ort and oddment, every cheese-paring and scum-drop as the seed-plot of new and joyous existence. Life, like an infinite nebulous spirit, bursts in through every nook and cranny of matter, squeezing itself into every possible and improbable mould, and even filling a chink in an existing creature rather than remain outside organisation. And each atom of spirit that achieves material existence takes its cramped horizons for the boundaries of the universe and itself as the centre of creation. Woe indeed to the creature that has seen beyond its own boundaries, that can weave no cosy autocosm to nestle in. This is what happens to your Shakespeares and your Schopenhauers; this is the "Everlasting Nay" of "Sartor Resartus." Life is become

"A tale
Told by an idiot, full of sound and fury,
Signifying nothing."

Such an autocosm is the shirt of Nessus. Hercules must tear it off or perish. And we are all the time changing our autocosms. That is the meaning of experience. Only the fool dies in the same cosmos in which he was born, and a great teacher or a great statesman changes the autocosm of his generation.

Here be the true weavings with which Time's Shuttle is busy, these endless patternings and re-patternings of mental worlds, adjusted to ever-changing creatures, and ever-shifting circumstances. The birth and death of planets is stability compared with this mercurial flux, which in the human world is known as movements of thought and religion, growths and decays of language, periods of art and politics. History is the clash of autocosms, and every war is a war of the worlds.

As I walk into Milan Cathedral, the modern autocosm fades out with the buzz and tingle of the electric cars that engirdle the great old building, and the massive walls of the mediæval autocosm shut me into a glowing gloom of unearthly radiance, whose religious hush is accentuated by the sound of soft bells. Only the dominating figure on the cross seems out of tone; this blood is too violent for peace. What a paradox that the Christians are such dominant races—perhaps they needed this brake. But even without the blood, the cruciform dusk of the interior is in discord with the lace-work of the exterior, recalls the sombreness below the glittering Renaissance. All this multitudinous microscopic work is waste, all this wealth of fretwork and final, for it is only at a distance, when the details have faded into the mass, that this mass appears noble. And this, too, is like the Catholic autocosm, with its rococo detail and its massive magnificence.

And round the Cathedral, as I said, rages the modern order—is not Milan the metropolis of Italian science and do not all tram-roads lead to the Piazza del Duomo?—and a ballet I saw in La Scala danced the carmagnole of the new world. "Excelsior" was its jubilant motto, the ascent being from Cathedrals to Railway Bridges and Balloons. A Shining Spirit of Light (Luce) inspired Civiltà and baffled the priestly powers of darkness (Tenebre), while ineffably glittering coryphées proclaimed with their toes "Eureka!"

But ah! my dear Corybants of Reason, an autocosm may be habitable and even comfortable in despite of Science. Its working value is independent of its containing false materials, or true materials in false proportions. And yet, my dear devotees of Pragmatism—that parvenu among Philosophies—its utility does not establish its truth. A false coin will do all the work of a true coin so long as it is not found out. Nevertheless there exists a test of coins independent of their power of gulling the public. And there exists a name for those who continue to circulate a coin after they know it to be false. The Pragmatist may apply his philosophy to justify past forms of belief and action, now outmoded, but he will do infinite mischief if he tries to juggle himself or the world into such forms of belief or action because they lead to spiritual and practical satisfactions.

Oh, what a tangled web we weave
When first we practise to believe!

Nay, it is doubtful whether satisfaction can come as the sequel of any but a genuine and involuntary belief. There is much significance in the story of the old Welsh lady who desired the removal of the mountain in front of her window and complained to her pastor that all her prayers had been unable to move it a single inch. "Because you have not real faith," was the glib clerical reply. Whereupon, resolved to have "real faith," the old lady spent a night of prayer on her knees opposite the mountain. When morning came, and she rolled up the blind, lo! the mountain stood as before. "There!" she exclaimed. "Just as I expected!"

This pseudo-faith is, I fear, all that the Pragmatist can beguile or batter himself into, for if he has real faith he needs no Pragmatism to justify it by.

I grant you—indeed I have always pointed out—that there is a large area of the autocosm given over to artistic, moral and spiritual truths which are their own justification. But it is only where there is no objective test of truth that Pontius Pilate's question may be answered with the test of success and stimulation. Wherever it is possible to compare the autocosm with the macrocosm, contradiction must be taken as the mark of falsity, and either our notion of the macrocosm must be amended, or our autocosm. Of course in the last analysis the macrocosm is only the autocosm of its age, but it is the common segment of all the individual autocosms. And while they are liable to shrivel up like pricked bladders, the objective universe can only expand and expand.

Despite La Scala and its dædal Modernism, it was, I fear, the Catholic autocosm which fascinated me most in Italy, with its naïve poetry, its grossness, its sublimity, and its daring distortions of the macrocosm. The very clock-wheels in their courses fight against reality. Read in the great church of S. Petronio the directions on the two clocks of Fornasini, one giving the solar time in the antique Italian style—when the hour varied with the daylight—and the other the mean time of the meridian of Bologna. "Subtract the time on the Italian clock from 24 o'clock, add the remainder to the time indicated on the other clock, but counted from 1 to 24 o'clock. The time thus obtained will be the hour of Ave Maria!" The hour of Ave Maria! Not some crude arithmetical hour. Not the hour of repose from work, not the hour of impending sunset, but the hour of the vesper bell, the hour of Ave Maria! How it circumlaps, this atmosphere, how it weaves a veil of pity and love between man and the macrocosm.

It is nearly three and a half centuries since Italy helped to break the power of the Paynim at Lepanto, yet the belief that the Madonna (who could not free her own land from the Turk) was the auxilium Christianorum, is as lively as on the day when the bigoted Gregory XIII instituted the Feast of the Rosary to commemorate her victory. At Verona I read in a church a vast inscription set up at the tercentenary of the battle, still ascribing the victory not only to the "supreme valour of our arms steeled by the word of Pius V," but also to "the great armipotent Virgin." Saints that I had in my ignorance imagined remote from to-day, shelved in legend and picture, retired from practical life, are, I found, still in the full exercise of their professional activities as thaumaturgists; and scholastic philosophers whose systems I had skimmed in my youth as archaic lore, whom I had conceived as buried in encyclopædias and monastic libraries, blossom annually in new editions. There is the Angelic Doctor—Preceptor as he was styled on the title-pages—whom I had thought safely tucked away in the tenth canto of the "Paradiso." In the Seminario Vescovile of Ferrara I beheld the bulky volumes of his "Summa Theologiæ" in the pious hands of the fledgeling priests, in a class-room whose ceiling bears the sombre frescoes with which Garofalo had enriched the building in its palmy days as a Palazzo. And the theology has decayed far less than the frescoes. Still, that which we look upon as the faded thought of the Middle Ages, serves as the fresh bread of life to these youthful souls. Little did I dream when I first saw Benozzo Gozzoli's picture of The Triumph of St. Thomas, or Taddeo Gaddi's portrayal of his celestial exaltation over the discomfited Arius, Sabellius, and Averroes, that I should see with my own eyes scholars still at the feet of the Magister studentium of the thirteenth century. Well may the Pope undaunted launch his Encyclicals, and the Osservatore Romano remark that "the evolution of dogma is a logical nonsense for philosophers and a heresy for theologians."

Pascal summed it up long ago: "Truth on this side of the Pyrenees, Falsehood beyond." What is true in the Piazza of St. Peter grows false as you pass the Swiss Guards. Catholic truth, like the Vatican, is extra-territorial. Why should it concern itself with what is believed outside? Even the Averroist philosophers taught that their results were true only in philosophy, and that in the realm of Catholicism what the Church taught was true. And though "impugning the known truth" be one of the sins against the Holy Ghost, the known truth and the Church truth show scant promise of coinciding. And the triumph of St. Thomas continues, as saint no less than as teacher. "Divus Thomas Aquinas" I found him styled in Perugia. His Festa is on March 7, as I read in a placard in the Church of S. Domenico in Ferrara.

"Festa dell' Angelico Dottore
S. T. d'Aquinas
San Patrono delle Scuole Cattoliche."

On the day of the Festa there is plenary indulgence for all the faithful. There was another indulgence "per gli ascritti alla Milizia Angelica." But whether the Angelic Militia are the pupils of the Angelic Doctor I am not learned enough to say.

His even earlier saintship, St. Antony, not only continues to dominate Padua from his vast monumental Church, and enjoy his three June days of Festa in his nominal city, but his tutelary grace extends far beyond. In the Church of San Spirito in the Via Ariosto of Ferrara, the famous preacher to the fishes was—after the earthquake of 1908—the target of three days of prayer. The house Ariosto built himself in the fifteenth century stands in the same street, but Ariosto's world of mediæval chivalry is shattered into atoms while St. Antony still saves Ferrara from earthquake.

Yes—allowing Messina and Reggio to be annihilated—the Saint in 1908 said to the seismic forces, "So far and no farther," and 'tis not for me, whose umbrella he recovered on the very day I mocked at his pretensions, to resent his preferences. Three days of thanksgiving (mass in the morning at his altar and prayers and Benediction in the afternoon), "per lo scampato flagello del Terremoto," rewarded his partiality for Ferrara. The town keeps doubtless a morbid memory of earthquakes, for from an old German book printed at Augsburg by Michael Manger, I learn that the terrible Terremoto of 1570, "in Welschland am Po," started in Ferrara on a 16th in the night and lasted till the 21st, during which time two hundred people perished, and many houses with a dozen churches, monasteries and nunneries were destroyed in Ferrara alone. Why St. Antony nodded on that occasion is not explained. Nor why he should have limited his protection to the Jews, not a man of whom was injured. Perhaps he had not yet recognised the claim of Ferrarese Christianity upon him. There is a wistful note in the prayer placarded in the Ferrarese church of San Francesco. "O great saint, commonly called the saint of Padua, but worthy to be called the saint of the world. . . . You who so often pressed in your arms the celestial Bambino!"

Happy Paduans, to whom this chronological prodigy is securely attached, who indeed hastened to build a Cathedral round him in the very year of his canonisation (1232). Here amid crudely worked flowers, crutches, photographs and other mementoes of his prowess, the faithful may find remission of their sins or expiation of the faults of their dead. For what limit is there to his intercessory power? Let me English the prayer hung up in his chapel. Every religion has its higher and more sophistic presentation, but it is well to turn from the pundits to the people.

"ORAZIONE A S. ANTONIO DI PADOVA.

"Great St. Antony, the Church glories in all the prerogatives that God has favoured you with among all the saints. Death is disarmed by your power; error is dissipated by your light. They whom the malice of man tries to wound receive from you the desired relief. The leprous, the sick, the crippled, by your virtue obtain cure, and the hurricanes and the tempests of the sea calm themselves at your command; the chains of slaves fall in pieces by your authority, and the lost things are found again by your care and return to their legitimate possessors. All those who invoke you with faith are freed from the evils and perils that menace them. In fine, there is no want to which your power and goodness do not extend."

Here the intermediary has practically superseded the Creator, even if dulia be still distinguished from latria.

Rimini was likewise safeguarded from the earthquake of 1908, but not by St. Antony. A saint of its own, the glorious Bishop and Martyr, St. Emidio, "compatrone della città, protettore potentissimo contro il flagello del Terremoto," received the Three Days' Solemn Supplication, and the Riminese were adjured in many a placard to repeat their fathers' glorious outburst of faith before the thaumaturgic images when the city was delivered from the frightful earthquake of 1786. But on the whole the saints can scarcely have done their duty by the old towered cities, for all Italy is full of the legend of toppled towers.

In war-perils it is the Archangel Michael who is the power to approach. A prayer, ordered by Pope Leo XIII to be said in all the churches of the world on bended knees after private mass, pleads to that Holy Prince of the celestial legions to defend us in battle and to thrust Satan and other roving spirits of evil back to Hell. "Tuque, Princeps Militiæ Cœlestis, Satanam aliosque spiritus malignos, qui ad perditionem animarum pervagantur in mundo, divina virtute in infernum detrude. Amen."

That Satan still has the entry of the Catholic autocosm, I was indeed not unaware. But I was certainly taken aback to find the Plague still curable by Paternosters. Yet this is what I was told in a little church in Brescia devoted to Moretto's works and monument, and summing up in letters of gold the whole duty of man.

"Christians! Bless the most holy name of God and of Jesus, Respect the Festas, Keep the Fasts and the Abstinences! In short, only by Prayer And Penitence will cease Great Mortality, Famine And every Epidemic."

I had regarded the Salute and the other Plague-Churches of Venice as mere historic curiosities, and written it down as an asset of human thought that the Plague of 1630 was due to the filthiness and congestion of the Levantine cities. That when 60,000 Venetians died—"uno sterminato numero" as the tablet in the Salute says—the Venetian Republic should with vermicular humility erect a gorgeous church in gratitude for the Death-Angel's moderation—this might pass in 1630, like St. Rocco's neglect in performing only the few desultory miracles recorded in the wooden bas-reliefs of his choir. In the seventeenth century one might even adore the angel of Piero Negri's staircase-fresco of Venice Relieved of the Pest, tardily as he came to relieve those ghastly visions of the plague-pit which Zanchi has painted, facing him. But that in 1836 Venice should have decreed a Three Days' Thanksgiving to the "Deiparæ Virgini salutari" for salvation from "the cholera fiercely raging through Europe" shows that two centuries had made no change in the Catholic autocosm, nor in the caprice of its Olympians. Venice had already passed under the Napoleonic reign of pure reason, and in an old poster of the Teatro Civico I read an invitation to the citizens to "democratise" the soil of the theatre by planting here the Tree of Liberty and dancing the graziosissima Carmagnola. But revolutions, French or other, leave undisturbed the deep instinct of humanity which demands that things spiritual shall produce equipollent effects in the physical sphere.

"E pur si muove," as Galileo said a hundred and thirty years after his death. The Catholic autocosm and the objective macrocosm begin to rub against each other even in the churches. Quaintly enough 'tis over the popular practice of spitting that science and religion come into friction. The priest who convoyed me through the Certosa of Pavia seemed to regard his wonderful church as a glorified spittoon, and notices in every church in Italy make clear the universality of the offence. But whereas at Pavia you are asked "For the decorum of the house of God do not spit on the pavement," in Brescia the deprecation is headed: "Lotta Contro la Tubercolosi," as though the most penitent and pious might be rewarded for church-going by consumption. The Cremona and Lucca churches compromise: "Out of respect for the house of God and for hygiene please do not spit on the pavement." In Verona the formula is practically the same: "Decency and hygiene forbid to spit on the pavement." In Bologna the modern autocosm was, I gather, even more victorious, for in time of plague, some frescoes in S. Petronio were whitewashed over. I trust for the sake of symbolic completeness these were frescoes of St. Sebastian and St. Rocco, the protective plague-saints.

A false cosmos, I said, like a false coin, may be as useful as a true one, so long as it is believed in. As long as the attrition of the macrocosm outside does not wear a hole in the Catholic autocosm, it will keep its spheric inflation. For there is nothing to wear a hole from inside, nothing contrary to pure reason, nothing inconsistent with something else. There is no à priori reason why saints should not control the chain of causation by spiritual forces as engineers and doctors control it by physical forces at the bidding of intelligence. There is no formal ground for denying that penitence puts cholera to flight. It is merely a matter of experience—and even Popes and Cardinals remove to cooler places when the pest breaks out at Rome. There is no conceptual reason why there should not be a Purgatory, nor why masses and alms for the dead (or still more the emotions of love and remorse which these represent) should not enable us to assist the posthumous destinies of those we have lost, nor why our sainted dead should be cut off from all fresh influence upon our lives. It seems indeed monstrous that they should pass beyond our yearning affection. In these and other things the Catholic autocosm gives hints to the Creator and shows how the "sorry scheme of things" may be moulded "nearer to the heart's desire." Nor is there any reason why there should not be a Trinity or a vicarious Atonement. These concepts, indeed, explain obscurum per obscurius—

"No light but rather darkness visible—"

and seem less natural and more complicated than the Jewish theory of a divine unity and a personal human responsibility. But complexity and incomprehensibility are not proofs of falsity. Tertullian, indeed, in his great lyric cry of faith, would make them proofs of truth. Certum est quia impossibile est. And it may be conceded to Tertullian that in a universe of mystery all compact, the word of the enigma can scarcely be a platitude. But there is a limit to this comfortable canon. Impossibility can only continue a source of certitude so long as transcendental theological conceptions are concerned. But when, leaving the tenuous empyrean of metaphysics, the Impossible incarnates itself upon earth, it must stand or fall by our terrestrial tests of historic happening, and the canon should rather run: Providing it has really happened, its mere impossibility does not diminish its certitude. So that, per contra, if it never happened at all, its mere impossibility cannot guarantee it. Impossibility is a quality it shares with an infinite number of propositions, and if it wishes to single itself out from the crowd, it must seek extraneous witnesses to character. And if it fails in this quest, its impossibility will not save it. We may believe the unproved, but not the disproved. The true interpretation of the universe must be incomprehensible, my interpretation is incomprehensible, therefore my interpretation is true—what tyro in the logics will not at a leap recognise the fallacy of the undistributed middle? Yet on this basis rest innumerable volumes of apologetics.

Nay, Sir Thomas Browne himself fell into this "Vulgar Error." "Methinks," he cries, basing himself upon Tertullian, "there be not impossibilities enough in Religion for an active faith . . . I love to lose myself in a mystery, to pursue my Reason to an O altitudo!" As if "O altitudo" is not pursuable by the simplest pagan, following the maze of Space and Time. The author of "Religio Medici" confesses that certain things in Genesis contradict Experience and History, but he adds: "Yet I do believe all this is true, which indeed, my Reason would persuade me to be false; and this I think is no vulgar part of Faith, to believe a thing not only above, but contrary to Reason and against the Arguments of our proper Senses." Pardon me, esteemed Sir Thomas. It is precisely the vulgar part of Faith—Religio Populi! It is putting the disproved and disprovable on the same plane as the unproved and the unprovable, where alone the ecstasy of the O altitudo may be legitimately pursued.

The friction between the Bible and Science has grown raspier since Sir Thomas's day, and by a new turn in human folly we are told that Science is bankrupt—with the implication that therefore the Bible is solvent. Poor old autocosms! They are both bankrupt, alas! Neither the ancient Bible nor the twentieth century Science can pay twenty shillings in the pound. Not that the Bible cannot meet its creditors honourably, nor that Science will not be permitted to go on dealing. The salvage from both is considerable. But neither can afford an autocosm in which the modern intellect can breathe and the modern soul aspire.

Nor was such work ever within the capacity of Science. She, the handmaid of religion, forgot her place when she aspired to the pulpit. And religion, with Time and Space and Love and Death for texts around her, stepped down from hers when she persisted in preaching from withered parchments of ambiguous tenor and uncertain authorship. What can be more pathetic than the joy of orthodoxy when the pick strikes some Old Testament tablet and it is discovered that there really was an Abraham or a Lot. As well might a neo-Pagan exult because the excavations in Crete prove that the Minotaur really existed—but as a fighting bull to which toreadors imported from conquered Athens sometimes fell victims. Not even Lot's wife supplies sufficient salt to swallow Genesis with. The Old Testament autocosm is dead and buried—it cannot be dug up again by the Palestine Exploration Fund. It is no longer literally true, even in the Vatican, where, if I understand aright, only the miracles of the New Testament still preserve their authenticity.

"Things are what they are, and the consequences will be what they will be," as the much-deluded Butler remarked. Wherefore, though you imagine yourself living in your autocosm, you are in truth inhabiting the macrocosm all the time and obnoxious to all its curious laws and inflexible realities. It is as if, playing cards in the smoking-room of a ship and fancying yourself at the club, you should be suddenly drowned. Only by living in the macrocosm itself can you avoid the stern surprises which await those who snuggle into autocosms. Hence the perils of the Catholic autocosm for its inhabitants. For in the real universe pestilences and earthquakes are not due to the wrath of God. The physical universe proceeds on its own lines, and the religious motives of the Crusaders did not prevent a Christian host from dying of the putrefying infidel corpses which it had manufactured so abundantly. Nor did heaven endorse the theory of the Children's Crusade—that innocence could accomplish what was impossible for flawed manhood. The poor innocents perished like flies, or were sold into slavery. These things take their course as imperturbably as Halley's comet, which refused to budge an inch even before the fulminations of Pope Callixtus III. Nor is the intermission of earthquakes or pestilence to be procured by the intercession of the saints or by the efficacy of their relics. A phial of the blood of Christ was carried about in Mantua during the plague of 1630, but there were not enough boats to carry away the corpses to the lakes. It was those marshes round Mantua that should have been drained. But it is in vain God thunders, "Thus and thus are My Laws. I am that I am." Impious Faith answers, "Not so. Thou art that Thou art not."

Pestilence—we know to-day—can be averted by closing the open cesspools and opening the sunless alleys of mediævalism; malaria can be minimised by minimising mosquitos, and earthquakes can be baffled by careful building after the fashion of Japan, which, being an earthquake country, behaves as such. After the Messina earthquake the Japanese Government sent two professors—one of seismology and the other of architecture—to study it and to compare it with the great Japanese earthquake of 1891, and they reported that although the Japanese shock was greater and the population affected more numerous, the number of Italian victims was four hundred and thirty times as great as the number of Japanese, and that "about 998 out of 1000 of the number killed in Messina must be regarded as having fallen victims to the seismologically bad construction of the houses." But where reliance is placed on paternosters and penitence, how shall there be equal zeal for antiseptics or structural precautions? The censer tends to oust the fumigator, and the priest the man of action. "Too easily resigned and too blindly hopeful," says the Messagero of Rome, commenting on the chaos that still reigns among the population of Messina.

"Trust in God and keep your powder dry" was the maxim of a Protestant. Cromwell but echoed the Psalmist, "Blessed be the Lord my strength, which teacheth my hands to war and my fingers to fight." This is the spirit that makes the best of both cosms. The too trustful denizen of the Catholic autocosm with his damp powder and his flaccid fingers risks falling a prey to the first foe.

But the balance-sheet is not yet complete. For it may be better to live without sanitation or structural precaution and to die at forty of the plague or the earthquake, after years of belief in your saint or your star, than to live a century without God in a bleak universe of mechanical law. True, the believer has the fear of hell, but by a happy insanity it does not interfere with his joie de vivre. He has had, indeed, to pay dearly for the consolation and courage the Church has sold him—since we are at the balance-sheet let this be said too—and seeing how in the last analysis all this overwhelming ecclesiastic splendour has come out of the toil of the masses, I cannot help wondering whether the Church could not have done the thing cheaper. Were these glittering vestments and soaring columns so absolutely essential to the cult of the manger-born God?

But perhaps it was the People's only chance of Magnificence. And after all the mediæval cathedrals were as much public assembly rooms as churches.

Dear wrinkled contadine whom I see prostrated in chapels before your therapeutic saints; dear gnarled facchini whose shoulders bow beneath the gentler burden of adoration; poor world-worn beings whom I watch genuflecting and sprinkling yourselves with the water of life, as the spacious hush and the roseate dimness of the great cathedral fall round you; and you, proud young Venetian housewife, whose baby was carried to baptism in a sort of cage, and who turned to me with that heavenly smile after the dipping and that rapturous cry, "Ora essa è una piccola Cristiana!"—and most of all you, heart-stricken mothers whose little ones have gone up to play with the Madonna's bambino, think ye I would prick your autocosm with my quill or withdraw one single ray from the haloes of your guardian genii? Nay, I pray that in that foreign land of death to which we must all emigrate, ye may find more Christian consideration than meets the emigrants to England or America. May your Christ be waiting at the haven ready to protect you against the exactions of Charon, to rescue you from the crimps, and initiate you into the alien life. Only one thing I ask of you—do not, I pray you in return, burn up my autocosm—and me with it. And ye, gentlemen of the cassock and the tonsure, continue, unmolested by me, your processions and your pageants and your mystic operas and ballets, your drinking ceremonials and serviette-wipings; for, bland and fatherly as you seem, you are the fiercest incendiaries the world has ever known—the arson of rival autocosms your favourite virtue. And I am not of those who hold your power or passion extinct. Even in your ashes live your wonted fires, and I may yet see the pyres of Smithfield blaze as in the days of Mary. For to hold the keys of Heaven and Hell is as unsettling as any other form of monopoly. Human nature cannot stand it. And by every channel, apert or subterranean, you are creeping back to power, carrying through all your labyrinths that terrible torch of faith. Already relics have been borne in procession at Westminster. But perhaps I wrong you. Perhaps your very Inquisition will make some concession to science and the age, and electrocute instead of burning.

But though ye burn me or electrocute, yet must I praise your Church for its three great principles of Democracy, Cosmopolitanism, and Female Equality. At the apogee of its splendour, in the days before its autocosm contradicted the known macrocosm, it made a brotherhood of Man and a United States of Europe, and St. Catherine and St. Clara ranked with St. Francis and St. Dominic. What can be more wonderful than that an English menial, plain Nicholas Breakspeare, should rise into Pope Adrian IV, and should crown Barbarossa at Rome as Emperor of the Holy Roman Empire, or that when this Empire's fourth Henry must fain go to Canossa, it was the reputed son of a carpenter that kept him waiting barefooted in the snow? Contrast all this with the commercial chauvinism, the snobbery, and the Mussulman disdain of woman into which Europe has fallen since the "Dark Ages."

I grant that the Papacy was as far from ensuring a human brotherhood as the Holy Roman Empire was from the ideal of Petrarch, yet both institutions kept the ideal of a unity of civilisation alive, and if they did not realise it better, was it not because two institutions aiming at the same unification are already a disturbing duality? The situation under which the Emperor elected the Pope who consecrated the Emperor, or the Pope excommunicated the Emperor who deposed the Pope and elected an anti-Pope, was positively Gilbertian, and the grim comedy reached its climax when Pope and anti-Pope used their respective churches as fortresses. The old duel persists to-day in the tug-of-war between Court and Vatican, and the Pope is so little a force for unification that he still refuses to recognise the unity of Italy. Yet no ironies of history can destroy the beauty of the Catholic concept.

"I lift mine eyes and all the windows blaze
With forms of Saints and holy men who died,
Here martyred and hereafter glorified;
And the great Rose upon its leaves displays
Christ's Triumph, and the angelic roundelays,
With splendour upon splendour multiplied;
And Beatrice again at Dante's side
No more rebukes, but smiles her words of praise.

"And then the organ sounds, and unseen choirs
Sing the old Latin hymns of peace and love
And benedictions of the Holy Ghost;
And the melodious bells among the spires
O'er all the house-tops and through heaven above
Proclaim the elevation of the Host."

That is the Catholic autocosm at its loveliest, as seen by the poet of the Pilgrim Fathers when under the spell of translating Dante. And 'tis, indeed, no untrue vision of its ideal.

I saw an old statue of St. Zeno in his church at Verona, and the saint, who began life as a fisherman, appeared as proud of his fish pendent as of his crozier. Can one imagine a British bishop in a fishmonger's apron? Even the Apostles are doubtless conceived at the Athenæum Club as a sort of Fishmongers' Company, with an old hall and a 'scutcheon. For England combines with her distrust of High Church a ritual of High Life, which is the most meticulous and sacrosanct in the world.

Nor is there any record of a British bishop behaving like St. Zeno when the Emperor Gallienus gave him the crown from off his own head, and the saint requested permission to sell it for the benefit of the poor. True, British bishops are not in the habit of exorcising demons from the daughters of emperors, but neither are they in the habit of dividing their stipends among curates with large families.

St. Zeno, by the way, came from Mauretania, and St. Antony was not really of Padua, but of Portugal. 'Twas a free trade in saints. There was no protection against protectors. Virgil and Boëthius themselves enjoyed a Christian reputation. One does not wonder that even Buddha crept into the calendar by an inspired error. It is heartening to come on an altar in Verona to St. Remigio, "apostle of the generous nation of the French," to find Lucca Cathedral given over to an Irish saint and honouring a Scotch king

("San Riccardo, Re di Scozia"), and to read of King Canute treating with Pope John and Emperor Conrad for free Alpine passes to Rome for English pilgrims. Universities too were really universal. The Angelic Doctor was equally at home in Naples, Paris, and Cologne.

What can be more nobly catholic than the prayer I found pasted outside Italian churches: "My God, I offer Thee all the masses which are being celebrated to-day in all the world for the sinners who are in agony and who must die to-day. May the most precious Blood of Jesus the Redeemer obtain for them mercy!" True, the poetry of this prayer is rather marred by the precise information that "every day in the universe about 140,000 persons die: 97 every minute, 51 millions every year," but not so grossly as by the indulgences accorded to the utterers. Why must this fine altruism be thus tainted? But alas! Catholicism perpetually appears the caricature of a great concept. Take for another example the methods of canonisation, by which he or she who dies "in the odour of piety" may pass, in the course of centuries, from the degree of venerable servant of God to the apogee of blessed saintship. What can be grander than this notion of taking all time as all earth for the Church's province? Yet consider the final test. The great souls she has produced must work two posthumous miracles, forsooth, before they can be esteemed saints. By what a perversion of the spiritual is it that holiness has come to be on a par with pills! Surely a true Church Universal should canonise for goodness of life, not for mortuary miracles. Joan of Arc, who must wait nigh five hundred years for saintship—did not the miracle of her life outweigh any possible prowess of her relics?

But despite, or rather because of, this grossness, the walls of the Catholic autocosm are still stout: centuries of friction with the macrocosm will be needed to wear them away. The love of noble ritual and noble buildings, of ordered fasts and feasts, of authority absolute; the comfortable concreteness of Orthodoxy beside the nebulousness of Modernism; the sinfulness of humanity, its helplessness before the tragic mysteries of life and death; the peace of confession, the therapeia of chance and hypnotism, the magnetism of a secular tradition, the vis inertiæ—all these are pillars of the mighty fabric of St. Peter. But even these would be as reeds but for the massive prop of endowments. 'Tis Mortmain—the dead hand—that keeps back Modernism. So long as any institution possesses funds, there will never be any lack of persons to administer them. This is the secret of all successful foundations. The rock on which the Church is founded is a gold-reef. And it is actively defended by Persecution and the Index, by which all thought is equally excluded, be it a Darwin's or a Gioberti's, a Zola's or a Tyrrell's. Who then shall set a term to its stability?

With such a marvellous machinery at hand for the Church Universal of the future—so democratic, so cosmopolitan, so free from sex injustice—it seems a thousand pities that there is nothing to be done with it but to scrap it. Surely it should be adapted to the macrocosm, brought into harmony with the modern mind, so that, becoming again the mistress of our distracted and divided world, moderating the frenzy of nationalisms by a European cult and a European culture, keeping in their place the mediocrities who are seated on our thrones, and the democracies when they stray from wisdom, it could send out a true blessing urbi et orbi. But this, I remember, is an Italian fantasy.

OF FACTS WITHOUT AUTOCOSMS: OR THE IRRELEVANCY OF SCIENCE

I did not need the lesson of the Scala ballet—Civiltà inspired by Luce and chasing Tenebre. I know that that light is electric. Have I not found it in the deepest crypt of the underground cathedral of Brescia, illuminating the two Corinthian pillars from the Temple of Vespasius? Have I not seen in the quaint sleepy alleys of rock-set Orvieto the wayside shrine of the Madonna utilised to hold an electric lamp? And have I not seen that ancient marble shrine between Carrara and Avenza supporting the telegraph wires, or the crumbling tower of Lucca the telephones? And did I not watch the thousand-year-old cathedral of Genoa—with St. Lorenzo's martyrdom on its façade—preparing to celebrate the fourth centenary of St. Caterina—"whose mortal remains in their urn have not felt the injury of time"—by a thorough cleansing with a vacuum cleaner? Ceaselessly throbbed the engine, like the purr of a pious congregation, and the hose extended to the uttermost ledges of the roof, sucking in dust immemorially undisturbed. And the cathedral clock of Verona that looks down on Charlemagne's paladins, Roland and Oliver, in rude stone—did it not tell me the correct time? Yes, 'tis the hour of Science.

And the contribution of Italy to Science is almost as great as her contribution to Art or Religion. A country that can produce St. Francis, Michelangelo, and Galileo, that founded at Verona the first geological museum and at Pisa the first botanical garden, has indeed all winds of the spirit blowing through her. But except in Da Vinci, Art and Science have not been able to lodge together. Him the sketches for his flying-machines in the Ambrosian library make a boon-fellow of Wright, Voisin, and Santos, as Luca Beltrami enthusiastically proclaims. Galileo had some pretensions to letters, writing essays and verses, and is even suspected of a comedy. But the life of Galileo practically divides Italy's art period from her scientific, so far at least as the material arts are concerned. His amanuensis, Torricelli, preluded the barometer, and the creation of electrical science by Galvani and Volta was a main factor in the evolution of our modern world of machinery. Venice and Florence founded statistical science, and if Sicily and South Italy have relapsed from the Arabic-Aristotelian stimulus administered by Frederick II— perhaps for fear of sharing the imperial Epicurean's furnace in the Sixth Circle of the Inferno—North Italy has remained a pioneer of the modern. It is not by accident that Marconi was born in Bologna, or Lombroso in Verona—which is to hold his statue—or that the most learned exponent of the dismal science of our day has been Luigi Cossa, Professor of Political Economy in the Universities of Pavia and Milan. But even Naples and Palermo have remained faithful to astronomy and the mathematics.

Far be it from me to say a word against Science as a magnified magical maid-of-all-work! But in so far as she pretends to set up in the parlour, ousting her old mistresses, Theology and Poetry, let me point out to her swains, the electro-plated youth of Lombardy, that the facts of Science, existing as they do outside autocosms, are as substantial to lean upon as the shadows of reeds. Of the need of a Scientia Scientiarum to put all these facts in their place, the average scientific specialist is as unconscious as a ploughboy of the calculus.

For it follows from the doctrine of autocosms that a fact cannot exist as such till it has settled to which autocosm it belongs. It must be born into the world of meaning. The same raw material may go to form part of autocosms innumerable, as the same man may be the butler at a duke's, the guest of honour at a grocer's, and the chief dish at a cannibal banquet. The same fire that beacons a ship from destruction sucks a moth to its doom, and the same election figures scatter at once delight and despair. The "fact," outside an autocosm, can only be regarded as a potentiality of entering into ratios; in other words, it is a "rational" possibility. But since there is a definite limit to its possibilities, and an election result cannot glut the cannibal appetite, nor a butler operate as a beacon-fire—except in the way of Ridley and Latimer—we are compelled to recognise an obstinate objective element fatal to the Pragmatic Philosophy. Potential facts are stubborn things. Pragmatism was a healthy reaction against the obsession of a world wholly gaugeable by Reason, like the reaction of Duns Scotus against Aquinas, but when it replaced Reason by Will, it fell into the other extreme of error. Both Reason and Will must enter into the Science of Sciences, and they must even be supplemented by Emotion.

For the human consciousness, our sole instrument for apprehending the world, is trinitarian. I should say we have three antennæ—Reason, Will, Emotion—wherewith to grope out into our environment, were it not that those antennæ are triune, and no knowledge of the outer world ever comes to us save with all the three factors intertwined in varying proportions. Why then should we throw away all that Will and Emotion tell us, putting asunder what God has put together? To represent the Report of the bare intellectual faculty as the Report of the whole Commission is fraudulence. Will and Emotion have too meekly contented themselves with a Minority Report. It is time they insisted on their views colouring and fusing into the Report Proper. Even Kant, having reached spiritual bankruptcy by his "Critique of Pure Reason," apologetically called in the Practical Reason to save the situation, thereby importing into his system an absurd dualism. Kant's Practical Reason is simply Will and Emotion restored to their proper rank as conjoint antennæ of apprehension. The effort to probe the universe with an isolated antenna was foredoomed to failure. The Practical Reason should have been called in, not after the bankruptcy as a sort of receiver to make the best of a bad estate, but before starting operations, as a partner with additional capital.

A fact, then, to be a fact, must be born into an autocosm, must be caught up not only into intellectual perception, but into emotional and volitional relations. The so-called scientific fact is thus two-thirds unborn. It is not a fact, but a facet of a fact. 'Tis only by a shorthand convention, indeed, that anything can be treated as purely an object of intellectual discrimination. Every substantive in the dictionary is a shrivelled leaf which requires the sap and greenness of a living sentence to restore it to life. This is best seen in words with more than one meaning, like "bark," which needs to be in a sentence to show whether it is canine or marine. But every word is in the same ambiguous case, and acquires its nuance from its relations with life. The molecule or structural unit of reality being thus triune, it is obvious that the isolated presentation of the material aspect of things in the shape of words under the name of Science can never be a presentation of Truth. It is a mere abstraction from the trinitarian wholeness of experience. Full life exists in three dimensions, Art in two, and Science in one, like a solid, a superficies, and a line, and the line as little reproduces the plenitude of being as the coast-line of a map the beetling cliffs and thundering seas.

But the subject-matter of the sciences is not even the universe treated as a material whole, but the universe cut up into abstract 'ologies and 'onomies, each of which insidiously tends to swell into a full-seeming sphere of Truth, as when Political Economy, having proved that Free Trade produces the cheapest article, tends to assume that humanity is therefore bound to buy in the cheapest market; so that even the Tariff Reformer, under the same hypnosis, seeks to deny this economic law, instead of admitting and overriding it by considerations from supplementary spheres of Truth. Similar fallacies spring from pathology, psychology, physiology, criminology, and other methods of vivisecting our noble selves. We are parcelled out among the professors, each of them magnifying his office.

"Hark, hark, the lark at Heaven's gate sings!"

says the beautiful song in Cymbeline. The sciences pounce upon that lark like hawks, and tear it to pieces between them. But the truth about the lark—is it in the unreal abstractions of the sciences, or is it in the poet's perception of the lark in all the fulness, colour, and richness of actual existence?

The little Gradgrinds, says Dickens, had cabinets in various departments of science. "They had a little chronological cabinet, and a little metallurgical cabinet, and a little mineralogical cabinet, and the specimens were all arranged and labelled, and the bits of stones and ore looked as though they might have been broken off from the parent substances by those tremendously hard instruments, their own names."

But it is only in the falsificatory museums of science that things exist in little cabinets, or that the butterfly is impaled on a pin and ranged in a glass case with other Lepidoptera. In the real universe it flutters alone amid the flowers. It is full of its own vivid life; it does not know it has been classified. This classification exists only in some student's mind; the truth is in the fluttering butterfly. And Truth really flutters like a butterfly, free and joyous, winged with iridescent splendours and subtle shades. Truth is not a dead formula, but an airy aliveness.

When I was a youth studying mathematics and the 'ologies, I became infected with the sense of superiority to the crowd which these pursuits bring: such cold, logical reasoning, such rare reaches of thought! To think that men eminent in these branches should remain unrewarded by popular fame, while every petty scribbler with a gift of invention commanded the applause of the mob! To be a novelist seemed a paltry affair; yet later on I came to recognise that the crowd is right, and that those who decry the predominance of the novel are wrong. All these sciences and speculations deal with human life, not in its living fulness, but with an abstractness which makes it dead, unreal, false. The world's instinctive distrust of pedants and students and mathematicians is justified. They isolate one aspect of life, one thread of the tangled skein, one motif in the eternal symphony, and sometimes drawing from reality the merest shred of tune, execute upon it an enormous fantasia—as in the higher mathematics—which plays itself out inaudibly in vacuo. The cold perfection of mathematics is due to our having eliminated in advance all the accidents of reality, and even the supposed infallibility of the proposition that two and two are four shatters itself upon the futility of adding two elephants to two speeches on the Irish question. And yet in those callow days it was to Number that I, like Pythagoras, was fain to look for the key of the riddle. But that was under the glittering spell of the late Monsieur Taine, who well-nigh persuaded me that a Science was only truly Scientific when it passed from the qualitative to the quantitative stage. If you could only express everything by mathematical formulæ, then at last you would catch that shy bird, Truth, by the tail. Strip away Truth's feathers, then the flesh, then even the bones, till you get a meaningless world of imaginary atoms, and that, forsooth, is the ultimate Truth. "The universe," said Taine triumphantly, "will one day be expressed in mathematical formulæ." In other words, strip away all there is to know, get rid of all that interests you, the colour and the form and the glow of life, and then you will really know the thing. The only way to know a thing is elaborately to prevent yourself from knowing it.

That invaluable institution the Post Office annually provides us with statistics. So many billion letters are sent a year, so many postcards, so many packages, and of these so many are left open, and so many unaddressed or unstamped, and so many go astray. These figures have as much to do with the realities implied in this correspondence as the figures of the quantitative sciences with the realities they are drawn from. Even could it be proved that the ratio of unaddressed letters to addressed is constant over a given area, or that the percentage of postcards varies inversely with the status of the senders, how much nearer are we to the hot passions and wild despairs, the commercial greeds and the loving humours which are the actuality of the phenomena under calculation?

Even the lines and angles of geometry, which have more body than statistics, are a poor substitute for the full, rich world, with its forests and skies. Mathematics may be indispensable to navigation, but on the sea of life we sail very well without it. Some of the most charming women I know count on their fingers. When

"A Rosalind-face at the lattice shows,
And Sir Romeo sticks in his ear a rose,"

it is indifferent to the situation that the rose is compact of chemical atoms dancing in complex figures, setting to partners, visiting and retreating.

Biron in "Love's Labour Lost," professing to derive his learning from women's eyes, which are

"the ground, the books, the academes, From whence doth spring the true Promethean fire,"

was, though the sentiment may be unpopular in this educational age, wiser than Faust in his study soliloquising on the curse of useless learning. Many of the statements of science are true for the abstract logical faculty; they are not actually conceivable. We laugh at the mediæval controversies as to how many angels could dance on the point of a needle, but surely our modern theory of the atomic constitution of the needle-point justifies the question. One angel per atom would exhaust the angelic hosts. Perhaps the sparks emitted for years by one drop of bromide of radium on the point of a needle are really a dance of demons. Or take the undulatory theory of light—that to produce the varying colours of the spectrum the luminiferous ether must vibrate from 458 to 727 million of million times per second. It might as well have been a thousand billions or ten trillions for all the difference to our understanding. To give us such figures is like offering a million-pound note to an omnibus conductor and expecting change. The best scientists admit that these conceptions are but working hypotheses. Nay, I find a worthy German actually calling them "useful fictions." Indeed, they cannot endure cross-examination, and if you want to see a scientific man as angry as a theologian of the Inquisition era, you will treat his mystic conceptions as Tom Paine treated the mysteries of religion. The world went very well ere we knew the fairy-tales of science and learned to dread death in every breath we took, every crumb we ate, every drop of non-alcoholic drink we drank. As if it were not tragic enough to read the newspapers, we are harassed with the life-histories of insects invisible to the naked eye, thirty generations or so of which live and die every day in a drop of ditch-water. At the same time such surface questions as why a man lives six times as long as a dog and a tortoise six times as long as a man are left in absolute darkness.

Men of science are to be admired for their patient and fearless groping after knowledge, the only reward of which is the applause of that splendid international brotherhood of learning. But this knowledge of theirs is never more than raw material for the philosopher at the centre to weave into his synopsis. No doubt there are men of science who preserve their perspective, who do not view the universe as heaven-sent material for a series of text-books, but this part of their thinking is done, not as scientists, but as poets or philosophers. Classification is all that Science Proper can do, and when the pigeon-holing is complete to the last Z, the universe will remain as mysterious as before. When the astronomers have determined the size, weight, orbit, speed, and spectrum lines of all the four hundred millions of visible stars, we shall still look up and say,

"Twinkle, twinkle, little star,
How I wonder what you are!"

But this pigeon-holing of the universe by Science is conspicuously incomplete. For by a paradoxical modesty the man of science too often forgets to include himself in the inventory.

In this way Herbert Spencer explained everything—except Herbert Spencer. Possibly the forgetfulness is wilful, because the existence of the man of science upsets so many of his explanations. "I find in the Universe no trace of Will or Reason," protested one of them to me. "I see only the blind movement of forces, mechanical as billiard-balls." "Naturally," I retorted, "if you omit to look in the one direction where Reason and Will assuredly exist—in your own self."

On the physical plane we get movement without will, on the animal plane the will to live, on the human plane the will to live divinely. These three strata cannot be reduced to a lowest common denominator of blind force. And if they could, the miracle of their differentiation would still remain. That blind forces should rise to consciousness and write books about themselves is even more wonderful than an eternity of spirit. Reduce all the seventy odd elements to one, as Chemistry hopes, and instead of an explanation you will only get the new puzzle of how the one could contain the seeds of the many. Even the popular Evolution theory is but a juggling with time. You do not get rid of Creation by shifting the beginning back to a billion years last Tuesday.

And with all my admiration for the fine qualities of the man of science I cannot away with his cocksureness, so curiously proof against the fact that scientific conceptions are always changing— witness the revolution wrought by radium. Even such a simple analysis as the composition of air has taken in many new and important constituents—argon, xenon, helium, krypton, neon, &c.—since the days when as a schoolboy I got full marks for stating them inaccurately. And yet to this day the scientist recounting the constituents of air forgets to wind up, "With power to add to their number."

As for those sciences which do not depend on intellectual conceptions and practical experiments, but on antiquarian research, those learned and dry-as-dust studies which academies delight to honour, they owe all their importance simply to antiquity's lack of self-consciousness and its failure to provide for the curiosity of posterity. Had the first man who evolved from the ape drawn up a note upon his ancestor, or, better still, made a picture of his ancestral tree, what controversies we should have been spared! Had the builders of the Pyramids or the delvers of the Roman catacombs put up little tablets to explain their ideas, what scholarship would have been nipped in the bud! The reputation of the Egyptologists depends on the fact that the writers of hieroglyphics apparently left no dictionary. If one were to turn up, the reputation of these savants would be gone. At present they are able to translate the same text by "The King went a-hunting" or "My grandmother is dead" without ceasing to be taken seriously.

But it is in the realm of Italian art-connoisseurship that the greatest havoc would be wrought did an official catalogue come to light, say in one of the recesses of the Vatican or in that wilderness of the Venetian archives. For the lordly neglect of the Old Masters to put their names to their pictures has flooded us with a tedious pedantry of rival attributions, and the thing of beauty, instead of being a joy for ever, is an eternal source of dulness.

"Ass who attributes it to Mantegna," I saw scribbled on a fresco, at Padua, of St. Antony admonishing Ezzelino, and connoisseurship is merely politer. As long ago as 1527 a quiz or a braggart of an artist, Zacchia da Vezzano, painted underneath a sacred picture of his, now in Lucca:

"His operis visis hujus cognoscere quis sit
Auctorem dempto nomine quisque potest."

As who should say, "Take away the name and anybody can tell the artist." But experience proves the contrary.

I do not say that the virtuosi would all be exposed, as by the pedigree of a Da Vinci bust, could we light on a source of certainty like the contemporary slatings in the Renaissance Review. Some of these sleuth-hounds might even be vindicated; and I opine that to you, amico mio, who of thirty-three Titians in a London exhibition pronounced no less than thirty-two to be hung on false evidence, the discovery of a set of Accademia catalogues would not be unwelcome. But your career as a connoisseur would close. Dead too would be the school of Morelli, collapsed the drapery students and ear-measurers, whose mathematics had, indeed, as little relation to Art as it has to life.

The Sherlock Holmeses of Science and Art dig up old cities, reconstruct forgotten civilisations, redistribute famous pictures, and amend corrupt texts or corrupt them more hopelessly. It is but rarely that they have imaginative and historic insight. "Learning is but an adjunct to ourselves," says Biron. Scholars are too often but an adjunct to learning. For men with real insight there are enough dead civilisations and forgotten customs still flourishing all about us. The taboo, the fetish, the totem, the oracle, and the myth are the very atmosphere of our being.

Our generation will leave newspapers and museums—nay, gramophone records and the films of bioscopes; the ghosts of our shapes and voices will haunt our posterity, and the only chance for scholars will be to condense the too, too ample materials—there are four miles of novels already in the British Museum—or perhaps a few beneficent fires will give scholarship a new lease of life. At their best and richest antiquarian studies only help to make the past present again, but how does that help us in essential insight? The past of to-morrow is here to-day and we are no wiser. In the hundredth century the excavator may exhume London, but we see London even more clearly to-day, and how does that help us in the real problems?

No; the only help for us lies in those elements of Truth which we draw from ourselves, not receive from without—in those emotional and volitional contacts with the essence of things which accompany all intellectual perception; in these motor aspects of reality which drive us along, these flashes of faith and spiritual intuition which, although they may vary from age to age under the spell of individual poets and prophets, and under the evolution of knowledge and civilisation,

"Are yet a master-light of all our seeing."

They may have been intertwined with incorrect intellectual elements, but because one antenna of the apparatus of consciousness functions falsely we are not therefore justified in wholly rejecting the joint report. When we think of the vast number of contradictory truths by which men in all ages and countries have lived and died, we shall find consolation in the thought that the emotional and volitional elements of Truth are more important than its intellectual skeleton.

But what a curious confusion that these emotional and volitional elements should themselves come to be treated as intellectual, and desiccated into dogmas! This is the result of their seeking expression in words, that unsuitable, impossible and fading medium. It is through their felicitous escape from words that verbally inarticulate artists and musicians paint and compose truer things than philosophers say, things that survive vicissitudes of thought and are as true to-morrow as yesterday. With the music of the Roman Catholic Church we all agree, and who shall contradict the Venus of Milo?

Yes, a statue or a symphony is safe from syllogisms, at least until it gets into the hands of the art critic and the programme-concocter. But the truth airily embodied in words is at the mercy of system-builders and deduction-squeezers. Taken with the hard definiteness of coins—as if, indeed, even coins did not vary from day to day in purchasing power and according to the country of circulation,—the words are added together to yield a specific sum of truth. Flying prophetic phrases and wingèd mystical raptures are shot down and stuffed for Church Catechisms and Athanasian Creeds. As if the emotional and volitional fringe of living words permitted them to be thus sterilised into scientific propositions! For just as facts are the skeletons of truths, so words are single bones, and the dictionary is a vast ossuary. Talk of the dead languages—all languages are dead unless spoken, and spoken with real feeling. A parrot always speaks a dead language. It is the folly of a universal language that it assumes the same vocabulary could be used over a vast area of varying conditions, its words never expanding nor contracting in meaning, nor ever changing in pronunciation or colour. As if Latin was not once universal in those countries which have gradually transformed it into French, Spanish, Portuguese, Italian, Provençal, Roumanian, and Rumonsch! Idiomatic expressions cannot be torn from the soil they grow in. Mañana has not the same meaning outside Spain nor Kismet outside Islam. Language lays such traps for fools; the fools have always spoiled and fossilised what the men of genius have felt and thought. They have made logic out of poetry and have deadened worship and wonder into theology. "What do you read?" says Hamlet. "Words, words, words."

A truth, then, may be formulated, but it is not true till it is felt and acted on, and ceases to be true when it ceases to be felt and acted on. Nor does this canon apply only to inner truths. Without an element of feeling and volition, however shadowy, even the simple realities of the outer world have never been perceived, and the omission of these elements invalidates the total reality. If so many readers skip scenery in novels, 'tis because the scene is described as though it existed in itself. The dead chunk of landscape bores and depresses. The reader subconsciously feels that so impersonal a vision is untrue to the actualities of perception. Nobody has ever seen a landscape without some emotion, if only the traveller's desire to be at the other end of it. A dozen persons—even omitting the colour-blind—would see it in as many different ways, each with different accompaniments of feeling, thought, and volition, potential or actual, just as every person in The Ring and the Book sees Pompilia differently. Let the novelist describe the scene, not for itself, but for its relation to the emotions and purposes of his personages, and it leaps into life. Similar is the case of Science, whose facts in divesting themselves of all emotion and individual error divest themselves likewise of reality. The dry scientific coldness with which the universe must be envisaged is an artificial method of vision. True, the scientist himself may be impelled by the most tingling curiosity. But the passion and thrill of his chase for truth does not appear in the quarry: that is a mere carcase. His report on his speciality is always carefully divested of emotion. But our emotional and volitional relations to the spectacle of existence are as much a part of the total truth of things as colour is of the visible world. The world is not complete without

"The light that never was on sea or land,
The consecration and the poet's dream."

When Lear cries to the heavens that they too are old, or Lamartine calls on the lake to remember his happiness, Ruskin would tell us that this suffusion of Nature with our own emotions is the pathetic fallacy. On the contrary, its absence is the scientific fallacy. Science registers the world as the phonograph registers sound or the camera space—without any emotion of its own. As the former with equal phlegm records a song or a curse, or the latter a wedding or a funeral, so does Science register its impassive observations. For once admit such a shifting subjective factor as emotion, and what becomes of the glorious objectivity of Science? Away, therefore, with all but the frigid intellectual view of things! Since the other elements of Truth elude our grasp, let us boldly declare them irrelevant. The bankruptcy of Science, you see, comes not at the end of its operations. Science starts bankrupt. It has not sufficient capital to begin trading. Its methods and apparatus are entirely inadequate for the attainment of truth. A cat may look at a king—but its observation will not be very profound. And Science is as little equipped for observing the universe as the cat for observing the king. All it can perceive or establish is chains of causation, or rather recurring sequences of phenomena, in an unconscious continuum. It is a post-mortem investigation to ascertain, not the cause of death, but the cause of life.

But the universe is not a quaint collection of dead things in a vacuum, not a museum of stuffed birds or transfixed butterflies, but a breathing, flying, singing, striving, and suffering process—an unfinished infinitude. This kinetic process cannot be expressed in terms of statics. "What is Truth?" says the jesting cosmos, and does not stay for an answer. But by an artificial abstraction parts of it can be expressed for the intellect in static 'ologies and 'onomies, on the understanding that the intellect never forgets to put back its results into the palpitating flux to which they belong and in which alone they have true significance. This understanding the intellect too frequently violates or forgets, and therefore for Truth we must go, not to the man of science, but to the poet, who registers his universe synthetically with soul as well as with brain. Tragedy, comedy, heroic drama, sombre suffering, majestic mystery, all these are in the flux—more surely than ether waves and dancing atoms—and the poet in painting the fulness of life with the fulness of his own emotion is giving us a fuller truth than any that Science can attain to. "We cannot really know the truth unless we love the truth," said Fénelon. "They who love well will know well." This is not mysticism but common sense, and Goethe repeated it when he said that "No one can write about anything unless he writes about it with love." "To see things in their beauty," said Matthew Arnold, "is to see them in their truth." It may be that the knowledge of things through pure intellect is pure delusion, that to pigeon-hole the universe is to make it into a cemetery. Instead of that "love is blind," the truth may be that only love sees. There is a sense in which every mother's babe is the most beautiful in the world.

Knowledge, then, as a mere function of the intellect, is only the dead knowledge that appears in school-books. But who shall say that knowledge was meant to be only a function of the intellect, that we do not know with our heart and soul as well as with our brains? Nay, as if to mock at mere intellect, the universe absolutely refuses to yield up its secret to the intellect. Hence the antinomies of Kant or Mansel or Plato's "Parmenides." Follow up mere thought, however apparently clear, and it lands us in nonsense. Perhaps wisdom does not lie that way at all. Perhaps the fear of the Lord is really the beginning of wisdom.

For if Science is Truth in one dimension and Art Truth in two dimensions, it is only when we complete emotional vision by volition that we arrive at Truth's full-orbed reality. Even love cannot bring wisdom unless the love translates itself into action. In short, the meaning of Truth must be changed from a dead fact of the intellect into a live fact of the whole being. The Truth is also the Way and the Life.

Aristotle in his "Metaphysics" tells us that Cratylus carried the scepticism of Heraclitus to such a degree that he at last was of opinion one ought to speak of nothing, but merely moved his finger. Aristotle does not see that in this moving of his finger Cratylus was asserting at least the volitional element of Truth and perhaps its most important. For the universe is not a museum, placarded "Look, but please do not touch." It says, "Touch, and then you will really see. Live, work, love, fight, and then you will really know what the nature of your universe is."

The world of the physical sciences is only the stage-setting for the spiritual drama. Though there is a truth of dead things called Science, the real truth is of live things—a triple truth in which intellect, will, and emotion are one. Our sense of this truth—obtained as it is during emotional volition—is individual, irreducible to the simpler planes of Science and Art, and thus incommunicable. And the measure of our attainment of it will be the measure of our sympathetic insight and of the depth to which we have penetrated by action into the heart of the phenomena. Then what seemed a mass of dull facts may break into music like a Beethoven score under the baton of a master.

The scientist who should say that a Beethoven symphony consisted of the atoms of the paper and ink which constitute the score, or even who expressed it mathematically as a sequence of complex air-vibrations made by strings and holes, would be talking truth; but as incomplete and irrelevant truth as the ignoramus who should say it was curious black strokes and dots on ruled paper, or the statistician who should count the semi-breves or fortissimo passages. The true truth of the symphony comes into being only when it is interpreted by the finest performers to souls whose life it enlarges.

And so with the universe, which is not a dead, complete thing outside of us, but a palpitating spiritual potentiality, for the fullest truth about which the co-operation of our own souls is needed, our souls that create a part of the truth they perceive or aspire to. The universe, in short, is a magic storehouse from which we may draw—or into which put—what we will to the extent of our faith, our emotion, our sense of beauty our righteousness. "Ask, and it shall be given you; seek, and ye shall find; knock, and it shall be opened unto you."

OF FACTS WITH ALIEN AUTOCOSMS: OR THE FUTILITY OF CULTURE

When I betake me to a zoological garden, equipped with a pennyworth of popcorn, a food strangely popular even among the carnivora, I am touched by a prescience of all the pleasure and dumb gratitude to be evoked by those humble grains. And in truth how many eager caged creatures are destined to have a joyous thrill of sniffing suspense, followed by the due titillation of the palate! My proffering fingers shall meet the gentle nose of the deer, the sensitive arching trunk of the elephant, the kindly peck of parrots, the mischievous hands of monkeys, the soft snouts of strange beasts. Not otherwise is it when, faring forth to Italy, I provision myself with a bag of coin. Into what innumerable itching tentacles these gilded or cuprous grains are to drop: white-cuffed hands of waiters, horny digits of vetturini and facchini, gnarled fins of gondoliers and hookers, grimy paws of beggars, shrivelled stumps of cripples, dexterous toes of armless ancients, spluttering mouths of divers, rosy fingers of flower-throwing children, persuasive plates of serenading musicians, deceptive ticket-holes of dishonest railway clerks, plethoric pockets of hotel-keepers, greedy tills of bargaining shopkeepers, pious palms of monks and sacristans, charity-boxes of cathedrals, long-handled fishing-nets of little churches, musty laps of squatting, mumbling crones, greasy caps of guides, official pyxes of curators and janitors, clutching claws of unbidden cicerones. All these—and how many more!—photographers and painters and copyists and forgers, modellers and restorers and lecturers on ruins, landlords and cooks and critics—live by Italy's ancient art. Great Cæsar dead—and turned to Show.

The beauty of Italy is elemental fodder for the autochthones; yet how strange the existence of the Neapolitan swimmer whose métier is to dive for coppers when the steamer sails for the witching cliffs of Sorrento, and to cry in enticing gurgles, "Money in the water!" the spluttering syllables flowing into one another as in the soft patois of Venice! Precisely when the Bay of Naples is a violet dancing flame, and Vesuvius, majestically couchant, sends her white incense to the blue, and you are tranced with beauty and sunshine, comes this monetary merman to drag you down to the depths.

"Nutritive chains" the biologists name the inter-related organisms whose existence depends on one another, and another link of this chain you shall count the boatmen waiting to show you the blue grotto of Capri. Their skiffs dart upon you like creatures whose prey comes only at a fixed hour; like creatures, moreover, shaped in the struggle for existence to the only function by which they can survive, for they are fittest to pass under the low arch of the cerulean grotto (the occupant consenting to crouch like an antenna drawn in). That ardent water in the Capri cave—that lovely flame of light blue in a bluer burning spirit—sustains likewise the naked diver who stands poised on a rock, ready to show its chromatic effects upon flesh; the culminating moment of whose day—the feeding-time, as it were—comes when the tourists glide in.

Apt symbol indeed of the tourist, that shallow skiff skimming over beauty with which the native is in deep elemental contact, from which, indeed, he wrests his living.

Since Goethe with his gospel of culture spent those famous Wanderjahre in Italy, a swollen stream of pious art-pilgrims has been pouring over the land. And coming into Florence from Lucca and a sheaf of quiet cities on an afternoon of this spring, I had a horrid impression of modern bustling streets and motors and trams and a great press of people, and ten thousand parasites battening on the art and beauty of the city, and it was not till I had won my way to my beloved Ponte Vecchio, with its mediæval stalls, that the city of the lily seemed to possess her soul again. Then as I saw her compose herself under her deep blue sky into a noble harmony, with her heights and her palaces and her river and her arches and arcades, and group herself round a tower, and brood in Venetian glamour over her water with her ancient rusty houses, and rise behind into a fantasy of quaint roofs and brick domes and steeples and belfries, all floating in a golden glory; and as I reflected on all she was and held within her narrow compass, how the names of great men and great days were written on every stone, and how every sort of art had been poured over her as prodigally as every sort of earth-beauty; and as I thought of the enchanting villages around and above her, where the cypress and the olive, the ilex and the pine slumbered in the sunshine, amid great rocks that shadowed cool glooming pools, and white roads went winding odorous with may and sweet with the song of thrush and blackbird, framing and arabesquing the faery city below in magic tangles of leafy boughs; and as I remembered that here to-day in this same city was not only spring, but Botticelli's Spring—then it seemed to me that her flowers and her palaces, her frescoes and the curves of her hills were pushed up from the same deep elemental core of beauty, and that she lay like some great princess of Brobdingnag on whose body a colony of all the culture-snobs of the world had dumped its masses of raw building, run up its hundreds of hotels and pensions, piled its pyramids of handbooks, biographies, Dantes, histories, essays, landed its hordes of guides and interpreters, encamped its army of lecturers and art critics, installed its cohort of copyists, dragged up its heavy battery of professional photographers, supplemented by an amateur corps of Kodak snapshooters; but that, breathing lightly beneath all this mountainous cumber, unasphyxiated even by the works on the Renaissance, she could still rise radiant in her immortal strength and beauty, shaking off the Lilliputian creatures and their spawn of print, ungalled by that ceaseless fire of snapshots, imperturbable amid the lecturing, unimpaired even by all that immemorial admiration.

The pioneers of this culture-colony blundered sometimes, as pioneers will, and even Goethe, one notes with malicious glee, spent himself upon the wrong pictures, gloating over Guercino, wrestling with Caracci, Guido and Domenichino, and passing Botticelli by, nay taking all Florence as an afternoon excursion. And Pater himself, the pontifical Pater, though he has the merit of a Botticelli pioneer, yet thought it necessary to apologise for criticising "a second-rate painter": which is as though one should apologise for discussing Keats.

Nor were Byron and Shelley more felicitous in their admirations. The Kunstforscher, that Being usually made in Germany, has been busy since their day. Amid the great movement of life, while men have been sowing and reaping, writing and painting, voyaging and making love, this spectacled creature has been peering at pictures and statues, scientifically analysing away their authenticity and often their charm. There is the Venus de' Medici, which generations have raved over, which innumerable processions of tourists have journeyed to admire and found admirable. The connoisseurs have now pronounced her "spurious and meretricious," and to-day nobody who respects himself would allow himself a thrill at the sight of her. Yet Childe Harold cried:

"We gaze and turn away, and know not where,
Dazzled and drunk with beauty, till the heart
Reels with its fulness."

I must admit that after the Venus of Milo the beauty of the Medici Venus does appear a trivial prettiness. But even the Venus of Milo—though we are still permitted to admire her—is "late and eclectic."

The unhappy Byron also wrote to somebody: "The Venus is more for admiration than for love. What struck me most was the mistress of the Raphael portrait." Alas! nobody believes now that the picture has anything to do with La Fornarina.

As for Shelley, when in 1819 he saw at Florence the Medusa attributed to Leonardo da Vinci, he broke into lyric raptures,

"Its horror and its beauty are divine,
Upon its lips and eyelids seems to lie
Loveliness like a shadow, &c. &c.

"'Tis the tempestuous loveliness of terror;
For from the serpents gleams a brazen glare,
Kindled by that inextricable error! . . ."

Kindled indeed by that inextricable error! For the Medusa is now given up by every connoisseur. It is a mere inartistic futility and to-day every lover of the arts must grow stony at the sight of it. That immortal line "the tempestuous loveliness of terror" is the only thing to its credit, though some might count, too, the passage in which Pater gloats over its beauty of conception.

Then there is that little matter of Leonardo's St. John in the Louvre. Michelet saw the whole Renaissance in it, and Pater alludes to it as "one of the few naked figures Leonardo painted," and builds upon it a complex theory of Leonardo's symbolic suggestive method, and is not surprised at the saint's "strange likeness to the Bacchus which hangs near it, which set Théophile Gautier thinking of Heine's notion of decayed gods, who, to maintain themselves after the fall of Paganism, took employment in the new religion." And now the St. John turns out to have been a pupil's or an imitator's, and probably not even a St. John.

The culture-pilgrims of to-day, armed with sacred text-books, verbally infallible, and canonical lists of authentic attributions, enjoy a suspicious superiority in æsthetic judgment over the greatest creative artists. For Goethe and Byron and Shelley did at least create, and Pater's interpretation of Mona Lisa is finer than the picture itself; whereas the pursuit of culture in the average pilgrim is a confession of sterility either in himself or in his own nation, which is not sufficiently vitalised to absorb his interests. "If the Romans had had to learn Latin," said Heine, "they would never have conquered the world." And were England free in thought and nobly artistic, there would be no need of this fervour for the preservation of Greek. Even Goethe, it is amazing to discover from his "Italiänische Reise," never saw the sea till he went to Italy. And his first glimpse of it was, of all places in the world, at the Lido in Venice! He with the German Ocean to draw from him, as it drew from Heine, the cry of "Thalassa!"; he who might have seen how

"Die weissen Meerkinder
Hoch aufspringen und jauchzen
Uebermut-berauscht,"

must fare forth to another land and behold a lazy, almost tideless lagoon lapping in shallow muddiness on the tamest and dullest shore in the world. Surely we have here an ironic image of the culture-pilgrim who sets out to see Art abroad before he has seen Nature at home.

When the Goths besieged Rome, Belisarius hurled down upon them the statues of the Mausoleum of St. Angelo, and the tomb was turned to a citadel. But against the siege of Rome by the Goethes there is no known defence. A rain of statues would merely aggravate their zeal, and the more hopelessly the statues smashed, the more would their admiration solidify. So to-day the Goethes and the Huns alike are invited up to see the statues—for a fee—and every citadel of reality is turned to a mausoleum-museum. St. Angelo, that has stood the storms of eighteen centuries, is the perquisite of a facetious warder who gabbles automatically of Beatrice Cenci, "la più bella ragazza d' Italia," as he points out her pitiful, if dubious, dungeon. In the stone cell of the Florentine monastery, on whose cold flags Savonarola wore his knees in fasting and prayer, a guide holds up a reflector to concentrate the light on the frescoes with which Fra Angelico glorified the rude walls. Where St. Catherine walked—in the footsteps of the Bridegroom—leaving the marks of her miraculous feet, a buxom native of Siena expects her obolus. Outside the pyramid-shadowed cemetery where Keats lies under his heart-broken epitaph, a Roman urchin turns supplicatory somersaults. Italia Bella, a paper published at Milan, adjured Arona to wake up and celebrate the tercentenary of the canonisation of its Saint Carlo, "if only because it pays." History, with its blood and tears, becomes æsthetics for the tourist and economics for the native. Of a truth quaint links concatenate Cæsar and the showman, the saint with the apple-woman who finds a profitable pitch for her stall at his church-corner. While we are fuming and strutting we are but providing popcorn for posterity. Buskined heroes of history, who walk the earth in tragic splendour, perchance your truest service to humanity has been done in affording occupation for the poor devil who expatiates upon the traces of your passing. This, at least, ye may be sure is good service; the rest of your work, who shall sever the good and evil strands of it? So much pother of prophets and politicians—and, lo! how poor a planet we still wander in.

The culture-pilgrim, too, apart from this scattering of popcorn, is a futile being. Culture as a mere excursion from a solid home-reality may be vitalising, but whoso thinks to batten on alien arts and letters is filling his belly with the sirocco. There is no reality in the travel-world, be it the world of Art or the world of Nature, for we have no true volitional relations with it. 'Twas Schopenhauer who discovered this for Art—though his World has only the two dimensions of Will and Idea. But he did not, if I remember, point out that everything seen with aloofness from action partakes of this art-quality. The landscape from the observation-car is a mere picture to us, however real to the peasants working in the fields.

The only "real" traveller is the commercial. We others, wandering through streets that our ancestors did not build, or sitting in alien apartments and gazing upon unhomely hills, are still spectators, not actors. We are not rooted in this soil, nor feel the deep intimacies that are the truest truth about it. I may partake in the annual festa of an Italian mountain village, hear the Mass, bear banner and taper in the procession, salute the saintly image, dance upon the plateau-piazza with a snooded peasant-girl, but how shall I feel the holiness and joy of this day of days?—I whose infant breath was not drawn amid these precipitous fastnesses, who have not lived in these human caves cut in the rock, who have not played in these steep stone streets, who know nothing of the dear narrowness, the vivid intensity that is born of cramped consciousness! There is in the very attitude of spectator something that stands between one and the object in its truth. This it is that makes the appreciations of cities by the school of Pater such hollow phantasy, such bastards of an accident by a temperament. This it was that begot Pierre Loti's monumental misreading of Japan as a Lilliput of the pretty-pretty. To lose the artistic Ego in the inner life of the phenomenon—how rare the critic who is capable of that! Listening to these parasites upon alien autocosms,

"Moving about in worlds not realised,"

one would imagine that a civilisation or a city existed, that its remote founders had fevered and its burghers toiled and its architects built, to the mere end that centuries after they were dust some exquisite vibrations should be registered on a sensitive soul.

Only less arrogant is it to place one's soul in patronising "appreciation" before some great historic structure—a cathedral, a mosque, a palace, a library. These works of man so immensely transcend any man's works that he fits into them almost as ludicrously as a mouse. A cathedral that represents the genius and labours and sacrifices of generations towers so immensely out of proportion to any individual that he can only recover a reasonable relation to it by fusing himself into the life and stature of the race. To be solely concerned with its impingement upon his own soul is an impertinence, to pass his life in contriving such impingements is to live by robbery, and to enjoy these secular products of human solidarity on the Paterian pretext that the only reality is the fleeting and isolated Ego, is peculiarly paradoxical.

Pater himself would even go so far as to study men, e.g. Pico di Mirandola, for their æsthetic flavours. This is, indeed, to live resolutely Im Schönen if not Im Ganzen, and it is, therefore, the more curious, that in citing Goethe's maxim in his "Winckelmann" Pater should, like Carlyle, have unconsciously substituted Im Wahren for Im Schönen. The æsthetic appreciation of Pico—as of most things—is a mere by-product. I do not deny that by-products are sometimes delightful. But let us not mistake them for central verities. And these churches, these pictures, these statues, these palaces, these monasteries which we see to-day in two dimensions, had once their third dimension of reality, nay often have it still to those who know them in their truth. How quaint that juxtaposition of Bibles and Baedekers in Italian churches! The image which, seen through tears, is soothing a worshipper's pain, is at the same moment finding exact appreciation at the eyes of a connoisseur. Who can read without emotion of how in thirteenth-century Florence Cimabue's Madonna, "the first Madonna the people could love," was borne in triumph from the painter's studio to its church by the whole population of the quarter, which henceforwards took the name of the Allegro Borgo! To-day the art-critic analyses its types and its composition, and it takes its place coldly in the history of painting as the link between the Byzantine and the Tuscan. But the citizens of the Joyous Quarter had the true flavour of the thing.

Despite the doctrine of Art for Art's sake it remains questionable if any maker of Art has ever escaped a desire to act—massively or diffusively—upon the life of his age. In vain he hides himself in the past, or flies to No-man's-land, he vibrates throughout to the present, touches living interests with their myriad indirect relations to action, to the third dimension. Every art-product holds, however subtly, something of that topical quality which makes the portrait of a contemporary celebrity, wet from the painter's brush, very different from the peaceful remoteness of an Old Master.

No half-deciphered face of dim sweetness, charming us from the magic casement of some fading fresco by some forgotten artist, as with the very image of Art aloof and absolute, but was once wrought for a specific market and born into a specific atmosphere. The forlorn stumps and torsos that litter the moss-grown courts of museums were hailed, as they fell from the craftsman's hand, by a definite clientèle, rejoicing in their beauty, stimulated by their freshness. Nothing, alas! is so old, so corroded with time, but it was once brand new, the pleasant novelty of the day to beings looking back upon an immemorial antiquity, and now long since mouldered to dust. Every blurred inscription, every crumbling pillar and shattered fragment had once its life, its meaning, its public.

The hand of time in eliminating the topical element and reducing a picture to pure Art—the inactive beauty that is its own end—removes from our perception the full reality of the art phenomenon as it fell from the artist's hand into time and space.

Some parts of this original plenitude were indeed better forgotten, for the Old Masters who were young once, young and impecunious, turned Renaissance art into a fancy dress ball of their patrons, the Magnificent Ones figuring as saints and patriarchs, Bethlehem shepherds and Magian kings, whom oblivious time has done well to mellow into a quasi-anonymity. But if the loss of such intellectual elements is a gain, I am less certain as to the evaporation of the emotional auras of works of art.

Andrea Orcagna worked ten years at the marble Gothic Tabernacle that stands in the fuscous Or San Michele of Florence, and men of other races and faiths gaze perfunctorily upon its decorative jewelled marvels, its pictorial reliefs, wrought after the plague of 1348 from the pious legacies of the dead or the thank-offerings of the survivors. The marble gleams in the immortal inactive beauty that is its own end—but where are the hope and the faith, the mourning and the anguish that made the atmosphere in which its beauty had birth? Ebbed to the eternal silence, like that great wave of popular rejoicing on which Cimabue's Madonna was carried to S. Maria Novella, or a picture of Duccio's to its due church in Siena. Can it be that Art, launched thus upon a sea of emotion, is only its true self when stranded high and dry upon the beach?

Is perhaps its most precious aspect precisely that by which it is related to life? And its least precious part that which remains over for the connoisseur of beauty? Oh but this is heresy, almost the philistinism of a Tolstoy or a Savonarola.

But believe me, my dear Virtuosi, that flavour which the citizens of the Joyous Quarter tasted, that wild-strawberry flavour of living, that dog-rose aroma of reality which you miss by your wilful avoidance of volitional relations, by your gospel of Art for Art's sake, is as exquisite as any of your hot-house flowers and fruitage. Are you rushing in pursuit of the new pleasure? Nay, it can only be captured by those who do not pursue it, who are even unaware that it exists. Mill's eudæmonistic paradox again, you see.

Has any professional hunter of the æsthetic ever, I wonder, had so exquisite a sense of the starry heaven as Garibaldi when he embarked from Quarto to redeem his country? "O night of the fifth of

May, lit up with the fire of a thousand lamps with which the Omnipotent has adorned the Infinite! Beautiful, tranquil, solemn with that solemnity which swells the hearts of generous men when they go forth to free the slave!"

"He never tampered with his sense of reality." These words came to me as the epitaph of an old Jewish pedlar when I heard of his passing away in far-off Jerusalem. He too knew this joy of the Allegro Borgo (though in his autocosm the Madonna was an idol) and gleams of it sustained him through long years of poverty and pain, and through the shadows of his closing hour. Pictures, songs, histories—all had no existence for him outside his religion. All were but ministers of faith, to feed its sacred flame. There was not in his whole life a moment of divorce between reality and consciousness. In such simplicity, what a unity, what a giant strength! Pitiful ye seem in comparison, ye unshelled æsthetes, wandering in search of an autocosm or yearning to inhabit every one in turn. Imagine it, to live the years of the Patriarch in our complex tortured era, and never to have had an art-emotion, never—save perhaps in childhood—to have known make-believe, never to have sundered vision and idea from actuality! Think of it, ye who have played such tricks with your souls as would make the angels weep, whose pious emotion has as much relation to religion as the enjoyment of a painted ocean to a struggle in the blind waters. You, Monsieur Loti of the Académie Française, with your vain literary vigil at the Holy Sepulchre, will you not envy this high seriousness which found an exaltation in forty fasts a year, without bite or sup, and drew a salty vitalisation from the tear of penitence? And you, sophisters of religion, who cling to your creed because it is good for the poor, or a beautiful tradition, or a branch of respectability; and above all, you, amateurs of "la volupté dans la dévotion," after the recipe of Barrès; you, neo-Catholics who mistake masturbation for adoration, bow your heads before one who worshipped God as naïvely as a dog adores his master, who did not even know that he believed, who was belief; who went to Jerusalem not because he was a Zionist but because it was Zion, whose tears at the Wailing Wall were tinctured with never a thought of the wonder and picturesqueness of weeping over a Zion lost eighteen hundred years before he was born! Poor Parsifal! Poor pure fool! Gone is thy restful simplicity. Persiflage is now our wisdom.

But because I have been privileged to see this sancta simplicitas of the old Jewish pedlar, I feel I know my Middle Ages better than the Protestant connoisseur whose learning flattens me out, or the pseudo-Catholic in search of sensations. I understand the Allegro Borgo, I say, and I am not appalled by the terrible list of Christian forgeries and legends, the apocryphal Gospels, the pseudo-Epistles, the hagiologies, for I know that 'tis the dry light of literary history that is false—like every other science—and that in life all these figments may have been the harmless nutriment of saintly souls. In this old Jew's autocosm, too, there were no physical impossibilities, no incredible miracles, no monsters or leviathans so strange but their names in Hebrew letters were a certificate of pedigree; the centuries were fused for him as by a cosmic cinematograph, the patriarchs and saints hovering over him in immortal synchrony. So am I not taken aback to see the Bambino still in his mother's lap by the time the Visconti present the Certosa to the Madonna, nor does it disconcert me to behold all the abbots and bishops of Christendom in attendance at the Crucifixion with consoling models of their churches. And as for the Madonna being an Italian grande dame dressed in Venetian silks or Florentine brocades, how else, pray, are we to preserve religion? True local colour and true Jerusalem costuming would have brought relativity into the absoluteness of belief, would have been a reminder that the Madonna was a foreigner. The truer truth is that she is Our Lady.

Art, you see, had in its palmy days to be a full-orbed reality, carrying conviction as well as beauty to the guileless beholder. To us too 'tis only the masterpiece attuned to our own macrocosm that can give us this plenary satisfaction. Even "Paradise Lost" is for us merely a magnificent banquet of words, the virgin bloom of Paradise truly lost with our faith in the groundwork of the epic. Tolstoy's attack on Art fails to differentiate between the Art of alien autocosms, the Culture Art which divides our soul against itself, and the real vitalising Art of our own epoch. For though we say, "Blessed are the simple, who live in the Absolute," 'tis no necessary converse to cry damnation on the complex. Art, we know, is in a sense a playing with life, an outcome, as Schiller said, of the play-impulse, the exuberance of energies not exhausted in the struggle for existence. This is what Carlyle felt when he denounced mere rhymesters and canvas-colourers; it was the secret of his "imperfect sympathies" (in Elia's phrase) with Shakespeare himself. 'Tis Hebraism versus Hellenism—the earnestness of the writers of the Bible, whose Art is an unconscious enhancement, a by-product struck off at white heat, versus the self-conscious manipulation of themes by Æschylus or Sophocles. A sense of futility and superfluity, if not of positive pravity, lies behind the eternal distrust of the Puritan for the make-believe of Art, his suspicion of the theatre and the nudities of Pagan sculpture. A prick of atavistic Calvinism caused the writer with the profoundest instinct for make-believe our generation has seen—Robert Louis Stevenson—suddenly to declare that the artist was no better than a fille de joie. But this was because the bulk of Stevenson's fiction—unlike his essays and his poetry—is Art in its anecdotage, without serious relation to the spirit. And there are moods in which a jejune elegance or an empty exhilaration is as unsatisfying as a lady's boudoir; and the artist, as a maker of beautiful toys, must sink into the same place as the contriver of perfumes and cushions. In Japan, where every workman is an artist, Art is in its proper place, and there is neither cant nor confusion. But besides the little Art of decorative line and melodious tinkle and romantic falsification of life there is the greater Art which has in it the unrest of the ocean and the silence of the starry night. Art, if in some instances it has sprung direct from the play-impulse, has largely come to us by way of religion, and where it is merely play for play's sake—as in rococo Art—it is doomed to sterility.

Although Art represents, yet, as photography came to prove, representation is not the aim of Art. The aim of Art is creation—creation that stimulates the soul. The artist has not to reproduce his model, but to create something new, living, and stimulating by help of it. He adds new creations to Nature. He marries her facts to his passion and pain, and the offspring is Art—Nature crossed by Man. The great odes of Keats and Wordsworth, the symphonies of Beethoven, the pictures of Bellini, the statues of Michelangelo, transmit to us the artists' spiritual exaltations, their ideals of beauty and energy. It boots not to point out that the artist is often selfish and licentious, irritable and vain. It is the greatnesses of his soul, not its pettinesses, which he puts into his art; his emotions and ideals into its content, his sincerity into its craftsmanship. And by greatnesses I do not mean only moral greatnesses, for life is larger than morality. It is his own temperament with which the artist crosses Nature. And that is why schools of Art can never yield more than craft: new creations can only be got by new crossings.

I would grant the Puritan, to whom all Art is of Satan, as I would grant his strange ally, Plato, that æsthetics may be abused, especially when divorced from life. There are young ladies who consume a novel a day, Sundays not omitted, by which process half their waking life is passed in a species of opium-eating. There are amateurs of music whose life is a surfeit of sweet sounds, and picture-lovers whose day is an orgy of line and colour. But when Tolstoy, perceiving what a sensual sty of Fine Art we may wallow in, ranged himself with the old Puritan iconoclasts, and launched his famous Platonic encyclical against music divorced from public psalmody, song sundered from harvest-festivity, or poetry that was not a marching song to the Millennium, he overlooked that even a healthy soul may have a surplusage of play-energy—nay, that this is the very child-soul—and that even from a Puritan point of view Fine Art may purify for fine Action, though it lack the direct nexus with Action. Tolstoy's tracts on religion may even be less vitalising for our age than "Anna Karenina" operating by way of the Aristotelian katharsis.

And the relation of so-called fiction to truth may be even closer than its nexus with Action. For it follows from our analysis of Science that novels and plays have the great initial veracity of reproducing the fulness of life as compared with the segregative sciences with their one-sided abstractions, which are to actuality as the conjugations in a Greek grammar are to a conversation with Helen of Troy. While the artificial selection of Science breaks a whole into parts, the artificial selection of Art can make a part truly represent the whole. And the greater the artist-soul the less will it play with its moods by the artificial and conscious refraction of Art for Art's sake. None should know better than Tolstoy that the highest Art is only Truth seen as Beauty. The great artist's registration and reflection of the universe in tone or colour, line or word, is, indeed, the highest form of Science at our command, fact and flower in one. "Beauty is Truth, Truth Beauty." Sophocles, Shakespeare, Dante, Michelangelo, Beethoven, Milton, Browning, were not playing with life. The world of Art may not be the world of Science, but it is the world we live in, the human world furnished with faith and emotion, no less "real" than the naked universe of physical law.

To accept Art for Art's sake, to divorce it from life, would be to pigeon-hole our souls, as most people put their religion into Sundays. The deepest analysis seems to conduct us back to a recognition that Art and Reality, though they have no necessary relation, do actually tend to approach each other in the greatest Art. The greatest writers—a Shakespeare or a Tourgénieff—in that selection from life which constitutes Art, select so as to give a sense of the whole, avoiding the one-sided selection which gives us on the one hand the disproportionate sexualities of the Palais-Royal farce or of the elegant bawdy-book, on the other the disproportionate sentimentalisms of goody-goody fiction. In painting, too, the Art which seizes the essence of places and people is the greatest, and I believe the greatest music seizes the essence of moods. Moreover, it is only by their relations to human realities that imaginative creations like Goethe's Mephistopheles or Swift's Lilliputians, the Prometheus of Æschylus, the Caliban of Shakespeare or the Jungle-Beasts of Kipling, have power to hold us. It may give us a useful distinction between Imagination and Fancy to connect the one with invention along the lines of life and born of insight into its essence—as in the creation of Hamlet; the other with artificial invention—as in the creation of Alice's Wonderland. Whether Hamlet existed or not, or that Prince Hal did exist, is irrelevant to Art. The transient reality has been replaced by the permanent creation. Per contra, what was meant as Truth may survive only as Art, like the mythological parts of the "Iliad," "Macbeth," "Paradise Lost," or the "Divina Commedia." Yet, as I have just pointed out, even these great artistic creations lose their hold in proportion as they cease to seem in correspondence with external realities. And if the supreme test of plastic and literary Art is its communication of a sense of life, is it not Truth we are really worshipping, Truth under another name? For lifelikeness, if it does not necessarily mean likeness to particular individuals, does necessarily mean likeness to universals. And Selection, though it omits portions of the truth, does not omit the whole truth—nay, sometimes reveals the whole truth by cutting away the obscuring details. Reality is the inexhaustible fons et origo of all great Art; apart from which there is no life in Art, but a rootless, sapless, soulless simulacrum. So that with the supreme artist, the Puritan antithesis of Truth and Art, Reality and Make-believe, Hebraism and Hellenism, disappears. A Sophocles is as earnest as a Socrates, a Michelangelo as a Savonarola, a Shakespeare as a Luther, a Beethoven as a Darwin.

As earnest, but not as limited. The biggest souls have never been able to express their sense of the multiform flowingness of things in neat packets of propositions; they have expressed it through the infinitude of Art. And Art, having once in human history been the medium of the spirit, must never sink back into a soulless toy. The Art of the future must vivify Science and take it up into Life; it must touch Truth with emotion and exalt it into Religion.

"Ludibria rerum humanarum cunctis in negotiis."
TACITUS.

I

So eccomi back in Assisi, after heaven knows how many years, and here is the same bland Franciscan—or his brother—to show me the same tiny monastery garden with the same rusty rose-bushes and tell me the same story of how its native thorns and briars turned into thornless roses with blood-specked leaves after St. Francis had rolled in them to subdue the flesh, and the same anecdote of the neophyte who refused to plant cabbages with their roots upward and was rejected by the saint as insufficiently simple and obedient, and I ask the same question as to the botanic results of planting cabbages topsy-turvy and receive the same beaming reassurance that they waxed to prize dimensions, while a blight fell on those whose roots had, with worldly-wise presumption, been planted in earth. And I am shown the same little hut which the saint occupied, with the same unnatural ecclesiastic vaulting and the same unnatural oratory above it, and I go again into the same Lilliputian church (twenty-two feet by thirteen) beloved of St. Francis, with its rude plaster and its wooden benches and its plain brass lamps, and receive the same shock at the thought of its asphyxiation beneath the giant grandeur of S. Maria of the Angels, that spreads over it like a golden eagle brooding a street sparrow. And from the door of this dear little Portiuncula I glean the same glad tidings that Pope Gregory XIII at the instance of the most illustrious Cardinal Sforza has conceded to every faithful Christian who will say (or pay for) a mass at its altar, the grace of liberating a soul from Purgatory. And I am given the same illuminated leaflet about St. Francis, with the same specimen of ensanguined rose-leaf—precisely like that which grows in my own garden—and I pay the same lira on the same spot where St. Francis, who called coins "flies," had some of these pests, innocently offered by a worshipper, thrown out upon asses' dung. The only change since my last visit is that a fig-tree has been planted "by request" in remembrance of the old tree in which Sister Grasshopper sang with the saint for eighty days.

And this "by request" is a vivid reminder that the Franciscan legend is flourishing more and more, like the topsy-turvy cabbage, and that shoals of pleasure-pilgrims, richly clad, come by carriage or motor to maunder over "the little poor man of Assisi," to gloat upon the cord of his tunic, stored up in a cupboard, and to gain an appetite for lunch by rhapsodising over the cell in which he fasted. Yes, the lover of poverty and of the brute creation has brought a good deal of money to the little hill-town, and no small sum of labour and lashings to its horses, and it is not surprising that the region round the poor little abandoned church of S. Maria in Portiuncula has grown up in the last quarter of a century into a big suburb, with eating- and lodging-houses, or that the successors of the saint who in his horror of property tried to tear down the chapter-house built for him, and who left even his cell because somebody referred to it as St. Francis's, have within the last ten years been able to enrich their vast basilica with three elaborate carven doors and an iron railing, not to mention the horrible modern fresco with six angels like ballet-girls hovering without the chapel where St. Francis died.

As I leave this musty S. Maria of the Angels and mount on this divine spring day towards the sunny hill-top where Assisi proper sits rock-hewn, with its towers, domes, and castles, and see beneath me the wonderful rolling Apennines, and the windings of white roads and silver streams, and around me the grey-green of olives and the bridal white of cherry-trees, and above me the cloud-galleons sailing in the great spaces of sky, a remark of the bland brother comes back to me with added significance. "We do not know where St. Francis's heart is," he said, grudgingly conceding that the rival church on high possessed his body. The fancy takes me, as I toil up to this tomb, that St. Francis's heart refused to be buried in a church, is here out of doors, at one with the spring and the sunshine.

And even more symbolic sounds to me the bland brother's boast that the colossal church built over the poor little Portiuncula is on the model of St. Peter's. Canonisation is a process that normally lasts centuries; our King Alfred's is not yet complete. But twenty months after his death Francesco Bernardone was hustled into formal saintship. The Pope crushed him by a loving embrace, and over his beloved doll's house of a church was erected a copy of St. Peter's! And far above, on the rival ridge of Assisi, as if to give a culminating irony to the symbolism, and as if one great church built over his body did not suffice to keep him down, a second church of S. Francesco has been built on the top of the first, and beneath these two churches, each supplied with its frescoed falsifications by the school of Giotto, the little brother of the poor who demanded only to lie among the criminals on the "Infernal Hill" was safely buried.

And yet not so safely but that his spirit has begun to penetrate through all the layers of stone and legend. Perhaps it has escaped through that portal of the upper church which, incautiously thrown open to illumine the painted miracles, tempers the austere gloom and the drone of ceaseless psalm-saying from below with a revealed greensward and a piping of birds. But one cannot imagine that his spirit has gone to occupy that large red throne between two yellow armchairs which the fresco depicts as the vision of his appointed seat in heaven, or that fiery chariot with which to bedazzle the brethren left behind. These twenty-eight wall frescoes, like the four triangular allegories on the ceiling below, hold little of the true St. Francis (notwithstanding that they are all drawn from Franciscan literature), and the least spiritual and the most mythical portions of the legend, the demons flying over Arezzo, or St. Francis hovering in the air while praying, figure on equal terms with his real activities, while the picture of his offering the Soldan the ordeal of fire is an imaginative amplification even of the literature. Setting aside all the fatuous monastic miracles, and the more tedious anecdotes of the Franciscan legend—and it must be remembered that the earliest dated manuscript of the Fioretti comes a hundred and sixty-four years after the death of St. Francis—we are yet able to extricate from it a kernel of personality sufficient to account for its genesis and growth, and it is this St. Francis who has at length burst through the three churches devoted to keeping him down and made his appeal to the modern mind. Yet the modern mind might easily misread itself into the mediæval mystic.

Despite his marriage to Lady Poverty, St. Francis was far from a conscious rebel against the glories of the Vatican. He was too humble-minded to be anything but a meek acceptant of the established Church and the ruling ritual. But there was in his literal translation into life of the Sermon on the Mount, the germ of a dangerous schism—a germ which duly developed into a sect of "Spirituals" for whom the Gospel of Assisi was the Eternal Evangel destined to supersede the Christianity of the Vatican—and it is not an accident that his followers, despite their popularisation of the idea of Papal infallibility, gravitated more to the Ghibelline cause than to the Guelph, and were, later on, formally condemned as heretics by John XXII. This unstatesmanlike Pope was not only ignorant that persecution is the seed of the sect, but he undermined the doctrine of his own Papal infallibility by thus reversing the bull of Nicholas III confirming their order. He alleged that Nicholas had framed it without his Cardinals, but the more logical Minorite Brothers contended that the contradiction of his predecessors proved him no true Pope, but a usurper. John and his successors retorted with the Holy Inquisition, and the Franciscans were burnt in stacks or tortured to death in dungeons; "martyrs," says Döllinger, "to the doctrine of Papal infallibility and the rule of poverty." And such is the comedy of Catholicism.

One wonders sometimes what St. Francis would have made of himself, had Christianity never come his way. His own genius would never have created the melancholy dogmas of the mediæval Church. There is neither Christ nor Atonement in his Canticle to the Sun—his most characteristic utterance. The Christianity he absorbed from his environment makes but a hybrid composite with his essential personality. There is thus no real unity in his spiritual being, no real reconciliation between his theory of utter abnegation and unworthiness, and his cheerful mystic oneness with the material universe and all its creatures. That everything God has created is laudable except one's self, and that all matter is sacramental except one's own body, is scarcely a congruous creed. And he followed his Christianity for the most part with a prosaic literality that showed that here he was but a passive receiver, as in his pharisaic prohibition against the brethren's practice of soaking pulse the evening before it was eaten, on the ground that this meant taking thought for the morrow. Not to soak it, is precisely taking thought, since it is concentrating attention on a triviality. But in his tender mystic universalism on the other hand he was a master, a creator. "Our Brother the Sun," "Our Sister the Moon," "Our Sister, Water," "Our little Brothers and Sisters, the Birds," "Our Sister, the Death of the Body"—these are the mintings of an original genius, not that tame subservience to texts which limited his wardrobe because of certain words in St. Matthew. And the originality of this genius consists, curiously enough, in the spontaneous reproduction of Hindu optimism and universality in a Western. How Hindu this thought is appears vividly from the story in the "Speculum Perfections," that when St. Francis's drawers caught fire about the knee, he would not put it out nor harm his brother Fire. From this point of view Hell would only be brother Fire enjoying himself. Yet we find St. Francis engaged all his life in thwarting the fraternal appetite. St. Francis would have been a greater man, had he been less of a Christian.

His distinctively Christian sayings are indeed comparatively poor. One scans the record almost in vain for any flash of the irony or sublimity of Jesus. The profoundest remark of the Fioretti—"everything, good or bad, that a man does, he does to himself"—belongs to brother Giles who, one is not surprised to find, left a book of Verba Aurea. Occasionally a superb transcendence of ritual as in St. Francis's remark that so far from not eating meat when Christ's nativity fell on a Friday, "the very walls should eat flesh on such a day, or if they cannot should at any rate be greased outside," recalls the flouter of Pharisaism, and we catch the voice of an authentic master in his exposition of a passage of Ezekiel to a peace-loving doctor of divinity perturbed about the text: "If thou proclaim not to the wicked man his wickedness, I will require his soul at thy hand." It was by the brightness of his own life and the perfume of his fame, said St. Francis, that the servant of God proclaimed their wickedness to the wicked. That was not precisely the method of Jesus, and herein St. Francis is more Christian than Christ. Nevertheless, if one had not his Hindu utterances to supplement his Christian, there would be little to distinguish the skinny black-eyed little strolling preacher from the numberless narrow-browed ascetics of the Church except his childishly dramatic delivery, his success in founding an Order and his redeeming weakness for talking bad French. It is that strange animism of his which gives him his hold upon us, which, not content with reading a soul into the bird, the fish, the grasshopper and the wolf, extends with half-savage, half-childish personalisation to fire and water, and even to wood and stone, nay to the very letters of the alphabet, so that he will not erase a letter even when he has set it down in error. Behind this divination of life in all things must have lain an exquisite sensibility, and it was thus his unfortunate fate to be supremely alive to beauty—even in woman—yet to be driven by his creed to the worship of sorrow, abnegation and self-inflicted pain, though even from these his subtle nervous system could snatch a rare moment of ecstasy, for so delicately was he strung that the mere words "the love of God" set up a sweet vibration like a plectrum striking a lute. How indeed should the gay knight, whom his comrades elected "King of the fools," change his sensitive skin, merely because he turned to be "God's fool?" If he now found his joy in the ecstasy of mystic communion and absolute abnegation, the joy was still at his core, and however he might afflict his body, with a sub-conscious sense of setting a model to his weaker brethren, it was impossible for him to subdue his sun-worship, or not to delight in the ripple of water, and the grace of birds and flowers and women. And herein he differs from the Buddha with whose life-story and tenderness for all creation he has so much in common, but to whom this world is merely a mistake to be endured till the nullity of Nirvana is attained. Even the pseudo-Christian theory of this vale of tears is not so pessimistic as Buddhism, for the lachrymose vale is merely the prelude to a mountain of bliss, and Schopenhauer's attempt to pair Christianity with Buddhism overlooked that the Buddhist saint lives to die and the Christian dies to live. Kuenen showed much deeper insight when he pointed out that Buddha does not value purity and renunciation as virtue—he is "beyond good and evil"—but as the best means of escape from life. But for St. Francis the world is not a vale of tears. Indeed the conception of a world of sorrow is contradicted by the sorrowful lives of the saints. For abnegation is pointless if there is no happiness to be surrendered. The pathos of the life of St. Francis lies precisely in his exquisite capacity for terrestrial happiness, and in his daily crucifixion of every natural desire at the bidding of a vicious theory of virtue, to which a natural want means something created by God in order to be thwarted, and which makes a vice of every necessity. Fortunately he had from his Hindu side the saving grace of joyousness, and could rebuke the saturnine visage of professional sanctity and even—towards the end—his own barbarity to that brotherly ass, his body.

His disciples, whose affinities with him were so imperfect that his most devoted biographer is the author of the "Dies Iræ," attempt indeed to harmonise the two halves of his personality by the mediation of texts. If he loves even the humble worm, it is because "he had read that word concerning the Saviour: 'I am a worm and no man,'" and if he treads reverently on the stone, it is not from some mystic sense of a stone-life or some sacramental sense of a divine immanence, but "for love of Him who is called the Rock." That his delight in water should be traced to its baptismal uses, and his prohibition against cutting down the whole of a tree to a reverence for the material of the cross, was, of course, inevitable. Nor is it impossible that St. Francis occasionally glossed himself over to himself, and it is quite probable that his special tenderness for the hooded lark was due to its quasi-monkish cowl, and that his comparative coldness to the ant reposed upon its providing for the morrow. For it was his tragedy to be torn between a blithe personal revelation of the divine and a stereotyped tradition of sorrow, to constrict his spiritual genius to a cut-and-dried scheme of salvation, and to be crucified on a second-hand cross. The stigmata which are the best proof of his hyperæsthesia are likewise the best evidence of his spiritual plagiarism and his comparative failure. For to be crucified is not to be Christ. Jesus did not set out to be crucified, but to do his and his Father's work. Crucifixion came in the day's work, but was its interruption, not its fulfilment. The true imitation of Christ is to do one's work though men crucify one. But deliberately to seek crucifixion—even crucifixion of one's natural desires—is to imitate the accident, not the essence. A still greater perversion is it to brood upon the crude insignia of the Passion till auto-hypnotism works miracles in the flesh.

The followers of St. Francis pushed the plagiarism so far as to adumbrate a parallel legend, with a descent into Purgatory and a John of the Chapel who fell away and hanged himself, and by the latter end of the fourteenth century the parallel was made precise and perfect in the Liber Conformitatum of Bartolommeo of Pisa. But the copy is only superficially true to the original. There is nothing in the story of the great Galilæan to justify the perpetual self-torture of St. Francis in his morbid quest of perfect humility and sinlessness. On the contrary, Jesus speaks with so god-like an assurance of righteousness that it has become one of the chief arguments for his divinity, as it is the chief stumbling-block to the efficacy of his example. For if God was made not man but superman, we can no more emulate this superman's goodness than his power of creating loaves and fishes in a crisis. Only if Jesus were not God is his example valuable. But man or superman, he did not sap his energies by brooding on his own vileness. Buddhism, with all the apathy that its pessimism engenders, is healthier here, since (according to the Mahâviyûhassutta) the Muni, the Master of renunciation, never blames himself.

I sympathise cordially with the perplexities of Brother Masseo, who, according to the "Analecta Franciscana," lost his naturally cheerful countenance under the difficulty of believing himself viler than the vicious loafer; and who, when this peak of humility was by grace attained, found himself in fresh despondency before the new Alp that rose on the horizon. "I am sad because I cannot get to the point of feeling that if any one cut off my hands or feet or plucked my eyes out, though I had served him to the best of my power, still I could love him as much as I did before, and be equally pleased to hear him well spoken of." Poor Masseo! Why should this worthy brother, a man, according to the Fioretti, of great eloquence and belonging to the inner circle of St. Francis, waste his time and spoil his valuable cheerfulness over such hypothetic absurdities? The humour of the last clause is worthy of Gilbert.

It is in face of such a heautontimorumenos as poor Brother Masseo that I revolt against all this strained ethics, this gymnast virtue demanding years of training to force the soul into some unnatural posture which it can only sustain at best for a few seconds. I could weep over all this wasted goodness when I think of the wrongs crying out for justice, the voice of lamentation that rises daily from the wan places of the world. How much there is for Hercules to labour at without standing on his head and balancing the seven deadly virtues on his toes! The beauty of holiness is often put on the same level as the holiness of beauty, as a self-sufficient ideal. But even as false ideals of beauty may impose themselves, so may false ideals of holiness. The static sanctity of a Stylites has long been relegated to those false ideals, and even a St. Francis cannot be accepted as a model for to-day, though a few satiated souls may yearn after abnegation as the last luxury of the spirit. There is much barren æsthetic admiration wasted upon religious maxims which it is admitted would overturn society if acted upon; and it is questionable, therefore, whether there is any real beauty in these, any more than in jewelled watches that will not go. Even when a rare saint acts upon them, they seem to produce spiritual sickliness rather than spiritual health. There is, perhaps, a finer beauty of holiness in the life of a wise and good man of the world with a sense of humour, than in the life of an ecstatic and underfed saint, whose very notion of the Fatherhood of God lacks the reality and fulness that come from paternity.

There are few things in literature more touchingly simple than those adventures in search of holiness, that picaresque novel of the spirit, known as "The Little Flowers of St. Francis." These gentle souls, who wander without food or knapsack, under the tutelage of the seraphic saint, through the enchanting valleys and hills of unspoiled thirteenth-century Italy, and adventuring in even more glamorous regions hold strange parleyings with the Soldan of Babylon, have upon them a morning light of innocence and that perfume of holiness which can never fail to justify the Master's exposition of Ezekiel. If anything could add to the sweetness of the idyll, it is the spiritual loves of St. Francis and St. Clara. And yet our adoration of St. Francis must not blind us to the questionable aspects of the chronicle. "I may yet have sons and daughters," he replied deprecatingly to one who proclaimed him blessed and holy. What a caricature of true ethics! Even the poverty for which he was "so greedy" is impossible if everybody is greedy for it, and the abnegation he practised he could not have preached. Otherwise when he tossed his own tunic to a shivering beggar, he should have inspired the beggar to toss it back to his now shivering self, and so ad infinitum. That game of tunic-tennis with nothing ever scored but "love" would have been true Franciscanism, but also its reductio ad absurdum. I do not wonder that Goethe smiled at the "Heiliger" of Assisi, for neglecting to visit whose shrine he was nearly arrested as a smuggler.

Yes, the bland brother does well to babble of the cabbage planted with its leaves in the ground. For he has blundered into the very essence of the Master's teaching: this topsy-turvydom, these roots in the air, are the secret of St. Francis's success. There is a tendency to blame our paradoxists, to deride their inversions as mechanical. But St. Francis is an inversion incarnate, a paradox in flesh and blood. While with other men Property is a sacred concept, a fetish guarded by a mesh of laws, he refuses to own anything and even disposes with blasphemous levity of other people's property. Theft he daringly defines as not to give something to anybody who has greater need of it than oneself. He hated Property, not as the Socialist hates it who covets its communalisation, but as something in itself evil. These practical inversions of his have the same excuse as those of the literary paradoxist. Nothing less than this violent antithesis will suffice to shake men's notions from the rigor mortis that overtakes even true ideas, or to offset the exaggeration which gradually falsifies them. One false extreme must be met by another, if the happy mean is to be struck.

Pray do not imagine I would endorse Aristotle's doctrine of the mean, or the popular platitude that truth always lies midway between two extreme views. On the contrary, truth is often the most violent and extreme of all possible propositions and right action the most violent and extreme of all possible forms of conduct. But the system of St. Francis needed as much contradiction from the world of common sense as the world of common sense needed from it. In so far as it was Christian, it was an imitation of early Christianity, minus the time-limit which justified its model. But the right course of action when the world is about to come to an end will not necessarily be the right course if the world is indefinitely to be continued in our next. In such a world the system of St. Francis is an impossibility, if only because it would bring the world to an end by lack of population. And if it really succeeded, it would bring itself to an end even before the world, for in the absence of owners there would be none to receive alms from, none to bake that bread which St. Francis naïvely regarded as coming by grace as simply as water. This absolute avoidance of money resembles, indeed, nothing so much as banking, which is possible only if the bulk of the investors do not ask for their money at the same time. It is on the certainty of his failure that the success of a saint reposes. His disciples will never be more than a miserable minority and so he will seem recuperative and not destructive to society. The exaggeration of his holiness will mitigate the materialism of the average man. Dives will not give up his dinner but he will drop a crumb for Lazarus and another for the saint, and perhaps eat only salmon and trout on Fridays. It is this reflection that he incarnates for the race an ideal of perfection, imperfect though it be in its impossibility, that reconciles me to the saint, as the reflection that the Church Fathers were engaged in fashioning that ideal reconciles me to their meticulous morality, in a world so given over to slaughter, sensuality and every abomination of injustice that their fine shades and their notion of an impassable infinity between right and the smallest wrong appear ludicrously disproportionate and academic.

The saint on this theory is a scapegoat, a victim on the altar of human selfishness; he does, suffers, or gives up, too much because most other persons do, suffer, or give up, too little. He is sacrificed to the balance of things, or as St. Paul put it, he is the leaven to the lump. Yet things would overbalance were he too successful, and too much leaven would spoil the lump.

If there is within St. Francis an unresolved discord between Hinduism and Christianity, still more jarring is the outer discord between Nature and Christianity which he tried so heroically to harmonise. Don Quixote tilting at windmills is a practical figure beside St. Francis trying to Christianise bird and beast. The consciously grotesque pathos of Cervantes is surpassed by the unconsciously grotesque pathos of the chronicles of St. Francis. The struggle for existence in Nature—the angler's hook and the birdcatcher's snare—can hardly be glossed over by sermons to the birds and the fishes. Doubtless St. Francis had—as some sinners have to-day—a strange power of fascination over the lower creatures, but the butcher was not eliminated because St. Francis occasionally bought off a lamb or a turtle-dove. We know too little of the psychology of wild beasts to deny that he tamed the Wolf of Agobio—though it is permissible to doubt the civil contract with Brother Wolf which in Sassetta's fanciful picture is even drawn up by a notary; nor is the stone record of the miracle you may read to-day on the façade of that little church in Gubbio which was set up three centuries later, nor even the skull of Brother Wolf himself, found—according to a lady writer on Gubbio—"precisely on the spot pointed out by tradition as the burial-place of the beast," and "now in the possession of a gentleman at Scheggia," as convincing a testimony as she imagines "to the indubitable truth of the tradition, and to the superhuman power of love towards every living creature." Love has no such power to turn lions and wolves into civil contractors or vegetarians. There is a battle of beneficent and sinister forces in the universe, which Persian speculation has always recognised frankly, but which Hebraic and Hindu systems, by their higher synthesis of Love or Good, unconsciously whittle away into a sham fight, or at best a tournament; a play of God with His own forces. 'Tis Docetism writ larger. But whether the fight be sham or real, the universe is not run on a Franciscan system, and it is this which makes the pathos and the grotesquerie of the saint's attempts to equate the macrocosm with his autocosm. Yes, St. Francis is as nobly mad as Don Quixote. Nay, towards the end, where the cavalier of Christ, broken by disease in the prime of his years—disease of the spleen, disease of the liver, disease of the stomach, disease of the eyes— macerated by senseless privations, a mere substratum for poultices and fomentations and cauterisations, scarcely even washing himself for fear of ostentating the stigmata, still sings songs of praise so blithely as to scandalise his companions' sense of death-bed decency, we touch a more Quixotic pathos than anything in Cervantes.

And these legends of his pious influence over the cicala and the swallow and the wolf, this tench that plays around his boat, this pheasant that haunts his cell, this falcon that wakes him for matins during his fast in the mountain, these birds that fly off in four companies like a cross after devoutly digesting his sermon, all make for the comity of creation, especially in Italy, where animals have no souls, only bodies that may be ill-used: indeed, St. Francis—with his disciple St. Antony of Padua—contributes to Christianity that missing note of respect for the animal creation which Hinduism expresses "in the great word Tat-twam-asi (This is thyself!)." And here at least modern thought is with St. Francis and his Hindu universalism. The evolution theory is usually considered a depressing doctrine, yet it has its stimulating aspects. For though we may doubt if St. Francis converted the wolf, we cannot doubt that Nature Christianised it, or at least some creature as low and savage. For from some gibbering ferocious brute there did, in the process of the suns, emerge a seraphic, selfless being with love for all creation. The wolf, in fact, became St. Francis; a more notable conversion than any in the missionary books.

But what did St. Francis become? Here the record is not so stimulating; here begins degeneration, devolution. Before he died he was an idol and the nominal centre of vast organisations, lay as well as monastic, female as well as male, and in this success lay his defeat. Lachrymæ rerum inhere even more in success than in failure. The portrait of St. Francis by Ribera which may be seen at Florence—a melancholy monk with his eyes turned up, holding a skull—was no sadder caricature of the blithe little man who swept out dirty churches with a broom than these gigantic and infinitely quarrelsome organisations were of his teaching.

A great man may either influence humanity by his solitary work or he may found an institution. The institution (if adequately financed) will live, but with himself squeezed out of it—for worship at a safe height. The squeezing out of St. Francis from Franciscanism began even before his death—the Papacy pressing from without and his own vicars from within. That very sensible fear of Brother William of Nottingham—evidently a practical Briton—that superfluities would grow up in the Order as insensibly as hairs in the beard, was more than verified. The dangerous rule of Absolute Poverty was relaxed, scholastic learning was reinstalled in its armchair, a network of rules replaced the rule of the spirit, and the little brotherhood that had lain on straw and tattered mattresses in the Portiuncula swelled and split into Conventualists and Observants, the majority established in magnificent monasteries. St. Francis lamented the degeneration of the brethren, though he characteristically refused to punish it. And when he was quite squeezed to death there began a fight for his body—holy body-snatching was a feature of the Middle Ages—and that vile enemy of the soul which he had battled against all his life took his place as the centre of the cult. Perugia, holding by force the body of St. Giles, removed from Assisi the only possible rival of his relics. His very poultice is still preserved as an object of edification.

II

Erasmus dreamed once—so he writes to Charles Utenhove—that St. Francis came to thank him for chastising the Franciscans. The Founder had not the scrupulous stage-costume of his degenerate followers: his brown frock was of undyed wool; the hood was not peaked, but merely hung behind to cover the head in bad weather; the cord was a piece of rope from a farmyard; the feet were bare. Of the five wounds of the stigmata there was as little trace in St. Francis as of the six virtues in the Franciscans. Obedience, poverty, chastity, humility, simplicity, charity—where had flown these "six wings of the seraph"?

Eheu fugaces! 'Tis the story of all founders, of all orders. St. Francis at his supreme moment of renunciation had not even the brown frock of Erasmus's dream. In the market-place of Assisi he stood in his shirt. And he desired to die even more naked, as Thomas of Celano and the "Legenda Trium Sociorum" testify. The first Franciscans were simple souls kindled by his love and ecstasy, "the minstrels of the dear Lord." They bore revilement and scourging; dragged along by their hoods, they never ceased to proclaim Peace. They lay a-cold in caves, with hearts careless of the morrow; they served in lepers' houses. And above all they worked; begging was only to be a last resort, and never was money to be asked for. "Beware of money," says the "Regula."

Brother Elias of Cortona, the immediate successor of St. Francis, is said to have lived like a prince, with valets and horses, and he readily got the Pope to sanction a device by which he obtained all the money he wanted per interpositas personas. Nor did the Master's teaching fare better at the hands of the more faithful faction—the Observants whom the Conventualists persecuted—for the rule of Absolute Poverty was applied without the genial concessions and exceptions he knew how to make; and under the guidance of the caustic and canonical Antony of Padua the ancient gaudentes in Domino hardened into slaves of the letter, while the more mystic degenerated into anchorites who retired to the mountains to save their own souls.

Nothing can point the tragedy of St. Francis's success more vividly than his own homely words in his "Testamentum." "And they who came to take up this life gave up whatever they might have to the poor and were content with a single tunic, patched inside and out (if they wished), together with a girdle and drawers: and we would have no more. We clerks said the office like other clerks; the lay-brothers said the Lord's Prayer. We gladly abode in poor and forsaken churches, and were simple folk and subject to all. And I used to work with my hands, and I desire to work, and my earnest wish is that all the brethren should work at some decent employment."

Only a century later Dante's eulogy of the Founder ("Paradiso," Canto XI) is qualified by the remark that so few of his followers cleave to his teachings that "a little stuff may furnish out their cloaks." And three centuries later the spectacle which these Fratri Minori represented to Erasmus was that of arrogant mendicants, often of loose morals, begging with forged testimonials, haunting the palaces of the rich, forcing themselves into families, selling the Franciscan habit to wealthy dying sinners as a funeral cloak to cover many sins. His little sisters, the swallows and the doves, fluttered over St. Francis's tomb, but from it issued the hawks and the vultures. An old, old moral, though humanity will never learn it.

Saint Francis was Francis Saint. The Lady Poverty "who for eleven hundred years had remained without a single suitor" found in him a spouse faithful unto death. His soul went out in fraternity to all the wonderful creation, in joyous surrender to pain and tribulation: even Death was his sister. To found an Order of St. Francis is to count upon a succession of St. Francises. As well found an Order of Shakespeare, a phalanstery of Da Vincis.

In religion no less than in literature or art the Master is ever a new individual—"Natura lo fece e ruppe il tipo"—but followers ever think to fix the free-blowing spirit. Alas! saints may be summarised in a system, but the system will not produce saints. Academies, churches, orders can never replace men; they too often serve to asphyxiate or assassinate such as appear. St. Dominic, the sterner founder of the other mendicant order, was not more fortunate in creating an apostolic succession of Poverty than his friend and contemporary; and as for his precursor, St. Bruno, contrast his marble image in the Certosa, gazing agonisedly at a crucifix, with the mosaics of agate, lapis-lazuli, amethyst, and cornelian worked over the altars by eight generations of the Sacchi family, or with the Lucullian feasts which the Carthusians could furnish forth at the bidding of the Magnificent Lodovico. St. Bruno retreated to the desert to fast and pray, and the result was Chartreuse. If he now follows the copious litigation he may well apprehend that his order has modified its motto and that for "Stat crux dum volvitur orbis" you should read "Stat spiritus."

Benedictine, too, is a curious by-product of the first of all the Western orders, and the one by which England was converted to Christianity. How pleased the founder of Monte Cassino must be to see a British bishop sipping Benedictine!

Religion has not, indeed, lacked saints aware of the tendency of followers to substitute the forms for the realities and the leader for the spirit. There was Antoinette Bourignon, with her love for the free flowing of the Holy Ghost and her hatred of the Atonement theory, but in the absence of forms her sect had not sufficient material framework to maintain itself by. If the Quakers still survive, it is because they have erected something into a system, if only colour-blindness. But the twaddle which is talked at Quaker meetings when an old bore is played upon by the spirit, turns one's thoughts longingly to a stately liturgy, independent on the passing generation. Humanity is indeed between the devil and the deep sea. Institutions strangle the spirit, and their absence dissipates it.

"Nec tecum possum vivere, nec sine te."

Even if by miracle a Church remains true to the spirit of its founder, this is a fresh source of unspirituality, for his spirit may be outgrown. An excellent definition of what a Church should be was given some years ago by a writer in the Church Quarterly: "A National Church, elastic enough to provide channels for fresh manifestations of spiritual life, yet anchored to the past." But where is such a Church to be found? "Anchored to the past"—yes, that condition is more than fulfilled. But spiritual elasticity? The Church Quarterly reviewer has the face to pass off his definition as that of the Church of England, and to say that such a National Church "might have saved the United States from many of those grotesque, and worse than grotesque, features which have at various times disfigured their spiritual life." But the Church of England has notoriously failed in elasticity—even the Archbishop of Canterbury is unable to make it express his view of the Athanasian Creed. And, far from its anchoring the spiritual life of the English people, they have violently torn themselves away from it in secessions of Baptists, Methodists, Quakers, &c. &c. As to its preserving them from grotesque religious features, the aberrations of English sectarianism fully equal those of America, when the difference of geographic area is considered and the absence of supervision over great spaces. Sandemanians, Walworth Jumpers, Joanna Southcottians, Seventh Day Baptists, Plymouth Brethren, Christadelphians, Peculiar People—such are a few of the British aberrations, some of which have counted distinguished followers. The bequests to foster even the Southcott mania were treated as sacred by the Court of Chancery. Jump-to-Glory-Jane is an English type put into poetry by an English poet. The sect to which Silas Marner belonged, with its naïve belief in drawing lots—the practical equivalent of the sortilege of the Pagan soothsayer—was not made in America. It was England which Voltaire ridiculed for its one sauce and its endless sects. The great scale of America magnifies the aberrations. But even Mormonism, Dowieism, and Christian Science have solid achievements to their credit. Salt Lake City is a paradise built over a desert reclaimed by Mormon labourers, Zion City is a handsome town without drinking-palaces, and Christian Science has made more advances in the last generation than Christianity made in its first two centuries, numbering as it does its temples and its teachers by the thousand. There is at least life behind these grotesqueries, while in the Established Churches there is asphyxiation by endowments.

Endowments—there is the secret of stagnation. It is an unhappy truth that man tends to become a parasite on his own institutions. Humanity is a Frankenstein that is ridden by its own creations. Its Churches, with their cast-iron creeds and their golden treasure-heaps, are the prisons of the soul of the future. The legal decision in the great Free Church fight serves as what Bacon calls an "ostensive instance" of this elemental truth, bringing out as it does that the legal interpretation of a Church involves, not the elasticity so glibly vaunted by the Church Quarterly reviewer, but absolute inelasticity. A tiny minority of ministers is able, for a time at least, to hold millions of money and hundreds of buildings, because the vast majority has elected, in a spirit of brotherly love, to join another body from which it is separated by a microscopic point. There can, at this rate, never be development in a Church. The faintest divergence from old tradition may justify the hard-shell orthodox in claiming all the funds and regarding the innovators as deserters of their posts and properties. All Church funds are indissolubly connected with the doctrines to which they were first tacked on, and changes in doctrine involve forfeiture of the belongings in favour of those who have had the fidelity or the shrewdness to cling to the original dogma. How much change is necessary to alter a creed is a delicate problem, known in logic as of the Soros order. For every day brings it subtle increments or decrements, and a dogma of imperishable adamant has not yet appeared in human history. Every dogma has its day. The life of a normally constituted truth is, according to Ibsen, twenty years at the outside, and aged truths are apt to be shockingly thin. Thus the danger which threatens all Churches—the danger of having to buy their ministers—is raised to infinity if the money is thus to be tied up by the dead hand of the past. A premium is placed upon infidelity and mustiness. There is no Church or religious body in the world which is not weighted with pecuniary substance, from Rome to the Order we have been considering, founded for the preachment of Absolute Poverty. The continuity of policy which the Church Quarterly applauds becomes a mere continuity of property, if progress is to be thus penalised. Nor are the Dissenting bodies immune from this pecuniary peril. A Calvinist chapel in Doncaster that was gravitating to the New Theology has found itself closed pro tem. under its trust deed of 1802.

The remedy for this clogging of spiritual life is clear. It was always obvious, but when Property is in danger one begins to consider things seriously.

Every Church and sect must be wound up after three generations. The time-limit needs elucidation.

The first generation of a Church or a heresy—the terms are synonymous, for every Church starts as a heresy—is full to the brim of vitality, fire, revolt, sincerity, spirituality, self-sacrifice. It is a generation in love, a generation exalted and enkindled by the new truth, a generation that will count life and lucre equally base beside the spreading of the new fire. The second generation has witnessed this fervour of its fathers, it has been nourished in the warmth of the doctrine, its education is imprinted with the true fiery stamp. It is still near the Holy Ghost. In the third generation the waves radiated from the primal fire have cooled in their passage through time; the original momentum tends to be exhausted. Now is the period of the smug Pharisees profiting by the martyrdoms of their ancestors, babbling rhetorically—between two pleasures—of their fidelity to the faith of their fathers. If the third generation of a Church can get through with fair spiritual success, it is often only because of a revival of persecution. But the third generation is absolutely the limit of the spiritual stirring. In the fourth generation you shall ever find the young people sly sceptics or sullen rebels, and the Vicar of Bray coming in for high preferment. Here, then, is the limitation dictated by human nature. The life of a Church should be wound up by the State. The birth of a heresy must be free to all, and should be registered like the birth of a child. It would expose its adherents to no disadvantages, either religious or political. But after three generations it must be wound up.

Of course, it should be perfectly open for the Church to reconstitute itself immediately, but it should do this under a new name. If it started again afresh, the compulsory winding-up would have acted as a species of persecution and thoroughly revitalised the content of the particular credo. The third generation would have strained every sinew to realise their faith and bring it home to the young and fourth generation. The latter, ere re-establishing the Church, would have rediscovered its truth, and thereby given it fresh momentum to carry it through another three generations. This simple system would allow children to continue the faith of their fathers from conviction instead of compulsion, and, by terminating the right to property, would save posterity from the asphyxiation of benefactions.

The life of a generation is computed by biological statisticians at thirty-three years. Three generations would thus make ninety-nine years. A century brings such changes in thought and things that the excerpts from the Times of a hundred years ago read like the journalism of another planet.

The bequests by which eleven old gentlewomen of a certain parish, that has been swept away, receive groats of an abolished currency, on a day that has disappeared from the calendar, to perpetuate the memory of a benevolent megalomaniac, would, on a similar principle, be limited to the natural run of a century. It is enough to be allowed a dead finger in the pie of proximate posterity; "a century not out" must never be written over any human will or institution.

If this time-limit seems a trifle harsh, apply it, dear reader, not to your own creed, but to something esoteric, like the doctrine of the Dalai Lamas of Tibet, which has for so many centuries paralysed a priest-ridden Asiatic population. Do you think this theory of reincarnation deserved a longer run than three generations?

THE GAY DOGES: OR THE FAILURE OF SOCIETY AND THE IMPOSSIBILITY OF SOCIALISM

"Dieses Prunkschiff ist ein rechtes Inventariënstück, woran man sehen kann, was die Venetianer waren, und sich zu sein dünkten."

I

But if Absolute Poverty is less worshipful than St. Francis imagined, Magnificence as an ideal will, I fear, always be found to connote defective moral sympathies, as of the Pharaohs building their treasure-cities on the labour of lashed slaves. For how in our world of sorrow and mystery can magnanimity and magnificence meet? What great soul could find expression in gilt, or even in gold? 'Tis a reflection on the character of the Doges of Venice that everywhere in their palace is a sense of over-gilded ceilings. Even when the Masters have made a firmament of frescoes, the massive flamboyant framing weighs like a torrid haze on a weary land. Art is overlaid and obliterated by gold. What wonder Religion too is soon asphyxiated in these flaming halls of Council—the Doge ceases to kneel to the Madonna, he stands before Venice Enthroned between Mars and Neptune. It is Juno who from a ceiling-fresco pours gold on Venice, and in the heavy gilded picture of Zelotti, the Magnificent Ten could behold Venice Seated on the World. What sly satirist was it who—over the choir of St. Mark's—crucified Christ on a cross of gold?

In "The Merchant of Venice," 'tis the Duke of Morocco who chooses the golden casket; I feel sure 'twas Bassanio, the Venetian. Not that I do not hate the leaden casket more. Portia should have gone with a field of buttercups in June.

Of all expressions of human greatness, metallic sheen is the most banal. I have never recovered from the shock of learning that the Greeks gilded their temples, and though I can now with even a spice of zest imagine them shining afar from their headlands in a golden glory, I would have preferred to keep my vision of austere columns and noble pediments; and I am grateful to Time, that truer artist, for having refined away that assertive aureola.

On the water, indeed—which is beneath one's feet, and not sagging on one's head—metallic sheen may exhilarate, subtilising and softening itself, as it does, in its own wavering reflections, and I find the Doge's gilded galley more endurable than his lacunar aureum. It may be because Shakespeare (or rather Plutarch) has reconciled me to Cleopatra's barge by those magnificent burnished lines. The Lord Mayor of London, too, had anciently his gilded barge, and if you will look at an eighteenth-century picture in the Guildhall by a pair of forgotten painters, representing the Lord of Cockaigne sailing in state on the Thames on the ninth of November, on the way to be sworn at Westminster, you will see how easily London, with her old boatmen and barges, and water-gates and water-parties, singing as in Pepys, might have paralleled the water-pomp of Venice, and how completely we have now thrown away the gorgeous possibilities of our proud water-way, lining it with warehouses in lieu of stately mansions, and cutting out of our lives all that shimmering vitality of ever-moving water. Man does not live by bread alone, and "Give us this day our daily water" were no unfitting prayer in our arid city. The Henley Week is our one approach to the colour of a Venetian festa. Yet what a Grand Canal the Thames might have been! I vow that at a distance I should take that old Guildhall picture, with its gay old costumes, its pageant of gilded galleys, each flying a brave array of rich-dyed flags and manned with rowers in white, its spires and turrets, and the noble dome of St. Paul's swelling into sunny spaces of air and cloud, all suffused in a golden mellowness, to represent the Doge of Venice going to a "solemn rite" at the Salute. Alas! the Lord Mayor has now only a gilded coach, and the Doge of Venice has vanished away, and only fragments of galleys in the Arsenal and a model of the last of the Bucentaurs remain to tell the tale of his marine glories, and his marriage to the Adriatic on Ascension Day.

One mast of the Bucentoro—the very mast that upbore the flag of the winged lion and the proud inscription, In hoc signo vinces—survives in tragic recumbency, while a morsel of frieze shows in gold, on a basis of dark wood, delicious angels playing trumpet and harp at the prow. The relics of other galleys, pranked with figures about half life-size, enable us to gather what exuberance of fancy and grotesquerie went to grace the Bucentoro which Napoleon burnt, while the fact that he extracted the gold of 80,000 Napoleons from its ashes shows with what prodigality the Republic blazoned its sense of itself.

But the marvellous model reconstructed by Ferdinand of Austria in 1837 at a cost of 152,000 francs, reveals, if it be exact, that seamy side which is always the obverse of Magnificence. At first the eye is taken up with its opulence of decoration, as it seems to take the water with its proud keel, and its great all-topping flag of the lion and the cross. For its upper deck is of mosaic, over-hinged by a huge lid, red velvet without and gold relief within, and from the water-line rise winged figures, and over the arch through which pass the many-flashing oars of red and gold is a frieze of flying horses, the rape of Europa, Centaurs, and what not; and above this are winged figures flying towards a gold sky, and gold figures on a balcony, which is supported at the prow by winged lions and a pair of mermen, and at the bowsprit couches the winged lion with two little angels playing behind him; and on the hull is a naiad pouring out her urn, and a merman blowing his trumpet, and the protrusive heads of alligators; and lest you should think Venice meant nothing but gold and fantasy and the pride of life, behold dominant over these Justice with her sword and her scales, and Peace with her dove and her olive-branch.

But below, hidden away behind and beneath the gilding, at the unseen end of the red and gold oars

"Which to the tune of flutes kept stroke,"

sat one hundred and seventy-eight galley-slaves, chained four to an oar; and here in this fuscous interior the benches are no longer of plush, but of rough deal; here is no play of Fancy—here in the hard seats we touch Reality. But not herein lies the supreme sordidness of the Bucentoro—the crowning touch is given by the oars, which, at the very point where they disappear over the rowlocks under the gay arches, turn from their red and gold into a plain dirty white, like shirt-cuffs that give on soiled sleeves. 'Tis the very magnificence of meanness! The horny-handed wretches, to the rhythm of whose tired muscles this golden vessel moved along in its music and sunshine, to whose caged gloom no glimpse came of the flags and the purple, the angels and the naiads, could not even be conceded the coloured end of an oar. But could there be an apter symbol of civilisation, ancient, mediæval, or modern, than this gilded oar, whose gaudiness fades as it passes from the bravery of the outer spectacle to the grimness of the inner labour? Upon such sweating slaves rested all the glitter and pageantry of the ancient world—not only Babylon and Carthage, but even the spiritual and artistic greatness of Greece. In hoc signo vinces—in the sign of slavery; in the sign of the lion and the cross—the lion for yourself and the cross for the people. And in every land of to-day the same State-Galley glides along in bannered pomp, parading its decorative images of Peace and Justice, and the radiant creations of its Art, while below are the hard bare benches and the labouring, groaning serfs. The serfs are below, even in another sense, for it is their unsightly hands that have built up every square inch of this splendour. Beatrice d'Este went to see a galley a-building, her velvet cap and her embroidered vest stuck full of jewels; complacently recording the ejaculations of admiration for her diamonds and rubies, while the Venetian women, and even children, were toiling at making the sails and the ropes. Yes, the social order too must be gazetted bankrupt. It has, indeed, never been solvent. It has never paid its real creditors, the slaves of the uncoloured oar.

Nor does our civilisation hold much hope of a change for the fairer. Despite prophets and poets, despite Socialists, dry-as-dust or dithyrambic, despite philanthropists and preachers, the revel on the top-deck amid the velvet and the mosaics grows ever wilder, the flutes ever more Dionysiac, the fantasies on prow and poop ever more grotesquely golden. America, shorn of monarchy and feudalism and rank, and all that the friends of man screamed against, divides with Russia the hegemony of hotels and outdoes the worst extravagances and debaucheries of the Renaissance. Where in the Cinquecento a few despots and "humanists" wallowed in lust and luxury, we have now ten thousand private tyrants and loose-livers, restrained hardly by the penal law. The deeds of the Cenci or the Baglioni must be done in a glass-house in the fierce light that beats upon local greatness. The ruffians of the Renaissance had no such free field for vagaries and vices as the vagrom son of a millionaire enjoys in this modern world, where property in growing fluid has become dissolved from duty; where in every pleasure-city palaces invite and women allure and slaves grovel; where every port swarms with white-winged yachts to bear his indolent irresponsibility to glamorous shores; where in a million halls of light his world-strewn flunkeys proffer unseasonable food cooked by unsurpassable artists, and rare champagnes, oscillated for months in a strange daily ritual by troops of underground elves.

They tell us that this New Year's Eve in New York alone some three million pounds were spent in suppers in the flaring restaurants, where between eleven and twelve o'clock only champagne could be served. Such is the New Era ushered in by the New World—the Era of Champagne. For this the Red Indian was uprooted and the wilderness tamed. For this Washington lived and Lincoln died. By the flood of champagne all standards of life and letters are swept away, save the one standard of financial success, save the ability to dine in that wonderful culinary cathedral where in a dim irreligious light as of a submarine world of faery, to a melting liturgical music, a fashionable congregation follows with absorbing zeal the lengthy order of service. What an Agapemone!

And this epidemic of vulgarity, spreading to our own country, has made the England of 1802, which Wordsworth denounced for "glittering like a brook," the England where "plain living and high thinking" were no more, appear like an island of pristine simplicity. Even the old families surrender to the new standard and—in the plaint of Dante—"non heroico more, sed plebeo sequuntur superbiam."

What is to be done? What is to be done about it all? We writing men, to whom the highest British manhood is still Wordsworth in that country cottage where visitors must pay for anything beyond bread and cheese, we to whom the greatest American personality is still Walt Whitman in his Camden shanty, must at least preserve our divine gift of laughter, our one poor power of laughing at these vulgarians, whom even the occasional smuggling of an Old Master out of Italy cannot redeem from barbarism.

The purple pomp of kings, blatant though it be in comparison with true grandeur, is at least the expression of a public dignity: it is an official costume like the judge's wig and gown. But because greatness must accept office at the hands of its otherwise helpless inferiors, and office must be suitably apparelled, a certain confusion has been established between splendour and greatness, as though because greatness means splendour, splendour must mean greatness. Of this confusion those are promptest to take advantage to whom the high road to consideration is closed. Private pomp is a confession of personal pettiness. The little soul must needs inflate itself by a great house-shell, and protract itself by a long retinue of servants. 'Tis almost too pathetic a meekness, this humility of the Magnificent Ones.

Cannot I breathe into you—O Magnificent Ones—a little proper pride? Ye buy the Past, watching one another in jealous competition; will no one buy the Future? Why not buy with your millions an earth renewed and regenerated, a solvent social order? Why not build a true civilisation on this malarious marsh, that shall rise like the spires and domes of Venice from her swamps? Surely that were a dream worthy of Magnificence! Come, let us build together a State-Galley where the oars shall be red and gold from blade to handle, and every man shall take his turn at them, and the fantasies of Art shall adorn the hull of Righteousness, and Justice and Peace shall no longer be ironic images carved for the complacency of the top-deck. So shall there dawn an Ascension Day on which the Doge shall go out with banners and music, not to marry the sea with a ring, but to celebrate the nuptials of Earth with Heaven.

Private pomp is surely a questionable thing. Mediæval life centred round the Cathedral, the Castle, the Palace. And the masses touched the life at each and all. The Cathedral gave them their religion, their laws came from the Palace, their protection from the Castle. Dominating a feudal population, the towers of law and war uplifted and unified the people. The lowliest were of this greatness. To-day palaces flaunt themselves, divorced from moral meaning, magnificence without significance. The world, as I said, is full of private autocrats, without duties or dangers: an unhappy consequence of the fall of feudalism, ere a system as human was ready to replace it. And to-day the Cathedral is our one feudal relic, reconciling magnificence with morality: the light streaming through the rose-window haloes the grey head of the market-woman, and her prayer equals that of the Magnificent One himself. It is significant that no villa—whoever the architect—can attain the poetic quality of the simplest village church. The palace of Moses is nowhere mentioned, but we read many minute instructions concerning the Tabernacle and the Temple. In truth, art treasures are essentially public: the furniture of cathedrals, libraries, law-courts, market-places, and parks. The owners of collections do indeed often allow the public to visit them at inconvenient times, but that anybody should have exclusive rights is an absurdity. If Art were a form of property like any other, the owner could destroy it, and the righteous indignation of the world at the destruction of a Botticelli or a Velasquez would mark the boundaries of private property. Land comes under the same canon. Nothing, perhaps, should be owned which might not be destroyed at will.

In literature and music—which are more spirits than bodies, and which can be multiplied without loss—monopolies are unnecessary. If I write a book against Socialism, the world will applaud, and communistically possess itself thereof after a brief term. And this legal limitation of copyright which forcibly wrests epics, operas, and novels from the heirs might be extended to pictures and statues.

II

But if the galley of old Venice stimulates my Socialism, the cinematograph of modern Venice torpifies it again. For be it known that in Venice there are scores of halls and theatres devoted to delectable visions at prices to suit the poorest, and open to ragazzi for a couple of soldi. And in every city of Italy the fever rages; one performance follows on the heels of another, and the wretched manipulator of the magic lantern must subsist on sandwiches while the theatre is clearing and re-filling. Every unlet dancing-hall or decayed rink or bankrupt building has blossomed out into a hall of enchantment where even the words of the play are sometimes given by the cunning juxtaposition of gramophones. In this way I heard Amletto, or the Prince of Denmark, its too, too solid flesh melted into a meat extract. But the most wonderful spectacle of all was soundless, save for the flowing music. For twenty centesimi the Teatro S. Marco passed before my eyes an exquisite vision of Le Ore—the hours in ten "Quadri animati," from the shiver of light that precedes the dawn to the last falling of night. In the Sala d'Aurora of the Castle of Ferrara, Dosso Dossi has depicted Tramonto, Notte, L'Aurora and Mezzogiorno, but not more poetically than the modern stage-manager who arranged these living pictures. As I watched these allegorical groupings of nymphs and fauns by their stream in the glade, I felt that the old pagan religion still lingered in the souls that could conceive and enjoy this nature-poetry.

And as I sat here, amid Venetian washerwomen and street boys, it was further borne in upon me that no State Bureau would ever have begotten this marvel for the joy and uplifting of the people, and that in the present imperfection of human nature individual initiative under the spur of gold or hunger could alone work these miracles of Socialism. "La propriété c'est la vol," said Proudhon, but "vol" in his sense implies a bullish acceptance of the very conception he is combating. Let us translate it by "flight." Property is the impulse of the aeroplane.

Therefore pray do not count my aspiration for a solvent social order as an adhesion to any cut and dried theory of the State owning and administering all social resources. For that sort of Socialism is—like science—bankrupt, even before it begins. It fails, not merely because it would substitute an external arrangement for a change of heart—and Socialism will either be a religion or will not be—but because no external arrangement is possible. The collective ownership of land and capital is feasible in Juan Fernandez so long as Robinson Crusoe and Friday continue exiled from civilisation, but impossible in our world of international finance, where private ownership extends to countries which the property holder will never even visit. Unless, therefore, every country in the world simultaneously adopted Socialism, there would be an inextricable tangle of Socialism and Individualism. Not to mention that capital—as every shareholder knows—means men as much as money. But even in Juan Fernandez, as soon as it became thickly populated, Socialism would be unmanageable, because the stock of concentrable human consciousness is insufficient to arrange a social order from a central bureau. Omniscience alone would be equal to the task, not to mention All Goodness and All Wisdom. Despite the vast loss by friction and absence of organisation, despite the vast suffering, the struggle for existence is the only agency capable of fitting the pegs into the holes. Shall the State, for example, select which man shall write poetry? And still more vital, which poetry the State Press shall print? We have already had experience of the State as a selector of Laureates and a censor of drama, and Milton knew it as a censor of literature. Our most brilliant Socialists, an they had their way, would be reduced to pasting pasquinades on the pedestals of our street statues.

But in a looser connotation, "we are all Socialists now," if indeed we ever were anything else. From the day of the first human grouping for co-operation and common defence, Socialism has been the rule of life, and the question of how the common work and the common products are to be apportioned is a mere question of organised distribution. That we have hitherto left this cumbrous and infinitely complex problem of distribution to solve itself by natural selection does not make society less socialistic. Nor would the discovery of a more excellent way of dividing up the labour and its results make society more socialistic. For compared with the assets of civilisation in which we share equally—the museums, picture galleries, libraries, parks, roads, schools, life-boat and fire-engine services, armies, navies, light-houses, weather-bureaus, asylums, hospitals, observatories—the assets in which we share unequally are relatively unimportant, and without sacrificing to a machine the zest and stimulus of liberty, and the fine flavour of individuality, it is a comparatively simple matter to minimise the waste and suffering produced by the struggle for existence, and to arrange that talent shall rise to the top, not for its sake but our own. It is no evil that one man should live in a palace and another in a cottage; these differences even add to the colour and joy of life. The evil is solely that any man willing to work should lack a cottage, or that the cottage should be a malarious hovel. Levelling up is the only reform necessary, as it is the only reform possible. For if the gradual consolidation of railways, land, mines, and a few leading industries in the hands of the State is not beyond practical politics, this would still be very far from "Socialism," and it is vastly amusing to witness the agony of apprehension with which respectable society looks forward to the advent of a social order which cannot possibly materialise, and which menaces us less than the flaming tail of a comet. Only less amusing is the awe with which society regards Property as something sacrosanct in quality and immutable in quantity. Why, even the King's shilling is as nimble and elusive as mercury, will buy you mutton to-day and only tripe to-morrow, and scarcely run to dog-sausage in a siege. Property is a Proteus, a shadow, a transient and generally embarrassed phantom. Property merely means a potential call upon human service—past or future—and if human service is unwilling or absent, Property shrinks or collapses, like the bag of pearls found by the thirsting Arab in the desert. Finance—like all other branches of science—has been treated as though its subject-matter had absolute existence. But the assets of the world's bankers incalculably outrun the world's power of service, and Property is merely a promissory note which can only be redeemed if there is not too great a run upon the labour bank at which it is presented. Still more elastic is the service that produces this right to call upon the service of others. A hundred thousand readers buy this book—instead of borrowing it—and I am a Crœsus; a hundred, and I am free of income tax. Motor cars are invented, and my house in Ascot falls to half its former value because the smart set need no longer stay overnight during the Ascot week. My unknown aunt remembers me in her will and I am a thousand pounds the richer. The Seine rises and my Paris flat is a ruin. I die and my land dwindles to six feet. Where in this foolish flux is room for holiness? And why may not society—the only source of values—mould Property as it will for society's ends? Why—among the many vicissitudes with which Property must reckon—should not social reform count equally with bad harvests, wars of conquest and Stock Exchange manœuvres?

To say that Property is sacred is to confuse the means with the end, like the miser who hoards his gold and forgets its uses. Society is sacred, not Property, and whatever sanctitude or stability has been attached to Property has been attached entirely for socialistic purposes; not that the individual may be enriched, but that he may not lose the spur that drives him to enrich society. Individual property is merely a by-product of labour for society. He who demands overmuch for his labour is under-moralised. The true citizen is anxious to be taxed for the general good, provided his taxes are used for social service. He is anxious that some form of distribution of the common products shall be organised to supplement natural selection and correct its over-harshness. Experience might prove that interference with natural selection saps the stamina and initiative of society more than it benefits the "submerged tenth," in which case we should reluctantly return to the present form of Socialism.

As for land, it is the one thing that I can conceive nationalised even under our present form of Socialism, nay, which is already nationalised to the extent that the private owners of British land may not sell it to Germany or Japan, as they may sell anything else of theirs. Every new State should doubtless begin by trying to nationalise its land. I say "trying," because it is by no means certain that it would succeed, since so far from the increment in land values being unearned, it is the very possibility of earning it that induces the pioneer to suffer peril, privation and isolation. Were Canada, for example, not to give away its land, the many adventurers who have flowed in from the United States would probably have remained at home, and all this Canadian territory have been still empty. And once you have made land quasi-private property, it cannot justly be subjected to any peculiar tax, since colossal as is the rise of land values in growing towns, the value of land is controlled by the same factors of luck and judgment as rule all other property values, and may be depreciated as well as enhanced by the operation of social forces beyond the owner's control or prevision. Wherefore all increments in value—in stocks and shares, copyrights, patents, &c. &c.—should be treated as potential matter for taxation equally with the so-called "unearned increment" on land.

One would imagine from the war cries in our latest political campaign that Socialism was already upon us, and that the only refuge from it lay in Tariff Reform. But it is precisely Tariff Reform which is Socialism; a taxation of the entire community in the interests of this or that industry. Nor should the entire community be averse from taxation for any provably good object; a moralised community would even be always looking round for fresh methods of self-taxation. Budget Day would be a national festival, a day of solemn joy, tense with the hope that new ways would be found of making England the Kingdom of God. Alas! it is a day of sick anxiety, with a sequel of farcical unfailingness, in which every section taxed sends a deputation to show that it is the one section that should have been left unburdened, while from the bloated gluttons and swillers at the great hotels arises the cry of "Red ruin and the breaking-up of laws." And the poor philanthropist we have always with us—he who threatens to stop his charity contributions. As if the abolition of charity was not the very object of social reform! Every benevolent activity means a sore in the social system, and charity covers indeed a multitude of our sins.

Strange that these sordid questions of money should so fever this mighty England of Shakespeare and Milton. Ship-money cost Charles the First his head, and a petty land tax changes the House of Peers. Poor humanity, so deluded as to the essential values of life, so peculiarly demented in all that concerns Property! But I bid you cast away your fears. I repeat to you my good tidings of great joy. Socialism is impossible. A perfect and just distribution of the goods and labours of life—"to each according to his needs, from each according to his powers"—is Utopian. Moreover envy, hatred and all uncharitableness prevent it: stupidity, sloth, selfishness, treachery and tyranny preclude it. Rejoice, therefore, and let us cry Hosanna!

Nor are these evil qualities confined to the capitalist, they are found in even uglier forms in the working man, who is merely a capitalist without means, and through his Trade Unions talks equally of rights and even less of duties and ideals.

But if Socialism is impossible, and Socialist parties consequently deficient in constructive potency, they yet perform in every country a critical and regulative function of the first importance. Our own Labour members are the only gentlemen in British politics. To all questions, national or international, they bring a broad spirit and a quixotic ideal, and while our Howards and our Percys cower in craven terror of Germany, or make prudent alliance with Holy Russia, or handle with correlative despotism India, Ireland or the woman question, our men from the pits and the factories sit free and fearless, the sole guardians of England's ancient glory.

THE SUPERMAN OF LETTERS: OR THE HYPOCRISY OF POLITICS

Arrestive was it in an aisle of Santa Croce—the Florentine Church of the Holy Cross—to come upon a monument to Niccolò Machiavelli, anathema alike for Catholicism and Protestantism, the "Old Nick" of the Hudibras rhyme. 'Twas as if Mephisto had managed not only to slip into the Cathedral, but to achieve canonisation. But even a devil is not given his due at the hands of his own countrymen: it was reserved for an English earl, more than two and a half centuries after Mephisto's passing, to provide his works with a splendid setting and his remains with a massive monument. And so, in the dim religious light, I pondered over the stately inscription:

"Tanto Nomini nullum par Elogium."

How, indeed, equate eulogy to so great a name? Machiavelli was our first modern—the first to exhibit the reign of law in human affairs, to read history as the play of human forces and not as the caprice of a cloudy Providence, modified by the stars. What an epic sweep in the opening sentences of his "History of Florence"—Gibbon in a nutshell, the whole "Decline and Fall," summarised as the economic emigration southward of the surplus population of the Goths into an Italy weakened by the removal of the seat of Empire to Constantinople. Vagarious chance, indeed, he admits, as a complication (to be minimised by prudence), but Providence is mentioned in "The Prince," only to be dropped, and astrology is not even mentioned. Machiavelli would have agreed that "the fault's in ourselves, not in our stars, that we are underlings," and for those who wished to prince it, he was prepared to point the conditions of success. And this indifference to the stars—to quadrangles and hexagons, sigils, conjunctions, and configurations—is not his least amazing merit.

Pico della Mirandola had, indeed, refuted astrology before him, but it was in the interests of that conventional theory of Providence and free-will which leaves the chaos of history irreducible to order. Machiavelli not only ignores astrology, but substitutes causation for the chaos.

'Tis true Comte suggested that astrology was, likewise, an attempt to reduce to law the chaos of human phenomena, but the remark is over-ingenious. Where there is no rational connection between causes and effects there is no science. The planetary conjuncture one was born under might, indeed, not impossibly affect temperament or internal destiny, just as the climate one was born under, but the notion that it could shape external destiny belongs to the mediæval megalomania. Galileo's discovery of new stars must have shaken it, falsifying as it did all previous horoscopes—indeed, Sir Henry Wotton, our ambassador to Venice, was more impressed by Galileo's injuriousness to astrology than to theology. "For the virtue of these new planets must needs vary the judicial part, and why may there not yet be more?" But Machiavelli belongs to the pre-telescope period; he wrote a whole century before Galileo, and thirty years ere Copernicus unsettled the ancient heavens by his Nuremberg treatise. True, even in the twelfth century, Maimonides had denounced astrology as "a disease, not a science," and the great Jew's letter "to the Men of Marseilles" had evoked papal applause. But not even Popes could arrest the disease. A century before Machiavelli was born Petrarch poured scorn on the astrologers. But the mockeries of this pioneer of humanism did not save a prince of the Renaissance like Lodovico from employing an astrologer advisory, under whose calculations he went from disaster to disaster. There were even Professors of Astrology at the Universities. Bodin, the next great political philosopher after Machiavelli, though half a century later, still dallies with astrology, still coquets with the theory of a connection between the planetary motions and the world's history, while Copernicus he regards as a fantast unworthy of serious refutation.

Earlier in the sixteenth century Luther had denounced astrology as "framed by the devil," and in his Table Talk had challenged the astrologers to answer him why Esau and Jacob, who were "born together of one father and one mother, at one time and under equal planets" were yet "wholly of contrary natures, kinds and morals." Nevertheless in the next century, Milton in "Paradise Regained" makes Satan predict truly to Jesus on the strength of

"What the stars, Voluminous or single characters,
In their conjunction met,"

give him to spell, and throughout the whole seventeenth century, as "Guy Mannering" reminds us, nativities continued to be cast. The child's horoscope in some parts of Europe hung side by side with his baptismal certificate. Even to-day such phrases as "Thank your lucky stars," conserve a shadow of the ancient belief, and the sidereal influence survives even more subtly in the word "consider." Through such banks of fog pierces the searchlight of the great Florentine, it turns its powerful beam even upon Church history. The Princes of ecclesiastical principalities, he remarks drily, are the only ones who can possess States and subjects without governing and defending them, but it would be presumptuous in him to discuss these matters, as they are under the superintendence and direction of an Almighty Being, whose dispensations are beyond our weak understandings. But the Church has likewise attained temporal power, and here Mephisto may intrude without blasphemy. Secular triumphs demand secular explanations. One is reminded of the dialogue on Julius II attributed to Erasmus. Our Mephisto notes grimly that no prophet has ever succeeded unless backed by an armed force. Hence the collapse of "brother Jerome Savonarola when the multitude ceased to have faith in him." In short, in the making of history Might and Right are partners.

Not in the exposition of this commonplace lay Machiavelli's offensiveness for his contemporaries. Had he remained the passionless observer of the pitiful human breed, the explicator of the tangled threads of history, he would have been acclaimed as a moralist, unveiling with ruthless hand the hypocrisies of princes. What changed angel to devil was that instead of fulminating against the partnership of Might and Right, he found that only by this firm could history be made. He wrote not science but art—the ars usurpandi. Not only had the Princes of the past combined Might with Right, guile with goodness, but whoso wished now to be a Prince must needs go and do likewise. The ethics springing from the social relations of citizen to citizen no longer holds in the relation of ruler to subjects.

It is true "The Prince" might also be regarded as an elaborate Swiftian irony—a negative Pulcinellian advice to those about to usurp—an exposition of Princedom as the service of the devil. "A New Prince cannot with impunity exercise all the virtues, because his own self-preservation will often compel him to violate the laws of charity, religion and humanity." But this Swiftian supposition does not tally with the dedication to Lorenzo de' Medici and his overt encouragement to the Most Magnificent to seize the reins. Machiavelli plainly believes in the sense he alleges hidden by the ancients in the myth of Chiron the Centaur, who was the educator of rulers because he had the double qualification of the brute and the man. In high politics crimes are only crimes when they are blunders. Unsuccessful cruelty is unpardonable. Wickedness should be pursued with an economy of means to end: like the causes in Occam's canon, crimes should not be multiplied præter necessitatem. Politics is a sort of bee-keeping, and the master of the hive will use the instincts and ethics of the little creatures for his own purposes, his kindness will be as cold-blooded as his cruelty. Thus, some three and a half centuries before Nietzsche, was expounded the doctrine of the Superman, the splendid blonde beast who had passed Jenseits von Gut und Böse. "The despised virtues of patience and humility have abased the spirits of men, which Pagan principles exalted." It is in such precisely Nietzschean terms that Sir Thomas Browne sums up, albeit unapplausively, "the judgment of Machiavel." But as a treatise on apiculture, "The Prince" is not rigidly scientific. The Superman, alone upon his dizzy height, Diabolists and neo-Dionysians as yet unborn to cheer him, has his moments of human weakness. Before the crimes of Agathocles he falters, and remarks with delicious gravity, "Still it must not be called virtue to murder one's fellow-citizens or to sacrifice one's friends, or be insensible to the voice of faith, pity or religion. These qualities may lead to sovereignty but not to glory." And there is a more general apologia in the concession that the times are out of joint—in the grim Tacitean explanation that "he who deviates from the common course of practice, and endeavours to act as duty dictates, necessarily ensures his own destruction." Super-morality lapses here into morality.

Moreover, Machiavelli did not himself play the Superman. He wrote the part—or founded it on Cæsar Borgia—but he did not act it. The Rubicon 'twixt thought and action he never crossed. His own morals appear to have been conventionally excellent. Like Helvetius, who traced virtue to the lowest roots of self-interest, he was of a rare magnanimity. As a scientific observer he advises the Tyrant, if he cannot live in the Republic he has conquered, to destroy it root and branch, but as a man he bore torture and imprisonment for the cause of liberty. Indeed, in his later years something of the sæva indignatio of Swift seems to have possessed his breast. It was Napoleon who was destined to incarnate the maxims of Machiavelli, though on a far grander stage than even Cæsar Borgia ever dreamed of: it was Napoleon who gave the greatest performance of "The Prince." And by a hitherto unnoted coincidence Napoleon was born exactly three centuries after Machiavelli. Exactly three hundred years (1469-1769) divided the nativities of the Superman of Letters and the Superman of Action—'tis almost enough to revive faith in the potency of planetary conjunctures. True, Nietzsche regards Napoleon as but "half-Superman," the other half being beast, but we have seen that the bestial portion is a necessary factor of the Machiavellian Superman, who is nothing if not super-dominant. What Nietzsche's Superman was to be, Nietzsche did not precisely know, though we may well suspect that the direction in which he strained his vision for him was not the horizon but the looking glass. Nietzsche has not even the credit of inventing the Superman, for when Nietzsche was six years old, Tennyson published "In Memoriam," with its prophetic peroration:

"A closer link Between us and the crowning race. . . .

No longer half akin to brute,
For all we thought and loved and did,
And hoped, and suffered, is but seed
Of what in them is flower and fruit."

Tennyson pressed home this idea of the further evolution of our race in his very last volume, in a poem called "The Making of Man."

"Man as yet is being made, and ere the crowning Age of ages,
Shall not æon after æon pass and touch him into shape?"

And again in "The Dawn."

"Ah, what will our children be,
The men of a hundred thousand, a million summers away?"

More self-conscious a disciple of Machiavelli than Napoleon was our own Thomas Cromwell, who carried "The Prince" as his political enchiridion, and who within three years of its publication chopped off Sir Thomas More's head as coolly as a knight captures a bishop on a chess-board. If you have to choose between love and fear, said the Master, then fear is the stronger weapon. With fear, Thomas the pupil hewed his way to the great ends he had set himself. Thomas Cromwell's application of the system was, however, vitiated by one radical mistake. By a paradox, worthy of Machiavelli himself—and repeated in our own day by Bismarck—"the Prince" he worked for was not himself but his sovereign. Howsoever Thomas Crommay have appeared the true gerent, the final profit was to the suzerain, and the axe of despotism which he had forged for Henry VIII was turned against his own neck. Of his canon that traitors should be condemned unheard, he was the sole victim. Possibly he might have triumphed even over the flaw in his practice, had Anne of Cleves been more personable. It was essential to his game to queen this pawn, and queen her he did. But at what a cost! It has been said that if Cleopatra's nose had been longer, the world's history would have been other. Of the German princess's nose it may be said that had it been prettier—or perchance had Holbein flattered it less before it was seen by the matrimonial agent—Thomas Cromwell would have continued to rule England, and Europe might have been spared the Thirty Years' War. But even Supermen cannot change the shape of ladies' noses, and in this surd of a world, where the best laid plans may "gang agley" over the tilt of a nostril, what avail your Supermen more than Supermice? The toasted cheese is but temporary, the end of Napoleon is the mouse-trap.

The phenomena of history are indeed too multifarious for consciousness, and the Machiavellian method of treating persons as things—in defiance of the moral maxim—shatters itself upon the impossibility of foreseeing all the permutations of the things. A bad prince is no more secure against assassination than a good prince. A religious reformer may arise and upset the snuggest peace. A failure of crops may precipitate rebellion. A child's arm may plug up a dam. In brief, lacking the necessary omniscience, the shrewdest of Supermen is driving in the dark. The upshot of Napoleon's career was to make Germany and mutilate France.

It is through lack of omniscience, too, that we cannot obey the frequent modern suggestion to breed the Superman—the Superman, that is, not as the cold-blooded manipulator of man, but as his moral superior and successor, Tennyson's Superman, not Nietzsche's. We are too abysmally ignorant for evolutionary eugenics. We breed horses and roses for higher types, but then we immeasurably transcend horses and roses. Who transcends us so immeasurably that he should breed us? In breeding we have a clear vision of our aim—to produce a thornless rose or a Derby winner. What clear vision has any one of the Superman? It is impossible to read even Nietzsche without seeing a spectral swarm of shifting types. Moreover we breed only for physical qualities. What experience have we of breeding for moral qualities? And what were all our breedings compared with Nature's inexhaustible experimentation, her thousand million men and women of all shades and psychoses, her endless blendings and crossings that yield now Nietzsches, now Isaiahs; yesterday Platos, to-day Darwins and Wagners.

The Superman will come of himself: already man rises as imperceptibly into him as he fades into the orang-outang. "This was no man," said Napoleon, reading the Sermon on the Mount—an involuntary admission by the Machiavellian of a finer species of Superman than his own.

And this brings us to the paradox that the defect in Machiavelli's system was not in his morals but in his intellect. In the hive he examined were creatures greater than he, obeying motives beyond his ken. To him Princes ruled primarily for their own glory, for the pomp and pride of power. Of the small but infinitely important class of rulers who assume mastership only because they have the greatest power to serve, he has no adequate conception. That there has sometimes been a Pope who felt himself literally servus servorum Dei passed his comprehension. This falsifies his treatment of history, this makes his vision imperfect, this throws his conclusions out of gear. The verse in St. Matthew, "he that is greatest among you shall be servant of all the rest," represents a more scientific generalisation. As Chapman's Don Byron (Act 3, Scene 1) reminds us, in his denunciation of "the schools first founded in ingenious Italy," the true

"Kings are not made by art
But right of nature, nor by treachery propt
But simple virtue."

But Machiavelli, that crude biologist, treats Moses and Cyrus as creatures of the same species, would run together the Attilas and the Buddhas. Hence the hard metallic sheen of his style as of an old Latin prose-writer; of spiritual iridescence, of Jewish tenderness, of Christian yearning, of even the Nietzschean ecstasy there is no trace. It is not astonishing that he should have turned a scornful ear to Savonarola's message, dismissed him as a compound of fraud and cunning. How dramatic is the picture of Mephisto listening to the preacher of San Marco that week of the Carnival of 1497! (What a pity "Romola" does not exploit that episode instead of using Machiavelli as a mere caustic conversationalist). But though Machiavelli's flair for crouching Cæsars was not utterly at fault, though the Dominican did indeed aspire to be "The Prince" of the Church, and even the power behind the thrones of the Princes of Christendom, yet 'twas all ad majorem Dei gloriam and for the greater confusion of the infidel, and George Eliot has understood this impersonal egotist infinitely better than his cynical contemporary understood him. And this intellectual limitation—this absence of the highest notes from his psychological gamut—must always keep Machiavelli out of the first rank of writers. He cannot rise above the notion that power is an end in itself and that those who can satisfy it "deserve praise rather than censure." If the King of France—he tells us—was powerful enough to invade the kingdom of Naples, then he ought to have done it. Though Machiavelli could see that the individual's crimes "may lead to sovereignty but not to glory," yet he did not question the right of a State to absorb or shatter another. He saw that the world went on

"The simple plan
That they should take who have the power,
And they should keep who can,"

and he admitted that the rule was indispensable—if you went into politics. This was his crime—High Treason against Idealism. Humanity prefers to be guided by rules which it disavows. The splendid blonde beasts who practised the maxims of Machiavelli shuddered at the scribe who merely stated them. Nowhere probably was disgust with the Florentine writer more vehement than in Venice, which employed assassins as a principle of polity. Could that Turkish "Prince" who decreed that each new monarch of his house must safeguard the dynasty by massacring his swarm of brothers, or that Persian "Prince" who invented the principle of blinding them, have seen the printed "Prince" of Machiavelli, they with their correct Islamic or Zoroastrian principles would have shared in the universal opprobrium.

That the world shudders still is shown by the apologetic attitude of his commentators and even of his panegyrists. Not one but repudiates his system, charitably traces it to the unhappy circumstances of his day, to the welter of force and fraud amid which his lot was cast. Yet are these circumstances essentially changed? The small urban republics have vanished, but in their stead are the Great Powers. Cæsar Borgia and Ezzelino are gone, but we have the Congo Ruler and the Trust Magnate. "Every country hath its Machiavel," says Sir Thomas Browne, and there is no spot on earth where the maxims of "The Prince" are not in daily operation. The voice may be the voice of Savonarola, but the hands are the hands of Machiavelli.

Nay, it is often the voice of Machiavelli even when it sounds like the voice of Savonarola. For, as Lord Acton subtly pointed out, Machiavellism lurks in many a seemingly innocent and even pious proposition. It is perhaps straining his point to find it in Jeremy Bentham's "greatest happiness principle," but who shall doubt but that it is involved in the popular idea that "Time tries all," and that everything happens for the best in the long run, and that history is, after all, the Will of God? What are all these nebulous notions but the acceptance of success—of the brute fact—as the moral standard? Less obvious than the proposition that "God is on the side of the biggest battalions," they are substantially identical with it. They simply mean that God was on the side of the biggest battalions. They imply that whichever party triumphed, God was with that party. So that many even of those who reject Machiavelli with loathing are found to be unconsciously Machiavellian.

Hallam in his "Introduction to the Literature of Europe" palliates the darker features of the Machiavellian teaching by the nature of the times, yet in his own "Europe during the Middle Ages," writing of the rapid decay of Charlemagne's Empire under his son Louis, "called by the Italians the Pious, and by the French the Debonair or Good-natured," he says "the fault lay entirely in his heart; and this fault was nothing but a temper too soft and a conscience too strict. It is not wonderful that the Empire should have been speedily dissolved." And Charlemagne, its peerless founder, is described as having divorced nine wives, beheaded four thousand Saxons in a single day, and executed all who ate flesh during Lent!

It is when I hear the words of Church or Press, Parliaments or Royal Proclamations, that I fall into a rage against language, and even as Sancho Panza blessed the man who invented sleep, I curse the man who invented speech. In the beautiful dumb days the strong rent the weak in sacred simplicity. Now the strong make pious speeches to show that the eupepsia of the universe is their appetite's aim, and the weak must listen to proofs that they are being eaten for their own good. Happily the serpent no longer talks, else were his slow slimy deglutition of the living rabbit accompanied by a sermon. The State has not only killed Christ but stolen his words. At the Hague the lion and the lamb lie down together, and the concordial words flow on like music, till the lamb suggests that the lion should pare his claws. And the lamb himself—is he anything but a wolf in sheep's clothing? Is he not at heart envious of claws, always feeling his paws for talons of his own?

"And when the Lord thy God shall deliver them before thee, thou shalt smite them and utterly destroy them: thou shalt make no covenant with them, nor show mercy unto them." Where outside Machiavelli shall you find a clean strong sentence like this of Moses? The Destroying Angel's sword shall be sharp and antiseptic as a surgeon's knife; he shall leave no writhing torsoes, no half-sawn limbs and festering wounds littering the purlieus of life. But this utterance is too strong for Christian stomachs, it belongs to the fee-fo-fum eye-for-eye period of the Old Testament: with the New entered the reign of ethereal mildness, lilies showering from full hands, festal fountains spouting the milk of human kindness. Well might Wordsworth cry out:

"Earth is sick,
And Heaven is weary, of the hollow words
Which States and Kingdoms utter when they talk
Of truth and justice."

But even the Old Testament is comparatively sophisticated. This extinction of the native tribes of Palestine is enjoined, not on political grounds but on religious. It is not that Palestine, which offers the most convenient territory for the refugees from Egypt, happens unfortunately to be densely populated. No, virtue must be vindicated, not brute force. But one cannot too much admire that the Biblical historian chose the less nauseous of the two morals open to him. "Not for thy righteousness, or for the uprightness of thine heart, dost thou go to possess their land; but for the wickedness of these nations the Lord thy God doth drive them out from before thee." By a remarkable exception in epics, Israel is the villain, not the hero, of his own story. But all the same, the story has to be coloured in the interests of righteousness. His successors in invasion have not been content to blacken the autochthones, they have brightened themselves. It is for their own uprightness that the Lord casts out the tribes before them or sets them to rule over the heathen. The Lord calls them to spread His word in countries closed to their commerce. He ordains they should bear the White Man's burden—the Black Man's ivory and gold are indeed no light weight. Pah! let us talk of politics like Machiavelli or forever hold our peace.

And yet something can be said for the world's hypocrisy. It is the homage which the Relative pays to the Absolute, part of that yearning of mankind for indefectible ideals, for Luther's "pearl of certainty." Its Right must be Right in all circumstances under the stars, nay, before the stars were born. Ethics shall not be a child of conditions; what holds between man and man, must obtain equally between ruler and ruled, even between State and State. But what is to be done when ethics demands one thing and necessity the opposite? Necessity wins of course, but on condition of not blazoning its victory. The Church, forbidden to shed blood, exacts an expiation from its indispensable warriors, or gravely invents the bloodless stake for its heretics, or with an even more humorous preference of the letter to the spirit forbids its priests to practise surgery. The negro, enfranchised by the Quixotic theory of the American constitution, is disestablished by the Sancho Panzas who miscount his votes. The Jew, commanded to rid himself of leaven during Passover, sells his stock of groceries to an accommodating Christian till the Festival be over. The Christian, to whom money-lending is a sin against nature, hands over the necessary function to the accursèd Jew with the sanction of St. Thomas Aquinas, or founds the Monte di Pietà which Leo X permits to exact a fee on its loans to cover the cost of its officials. Ethics, like the old astronomy, complicates itself with the cycles and epicycles of practice, but the theory of the perfect circle of planetary motion remains immutable. In Lombardy, in Florence, under the very eye of the Pope, the industrial system of modern Europe founds itself on money-lending, but no Encyclical removes the prohibition or condones the sacrilege, or grants Christian burial to the impenitent financier. The irresistible force of facts comes into collision with the immovable body of principles, but the crash is soundless, and by a delicate instinct Society looks the other way. The immortal principle is buried silently—not a drum is heard, not a funeral note. For later generations its deadness is a matter of course.

Even so mankind founds its social systems upon beautiful ideals and averts its eyes from the rotten places of the fabric. It will concede almost anything to practice, if practice will only remain under the rose. This Social Conspiracy is sub-conscious. In war or in religion, in sex or even the smaller animal functions, it works towards a harmony of seeming, an artistic selection of the beautiful or the perfect with rejection of the ugly or the jarring. Is not this indeed our highest art, this art of civilisation, which, out of the raw stuff we are, fashions us into the figures of an heroic and poetic masque? Costumed in the skins of our fellow beasts or in the spoils of our vegetable contemporaries, our dames pranked in the web of a worm, we ruffle it in drawing-rooms as gods and spirits, no terrestrial weakness bewrayed. Our true superiority to the brutes is that we are artists, and they are naturals. Man will not be a creature of Nature, as Coleridge noted. All the world's a stage and all the men and women players, or—to say it in Greek—hypocrites. It is for bad manners that Machiavelli has been boycotted.

LUCREZIA BORGIA: OR THE MYTH OF HISTORY

I

It was with a thrill that I came upon a holograph of Lucrezia Borgia in the library of the University of Ferrara. I had already seen in a little glass case at Milan, in the Ambrosian library, a lock of her notorious yellow hair, and this wishy-washy tress, so below the flamboyance of its fame, should have prepared me for the Ferrara relic. For the document was—of all things in the world—a washing list! The lurid lady—the heroine of Donizetti's opera, the Medea of Victor Hugo's drama—checked, perhaps mended, her household linen! It has been sufficiently washed in public since her day. But this list alone should serve to cleanse her character. Indeed Pope Alexander's daughter does not lack modern whitewashers—what ancient disrepute is safe from them? Roscoe, Gilbert and Gregorovius defend her, and even in her lifetime she had her circle of court laureates that included Ariosto himself. Her platonic friendship with Cardinal Bembo is rather in her favour. The copiously grey-bearded ecclesiast in cap and robe, whose portrait may be seen at Florence in the corridor between the Pitti and the Uffizi, does not look like a man who would consort with the legendary Lucrezia. Yet even a man of letters of Bembo's status is liable to colour-blindness when the Scarlet Woman is a reigning duchess. Bembo, we know, was afraid to read the Epistles of St. Paul, for fear of contaminating his Latin; we are less certain that any fear of contaminating his character would keep him from reading the epistles of Lucrezia. But it seems fairest to accept the view that once freed by her third marriage from the vicious influences of the Vatican and the company of the Pope's concubines, she became rangée, steadying herself into an admirable if pleasure-loving consort of the ruler of Ferrara! Nevertheless even in Ferrara rumour connected her with the murder of the poet Ercole Strozzi, and the guides used to count among their perquisites the blood-flecked wall of the Palace in which, by way of revenge for her extrusion from a respectable Venetian ball-room, she poisoned off at a supper-party eighteen noble Venetian youths, including a natural son of her own whom she poignarded in the frenzy of the discovery.

And Addington Symonds, even after the huge monograph of Gregorovius in her favour, can only exchange the idea of "a potent and malignant witch" for "a feeble woman soiled with sensual foulness from the cradle," a woman who could look on complaisantly at orgies devised for her amusement, applauding even when Cesare chivied prisoners to death with arrows.

But it was reserved for the latest biographer of the Borgias (Frederick Baron Corvo) to write of her: "She was now the wife of royalty, with a near prospect of a throne, worshipped by the poor for her boundless and sympathetic charity, by the learned for her intelligence, by her kin for her loving loyalty, by her husband for her perfect wifehood and motherhood, by all for her transcendent beauty and her spotless name. Why it has pleased modern writers and painters to depict this pearl among women as a 'poison-bearing mænad,' a 'veneficous Bacchante' stained with revolting and unnatural turpitude, is one of those riddles to which there is no key." As for there being no key to it, that is nonsense, for naturally Lucrezia Borgia would share in the opprobrium due to the pravity of Cesare Borgia and Pope Alexander VI, and Corvo himself claims that Gregorovius proves that these calumnious inventions came from the poisoned pens of her father's enemies. This judgment of a reckless writer may however be discounted, for Corvo throughout defends that papal Antichrist, Lucrezia's father, in a spirit which Machiavelli, to whom "virtù" and "magnanimità" meant efficiency whether for good or evil, could not possibly better. And he gaily announces in his preface that he does not write to whitewash the House of Borgia, "his present opinion being that all men are too vile for words to tell." In such a darkness, in which all cats are grey, Lucrezia Borgia might well seem as white as a blue-eyed Persian. But the paradox remains that Corvo may not impossibly be right. As, but for superhuman strainings, Dreyfus might have gone down to history as a traitor to France, so may the Borgian Lucrezia have been as blameless as the Tarquinian to whom indeed Ariosto boldly compares her. The woman who protected the Jews during a famine, provided poor girls with dowries, passed evenings over her embroidery frame and held the esteem of the greatest poet and the greatest stylist of her day, may really have lived up to that washing list. Chose jugée is never absolutely true in history, and there is no trial but is liable to revision. Even the saints are not safe; the devil's advocate may always appeal. Sir Philip Sidney himself has been sadly toned down in his latest biography, and per contra it may well be that Lucrezia Borgia has innocently shared in the blackness of the Borgias. But how shall we ever know? How is it possible—especially considering the public and private conspiracy of falsification and suppression—to uncover the truth even about our contemporaries? Our very housemates elude us. The simplest village happening is recounted by the onlookers in a dozen different ways; an historic episode varies according to the politics of the recording newspaper. Matthew, Mark, Luke and John recount their great story, each after his own fashion, so that even "gospel truth" is no synonym for objective veracity. Letters are taken as invaluable evidence in past history, yet every letter involves a personal relation between the writer and the receiver, is written in what the logicians in a narrower sense call "the universe of discourse," so that words written to one man differ from the same words written to another man, and still more from the same words written to a woman. Facetiousness, exaggeration, under-statement, pet-words, words in special meanings, are the note of intimate intercourse. 'Tis a cipher to which nobody else has the key, and which can never be read by the chronicler. "Our virtuous and popular Gloster" might mean "our vicious and universally odious Gloster." How shall the peering student of musty records behold the wink in the long-vanished eye of the writer, the smile on the skull of the reader? A frigid note may veil a burning love; a tropic outburst disguise a dying passion. Who has the clue to these things? And in the literature of an age the things that are understood are exactly the things that are not written down, and thus the things that are written down are the things that are not understood. What would we not give for a little realistic description of houses, clothes and furniture in the Bible! But such information only drifts into the text indirectly and by accident. Official documents are the bed-rock of history, yet even such formal things as birth-certificates are unreliable, for did not the wife of my dearest friend momentarily forget where her own baby was born? Suppose Peggy grows up a celebrity, an Academician or even a Prime Minister, what is to prevent her birth-plaque being affixed to the wrong house?

Once, and once only, did I strive to penetrate to the sources of history—it was the life of Spinoza—and I found to my amaze that the traditional detail of his doings and habits rested on little more solid than the mistranslated scribblings of a Lutheran pastor who had occupied his lodging a generation after his death. And once in my life did I examine State papers. It was in the Archives of Venice; and as I wandered through the two hundred and ninety-eight rooms of the Recording Angel—though I did not verify the statement that there are fourteen million documents—I saw enough chronicles and certificates, enough Orators' letters in cypher from every court in Europe (with inter-bound Italian translations) to keep in life-long occupation a staff of Methuselahs. And this for only one town, or, if you will, for one empire! Who is it that has the patience to sift this mammoth dust-heap, or who, having the patience, is likely to have the insight to interpret, or the genius to embody its essence? How shall we know which ambassador lied abroad for his country's good, and which for his own? How shall we abstract the personal equation from their reports? How allow for their individual prejudices, jealousies, stupidities, rancours, mal-observations and dishonesties?

As the wise Faust pointed out,
History is a subjective illusion.

"Mein Freund, die Zeiten der Vergangenheit Sind uns ein Buch mit sieben Siegeln; Was ihr den Geist der Zeiten heisst, Das ist im Grund der Herren eigner Geist In dem die Zeiten sich bespiegeln."

Or as honest Burckhardt puts it more prosaically in his preface to his "Renaissance in Italy": "In the wide ocean upon which we venture, the possible ways and directions are many; and the same studies which have served for this work might easily, in other hands, not only receive a wholly different treatment and application, but lead also to essentially different conclusions."

This would be the case even were our information on the past complete. The reduction of this wilderness of material to ordered statement and judgment would permit innumerable ways of seeing and summarising. But consisting as our knowledge does for the most part of mere ruins and shadows, or worse, of substantial falsities, such infinite perspectives of misreading are opened up that the bulk of written history can be only an artistic manipulation of hypotheses. What wonder if the original research and original insight of successive historians is constantly changing the colours and perspectives? Read Pope Gregory's letter to the German princes describing the humiliation of Henry IV, and judge for yourself whether the famous story of the three days' penance can really be built up out of "utpote discalciatus et laneis indutus," &c. or whether it should be blotted out from the history-books as some modern writers demand. Is there, indeed, any episode to which we can pin a final faith? Has history bequeathed us anything on which the duty to truth is not so large as almost to swallow up the legacy? Popular wisdom in insisting that "Queen Anne is dead" selects the only sort of historic affirmation which can be made with certainty. As for any real picture of a period, how can the manifold currents of the ocean of life be represented in a single stream of words?

No; the truth about Lucrezia Borgia will never be known. But what imports? Our librettists and dramatists need themes, our novelists cannot do without "veneficous Bacchantes." If Lucrezia Borgia was not a "poison-bearing Mænad," somebody else was. Perhaps that other has even annexed the reputation for virtue that should have been Lucrezia's! What matters who is which? Let them sort themselves out. If the Mænad or the Bella Donna is indispensable to the novelist or the dramatist, so is the Vestal Virgin and the Saint, and though his models may have exchanged names, he keeps his canvas true to reality. Cleopatra, to judge by her coins, had a face of power, not beauty, but shall the artist therefore surrender the conceptual Cleopatra? Assuredly there has been no lack of beautiful women to sterilise statesmen! Great figures are even more necessary in life than in art. Life would indeed be a "Vanity Fair" if it were "a novel without a hero." We need monuments, memorials, masses, days of commemoration—for ourselves, not for the heroic dead. Dead men hear no tales. Posthumous fame is an Irish bull. We cannot atone to the dead for our neglect of them in their lives, but we need the memory of their lives to uplift ourselves by, we need the outpour of reverence for nobility of soul, we need to lose ourselves in the thought of greatness. But whether we are worshipping the right heroes is comparatively immaterial. Let us not be depressed, then, at the dubiety of history or at that labyrinth of Venetian archives. We can do without the belief that history is a just tribunal, so long as we preserve the belief in justice, and keep a sufficient store of heroes to applaud and villains to hiss. "La vie des héros a enrichi l'histoire," said La Bruyère, "et l'histoire a embelli les actions des héros." It is a fair give and take.

Peculiarly immaterial, so long as we preserve an ennobling conception of majesty, is the real character of that most embellished class of heroes—the Kings. Were we pinned down to drab reality, popular loyalty would not infrequently be paralysed. For that on the hereditary principle a constant and unfailing succession of genius and virtue should be supplied to a nation, contradicts all biological experience, yet nothing less than this is demanded by the necessities of State and the yearning of every people for wise and righteous leadership. In truth heredity is ruled out of court. Kings are not born but made. By a marvellous process of mythopoiesis the monarch is manufactured to suit the national need, and from the most unpromising materials prodigies of goodness and genius are created, or, in the case of female sovereigns, paragons of beauty. It is wonderful how far a single feature will go with a princess, and what crumbs of sense and courage will suffice for the valour and wit of a prince. Bricks can be made—and of the highest glaze—without a single wisp of straw. Of course a neutral character supplies the best basis for apotheosis: traits too positive for evil or for ugliness would render the material intractable. But there are few things too tough for the national imagination to transform. Perhaps the manufacture of monarchs is thus facile because the article is not required to last. The duration of the myth need not exceed a couple of reigns, nor need it be robust enough for exportation. Humanity, while insisting on the perfection of its own monarchs, is prepared to admit that prior generations and foreign peoples have not been so fortunate: indeed my school history of England made out that the country had been governed up till the Victorian era by a succession of monsters or weaklings. 'Tis distance lends disenchantment to the view. Even, however, when the hero is real, he never bulks as large as the phantasy of his idolaters. Napoleon himself was a pigmy, compared with the image in the heart of Heine's "Zwei Grenadiere."

II

Parisina, the Marchioness d'Este, that other heroine whom Ferrara has contributed to romance, or—if you will—to history, for she makes her first English appearance in Gibbon's "Antiquities of the House of Brunswick," has been less fortunate in finding defenders; perhaps because her guilt was less. Very shadowy appears that ill-starred Malatesta bride, of whom nothing seems recorded save that she and her paramour, Hugo, her husband's natural son, were beheaded by her righteously indignant spouse. Yet she grew suddenly solid when I found a scribble of hers neighbouring Lucrezia Borgia's washing-list. "Mandate per lo portatore del presente dieci ducati d'oro per una certa spesa la quale habiamo fatto." It sounds suspiciously vague, I fear. "For a certain expense." What could Parisina have bought with those ten ducats?

But for aught we know they may have been dispensed in charity. And for aught history can tell us, she may have been as spotless as Desdemona. Gibbon, mark you, is by no means convinced of her guilt. If the couple were innocent, he observes oracularly, the husband was unfortunate; if they were guilty, he was still more unfortunate. "Unfortunate" is a mild word for the Margrave, as if his begetting of Hugo were a mere casualty. It is true that at this period in Italy there was little discrimination against bastards, especially those of Popes and Princes. Still Nicholas had only himself to blame for thrusting his Hugo into the contiguity of his wife. Byron, indeed, in his mediocre poem of "Parisina," makes Hugo offer vivid reproaches to his father (mellifluously transformed to Azo, which the poet omits to say was really the name of the first Margrave of the line). But though these reproaches are comprehensive enough:

"Nor are my mother's wrongs forgot,
Her slighted love and ruined name,
Her offspring's heritage of shame,"

and embrace even the charge that Parisina was originally destined for Hugo himself, but refused to him by the father on the brazen ground that his birth was unworthy of her, nevertheless Byron, like most vicious men, preserves the conventional view of the husband's rights.

In his poem Parisina's fate is left artistically uncertain.

"No more in palace, hall, or bower
Was Parisina heard or seen."

But the guides know better. She was beheaded in her dungeon, and the original door leading to that dungeon is still standing in the mighty old castle, and I passed through it. The cell is two storeys below this grim portal, and is reached through a trap-door and passages, and then a second trap-door and more passages, and then a door of iron on wood, and then a door wholly iron, with an iron flap through which her food was pushed. Poor Parisina, poor fluttering bird, caught in that cage of iron! The very light filters into this cell only through a series of six cobwebbed gratings, tapering narrower and narrower, as though some elf of a prisoner might squeeze his way out into the moat. Through such peep-holes, and as fuscously, filters the light of history to us adown the cobwebbed centuries.

SICILY AND THE ALBERGO SAMUELE BUTLER: OR THE FICTION OF CHRONOLOGY

I

To cycle in Sicily is to experience the joys or the sorrows of the pioneer, to pedal backward on the road of Time, and revisit the pre-bicycle period ere man had evolved into a rotiferous animal. Palermo has witnessed the landing of many tribes and races: Phœnician and Greek, Roman and Goth, Saracen and Norman, Spaniard and Savoyard. But not till my comrade and I disembarked with our wheels had any cyclist troubled the Custom House. Others, indeed, had preceded us by land, but we hold the record by sea—the first marine invaders. And our arrival, by way of Tunis, fitly fluttered and puddered the guardians of the port. Three or four officials and a chaos of bystanders, quidnuncs, and porters, entered into excited discussion. The recording angel—a mild and muddled clerk, whose palsied pen shook in his fingers—turned over not only a new leaf, but a new book, and made us sign in three wrong places of the immaculate tome; we had to answer a world of questions, and await innumerable calculations and consultations. Meantime, without, the rich, romantic harbour fretted our curiosity, and the painted Sicilian carts gave an air of fairyland. The very dust-carts were perambulating art-galleries, pompous with grave historic themes, or pious with carven angels or figures of the Virgin; the horn of the horses was exalted, springing in scarlet from the middle of their backs, their blinkers and headpieces were broidered in red. The workaday world was transfigured to poetry, and the old Church-poet's maxim,

"Who sweeps a room, as for Thy laws,
Makes that and th' action fine,"

seemed translated into visual glorification of the dignity of labour and the joy of common life.

Everything combined to make us kick our heels with unusual viciousness. Finally we were condemned to pay about fourpence each, and, mounting our ransomed machines, we rode forth into the strange new world.

Palermo itself proved a disappointment; a monstrous, straggling, stony, modern city, wedged between mountain and harbour, as difficult to escape from as a circle of the Inferno. Miles on miles of hard riding still leave you hemmed in by unlovely houses, harried by electric trams. But at last, by muddy byways, you come upon fluting shepherds, grey olive-trees, flowering almonds, orange-groves, gleaming like fairy gold through bowers of green, and beyond and consecrating all, the blue-spreading, sun-dimpled sea. You have reached the land of Theocritus—though Theocritus himself, by the way, is quite unknown to the Palermese booksellers. And if Palermo is prosaic, Monreale, not five miles off, is one of the remotest towns in Europe. Perched eleven hundred and fifty feet above the sea, over which it looks superbly across a pastoral landscape, it is a dirty network of steep and ancient alleys, with shrines at street-corners, and running fountains down steps, and large yellowish jars on the house-ledges by way of cisterns. The roadway swarms with morose, shawled, swarthy men, lounging and gossiping, while the busy women stride along, bearing brimming vase-pitchers on their gracefully poised, kerchiefed heads; goats, greedy of garbage, feed ubiquitously, some rampant on tubs of squeezed lemons; poultry peck and scurry through the slime; the milkman passes with his mobile milk-can, the she-goat, to be tapped at every door; on the mouldering façades stream flaring insignia of orange-peel, strung together for sale to confectioners, or macaroni hangs a-drying in the sun. And, for crowning assurance of mediævalism, the magnificent Roman-Saracen cathedral, surely one of the seven wonders of Christendom, offers its bronze portals and its Byzantine blaze of mosaics, Bible illustrations naïve as a Noah's ark. Monreale is already the true Sicily, with its aloofness from the modern age, and with its architecture carrying like geological strata the record of all the influences to which it has been exposed. Presently the cyclist or the motorist will leave a new imprint upon the historic soil, saturated with the blood of rival races, and with the finest poetry of Pagan mythology. At present there are few roads for him to follow, and fewer inns to lodge him, and the rumour of brigands dogs his footsteps, though we ourselves never encountered even an exorbitant landlord. Like Blondins of the bicycle, we pursued our unmolested way over tenuous ridges, 'twixt ditch and rut, daring to swerve no hair's-breadth, and the only terror of the countryside was that which we ourselves produced. Wherever we passed, pigs scuttered and poultry fluttered, and goats bleated and kids scampered; horses reared and broke from their traces, mules stampeded in craven terror, dogs fled howling or dumb-struck, whole populations crowded to the doors and balconies, children escorted us literally by hundreds, racing by short cuts across the mountain-paths to get additional glimpses of us from parallel parapets. Like ominous comets we flared through the old Sicilian villages, scattering awe and wonder. The only sensible creatures were the donkeys; they regarded us stolidly, or turned a head of mere intelligent curiosity upon our receding mechanisms. Our wheels had become Time-machines, tests of the difference from standard central-European time, and they showed Sicily half a century—nay, a whole cycle—slow.

Chronology is indeed a metaphysical figment, and even this little globe still offers all the centuries simultaneously to the traveller.

Fantastic is the common reckoning of time by which our globe revolves in a temporal continuum, so that it is the same date—within twelve hours—all over its surface. The Irishman who spoke of the so-called nineteenth century was severely logical. The nineteenth century has not even yet dawned for the bulk of our planet, which presents in fact a bewildering diversity of dates. The Pyrenees divide not merely right from wrong, as Pascal was puzzled to find, but even century from century.

Meals in the byways of Sicily were rather haphazard. The hotels had often nothing in the house, and even when one advanced the money to get something, there might be a dearth in the neighbourhood. Macaroni is, however, a standby. But a single bed-sitting-dining-and-coffee-room spells adventure rather than accommodation. The possession of one spare room sets up the hardy Sicilian peasant-woman as a hotel-keeper. Ceres wandering through Sicily in search of Proserpina must have had a poorish time, unless she fell back upon her own horn of plenty. It was a voluptuous emotion to glide one evening into the broad white streets of Castelvetrano under a crescent moon and into the haven of a real hotel.

Castelvetrano was the nearest town to one of the great goals of our pilgrimage—the ruins of Selinunte. The Normans did not conquer Sicily as permanently as those old Greeks, and even in their decay the Greek temples of Sicily rank with the most precious vestiges of ancient art. Some hours of cycling brought us to the magnificent chaos of graven stone that fronts eternity on a barren field by a lonely shore. There they lie, seven temples, sublime in their very huddle and pell-mell, a wilderness of snapt and tumbled columns, Ossa piled on Pelion. Only one of Vulcan's freaks—and the fire god had a workshop under Etna—could have wrought this mighty upheaval. In utter abandonment the land stretches towards the empty sea, and where priests sacrificed and worshippers trod, spring the wild parsley, the purple anemone, the marigold, and the daisy. From clefts of the great broken bases or in hollows of the fallen capitals push dwarf palms and myrtles, like the lower world of the vegetable reasserting itself over the stone that had mounted to beauty by alliance with man's soul. An odd monolith left towering here or there but accentuates the desolation.

The temples of Concord and of Juno Lacinia still stand four-square to the winds at Girgenti. But of all the temples that preserve for us "the glory that was Greece," that of Segesta stands predominant, if only by reason of its situation. From afar it draws the eye upwards, gleaming almost white on its hilltop. But, standing amid the wild fennel in its grassy court, you see that the noble Doric pillars, though marvellously preserved through three-and-twenty centuries, are corroded in great holes and bear the rusty livery of Time. Behind the temple the earth sinks into a gigantic cup, forming a natural theatre, and in front stretches a vast spread of rolling hills, with beautiful cloud-shadows of purple and brown and silver, and a little glimmer of the Gulf of Castellamare. The few cultivated patches, the faint trees and solitary farms in the dim background, scarcely modify the impression of Nature unadorned. Nothing is given you but the largest elemental things—the sun, the sea, the barren mountains, and the sternest, sublimest form of human architecture. Nothing is known even as to the god to whom the temple was dedicated.

One could wish that mighty Syracuse, with its memories of Æschylus and Pindar, had lapsed to such a wilderness instead of surviving as a small modern town for tourists. A Babylon with restaurants and cab-fares is bathos. But Taormina—the first Greek settlement—still remains, despite its pleasure-pilgrims, the culminating point of a visit to Sicily. Culminating, too, in a sense that will not recommend it to cyclists. Ours are perhaps the only machines that have laboured steadily and daily up this forbidding steep, some four hundred feet above the sea and the railway station. The road mounts even higher— past walled gardens of roses and lemons and almonds, till from the ruined castle at Mola you command a marvellous scape of land and sea. But the mere every-day view from Taormina itself is one of the greatest pictures of the Cosmic Master, for out beyond the sunlit straits shows the Calabrian foot of Italy, generally muffled in a fairy mist, while the Sicilian shore is washed by a pale rainbowed streak of sea. And for eternal background Etna towers, infinitely various, now in snow-white majesty, now cloud-veiled and sombre, now ablaze with an apocalyptic splendour of sunset. But it is in the wooded gorges around Taormina, with their tumbling rock-broken streams, that the climax of Sicilian picturesqueness is reached: here is all the wild witchery of romantic landscape, set to music, as it were, by the piping and trilling of some solitary, far-off shepherd, whose every note travels clear-cut in the lucid air. In the grove below you passes a procession of young women, their right hands supporting lemon-baskets on their shawled heads. Their feet are bare, and they sing a wistful Eastern melody as they move slowly on. A boy leads a black cow by a string round its horns. All is antique and pastoral. Or rather, the Eclogues of Virgil and the Idylls of Theocritus seem contemporary.

At the Greek Theatre, too, that naked majestic amphitheatre, how tinkling and trivial would have sounded the dialogue of modern drama. Sophocles and Æschylus alone could fill the spaces with due thunder. Or was not the large drama of the Greeks positively forced upon them by this great natural theatre, o'er-towered by mountains, roofed by the sky, and giving on the sapphire sea? The infinities and the eternities conspired with the dramatist in a religious uplifting, and his utterance must needs be spacious and noble.

I was not aware that any English writer had achieved the distinction of stamping his name upon a Sicilian street, or even—quainter, if lesser glory—upon a Sicilian inn. Yet at Calatafimi, a little town so obscure (despite its heroic Garibaldi memories) that it had not yet reached the picture-postcard stage, a town five miles from a railway station, up one of the steepest and stoniest roads of the island, I lodged at the Albergo Samuele Butler, and walked through the Via Samuele Butler. Yes, this peculiar immortality was reserved in a Catholic land for our British iconoclast. It was the Communal Council that resolved that the street leading from the Nuovo Mercato towards Segesta should "honour a great man's memory, handing down his name to posterity, and doing homage to the friendly English nation." But the change in the name of the inn, which is in another street, must have been due to the personal initiative of the proprietors, in commemoration of their distinguished client. Meantime "the friendly English nation" cares even less about Samuel Butler of "Erewhon" than about Samuel Butler of "Hudibras," if indeed it distinguishes one from the other.

Thus the super-subtle satirist, understood not of the British people, paradoxical in death as in life, has left his highest reputation in the hearts of Sicilian peasants. The recluse of Clifford's Inn, the stoic and cynic of civilisation, was hail fellow well met with the cottagers of Calatafimi.

It was only natural that the pundits of Trapani should welcome with complacent acquiescence the theory of "The Authoress of the Odyssey," which was received in England with such raised eyebrows; for did not Butler locate the adventures of Ulysses as a voyage round Sicily, and identify Trapani as the place where the lady writer composed the Odyssey? Butler won equal gratitude in Italy by his exhumation and glorification of the sculptor Tabachetti, whom he identified with the Flemish Jean de Wespin. But these learned lucubrations of his would not have sufficed to enthrone Butler in the hearts of the simple. That was the reward of his Bohemian bonhomie. "He always remembered all about everybody," says his friend, Mr. Festing Jones, "and asked how the potatoes were doing this year, and whether the grandchildren were growing up into fine boys and girls, and never forgot to inquire after the son who had gone to be a waiter in New York."

"He called me la bella Maria," the septuagenarian landlady of the Albergo Samuele Butler told me, as she showed me the photograph he had given her—the portrait of the melancholy tired thinker, whom she survives with undiminished vitality and fire. He was done in a group, too, with her and her husband, and altogether appeared to have found a rest from the torture of thought and the bitterness of "The Way of All Flesh" in these primitive personalities.

And here again I had occasion to note the absurdity of chronology, the first century and the fortieth lodging under the same roof—for Butler was at least as far ahead of the twentieth century as his hostess was behind it. Pleasant it is to think that there is a possible human community between epochs so sundered.

Spring after spring came Butler to the inn that now bears his name, and having followed unconsciously in his footsteps, and slept in his very bed, I wonder how he could have found life tolerable there. The Admirable Crichton of his day, novelist and poet, musician and painter, scientist and theologian, art critic and sheep farmer, and perhaps the subtlest wit since Swift, Samuel Butler seems to have reduced his personal demands upon the universe to a smaller minimum than Stevenson in his most admired moments. And that not from poverty, for his resources in later life were adequate, but from sheer love of "plain living and high thinking." The walls of his bedroom in the formerly yclept Albergo Centrale are whitewashed, the ceiling is of logs, the washstand of iron, and even if the water-jug is a lovely Greek vase with two handles, and the pail a beautiful green basin, this is only because Sicily supplies no poorer form of these articles. The bed is of planks on iron trestles. The Albergo itself, with its primitive sanitation, is in keeping with its best room. For Sicily it is, perhaps, a Grand Hotel, embracing as it does an entire flat of three bedrooms on the second floor (a cobbler occupies the ground floor, and the mystery of the first floor I never penetrated). This three-roomed hotel is shut off from the rest of the house by a massive portal. On the first night there appeared to be even a dining-room, but morning revealed this as a mere ante-chamber, windowless, and depending for its light upon the bedroom doors being open. On the second night even this substitute for a dining-room vanished, owing to the advent of another traveller, and the ante-room became a bedroom, so that I had to make my entrances and exits through the new lodger's pseudo-chamber. The landlady also passed through it on her morning visit to me, which was made without any regard for my morning tub. "È permesso?" she asked gaily, as she sailed in. This was her ordinary formula—first to come in, and then to ask if she might.

When I opened my door I had a curious double picture impressed upon my memory: the shirted backs of two young men dressing, each in his room; the one in the bedroom proper was seen in a pale morning light, the occupant of the windowless ante-room was vividly Rembrandtesque under his necessary lamp. Each was singing cheerily to himself as he made his toilette.

Nor was the food superior to the accommodation. Butter was unobtainable during my stay, and breakfast consisted of dry bread, washed down by great bowls of coffee. Fish was not, and the meat had better not have been. I must admit that the dry bread was served with an air that made it seem wedding-cake. "Pane!" la bella Maria would exclaim ecstatically, dumping the coarse, scarce edible loaf on the table with a suggestion of Diana triumphant in the chase. "Caffè!" was another hallelujah, as of a Swiss Family Robinson discovering delectable potions. And "Latte!" bore all the jubilation of a cow specially captured and despoiled for the first time in human history of the treasure of its dugs. Maria's manner of waiting revitalised the common objects of the breakfast table, made them a fairy-tale again; under her magic gestures every piece of sugar grew enchanted and every spoon an adventure. And Butler's tastes were of the simplest, even in Clifford's Inn, where, out of consideration for his old laundress, he made his own breakfast before she turned up. All the same, the attraction of Calatafimi for Butler is difficult to explain. It is one of the dingiest Sicilian towns, littered with poultry, goats, children, and refuse, though, of course, you are soon out of it and amid the scenery of Theocritus. But the view from Butler's own balcony—often a paramount consideration for a writer—was not remarkably stimulating; hemmed in by the opposite houses, though rising into hills and a ruined castle.

Nor was he a student of the campaign of the Thousand, Homeric as was the battle of Calatafimi. It may be that he found the spot more secluded than a seaport like Trapani for pursuing his topographical investigations into the wanderings of the woman-made Ulysses; or it may be that he found unceasing rapture in the contemplation of the aforesaid temple of Segesta that dominates the landscape from its headland, albeit a closer contemplation of its noble columns costs a five-mile walk and climb. Here Goethe came and philosophised on the passing show of human glory, and here, too, Butler may have loved to muse.

In a fine sonnet on Immortality, published in the Athenæum a few months before mortality claimed him, Butler expressed his belief that the only after-life for the dead lay in the hearts of the living, and only upon their lips could those meet whom the centuries had parted.

"We shall not even know that we have met,

Yet meet we shall, and part, and meet again
Where dead men meet, on lips of living men."

It is strange to me, who lived—as chronology would say—in the same age as Butler, and in the same London, and only a minute's walk from him, to think that I should yet never have met him save on the lips of the peasants of Calatafimi, lips that spoke only Sicilian.

INTERMEZZO

I

Here have I been in Italy half a book, and scarcely a page about the Pictures or the "National Monuments." Ci vuol pazienza. I fear you will soon cry "hold enough," as I have cried many a time in these endless galleries congested with bad pictures, yet apparently never to be weeded. For the bad Masters were just as prolific as the good, besides having the advantage of numbers. Civerchio, Crespi, Garofalo, the Caracci, Penni, Guercino, Domenichino—the very names recall acres of vast glaring canvases, and the memory of Pistoja with only one picture to see—and that a Lorenzo di Credi—is as the shadow of a great rock in a weary land. Berenson, that prince of connoisseurs and creative critics, has done brave service both in dethroning and uplifting. Yet am I convinced there is still a wilderness of invaluable pictures by unvalued artists, who, to-day obscure, shall to-morrow be exalted in glory. Mutations of taste are not yet foreclosed: Michelangelo himself with his Super-statues, may recede and rejoin the mellifluous Raphael, while Siena replaces Florence. The art of Japan may win further victories, or we may follow the great expounder of Renaissance painting to his Chinese Canossa. Or the revolt against anecdote may spread to sacred anecdote, and disestablish the bulk of Christian art. I can imagine a newer Pre-Raphaelitism ruling the vogue, and Stefano da Zevio's St. Catherine in the Rose-Garden becoming the centre of the world's desire. I have a weakness myself for this Veronese picture, just because it is so frankly free from so many artistic virtues, so unpretentious of reality, so candidly a pattern, a reverie in roses and birds and angels and gold, a poem, a melting music. I like this new chord of roses and haloes, it is a rare harmony, a lovely marriage of heaven and earth. I can well imagine a visual art arising which will repudiate realities altogether. The cinematograph has come to complete the lesson of the camera, and to throw back the artist on his own soul.

But whatever revolutions in taste await us, my peregrinations have convinced me that there is no single consciousness in the world that holds a knowledge of the treasure of art, even though we limited the art to Italian, nay though we omitted sculpture and architecture and tapestries, and the delicious terra-cottas of Luca della Robbia, and ivories and bronzes and goldsmiths' work, and the majolicas of Urbino and Pesaro, and cameos and medallions and glass-work, and book-binding and furniture, and the intarsiatura of cassoni and pulpits and choir-stalls and lecterns, and the pavement art of the graffiti, and everything save drawing and painting. For when every church, house, and gallery in the world had been ransacked for every trace of Italian brush or pencil on plaster, canvas or paper, and all this registered in the one poor human brain, there would still remain the unexplored ocean of illumination—the manuscript books and missals, and decrees and charters of guilds and confraternities and Monti di Pietà, and lists of monks and rules of monasteries, and matricular books of Drapers and Mercers, and even decorative wills and deeds of gift—all that realm of beauty so largely extinguished by printing.

Upon which fathomless ocean embarking, we may well behold without too much of awe or envy the sails of the master-mariners. Sufficient to drift and anchor at the first enchanted isle.

Less enchanted, however, are even the galleries of masterpieces than the quiet bowers one finds for oneself—like that chapel in Arona where, unveiling an altar-picture in despite of a tall candle-stick, I caught my breath at the sudden serene beauty of Gaudenzio Ferrari's Holy Family; or like that reclusive Venetian church, where the luminous unity of Bellini's Madonna and Saints pierces the religious gloom. Pictures in collections are as unreal as objects in museums, less so perhaps to-day than when each was painted for a definite altar, refectory, wall or ceiling, yet none the less destroying one another's beauties. 'Tis only in the visual arts that we surrender ourselves to a chaos of impressions; imagine Beethoven, Wagner, Verdi, Rossini, Gounod, sounding simultaneously. I could have wept to see how Simone Martini's Annunciation in the Uffizi had suffered by being transplanted to more gilded society. Gone was that golden and lilied purity which used to illumine the corridor.

And yet to see a picture in its own place is often equally heartbreaking. Some of the greatest pictures have carefully selected the most sombre and inaccessible situations.

Europe has perhaps no more melancholy chamber than that art-shrine in Rome in which the pleasure-pilgrims of the world crick their necks or catch bits of frescoed ceiling in hand-mirrors. 'Tis not merely the bad light—for even in the best morning light the Sistine Chapel is fuscous—nor the sombre effect of the discoloured and chaotic Last Judgment, with its bluish streakiness and dark background—nor the dull painted hangings, nor the overcrowding of the ceiling with its Titanic episodes and figures, nor even the Signorellis and Botticellis round the walls, though all contribute to the stuffy sublimity.

The oppressiveness is partially due to the fact that the architectural ceiling that Michelangelo painted—as artificial as the hangings—has faded rather more than the frescoes themselves, so that the figures seem to droop higgledy-piggledy upon the spectator's head instead of standing out statuesque in their panels and spandrils. I dismiss the specious theory of a painting friend that they thus only hover the better, as prophets and patriarchs should. I refuse to be crushed even by Michelangelo. I know that a ceiling can soar, not menace, for have I not expanded under the gay lightness of the Pintoricchio ceiling in the Borgia apartments! Even the heavy and gilded ceiling of the Scuola di San Rocco at Venice, sombre enough in all conscience, by preserving architectural plausibility, and resting on painted pillars, escapes seeming to fall upon one's head. Yet at best a ceiling is a poor place for any save the most simple design. Michelangelo, or rather his papal employer, went against the principle of decoration. A room with such massive masterpieces on its ceiling could not but be top-heavy. Moreover the art feeling can only be received in comfort. If we are to be transported outside our bodies, we must not be distressfully reminded of them by the straining of neck muscles. How foolish and provoking of Correggio to put his finest soaring figures not only into a cathedral cupola, but into a cupola lit only by a few round windows. And his frescoes in the other dome at Parma are equally invisible. One is reduced to enjoying them in the copies. Michelangelo himself undertook the dizzying task of vault-painting with vast reluctance, and complained in a sonnet that he had grown a goitre, and that his belly had been driven close beneath his chin. He achieved a miracle of art—in the wrong place. Perhaps Julius II was not so Philistine in thinking more ultramarine and gold-leaf would have brightened it up.

II

A prophet is never without honour in his own country after his fame has been recognised by the world; indeed, his own country will cling piously to him after the tide of his larger reputation has receded, being as slow to unlearn as to learn. Particularly is this true of painters. And when the artist has achieved the feat of substituting himself for a town in the popular imagination, like Bassano, Garofalo, Luini, Sassoferrato, Correggio, the town thus snubbed is usually prudent enough to identify itself with his glory. But it must be humiliating for a town like Correggio, once the capital of a principality, to owe its only hold upon the present to a painter who did not live there, and of whom it does not possess a single picture. Let arrogant cities take warning: the time may come when their only niche in history will be provided by some obscure citizen now neglected, if not ill-treated or repudiated.

Once arrived, then, the Old Masters are not to be shaken off, even after they have departed again. Their birthplace or their working centre makes a cult of them, and it is touching to see them at home, each presiding over a sala at least of his works, and though depreciated abroad, yet still at an exorbitant premium in his local shrine, like some obscure paterfamilias basking and burgeoning at the family hearth. Guercino is still a god at Cento, his statue in the piazza, his pictures in the gallery. Possagno has a shrine with casts of all Canova. With what a gusto did the cicerones of Mantua talk of Giulio Romano! How the name rolled from the tongue, how it brightened a dingy fresco and glorified a dubious canvas. Si! Si! Tutto di Giulio Romano! Poor Giulio Romano! Not that those giants of yours tumbling on their heads in the Palazzo Te are as detestable as Dickens said. Those of David and Goliath in the great courtyard are even charming. And more fortunate than poor Guido, who must share his Bologna with Francia, you have a town to yourself. Even in his own sala poor Guido is put in the shade by the poetry of Niccolò da Foligno.

Moretto is properly the hero of Brescia, though not born there, and he dominates the Palazzo Martinengo with his charming St. Nicholas presenting the School Children to the Virgin, and a dozen other pictures, as he dominates the bishop's palace and the churches. It is rare that so large a proportion of a painter's work should remain at home, even when the painter himself is as homekeeping as was Moretto.

Very proud are they in Forli of Melozzo, exhibiting engravings of all his works, and even a rescued shop sign of his representing a pepper-brayer banging with his pestle. Marco Palmezzani, too, is high in honour in Forli. Correggio, who made his home in Parma, has been adopted by that city, and it is one of the few things to the credit of Marie Louise that she inspired this sacrosanct treatment of his work, in rich pilastered frames, under sculptured and vaulted ceilings, with two pictures to a room, or in the case of the Madonna della Scodella a room to itself. Poor Parmigiano, the real native of Parma, is thrown into the shade, though there is a Parmigiano room in the Pinacoteca and a Parmigiano statue in the Piazza della Steccata.

Urbino, a city as dead as Correggio, except for the fame of its ancient majolica, resembles it further in not possessing a single example of the work of its greatest son, so that Raphael's father, who had the talent which so often sires a genius, pathetically holds the place of honour with his Santa Chiara and other more or less mediocre pictures. And yet there were five years at least in which Guidobaldo Montefeltro might have summoned Raphael to that famous Court which Castiglione depicted as a model. To-day, of course, the steep cobbled old city is all Raphael, with the exception of Polidoro Virgili, "the most learned man of letters of the fifteenth century," and Gianleone Semproni, "Epic Poet"(!). A Contrada Raffaello, and a bronze bust, and a monument 36 ft. high, all attest his glory. But it would have been far wiser to have perpetuated his exclusion from the Montefeltro Palace than to represent him by a hideous complete set of cheap tiny photographs of his works, all set side by side in a large frame which stands in the chapel, together with his skull in a glass case! At least, it is not really his skull—it has not even that excuse—it is merely a cast in clay, though the clay was taken from his skeleton, from the cavity where once the heart that loved all beauty had pulsed. And here, looking upon the scenes his youthful eye had dwelt on; here, where one would wish to surrender oneself to memories of his magical creations, this skull with its perfect teeth is set to grin its mockery of art and life.

An anthropologist, we are told by an eminent historian of art, supposed this cast to be that of a woman, and we are invited to see in it the explanation of Raphael's suavity. But I had been satisfactorily explaining this suavity myself by the amenities of the tame landscape—olives, poplars, hawthorn, a half-dried river, pairs of white oxen—as I trudged the forty kilometres from Pesaro to Urbino, till to my chagrin the character of the country changed and grew wilder and wilder as I approached his birthplace.

At dusk I was climbing up to an Urbino towering romantically above me with its few twinkling lights and wafting down the music of its vesper bells. My persuasion that I had explained Raphael dwindled with every painful step up the "Contrada Raffaello," probably the steepest and worst-paved street in the world, and vanished altogether by the time I had climbed one of the gigantic stone staircases of the rock-hewn fortress city. And next morning I looked from the loggia of the great hook-nosed Duke upon wonderful rolling mountains, range upon range, snow-capped at the last, and winding paths twisting among them in a great poetry of space. Ha! Poetry of space! Was not that now set down as Raphael's one real claim to greatness? And it was here no doubt he had found it, just as Piero dei Franceschi had found it, when here at the Duke's invitation. But a hundred thousand other people—I suddenly remembered—have been born or have lived at Urbino, and why—I asked myself—were they not inspired to paint like Raphael? And a hundred thousand other men have had feminine skulls (not to mention women), and why have they not produced Transfigurations and Schools of Athens? Alas! I fear the Taine method has its limitations. Rousselot in his "Histoire de l'Évangile Éternel" talks as if Calabria with its solitary mountains and valleys could not help producing Joachim of Flora, nor Assisi St. Francis. But why do these places not go on producing saints and mystics?

III

If a painter's skull is so offensive artistically and so futile scientifically, what shall we say of a poet's heart? "Look into thy heart and write" may be a sound maxim, but to look into somebody else's heart, is another matter. Separate sepulture for the poet's heart is not unknown. But the exhibition of a poet's heart as a literal literary asset, or library decoration, is, I imagine, only to be seen in the University of Ferrara. 'Tis the heart of the poet Monti who died in 1828, after having frequently resided in Ferrara, as a local tablet to "the sovereign poet of his age" testifies. Be it known that to Ferrara's University turn the hearts of all poets, inasmuch as hither were transported the bones of Ariosto—and here a beautifully bound Ariosto album by all the poets of the day still awaits Napoleon's promised attendance at the osseous installation, side by side with a lonely phalange of Ariosto that was equally belated for the ceremony. Monti could not resist the desire to bequeath his heart to this shrine of the Muses, and lo! there I beheld it, in a sort of air-tight hour-glass, a little brown heart, preserved in alcohol like a physiological specimen. Could anything be more prosaic of a poet, nay, more heartless? Fie upon you, Vincenzo! Was it not enough that your side-whiskers are perpetuated in the bust in the Ambrosian library? Are you an Arab that you should hold the heart the centre of the soul? Would you persuade us that this quaint ounce of flesh was the heart that contracted and dilated with tragic passion as you wrote your "Aristodemo," the heart that beat out the music of "Bella Italia, amate sponde," the heart that swelled with the tropes of the Professor of Eloquence at Pavia? Was it with these auricles and ventricles that you pumped up your poetry, was it these cardiac muscles that wrested the laureateship from Foscolo and Pindemonte? Was this "the official organ" of Napoleon?

Go to! Wear your heart on your sleeve, if you will, so long as it throbs with your life, but foist not upon us this butcher's oddment as the essential you. Is it that you would abase us like Hamlet's gravedigger with abject reminders of our mortality? Pooh! a lock of your hair during your lifetime were no more distressing. Not with this key did Shakespeare unlock his heart. And if we wish to behold your heart, we shall turn to your poems, and see it divided among many loves, equally susceptible to Dante and Homer. But this offal—let it be buried with Ariosto's phalange!

Indeed, in justice to Italian taste, it should be stated that this heart has already been buried once. The courteous librarian of the University informed me that at Monti's death in 1828, it was sent to the library by a beloved friend who had placed it in a pot of alcohol. But Cardinal Della Genga vetoed its exhibition and it was interred in the Certosa, under the poet's monument. There it remained till 1884, when it was decided to carry the lead case in which the heart was buried to the library. In 1900 the case was opened in the presence of the authorities and the heart found splendidly preserved. It was therefore placed on view in a chest belonging to the poet, and containing papers of his. But the sooner it is removed again the better. That sort of "literary remains" scarce goes with the atmosphere of libraries.

IV

But from the heart in a more romantic sense the most learned atmosphere is not safe, and I am reminded of another University affair of the heart which I stumbled upon in Bologna.

As we know from old coins, Bononia docet. But somewhere about 1320 Bologna ceased to teach. For there was a strike of students. An old stone relief in the Museo Civico, representing a crowned figure holding a little scholar in his lap and stretching his hands to a kneeling group, celebrates the reconciliation of the Rector with his scholars and sets down in Latin a record of the episode. "The scholars of our University being reconciled with the city, from which they had departed in resentment at the capital punishment inflicted upon their colleague Giacomo da Valenza, for the ravishing of Constanzia Zagnoni, by him beloved, the Church of Peace was erected in the year 1322, in the Via S. Mamolo and this memorial was placed there."

What a tragic romance! What a story for a novelist, the Church, the World, and the University all intermingled, what a riot of young blood all stilled six hundred years ago!

The Doctors of that day still sit in carven state beside this memorial; learned petrifactions, holding their stone chairs for a term of centuries, Bartoluzzo de' Preti, Reader of Civil Law, who died in 1318, and Bonandrea de' Bonandrei, Reader of Decretals, who died in 1333. The "pleasant" Doctor this Bonandrea is styled; seasoning, no doubt, his erudition with graces of style. I figure him deeply versed in the decisions published by Gregory IX in 1234, and a profound expounder of the Isidorian Decretals.

Befitting was it at Mantua to feel so poignantly the lachrymæ rerum. I should perhaps have felt it at Virgil's own tomb at Naples, had that not been so vague and rambling a site that no moment of concentration or even of conviction was possible. But the ancient Ducal Palace of the Gonzagas in the Piazza Sordello had the pathos of the unexpected. Nothing in its exterior suggested ruin and desolation, nay the scaffolding across the façade spoke rather of restoration and repair. The tall red brick arches of the portico beneath, the double row of plain straight windows in the middle, and the top tier of ornamental arched windows, surmounted by the battlements, conveyed an impression of Gothic solidity and moderate spaciousness. It was not till I had walked for many minutes through an endless series of dilapidated chambers and mutilated magnificences—propped-up ceilings and walled-up windows and rotting floors, and marble and gold and rich-dyed woods and gorgeous ceilings, and mouldering tapestries and paintings, and musty grandeurs multiplied in specked mirrors, and faded hangings and forlorn frescoes, and chandeliers without candles, and fly-blown gilding and broken furniture and beautiful furniture and whitewash and blackened plaster and bare brick and a vast unpeopled void—that there began to grow upon my soul the sense of a colossal tragedy of ruin, a monstrous and melancholy desolation, an heroic grandeur of disarray, a veritable poem of decay and destruction. Not the Alhambra itself is so dumbly eloquent of the passing of the Magnificent Ones.

"Babylon is fallen, is fallen."

For the interior answers not to the exterior, whether in preservation or in character. It is renaissance and ruin, with a minor note of the Empire; all the splendours of the world fallen upon evil days. Only by remembering the mutations of Mantua can one account for this hybrid Cortile Reale of dishevelled grandeurs, whose face so belies its character and its fortunes.

The Palace was begun under the dynasty which preceded the Gonzagas, it saw all the glories of the Renaissance, saw Mantua sacked by the Germans, and the Gonzaga dynasty extinguished by the Austrians, and the city fallen to the French, and re-fallen to Austria, and caught up into the Cisalpine Republic, and then into the Napoleonic Kingdom of Italy, and then Austrian again till the yoke was broken by Victor Emmanuel and the stable dulness of to-day established. It is in fact a microcosm of Mantuan history from the day Guido Bonacolsi laid the first stone somewhere near the year 1300. The building had not proceeded very far before the Gonzagas came into power in 1328, in time to stamp the apartments with their character, and it is with Isabella d'Este that its most inventive features are associated.

A hundred and eighty rooms, said the janitor, and when one remembers the crowd of resident courtiers and the great trains with which the Magnificent Ones travelled, one should not be astonished at the resemblance of an ancient Palace to a modern Grand Hotel. Isabella d'Este's brother-in-law, Lodovico the Moro, once visited her here with a suite of a thousand persons, and that was only half the number with which Lodovico's brother, Galeazzo, Duke of Milan, descended upon Florence in 1471. But no modern hotel could keep open a week with such apartments. I do not refer merely to their dearth of conveniences, but to their mutual accessibility, their comparative scarcity of corridors. I do not see how a man could go to bed without passing through another man's bedroom. Grandeur without comfort, art without privacy, such was the Palace in its peopled prime. Think of it to-day—grandeur in rags, art torn from its sockets, and a lonely scribe trailing through vaulted and frescoed emptiness.

The portraits of the Gonzagas are still in the Hall of the Dukes, but when I ascended the beautiful staircase to the vast armoury, I found an aching void. The weapons had been carried off in the sack of Mantua—a sack so complete that Duke Carlo on his return had to accept a few sticks of furniture from the Grand Duke of Tuscany. The Hall of the Caryatides preserves its paintings but the Apartment of the Tapestry is a chandeliered vacancy. The Apartment of the Empress (for Maria Theresa crossed Mantua's line of life) is in yellow silk upholstery with gilded ceilings and an antique chandelier from Murano, but one wall is relapsed to rough brick, in sharp contrast with the white medallioned ceiling. The Refectory or Hall of the Rivers survives, a curious symphony in brown, a long vaulted room with frescoes of Father Po and his brother-rivers and lakes, with grottoes, and caryatides, and marmoreal mosaics, its windows looking on a hanging garden—yea, Babylon is fallen!—with a piazza of Tuscan columns and a central temple.

A sense of passing through a fantastic dream-world began to steal upon me as I wandered through the Hall of the Zodiac with its great blue roof of stars and celestial signs and ships drawn by dogs, and its walls gay with figures in green and gold, and came to a bed with tall green curtains, in which the inevitable Napoleon had once slept. He was not, I mused, of those who could not sleep in a new bed. Followed a suite of three rooms of the Emperor, decorated with painted tapestry, the real removed to Vienna.

And the nightmare continued—one long succession of cold stone floors below and crystal chandeliers on high, bleakly glittering. There was a Hall of the Popes, bare as a barrack. There was a long shiny gallery of bad pictures, which was once a shrine of the Masters. There was a Ducal Apartment modernised, but with the old gilded and bossed ceiling, and dark cobwebbed canvases of the Flemish school. There was the Hall of the Archers, picturesque with the great wooden rafters of its ruined roof and still painted with illusive white pillars, statues, and scenes. Most monstrous of all was the many mirrored, many chandeliered Ball-room—its rows of mirrors reflecting what dead faces, its gold frieze of putti still echoing what madrigals and toccatas, the gods of Olympus looking down from its frescoed ceiling, Apollo driving his chariot and four, and the Arts, the Sciences, Parnassus, Virgil, Sordello, peeping from every arch and lunette. And from the Hall of the Archers my nightmare led me through Ducal Halls and still other Ducal Halls, till I had passed through seven—vasty Halls of Death, with marvellous gilded ceilings and unplastered walls, or with plaster or whitewash over frescoes, or with a sixteenth-century ceiling swearing at an elegant Austrian bathroom (hot and cold). Vivid, even in this strange dream, stood out a ceiling intaglioed with a labyrinth of gilded wood recording the victory of Vincenzo over the Turks:

"Contra Turcos pugnavit
Vincenzo Gonzaga"

—and intertangled repeatedly with the labyrinth the device which d'Annunzio has borrowed for his latest novel—Forse che si, forse che no—and reproduced upon the cover. An old mirror with the glass half-sooted over reflected these glories drearily and showed me the only living face in this labyrinthine tomb.

And so at last by many rooms and ways and up a little staircase of eleven steps under a painted ceiling, I came, like a soul that has travailed, to the Apartment of Paradise, the bower of the beautiful sweet-voiced Isabella d'Este, where, under her ceiling-device "nec spe nec metu," she lived her married life and her long years of widowhood, with her books and her pictures and her antiquities, playing on her silver lyre and her lute and her clavichord, and corresponding with her scholars and poets, "the first lady of the Renaissance." Piety for this legendary "dame du temps jadis" seems to have preserved her six-roomed apartment much as it was, with her wonderful polychrome wooden ceilings and her wonderful doors fretted with porphyry and marbles and her bird's-eye views of great cities she had not seen—Algiers, Jerusalem, Lisbon, Madrid—and her real view of the panorama sloping towards the Po; this combination of a river, a garden and a lake being so stupendo to the inhabitants of that melancholy region of Italy that Isabella's apartment took thence its name of Paradise, much as that dull Damascus is "the pearl of the East." Her music-room, too, is intact, save for the rifling of its pictures. Its intarsia depicting dulcimer, virginal, harp, and viol, and musical notation, its heavy-gilded vaulted ceiling with its musical staves and other decorations, and the little bas-relief showing herself with her beloved instruments, remain as in the days when Gian Trissino wrote a canzone "To Madonna Isabella playing on her lute." But the Mantegnas she commanded, the Lottos and the Perugino, are at the Louvre, doubtless at the behest of Napoleon, that despot of a greater Renaissance to whom even Isabella's formidable brother-in-law, the Moro, was a pigmy, though both of them died in prison and exile, as is the habit of the Magnificent Ones.

Did my nightmare end in this Paradise, softening in this quiet bower into a sleep

"Full of sweet dreams and health and quiet breathing"?

Nay, it grew only more incoherent—vast Halls ruined by being turned into barracks, the statues smashed by a rude soldiery, the pictures slashed, and only the inaccessible splendours of the ceiling safe—though not from the damp; in the Hall of the Triumphs no Triumph remaining save the Triumph of Time and of Fate, Mantegna's pictures of the Triumphs of Cæsar haled to Hampton Court, only their empty oaken frames here gaping; corridors, empty and long, corridors echoing under the footstep, corridors adorned with stuccos and rafaellesques; the Hall of the Moors with a splendid old ceiling and figures of Moors on a frieze of gilded wood; the Corte Vecchia; the Apartment of Troy, with crowded wall-frescoes by Giulio Romano, Mantegna, Primaticcio; the lovely salon of Troy, dismantled, discoloured, its frescoed legend of Troy undecipherable, its ceiling of intaglioed wood dilapidated; the Hall of the Oath of the Primo Capitano, the Hall of the Virtues, Halls anonymously mouldering; the Saletta of the Eleven Emperors denuded of Titian's portraits, to the profit of the British Museum; the Hall of the Capitani with a Jove of Giulio Romano thundering from the ceiling but ironically damaged by real rainstorms; the Saletta of Troy, with more Homer and Virgil—do you begin to have a sense of the monumental desolation? But you have yet to figure me drifting in my dream through the Court of the Marbles and the empty Sculpture Gallery with its great ruined ceiling and the Cavallerizza, or Hippodrome, the largest of its time, now stilled of the clangour of tournament and the plaudits of ladies, and the Apartment of the Boots and the Gallery over the lake, and another garden hanging dead, with a Triton for a tombstone and owls for mourners, the Apartment of the Four Rooms, blackened by the smoke of days when they were let as lodgings, and Halls and more Halls, and still more Halls and Cabinets, and the Hall of the Shells, with its tasty pictures of fish and venison, and the Hall of the Garlands, and the Apartment of the Dwarfs, with their miniature chambers and their staircases with small squat steps—a quarter in itself!

Basta! The nightmare grows too oppressive. Why wake the buffoons from their pigmy coffins of dwarf oak?

Poor little jesters! Are their souls, too, I wonder, stunted, and is there for them in heaven some Lilliputian quarter, where the Magnificent Ones must make sport for them?

"Isabella Estensis, niece of the Kings of Aragon, daughter and sister of the Dukes of Ferrara, wife and mother of the Marquises of Gonzaga, erected this in the year 1522 from the Virgin's bearing."

So runs—O rare Renaissance lady—the Italian vaunt in the frieze round thy Grotto, and I reading it from thy little courtyard, sit and chew the cud of bitter fancy. Poor Madonna Isabella, whose inwoven name still clings so passionately to thy bourdoir walls, in what camera of Paradise dost thou hold thy court? Methinks thy talent for viol and harp, and that lovely singing voice of thine, should find fit service in that orchestral heaven, where thou—always desiderosa di cosa nuova—enjoyest perchance an ampler pasture for thy sensibilities. Forse che sì, forse che no. But from earth thou art vanished utterly, and Renaissance for thee is none. Where be thy pages and poets and buffoons, thy singing seraphs, thy painters and broiderers, thy goldsmiths and gravers, thy cunning artificers in ivory and marble and precious woods? Where is Niccolò da Correggio, thy perfect courtier? Where be Beatrice and Violante, who combed thy hair, and Lorenzo da Pavia who built thy organ, and Cristoforo Romano who carved thy doorway and designed thy medal, and Galeotto del Carretto who sent thee roundelays to carol to thy lute? Have all these less substance than the very brocades in which thy soul was wont to bask? Can these chalcedony jars of thy Grotto outlive them, these shells mock their flippant fleeting? And thy rhyming and thy reasoning, and thy gay laughter and that zest to ride all day and dance all night—could all this effervescence of life settle into mere slime? And this hideous doubt—this fluctuant forse—can we really face it nec spe nec metu?

A horn sounds and steeds clatter up and down thy graded staircase. The hounds give tongue, the hawk flutters on thy wrist. The great spaces of the Cavallerizza fill with jousting paladins; dames in cloth of gold and silver look down from the balconies, princes and ambassadors dispute their smiles. Where has it vanished, all that allegro life—for I must speak to thee by the stave—that gay gavotte that went tripping its merry rhythm through the vasty vaulted halls? Whither has it ebbed? On what shore breaks that music?

And that Mantuan populace that poured in like a stage-crowd to hear its Dukes take the oath of fidelity—are the supers, too, dismissed for ever with the run of the dynasty? And the Dukes themselves, the haughty Gonzagas, is it possible that they are crumbled even more irredeemably than those plasterless walls of their palace? Can it be that Mantegna's portraits are less phantasmal than the originals?

"For the honour of the illustrious Lodovico the Magnificent and Excellent Prince, and unconquered in Faith, and his illustrious Consort Barbara, the incomparable glory of women, his Andrea Mantegna, the Paduan, executed this work in 1473."

At last, at last something lives and breathes in this vast wilderness of shadows. Bless you, Barbara, incomparable glory of women, with your strong masculine face; and you, too, Magnificent long-nosed Lodovico. Far have I been driven in my dream—I am wandered even to the adjoining ruin of the Ducal Castle—but now I am with the quick, with pigments whose life, though it has its fading, is a quasi-immortality compared with our transience. Go, get you to my lady's chamber, and tell her to be painted, for this canvas complexion is the sole that will last.

Isabella d'Este lives at Vienna, recreated by Titian, and at Paris Vittore Pisano shows us what a princess of her house was like, painting beauty of face and brocade against a Japanese background of flowers and butterflies. A more shadowy life she lives in this legend of the princess of the Renaissance, which the prince of Italian writers has revived in his novel, "Forse che sì, forse che no," a book in which my Italian friends tell me d'Annunzio has won yet another triumph of language, old words being so cunningly mingled with new that they do not jar, but chime. D'Annunzio is a demi-incarnation of the Renaissance spirit, exanimate of the Christian half, and it is characteristic that the qualities round which his adoration of Isabella plays are the qualities not of a great lady, but of a great courtesan; a leader of the demi-monde. But as d'Annunzio lives in a half-world, what can his heroines do but lead it? His

Isabella d'Este—as re-created through the worshipful eyes of Aldo—is the rival in dress of Beatrice Sforza, Renata d'Este, and Lucrezia Borgia; marchionesses borrow her old clothes as models, Ippolita Sforza, Bianca Maria Sforza, and Leonora of Aragon are hopelessly out-dressed. Her sister Beatrice alone sticks like a thorn in her side—Beatrice whose wardrobe had eighty-four accessions in two years! But Isabella squeezed ninety-three into one year!! Lucrezia Borgia, when she went to marry Alfonso d'Este, had two hundred marvellous chemises; Isabella outdid her, and even Lucrezia must have recourse to her for a fan of gold sticks with black ostrich feathers. Isabella invented new styles and new modes, and the fashion of the carriage at Rome. Isabella loved gems, particularly emeralds, and succeeded in obtaining the most beautiful in existence. She had her goldsmiths at Venice, at Milan, at Ferrara. She possessed not only the finest jewels, but the finest settings, rings, collars, chains, bracelets, seals, and so through the list of gewgaws and baubles. She was the admiration of France. She adored perfumes and compounded them, and masks, and sent Cæsar Borgia a hundred, and had the most exquisite nail-files for manicuring, and was head over ears in debt—per sopra ai capelli—for she had a mad desire to buy everything that took her whimsy. Has any one ever better summarised the eternal courtesan?

Not a word about the nobler Isabella, the kind-hearted lady who was always interceding for criminals or unfortunates; not a word of the Isabella of unspotted reputation in an age of demireps (naturally d'Annunzio would hush this up); not a whisper of the Isabella who felt the defence of Faenza against Cæsar Borgia "as a vindication of the honour of Italy." Scarce a hint of the inspirer of humanism, the patroness of some of the finest artists of all time; still less any suggestion of the other Isabella, the housewife who sent salmon-trout to her friends, the philosopher who, when the King of France had entered Naples, pointed out to her lord that the discontent of the people is more dangerous to a monarch than all the might of his enemies on the battlefield, and the worldly wise woman who, when he was hesitating over an inglorious military appointment, bade him take the cash and let the credit go.

So complex an Isabella is beyond the scope of d'Annunzio, whose Isabella Inghirami is an elemental creature of passion and tragedy.

"Forse che si, forse che no." An inhabitant of the full world, beholding this motto written and rewritten in the ceiling-labyrinth of the Gonzaga Palace, might fall into contemplation of the labyrinth of human life, and see this device scribbled all over it; he might hail it as the philosophy of Montaigne in a nutshell, and jump, if he were a novelist, at this magnificent setting for some tale of high speculative fantasy. But for d'Annunzio there can be only one problem lying between these mighty opposites. Will a woman yield to her lover, or will virtue resist him? To this petty issue must these measureless words be narrowed. 'Tis not even a forse. With d'Annunzio there can be no negative in such an alternative. And so the mighty Mantuan ruin which has known so many desolations receives its last humiliation, and passes into literature as a background for lust. Sunt lachrymæ rerum.

The true Isabella d'Este has been as much rarefied by the Renaissance legend as she has been materialised by d'Annunzio. For she cannot be wholly exonerated from d'Annunzio's panegyric. "Would to God," she cried at sight of her brother-in-law's treasure, "that we who are so fond of money possessed as much." It was this treasure of the Duke of Milan's that did, indeed, make her sister Beatrice a thorn in her side, if also a rose in her breast, since darling Duchess Beatrice set the pace at a rate ruinous to the Marchioness of Mantua. Isabella could not even go to Venice at the same time as Beatrice, lest all that magnificence (whose very leavings overwhelmed me in her Palace) should appear shabbiness. And when she lost her mother, she appeared more anxious about the proper shade of mourning than the proper sentiment of grief. (How came d'Annunzio to have missed this trait? What a chance for analysis of the æsthetic temperament!) More pardonable was her anxiety as to the colour of the hangings in the Moro's rooms, her hurried borrowing of plate and tapestries, when he impended with that suite of a thousand. But even for Beatrice's death she seemed to find some satisfaction in the ultimate reversion of her much-coveted clavichord, and she found it possible to borrow a Da Vinci portrait from the Duke's former mistress—her sister's cross. Nor—after the Duke was in exile—does it seem very loyal to that fallen idol and faithful admirer, to have ingratiated herself with the French conqueror. That she should rejoice in the election to the papacy of her profligate kinsman, Cardinal Rodrigo Borgia, was perhaps not unnatural, but when every allowance is made for her virtues, it must be admitted that she was not utterly unworthy of d'Annunzio's admiration.

She was, in brief, a Magnificent One, and if the Magnificent Ones are, as a rule, less monstrous when they are women, at the best they are a seamy shady lot, grinding the faces of the poor, that their babes may lie in foolish cradles of gold, and building themselves lordly pleasure-houses designed by hirelings of genius. Even Da Vinci prostituted his genius to plan a bathroom for that minx of a Beatrice, and a pavilion with a round cupola for the castle-labyrinth of his Most Illustrious Prince, Signor Lodovico. Yet Lodovico must be commended for his taste, which is more than can be said for the Magnificent Ones of to-day, who are apt to combine the libertine with the Philistine. Save for the mad King of Bavaria, I can recall no modern monarch who has had a man of genius at his Court. The late King Leopold exacted gold and executed evil on a scale beyond the dreams of the Moro, but where were his Leonardos and Bramantes? Burckhardt tells us that the Renaissance Despot, whose sway was nearly always illegitimate, gathered a Court of genius and learning to give himself a standing; the pompous dulness of our modern Courts shows that Gibbon's plea for stability of succession failed to reckon with the stagnation of security.

Prosaic compared with the fate of the Palace at Mantua is the fate of the Castle of Ferrara, the cradle of Isabella d'Este. 'Tis one of those gloomy massive four-towered structures that recall the fables of the giants, with its moat still two yards deep and its drawbridge intact—a barbarous mediæval pile, forbidding by daylight and sinister in the moon, with a great clock that has so much leisure that it strikes the hour before every quarter.

Yet this grim fortress, originally built by a despot as a refuge from his subjects, is merely the seat of telegraph and other civic offices; like some antediluvian dragon tamed and harnessed, instead of wastefully slain, by the St. George who gleams above the portcullis.

In the piazza before the castle, where I saw only a cab-rank of broken-down horses, the festa of this patron-saint of Ferrara was wont to set Barbary horses racing for the pallium, and splendid battle-chargers ramped in that great tournament which was held by Duke Ercole, Isabella's father, in honour of his son-in law, the Moro, and which was won by Galeazzo di Sanseverino, the model of the Cortigiano. Isabella d'Este in her glad virginal youth walked her palfrey up and down the great equine staircase, now given over to messenger boys and clerks. Under the sportive ceilings and adipose angels of Dosso Dossi, or within that girdling frieze of putti driving their teams of birds, beasts, snakes or fishes, pragmatic councillors hold debate. In the castle ball-room are held—charity dances!

But infinitely the saddest relic of the Magnificent Moro is his former palace in Ferrara. Why he needed a palace in Ferrara I do not know, unless to accommodate the overflowings of his suite when he visited his ducal father-in-law. Of this palace the excellent Baedeker discourses thus: "To the S. of S. Maria in Vado, in the Corso Porta Romana, is the former Palazzo Costabili or Palazzo Scrofa, now known as the Palazzo Beltrami-Calcagnini. It was erected for Lodovico il Moro, but is uncompleted. Handsome court. On the ground-floor to the left are two rooms with excellent ceiling-frescoes, by Ercole Grandi; in the first, prophets and Sybils; in the second, scenes from the Old Testament in grisaille."

It could not have been done better by an auctioneer. Here is the reality. A courtyard with arches, dirty, refuse-littered, surrounded by a barrack of slum-dwellings. The first room I penetrated into was palatial in size but occupied by three beds, and a stove replaced the old hearth. The floor was of bare brick. Sole touch of colour, a canary sang in a cage, as cheerfully as to a Magnificent One. The crone whose family inhabited this room conducted me at my request to the chamber with the ceilings by Ercole Grandi. She opened the door, and—like Maria of Sicily—entered crying, "È permesso?" with retrospective ceremoniousness, and I followed her into a vast lofty room, dingy below, but glorious above, though more to faith than to sight, for the firmament of fresco was difficult to see clearly in the gloom. The floor was of stone, and held two beds, a chair or two, a cradle, a stout dwarfish old woman and a sprawl of children with unkempt heads. In the adjoining room sat a sickly and silent woman working a sewing machine under the hovering Sybils and Prophets, dim and faded as herself.

For those who covet a Renaissance chamber, even after this exposure of the auctioneer, let me say that the rent of this last room was thirty-two scudi a year, Sybils and Prophets thrown in.

The entire Palace Beltrami-Calcagnini is, I imagine, to be acquired for a song. When I first read in Ruskin's "A Joy for Ever," his exhortation to Manchester manufacturers to purchase palaces in Verona so as to safeguard stray Titians and Veroneses, I felt that the Anglo-Saxon aspiration to play Atlas had reached its culminating grotesquerie. But now that I have seen the state of the Ercole Grandi frescoes, I feel that the Anglo-Saxon might do worse than step in, and I cannot understand why Italy, so rigid against the exportation of her treasures, is so callous to their extinction.

And this is the Palace built by the great Moro, who "boasted that the Pope Alexander was his chaplain, the Emperor Maximilian his condottiere, Venice his chamberlain, and the King of France his courier"; for whose wedding procession, which was preceded by a hundred trumpeters, Milan draped itself in satins and brocades; who patronised the immortals of Art; and who wore to death in an underground dungeon in France.

An older than Virgil hath spoken the final word: Vanitas vanitatum, omnia vanitas.

OF DEAD SUBLIMITIES, SERENE MAGNIFICENCES, AND GAGGED POETS

There are few livelier expressions of vitality than tombs, especially tombs designed or commissioned by their occupants. These be projections of personality beyond the grave, extensions of egotism beyond the body. The Magnificent Ones have invariably the mausolean habit. It is another of their humilities. The majesty of death, they know, is not enough to cover their nakedness. Moses, the true Superman, had his sepulchre hidden that none might worship at it. The false Superman ostentates his sepulchre in the hope that some one may worship at it. His Magnificence is only Serene in his tomb: his life passes in uneasy tiptoeings after greatness. Sometimes his mortuary tumefactions are softened by his spouse being made co-tenant of his tomb, as in the Taj Mahal of Agra, or in that beautiful monument ordered by Lodovico of Milan for himself and Beatrice d'Este. And sometimes when "the Bishop orders his tomb" it may be with an extenuating design to beautify his church—"ad ornatum ecclesiae" as "Leo Episcopus" says of the monument he designed for himself in Pistoja Cathedral. Unfortunately Bishop Leo's worthy object is scarcely attained by the two fat angels leaning sleepily against his sarcophagus, or by the skull and the shell-work over it, though in comparison with Verrocchio's adjacent monument of Cardinal Forteguerra—or rather the bust and the black sarcophagus superimposed upon the original marble—the Bishop's tomb is a thing of beauty.

But it is only when the corpse has not commanded the monument that I am able to endure its magnificence. The Cardinal of Portugal in San Miniato, the poisoned Pope Benedict in Perugia, St. Dominic in Bologna, St. Agatha in Venice, and even the mysterious Lazaro Papi, "Colonel for the English in Brazil," the "esteemed writer of verses and history," whose friends raised him so elaborate a memorial in the cathedral of Lucca in 1835, all lie as guiltless of their monumental follies as Mausolus himself, who, it will be remembered, was the victim of his designing widow. Nor could the Ossa Dantis well escape that domed mausoleum at Ravenna, though they lay low for a century and a half.

Still further removed from responsibility for his own posthumous pomp is St. Augustine, who with all his inspiration could not foresee the adventures of his corpse; how from Hippo it should come to rest at Pavia, by way of Sardinia, and there, a thousand years after his death, have that marvellous Arca erected over it by the Eremitani. Nor could St. Donato, when he slew the water-dragon of Arezzo by spitting into its mouth, foresee the great shrine embodying this and other miracles of his which the millennial piety of the town would rear over his desiccated dust.

But the Medici, the magnificent Medici! Not their chapel in Santa Croce, full though it be of the pomp of marble and majolica; not their San Marco monastery with their doctor-saints—St. Cosmo and St. Damian—not their Medici Palace, despite that joyous Benozzo fresco with its gay glamour of landscape and processions; not the Pitti with its incalculable treasures; not the Villa Medici, nor even the Venus herself, so reeks with the pride of life as all that appertains to their tombs. When I gaze upon the monuments of these serene Magnificences in the Old Sacristy of Florence, with the multiple allusions to the family and its saints—in marble and terra-cotta, in stucco and bronze, in fresco and frieze, in high-relief and low-relief—I feel a mere grave-worm. And when I crawl into the Capella dei Principi where stand the granite sarcophagi of the Grand Dukes, there glances at me from every square inch of the polished walls and the pompous crests and rich mosaics a glacial radiation of the pride of life—nay, the hubris of life. That hushed spaciousness is yet like an elaborate funeral mass perpetually performed by an orchestra opulently over-paid.

I wonder how in their life-time men dared to apply to these Magnificent Ones the common Italian words for the body and its operations and why there was not evolved for them—as for the bonzes of the Cambodgians—a specific vocabulary to differentiate their eating and drinking from the munching and lapping of such as I. And yet in the New Sacristy I find consolation. For, inasmuch as the genius of Michelangelo was harnessed to the funeral car of his patrons, I perceive that here at last they are truly buried. They are buried beneath the majestic sculptures of Day and Night, Evening and Dawn, and 'tis Michelangelo that lives here, not they. Peace to their gilded dust.

Far more reposeful, at least for the spectator, is Michelangelo's own burial place in Santa Croce, which is the most satisfactory church the Franciscans have produced, and in its empty spaciousness an uplifting change from the stuffy, muggy atmosphere, the tawdry profusion of overladen chapels, which make up one's general sense of an Italian church. It is not free from poor pictures and monuments, and only some of the coloured glass is good, but the defects are lost in the noble simplicity of the whole under its high wooden roof. Michelangelo's monument is unfortunately impaired by one of the few errors of overcrowding, for the frescoes above it make it look inferior to the Dante cenotaph, though it is really rather superior. Curiously enough the line anent the "great poet"

"Ingenio cujus non satis orbis erat,"

does not come from Dante's monument, but from that of a certain Karolus, presumably Carlo Marsuppini!

I have spoken of the museum as the mausoleum of reality. But mausolea too, turn into museums; in losing their dead they, too, die and become a mere spectacle. Such is the melancholy fate of the Mausoleum of Theodoric the Great outside Ravenna, robbed of its imperial heretical bones by avenging Christian orthodoxy. Infinitely dreary this dead tomb when I saw it in the centre of its desolate plain, to which I had trudged through sodden marshland that would have been malarious in summer; snowbound it lay, its arched substructure flooded, its upper chamber only just accessible by a snow-crusted marble staircase: a bare rotundity, a bleak emptiness, robbed even of its coffin, uncheered even by its corpse. O magnificent Ostrogoth, conqueror of Italy, O most Christian Emperor, when you turned from the splendour of your court at Ravenna to build your last home, you with your imperial tolerance could hardly foresee that because you held Christ an originated being, as Arius had gone about singing, a Christian posterity would scatter you to the four winds. And that rival gigantic tomb in the Appian Way at Rome, does Cæcilia Metella still inhabit it, I wonder? I mourn to see such spacious tombs stand empty when there are so many living Magnificences whom they would fit to a span. Very proper was it to bury Beatrice, the mother of Matilda, in the sarcophagus of a Pagan hero. Mausolea no more than palaces should remain untenanted. Let them be turned into orts and castles, an you will, like Hadrian's Tomb into Sant' Angelo, or into circuses, like the Mausoleum of Augustus—sweet are the uses of Magnificence—but to keep them standing idle when there must be so many Magnificences in quest of a family sepulchre is a crime against America. The tomb of Theodoric is, I fear, too secluded for American taste, but the Exarch Isaac's in such cheerful contiguity with town and church may arride the millionaire more. For a consideration the Exarch's own sarcophagus might be had from the Museum, and the Exarch scrapped. Or there is Galla Placidia's Mausoleum, with its Byzantine mosaics thrown in. Come! Who bids for these rare curios, one of the few links between Antiquity and the Renaissance, with their grotesque mediæval sincerity. Remark, Signori, that prefiguration of the Index Expurgatorius, that bearded Christ or S. Lorenzo (you pay your money and you take the choice) who is casting into a crate of serpentine flames one of those Pagan volumes for which the Cinquecento will go hunting madly. No, that cabinet does not contain cigar-boxes—what did the saints know of cigars?—nor are Marcus, Lucas, Matteus, Joannes, the names of brands. Those apparent cigar-boxes, as you might have seen from the strings, are holy manuscripts triumphant over the Pagan volume. This naïve draughtsmanship, Signora, is just what makes them so precious and your petty bids so amazing. What is that you say, Signorina? Galla Placidia is still in possession? And two Roman Emperors with her? Nay, nay, a nine hundred and ninety-nine years' lease is all that a reasonable ghost may desire; after that, every tomb must be esteemed a cenotaph; unless indeed the heirs will pay the unearned increment. Choose your sarcophagus, Signori, an Emperor's sarcophagus is not in the market every day.

But I do not think that even the vulgarest millionaire would desire his ashes to dispossess the Doges of Venice, or at least not Giovanni Pesaro. The most romantic auctioneer might despair of disposing of that portal wall of the Frari which is sacred to the Gargantuan grotesquerie of his colossal memorial. Does the whole world hold a more baroque monument? Going, going—and how I wish I could say gone!—that portal upheld by bowed negro giants on gargoyled pedestals, with patches of black flesh gleaming through holes in their trousers. Item, one black skeleton surmounted by other unique curios, including two giraffes. Item, His Sublimity, the Doge himself, sitting up on his sarcophagus, holding up his hands as if in expostulation, gentlemen, against your inadequate bids. Item, a wealth of heroic figures, and an array of virtues and vices, all life-size. (Could be sold separately as absolutely incongruous with the negro portions of the monument.) Also, in the same lot if desired, two hovering angelets, holding a wreath, suitable for any Christian celebrity.

Alas, Barnum is no more and bidding languishes. And yet I do not see why the lot should not be knocked down. Who was this Pesaro that he should have the right to impose this horror on posterity? Why should generations of worshippers at the Frari be obsessed by this nightmare? There can be no sacredness in such demented mural testaments. And Time, who preserved this, while he has destroyed so many precious things, who shattered Leonardo's horse and melted Michelangelo's bronze Pope, is hereby shown of taste most abominable. History must get a better curator.

The black skeleton—I had not thought before that skeletons could be negro—flourishes a scroll which ascribes to the Doge the wisdom of Solomon and an implacable hostility against the foes of Christ, while a tablet held by one of the giant negroes announces

"Aureum inter optimos principes vides."

Aureum indeed! Doubtless only some faint sense that sheen and death are discrepant held back the Doges from being buried in golden caskets. The Doge lives again in this monument, boasts the Latin, and one can only reflect that if the dogal taste reached this depravity by the middle of the seventeenth century, actum est de republicâ might have been written long before Napoleon. Fortunately for the memory of the Pesaro family it finds a nobler, if no less bombastic expression, in the great Titian altar-piece, the Madonna di Casa Pesaro, in which the Queen of Heaven bends from her throne to beam at its episcopal representative, and St. Francis and St. Anthony grace by their presence the symbols of its victory over the Turk, while St. Peter pauses in his pious lection.

But the dead Doges lie mostly in S. S. Giovanni e Paolo, where their funeral service was performed. It is the very church for Their Sublimities—floods of light, pillared splendour, imposing proportions. Their tombs protrude from the walls, and their sculptured forms lie on their backs, their heads on pillows, their feet comfortably on cushions. Even when we are reminded of the finer things for which the Republic stood, there is an echo of material opulence.

"Steno, olim Dux Venetiorum, amator
Justitiæ, Pacis, et Ubertatis anima."

Ubertatis anima! The soul of prodigal splendour! Even spiritual metaphor must harp on images of Magnificence.

But not every dead Doge consents to be couchant. Horatio Baleono, who died in 1617, "hostes post innumeros stratos," has for monument a cavalier (of course, gilded) riding rough-shod over writhing forms and a broken-down cannon, and Pietro Mocenigo, whose mausoleum vaunts itself "ex hostium manubiis," stands defiant on the summit of his sarcophagus, which is upborne by a trinity of figures.

What a family this Casa Mocenigo, with its record of Doges! Remove their memorials and mausolea from this church and you would half empty it of monuments. Tintoretto, no less than Titian, was dragged at their triumphal car. There is an Adoration of the Saviour at Vicenza, which might just as well be the adoration of the Doge, Alvise Mocenigo, who is in the centre of the picture. For though he is kneeling, he has all the air of sitting, and all the other figures—the worshippers, the angel flying towards him, and the Christ flying down to him—converge towards him like a stage-group towards the limelit hero. Compare all this posthumous self-assertion with the oblivion fallen on Marino Faliero, the decapitated Doge of Byron's drama, whose dubious sarcophagus was shown to the poet in the outside wall of this church.

Nor could Padua, Venice's neighbour, fall behind her in mortuary magnificence.

"Nequidque patavino splendore deesset"

says a monument to Alessandro Contarini in the nave of the cathedral, a monument supported by six slaves and embracing a bas-relief of the fleet. Another in the worst dogal style exhibits Caterino Cornaro, a hero of the Cretan War (who died in 1674) in a full-bottomed wig and baggy knee-breeches, holding a scroll as if about to smack the universe with it. Sad is it to see so many "eternal monuments" of faded fames.

The Scaliger street-tombs in Verona are at least artistically laudable, however ironically their Christian ostensiveness compares with the record of the Family of the Ladder, whose rungs were murdered relatives. But even had Can Signorio lived the life of a saint, it would have needed a considerable conquest of his Christian humility before he could have commissioned that portentous tomb of his from Bonino da Campiglione. Knowing the Magnificent One, Bonino gave him solidity and superfluity, a plethora of niched and statued minarets of saints and virtues armed warriors, and bewildering pinnacles clothed with figures, all resting on six red marble columns springing from a base which supports the tomb, and is itself upborne by angels at each corner and adorned with pious bas-reliefs. And while the dead man lies in stone above his tomb, guarded by angels at head and foot, he also bestrides his horse and sports his spear on the uttermost pinnacle of his ladder-crested memorial, as though making the best of both worlds; which was indeed the general habit of the Magnificent, who desired likewise the beatitudes of the Meek, and often shed tears of sincere repentance when they could sin no more. Mastino della Scala's tomb is more gilded and elegant than Can Signorio's, though not less assertive and bi-worldly. And as for the tomb of Can Grande—"Dog the Great," as Byron translated him in "The Age of Bronze,"—which is perched over the church door and soars up into a turret, it was—on the day I first saw it—provided with a long and dirty ladder for repairing purposes. So that I say Father Time—if he be a poor curator—is at least a fellow of infinite jest. One of his jests is to hound the Magnificent dead from pillar to post, from church to monastery, from crypt to chapel. In the grave there is rest? Fiddle-faddle! No body is safe from these chances of mortality. Stone walls do not a coffin make, nor iron bars a tomb. Call no body happy until it is burnt. After five centuries of rest Matilda of Tuscany was carried off from Mantua in a sort of mortuary elopement by her great admirer, Pope Urban VIII, and hidden away in the castle of S. Angelo, till she could be inhumed in St. Peter's, and it was only the pride of Spoleto that saved Lippo Lippi from being sold to Florence. Napoleon, in suppressing churches, disestablished many an ancient corpse, and the pious families of Verona hastened to transport their sarcophagi to the church of S. Zeno on the outskirts. Hither must ride the dead Cavalli with their equine scutcheons, flying before the World-Conqueror on his white horse.

Dismemberment, too, befalls tombs at the hands of the merry jester. The friars of S. Maria delle Grazie who owed so much to the great Sforza Duke, broke up his monument and offered his effigy and his wife's for sale. The more loyal Carthusians snapped up Cristoforo Solari's beautiful sculptures for the beggarly price of thirty-eight ducats, and Lodovico and Beatrice in marble must leave their dust and make a last journey to Pavia. A last journey? Chi sa?

"Iterum et iterum translatis," sighs the monument over the bones of Cino in Pistoja Cathedral, and who knows that the "pax tandem ossibus" is more than a sanguine aspiration? Cino was not the only Italian poet to be thus "translated," though neither Petrarch nor Ariosto was "translated" so often. Petrarch indeed was rather pirated than "translated," for his right arm was stolen from his sepulchre at Arquà for the Florentines, and the rest of him is now supposed to be in Madrid—a town which also holds that monarch of sanctity, Francesco di Borja, likewise minus an arm, for the Gesù of Rome kept back that precious morsel of the Duke who had entered the kingdom of heaven by the rare gate of abdication.

But stranger than these mutations of mortality is the fact that Italy holds the ashes of our Shelley and Keats, as it held so much of the life of Byron and Browning. As if Rome had not riches and memories to super-satiety! A Protestant cemetery seems indeed out of key as much with these poets as with Rome, but that overshadowing Pyramid of Cestius restores the exotic touch, and violets and daisies blot out all but the religion of beauty, so that Shelley could write: "It might make me in love with death to think that one should be buried in so sweet a place." It is pleasant to think that only a year later Shelley, however exiguous his ashes, found in that sweet place the rest and re-union for which his cor cordium yearned.

"'Tis Adonais calls! oh hasten thither,
No more let life divide what Death can join together."

With what a wonderful coast Shelley has mingled his memory—fig-trees, olives, palms, cactus, hawthorn, pines bent seaward, all running down the steep cliff. What enchanting harmonies they make with the glimpses of sea deep below, the white villages and campaniles, seen through their magic tangle. As you pass through the sunny dusty village roads, the girls seem to ripen out of the earth like grapes, both white and black, for there are golden-haired blondes as well as sun-kissed brunettes. They walk bare-footed, with water-jars poised on their heads, sometimes balancing great russet bundles of hay. And the old peasant women with Dantesque features sit spinning or lace-making at the doors of their cottages, as they have sat these three thousand years, without growing a wrinkle the more, if indeed there was ever room for another wrinkle on their dear corrugated faces. What earth lore as of aged oaks they must have sucked in during all these centuries!

It is here that one understands the Paganism of d'Annunzio, whose soul lies suffused in these sparkling infinities of sun and sea and sky, whose marmoreal language is woven from the rhythmic movement and balance of these sculptural bodies.

Viareggio, which holds Shelley's monument, is a place of strange twisted plane-trees. The Piazza Shelley is a simple quiet square of low houses fronting a leafy garden and the sea. It leads out, curiously enough, from the Via Machiavelli. There is a bronze bust, which admirers cover with laurel, and an inscription which represents him as meditating here a final page to "Prometheus Unbound." (Baedeker, comically mis-translating "una pagina postrema," represents him as meditating "a posthumous page"!)

Not here, however, but in La Pineta is the place to muse upon Shelley. It is a thick, sandy pinewood with an avenue of planes. The pines are staggering about in all directions, drunk with wind and sun. Very silent was it as I sat here on a spring evening, watching the rosy clouds over the low hills and the mottled sunset over the sea. The birds ventured scarcely a twitter; they knew they could not vie with Shelley's skylark.

Shelley's epitaph in the Roman cemetery is like a soft music at the end of a Shakespeare tragedy.

"Nothing of me that doth fade
But doth suffer a sea-change
Into something rich and strange."

What a curious and pacifying fusion of poetry and wit! It reconciles us to the passing back of this cosmic spirit into the elements by way of water. But what a jarring perpetuation of the world's noises on the tombstone of Keats!

"This grave contains all that was mortal of a young English poet, who on his death-bed, in the bitterness of his heart at the malicious powers of his enemies, desired these words to be engraven on his tombstone: 'Here lies one whose name was written in water.'"

Water again! But water as chaos and devourer. How ill all this turbulence accords with the marble serenity of his fame, a fame that so far as pure poetry is concerned stands side by side with Shakespeare's! We are a good way now from the twenty-fourth of February, eighteen hundred and twenty-one. A few years more and Keats will have been silent a hundred years, and we know that his nightingale will sing for ever. What profits it, then, to prolong this mortuary bitterness, to hang this dirty British linen on the Roman grave? The museum is the place for this tombstone—I could whisk it thither like the Doge Pesaro's wall. Will it save the next great poet from the malice of his enemies? Will they speak a dagger less? Not a bodkin! The next great poet, being great and a poet, will appeal in novel and unforeseeable ways, and be as little read and as harshly reviewed as the marvellous boy of Hampstead whose death at twenty-five is the greatest loss English literature has ever sustained. Were it not fittest, therefore, to celebrate the centenary of this death by changing his epitaph for a line of "Adonais"?—

"He lives, he wakes; 'tis Death is dead, not he."

The tragedy of Keats is sufficiently commemorated in Shelley's preface and in the pages of literary history and in the doggerel of Byron.

"'Who killed John Keats?' 'I,' says the Quarterly,
So savage and Tartarly 'Twas one of my feats."

And Byron lamented and marvelled

"That the soul, that very fiery particle,
Should let itself be snuffed out by an article."

I do not share this discontent. To be snuffed out by an article is precisely the only dignified ending for a soul. This dualism of body and spirit which has been foisted upon us has degradations enough even in health. No union was ever worse assorted than this marriage of inconvenience by which a body with boorish tastes and disgusting habits is chained to an intelligent and fastidious soul. No wonder their relations are strained. Such cohabitation is scarcely legitimate. Were they only to keep their places, a reasonable modus vivendi might be patched up. The things of the spirit could exercise causation in the sphere of the spirit, and the things of the body would be restricted to their corporeal circle. But alas! the partners, like most married couples, interfere with each other and intrude on each other's domain. Body and soul transfuse and percolate each other. Too much philosophising makes the liver sluggish, and a toothache tampers with philosophy. Despair slackens the blood and wine runs to eloquence. Body or soul cannot even die of its own infirmity; the twain must arrange a modus moriendi, each consenting to collapse of the other's disease. Thus a body in going order may be stilled by a stroke of bad news, and a spiritual essence may pass away through a pox.

Think of the most powerful of the Popes, the head of Christendom, the excommunicator of the Kings of France and Spain, having to succumb to a fever; think of the great French writer, in whose brain the whole modern world mirrored itself, having to die of a gas from which even his dog recovered; think of the giant German philosopher, who had announced the starry infinitude of the moral law, degenerating into the imbecile who must tie and untie his necktie many times a minute. Surely it were worthier of man's estate had Innocent III perished of an argument in favour of lay investiture, had Zola been snuffed out by an anti-Dreyfusard pamphlet or a romantic poem, had Kant succumbed to the scornful epigram of Herder, or even to the barkings of the priests' dogs who had been given his name. And far worthier were it of a poet to die of a review than of a jaundice, of a criticism than a consumption. Infinitely more dignified was the death of Keats under the Quarterly than the death of Byron himself under a fever, which some trace to a microbe, itself possibly injected by a mosquito. That were an unpardonable oversight of Dame Nature, who in her democratic enthusiasm forgets that mosquitos are not men's equals, and that these admirable insects should be blooded more economically. Assuredly the author of "The Vision of Judgment" would have preferred to die of a stanza or a sting-tailed epigram.

Dame Nature had the last word; but was Byron, foreseeing her crushing repartee, so absolutely unjustified in his criticisms and questionings of a Power that held him as lightly as the parasite on the hind leg of any of the fifty thousand species of beetles? For if Fate treads with equal foot on a Byron and a beetle, the bard may be forgiven if he takes it less christianly than the coleopteron.

Byron is "cheap" to-day in England, and while Greece celebrates the centenary of his arrival and Crete calls on his name, while Italy is full of his glory, his hotels and his piazzas, while Genoa is proud that he lived in Il Paradiso and the Armenian Monastery at Venice still cherishes the memory of his sojourn there to learn Armenian, and every spot he trod is similarly sacred, the Puritan critic reminds us that

"The gods approve The depth and not the tumult of the soul."

Yes, we know, but when a poet is disapproving of the gods their standards matter less. And we are men, not gods, that their standards should be ours. Humani sumus, and nothing of Byron's passion and pain can be alien from us. This tumult of the soul, who has escaped it? Not Wordsworth, assuredly, who wrote those lines. Only the fool hath not said in his heart, "There is no God." Even Cardinal Manning said it on his death-bed. Not that death-bed conversions are worth anything. Matthew Arnold was apt to give us Wordsworth as the reposeful contrast to the bold, bad Byron. But the calmness of Wordsworth is only in his style, and if his questionings are cast in bronze, they were often forged in the same furnace as Byron's, and fused through and through with the pain

"Of all this unintelligible world."

Poets, even the austere, have to learn in suffering what they teach in song. Only the suffering is always so much clearer than what it teaches them. And then, as Heine says, comes Death, and with a clod of earth gags the mouth that sings and cries and questions.

"Aber ist Das eine Antwort?"

Among these multitudinous Madonnas, and countless Crucifixions, and Entombments innumerable, who shall dare award the palm for nobility of conception? But there is a minor theme of Renaissance Art as to which I do not hesitate. It is the Pietà theme, but with angels replacing or supplementing the Madonna who cherishes the dead Christ, and it is significant that the finest treatment of it I have seen comes from the greatest craftsman who treated it—to wit, Giovanni Bellini. His Cristo Sorretto da Angioli you will find painted on wood—a tavola—in the Palazzo Communale of Rimini. The Christ lies limp but tranquil, in the peace, not the rigidity, of death, and four little angels stand by, one of them half hidden by the dead figure. The exquisite appeal of this picture, the uniqueness of the conception, lies in the sweet sorrow of the little angels—a sorrow as of a dog or a child that cannot fathom the greatness of the tragedy, only knows dumbly that here is matter for sadness. The little angels regard the wounds with grave infantile concern. Sacred tragedy is here fused with idyllic poetry in a manner to which I know no parallel in any other painter. The sweet perfection of Giovanni Bellini, too suave for the grim central theme of Christianity, here finds triumphant and enchanting justification.

It is perhaps worth while tracing how every other painter's handling of the theme that I have chanced on fails to reach this lyric pathos.

Bellini himself did not perhaps quite reach it again, though he reaches very noble heights in two pictures (one now in London and the other in Berlin), in which the reduction in the number of angels to two makes even for enhancement of the restful simplicity, while in the Berlin picture there is a touching intimacy of uncomprehending consolation in the pressing of the little angelic cheeks against the dead face. But the fact that in both pictures one angel seems to understand more or to be more exercised than the other contributes a disturbing complicacy. The serene unity is, indeed, preserved by Bellini in his Pietà in the Museo Correr of Venice. But here the three young angels supporting the body are merely at peace—there is nothing of that sweet wistfulness.

For a contrary reason the woodland flavour is equally absent from its neighbour, a picture by an unknown painter of the Paduan school. Here the peace is exchanged, not for poetry but tragedy. The Christ is erect in his tomb, and the two haloed baby angels who uphold his arms are the one weeping, the other horror-struck. The horror is accentuated and the poetry still further lessened in an anonymous painting in a chapel of S. Anastasia in Verona, where boy angels are positively roaring with grief. Nor is the poetry augmented in that other anonymous painting in the Palazzo Ducale of Venice, where one angel kisses the dead hand and the other the blood-stained linen at the foot. In Girolamo da Treviso's picture in the Brera one child angel examines the bloody palm and the other lifts up the drooping left arm with its little frock. Great round tears run down their faces, which are swollen and ugly with grief. Still more tragic, even to grotesquerie, is an old fresco fragment in an underground church in Brescia, where the little angels are catching the sacred blood in cups—those cups invented by Perugino and borrowed even by Raphael. Francesco Bissolo, in the Academy of Venice, preserves the tranquillity of Bellini, but by making the angels older loses not only the seductive naïveté but the whole naturalness, for these angels are old enough to know better, one feels. They have no right to such callousness. Raphael's father in his picture in the cathedral of Urbino escapes this pitfall, for his adult angels bend solicitously over the Christ and support his arms from above. But Lorenzo Lotto, though he gives us innocent child-angels, tumbles into an analogous trap, for he forgets that by adding a Madonna and a Magdalen in bitter tears he transforms these untroubled little angels into little devils, who have not even the curiosity to wonder what in heaven's name their mortal elders are weeping over. In Cariani's so-called Deposizione at Ravenna one little angel does weep in imitation of the mortals, leaning his wet cheek on the Christ's dead hand—"tears such as angels weep"—but he only repeats the human tragedy, and might as well be a little boy. Two older angels howl and grimace in Marco Zoppo's picture in the Palazzo Almerici of Pesaro, while the haloed, long-ringleted head of the Christ droops with slightly open mouth and a strange smile as provoking as Mona Lisa's. Francia in the National Gallery gives us a red-eyed Madonna with one calm and one compassionate angel, and Zaganelli in the Brera vies with Bellini in the vague, tender wonderment of the child angels who lift up the arms, but the picture is second-rate and the angels are little girls with bare arms and puffed sleeves. Nor is it a happy innovation to show us the legs of the Christ sprawling across the tomb.

Marco Palmezzano, with inferior beauty, also trenches on Bellini's ground; but not only is the Christ sitting up, not quite dead, but one of the two child angels is calling out as for aid, so that the restful finality of Bellini is vanished. Still nearer to the Bellini idea approaches a picture in the Academy of Venice attributed to Marco Basaiti and an unknown Lombardian. But if this avoids tragedy, the turn is too much in the direction of comedy. The child angels are made still more infantine, so that there is neither horror nor even perturbation, merely a shade of surprise at so passive a figure. One plays with the Christ's hair, the other with his feet—the Blake-like tenderness is not absent, but the poetry of this utter unconsciousness is not so penetrating as the wistful yearning of the Bellini angels before some dim, unsounded ocean of tragedy. This precise note I did, indeed, once catch in a corner of Domenichino's Madonna del Rosario, where a baby surveys the crown of thorns; but this is just a side-show in a joyous, thickly populated picture, and the Christ is not dead, but a live bambino, who showers down roses on the lower world of martyrdom and sorrow.

He is almost too dead in the fading fresco of the little low-vaulted, whitewashed, ancient church of S. Maria Infra Portas in Foligno. A great gash mutilates his side, his head, horribly fallen back, lies on the Madonna's lap, his legs and arms droop. The mother's long hair hangs down from her halo, she clasps her hands in agony, and a child angel on either side looks on commiseratingly. Strange to say, this conserves the poetry, despite the horror, though the horror removes it out of comparison with Bellini's handling.

In Genoa I found three more variations on the theme, two in the cathedral, the first with four angels, all gravely concerned, and the second with quite a crowd of little boys and angels, nearly all weeping. One of the little angels has taken off the crown of thorns—a good touch in a bad picture. The third variant is by Luca Cambiaso, and in the Palazzo Rosso, with a single agitated boy angel. A Pietà in Pistoja takes its main pathos from its lonely position on the staircase of the fusty town hall: a last rose of summer, all its companions are faded and gone, all save one pretty lady saint blooming in a vast ocean of plaster. Even its own Madonna and Apostles are half obliterated; but the boy angel remains in a curious posture: he has got his head betwixt the legs of the Christ, and with his arms helps to sustain the drooping figure. Still more original touches appear in Andrea Utili's picture in Faenza. Here the Christ has his arms crossed, and his halo, tilted back over his crown of thorns, gleams weirdly in red and gold, and on his tomb rest pincers and a hammer. The two youthful angels are deeply moved; one holds a cross and the other three nails.

If any painter could vie in enchantment with Giovanni Bellini it is Crivelli, and, indeed, there are fascinating things in his Pietà in the Brera, idyllic sweetness in the angels, original decorative touches in the book and burning taper, and masterly imagination in the ghastly lack of vitality with which each dead hand of the Christ droops on the tender living hand of an angel. Had only the angels been a little younger, this would have been as sweetly lyrical as Bellini. From Michelangelo we have only a sketch of the subject, with his wingless child angels, over whom stands the Mater Dolorosa with useless outspread arms, that should have been helping the poor little things to support their burden. In Guido Reni's Pietà at Bologna her hands droop in folded resignation, while one angel weeps and one adores and pities. I fear the presence of the Madonna and other mortals destroys the peculiar celestial poetry, though of course the conjunction of mortals and angels brings a poetry of its own.

Tura's treatment of the theme in Vienna I have not seen. But Vivarini breaks out in a new direction. His two angels fly from right and left towards the tomb, under full canvas, so to speak. But it is a pattern et præterea nihil. More poetic in its originality is a picture of the Veronese school in the Brera, showing us two baby angels, half curious, half apprehensive, unfolding the Christ's winding-sheet. But it is a dark, poorly painted picture. Another new invention is Garofalo's in the same gallery. He gives us a crowd of commonplace weeping figures in a picturesque landscape, and his angel is a sweet little cherub aloft on a pillar over the heads of the mourning mob. But the angel might be a mere architectural decoration, for all his effect upon the picture.

Thus have we seen almost every possible variation tried—adult angels and young angels and baby angels, calm angels and callous angels, lachrymose angels and vociferous angels, helpless angels and hospital angels, boy angels and girl angels, and only one artist has seen the sole permutation which extracts the quintessential poetry of the theme—the high celestial tragedy unadulterated by human grief, and sweetened yet deepened by angels too young to understand and too old to be unperturbed, too troubled for play and too tranquil for tears.

And it is to that incarnation of evil, Sigismondo Malatesta, that we owe this masterpiece of lyric simplicity, for 'twas the Magnificent Monster himself that commissioned it—His rolling and reverberating Magnificence, Sigismondo Pandolfo Malatesta di Pandolfo—whose polyphonous, orotund name and the black and white elephants of whose crest pervade the splendid temple which he remodelled at Rimini for the glory of God. And lest the world should forget 'twas he to whom heaven owed the delicious Pagan reliefs by the pillars, or the now-faded ultramarine and starry gold of the chapels, each first pilaster bears in Greek the due inscription:

TO THE IMMORTAL GOD
SIGISMONDO PANDOLFO MALATESTA DI PANDOLFO

(Pray do not pause here—epigraphs, like telegrams, are not punctuated)

PRESERVED FROM MANY OF THE GREATEST PERILS OF THE ITALIAN WAR
ERECTED AND BEQUEATHED MAGNIFICENTLY LAVISH
AS HE HAD VOWED IN THE VERY MIDST OF THE STRUGGLE AN ILLUSTRIOUS AND HOLY MEMORIAL

No less reflexive was his apotheosis of the frail Isotta, of whom he first made an honest woman and then a goddess. What wonder if his critics carped at the "Disottæ," the "divine Isotta," he wrote over her tomb, in lieu of the conventional "Dominæ Isottæ Bonæ Memoriæ"! But one must do the bold, bad condottiere the justice to say that while two angels bear this inscription over her in gold, his own tomb is comparatively modest. It is Isotta whose tomb is supported by shield-bearing elephants and culminates in flourishes as of elephants' trunks, Isotta who stands over her altar in the guise of a gold-winged angel. Malatesta's patronage of Giovanni Bellini was not his only contribution to the arts, for a cluster of poets found hospitality at his court and burial at his temple—with a careful inscription that it was Sigismondo Pandolfo Malatesta di Pandolfo who buried them—though these seem to have plied the trade of Laureate, if I may judge from the volume published at Paris, "L'Isotteo." I cannot pretend to be read in Porcellio de' Pandone or Tommaso Seneca or Basinio of Parma. But Bellini's tavola suffices to make me say with riddling Samson, "Out of the strong cometh forth sweetness."

For this is perhaps the teleological purpose of the Magnificent Ones, to play the Mæcenas to some starveling artist or penurious poet. There is in the santuario of the Malatesta temple a fresco of this Sigismondo. He is seen in the flush of youth, gay in a brocaded mantle and red hose, but somewhat disconcertingly on his knees before a crowned figure—his patron saint according to some, the Emperor Sigismondo more probably. Let us call it that sovereign fate to which even megaphonious Magnificence must bow. Almost divine in his lifetime, within a few years the Magnificent One's character commences to decay, as if that too could not resist the corruption of death. Happy the prince of whom some not malodorous shred of reputation remains a century after his death. The evil that men do lives after them, the good they have not done is oft interred with their bones.

Yes, there is a pathos in the Magnificent Ones. When I consider how their autocosm ensnared them with a sense of their own perdurability, lured them into engaging painters and architects and statuaries to express their triumphant sense of timeless energising, and then ebbed away from them, leaving them putrid carbonates, phosphates, and silicates, while the work of Beauty lived on and lives, having used these momentarily swollen creatures as its channel and tool, then I find it in me to pity these frog-bulls of egotism, so cruelly bemocked and deluded.

Before parting with the Pietà theme I would remark that in the Italian galleries the name Pietà is often—with apparent inaccuracy—given to pictures of the dead Christ alone in his tomb. One of the most curious pictures of this sort I came upon in the gallery of Faenza, where Christ stands in his tomb, yet still nailed on the Cross, from either end of which depends a scourge. I found the same design in the centre of a little stone shield over a building marked as the "Mons Pietatis" of Faenza. And this set me speculating whether such an image as a symbol of the Monte di Pietà was due to the mere suggestiveness of the word Pietà, or whether there was a more mystical connection implied between the Crucifixion and the loan-offices instituted in Italy by Bernardino da Feltre to frustrate the usury of the Jews. It is the Monte di Pietà of Treviso that shelters the Entombment ascribed to Giorgione. It seems a long way from Golgotha to the pawn-shop, yet we still talk of pledges being redeemed.

HIGH ART AND LOW

"Pictures
Of this Italian master and that Dutchman."
JAMES SHIRLEY: The Lady of Pleasure.

To come in the Uffizi upon a Dutch collection, to see the boors of Jan Steen, the tavern peasants of Heemskerck, the pancake-seller of Gerard Dou, the mushrooms and butterflies of Marcellis Ottone, is to have, first a shock of discord and then a breath of fresh air and to grow suddenly conscious of the artificial atmosphere of all this Renaissance art. Where it does not reek of the mould of crypts or the incense of cathedrals or the pot-pourri of the cloister, it is redolent of marmoreal salons, it is the art of the Magnificent Ones. Moroni's Tailor marks almost the social nadir of its lay subjects, and our sartor was no doubt a prosperous member of his guild. There are two courtesans in Carpaccio but indistinguishable from countesses, in a rich setting of pilasters and domestic pets. Guido Reni painted his foster-mother, but it is the exception which proves the rule. And the rule is that Demos shall appear in Art only as the accessory in a sacred picture, like the old woman with the basket of eggs in Titian's Presentation in the Temple, or the servants in the many sacred suppers and banquetings beloved of Veronese. That the Holy Family itself was of lowly status is, of course, ignored except here or there by Tintoretto or Signorelli or Giovanni Bellini, and the wonderful gowns and jewels worn by the carpenter's wife, according to Fra Angelico or Crivelli, would be remarkable even on a Beatrice d'Este or a Marie de' Medici. Who would ever think that Raphael's Sposalizio of the Virgin was the marriage of a Bethlehem artisan to a peasant girl? Even the carpenter's barefootedness—the one touch of naked truth—seems a mere piece of hymeneal ritual, in face of that royal company of princesses and their suites, that functioning High Priest. No; insistence on the humbleness of the Holy Family hardly tallied with the Christianity of the Renaissance, or even with the psychology of the poor believer, who loves to dress up his gods as Magnificent Ones and for whom to adore is to adorn. Aristocracy is the note of Italian painting—the Holy Family takes formal precedence, but the Colonnas and the Medicis rank their families no less select. The outflowering of Dutch art was like the change from the airless Latin of the scholars to the blowy idioms with which real European literature began. Italian art expressed dignity, beauty, religion; Dutch art went back to life, to find all these in life itself. It was the efflorescence of triumphant democracy, of the Dutch Republic surgent from the waves of Spain and Catholicism as indomitably as she had risen from the North Sea. Hence this sturdy satisfaction with reality. Rembrandt painted with equal hand ribs of beef and ribs of men. The Low Countries invented the fruit and flower piece and the fish and game piece. That Low Art hails from the nether lands is not a mere coincidence. Holland was less a country than a piece of the bed of the sea to which men stuck instead of limpets. Cowper says, "God made the country and man made the town," but the Dutch proverb says, "God made the sea and we made the shore." 'Twas no braggart boast. The Dutchman had made for himself a sort of anchored ship, and the damps and vapours drove him oft from the deck to the warm cabin, where, asquat on plump cushions with buxom vrow and solid food and stout liquor, he met the mists with an answering cloud from his placid pipe. And the art he engendered reflected this love for cosy realities, and found a poetry in the very peeling of potatoes. No voice of croaking save from the frogs of his marshes. Let your Leopardis croak 'mid their sunny vineyards, let your Obermanns sulk on their stable mountains Mynheer is grateful to be here at all, to have outwitted the waters and dished the Dons. And so never has earthiness found more joyous expression than in his pictures. What gay content with the colours of clothes and the shafts of sunshine, and the ripe forms of women, and the hues of meats and fishes! O the joy of skating on the frozen canals! O the jolly revels in village taverns! Hail the ecstasy of the Kermesse! "How good is man's life, the mere living." "It is a pleasant thing to have beheld the sun." These are the notes of Dutch art, which is like a perpetual grace to God for the beauty of common things. And if the painters are concerned so much with the problems of light, if Rembrandt was the poet of light, was it not because the Dutchman had always in his eye varying effects of light, shifting reflections and scintillations in the ubiquitous canals, kaleidoscopic struggles of sunlight with mist and fog? The Venetians too, those Hollanders of Italy, are notable for their colour, in contrast with the Florentines.

Even in the Dutch and Flemish images of doom I have thought to detect a note of earth-laughter, almost an irresponsible gaiety. Pierre Breughel paints the Fall of the Angels as a descent to lower forms—the loyal angels beat the rebels down, and they change as they fall into birds, beasts, and fishes, into frogs and lizards, and even into vegetables. There are bipedal carrots, and winged artichokes and bird-tailed pomegranates. 'Tis as if the worthy painter was anxious to return to the kitchen, to his genre subjects.

Or may we sniff a belated Buddhism or a premature Darwinism? Instead of a sacred picture we get a pantomimic transformation scene: metamorphosis caught grotesquely in the act. This Fall of the Angels seems a favourite Flemish subject—one reads almost an allegory of Art hurled down from heaven to earth.

The same sportive fantasy frolics it over the Flemish hell. De Vos gives us a devil playing on the fluted nose of a metamorphosed sinner. In a triptych of Jerome Bosch, the Last Judgment is the judgment of a Merry Andrew who turns the damned into bell-clappers, strings them across harp-strings, or claps their mouth to the faucets of barrels till they retch. So far goes the painter's free fancy that he invents air-ships and submarines for the lost souls to cower in, unwitting of the day when these would hold no terrors for the manes of erring aeronauts and torpedoists.

Italian art even in the childish grotesqueries of its Inferno never falls so low as this freakish farrago. One cannot help feeling that the Italians believed in hell and the Netherlanders made fun of it.

One of these extravaganzas of Bosch has drifted to Venice, though this Temptation of St. Antony (of which there is a replica in Brussels) is also attributed to Van Bles. The nude ladies coming to the saint with gifts are most unprepossessing, and what temptation there is in the whirl of carnival grotesques I cannot understand. No doubt some allegory of sin lurks in these goblin faces, with their greedy mouths full of strange creatures, and in this great head with black-tailed things creeping in through eye and mouth, with frogs suspended from its earrings and a little town growing out of its head. Such uncouth ugliness has no parallel in Venice, unless it be a German Inferno with a belled devil. From such puerilities one turns with relief to the coldest and stateliest conventions of High Art.

And yet Dutch art and Italian are not wholly discrepant the link, as I have said, comes through the minor figures of religious scenes, or even occasionally through the major. A Dutch homeliness lurks shyly in the background of Italian art, and at times appears boldly in the foreground. From one point of view nothing could be more Dutch than the innumerable Madonnas who suckle their Bambini. Nor do their haloes destroy their homeliness. The peasant girl of Tintoretto's Annunciation in S. Rocco wears a halo, but neither that nor the angel bursting through the crumbling brick of the door can prevent this scene from being a Dutch interior with a cane chair. Realism, smuggled in under the cloak of religion, is none the less realism, and when Moretto shows us the Bambino about to be bathed by mother and nurse, and paints us a basket of belly-bands, he has given us a genre picture none the less because rapt saints and monks look on in defiance of chronology, and, perched on a bank of cloud over a romantic landscape, angels sing on high. Even as early as Giotto the nurse who presides at The Birth of the Virgin is washing the baby's eyes. Very curious and realistic is the pastoral study which Luca Cambiaso styled Adoration of the Shepherds. And in Veronese, for all his magnificence, and in Carpaccio, for all his fairy-tale atmosphere, and above all in Bassano, for all his golden glow, we get well-established half-way houses between High Art and Low. Under the pretext of The Supper in Emmaus Bassano anticipates all Dutch art. Here be cats, dogs, plucked geese, meat in the pan, shining copper utensils scattered around, the pot over the glow of the fire, the rows of plates in the kitchen behind. What loving study of the colour of the wine in the glasses of the guests, and of their robes and their furs! These things it is that, with the busy figures behind the bar or stooping on the floor, fill up the picture, while the Christ on a raised platform in the corner bulks less than the serving-maid, and the centre of the stage is occupied by a casual eater, his napkin across his knees. If this sixteenth-century picture is Venetian in its glowing colour and its comparative indifference to form, it is Dutch in its minuteness and homeliness.

The same love of pots and pans and animals glows in The Departure of Jacob, with his horse and his ass and his sheep and his goats and his basket of hens, and even beguiles Bassano into attempting a faint peering camel. But not even the presence of God in a full white beard can render this a sacred picture. It is, however, in his favourite theme of The Animals going into the Ark that Bassano brings the line between the sacred and secular almost to vanishing point. Although Savonarola preached on the Ark with such unction, as became the prophet of a new deluge, the just Noah himself seems the least religious figure in the Old Testament, perhaps because—after so much water—he took too much wine. There is even a tradition recorded by Ibn Yachya that after the Flood he emigrated to Italy and studied science. At any rate Bassano always treated him as a mere travelling showman, packing his animals and properties for the next stage. In a picture at Padua Noah's sons and daughters are doing up their luggage—one almost sees the labels—and Noah, with his few thin white hairs, remonstrates agitatedly with Shem—or it may be Ham or Japhet—who is apparently muddling the boxes. A lion and lioness are treading the plank to the Ark, into which a Miss Noah is just pushing the leisurely rump of a pig, which even the lions at its tail fail to accelerate. Countless other pairs of every description, including poultry, jostle one another amid a confusion of pots, wash-tubs, sacks, and bundles, the birds alone finding comfortable perching-room on the trees. Mrs. Noah wears her hair done up in a knot with pearls just like the Venetian ladies, and a billy-cock hat lies on one of the bundles. In his Sheep-shearing (in the Pinacoteca Estense of Modena) Bassano throws over all pious pretences and becomes unblushingly Dutch—nay, double-Dutch, for he drags in agricultural operations and cooking as well as sheep-shearing.

But it is in Turin that Bassano's Batavianism runs riot. For his market-place is a revel of fowls, onions, prezels, eggs, carcases, sheep, rams, mules, dogs gnawing bones, market-women, chafferers, with a delicious little boy whose shirt hangs out behind his vivid red trousers. And his Cupid at the Forge of Vulcan is an extravaganza in copper pots and pans; and yet another market masterpiece is an inventory of all he loved—butcher's meat and rabbits and geese and doves, and lungs and livers, and gherkins and melons, and cocks and hens, and copper pans and pewter spoons, and a cow and a horse and an owl and lambs, all jostling amid booths and stalls on a pleasant rustic background as in a Tintoretto Paradise of luscious paintabilities.

Gaudenzio Ferrari has the same love of sheep, and these, with horses and dogs, force their way into his pictures. The Bible is an encyclopædia of themes, and even had any subject been wanting, apocrypha and sacred legend would have provided it. For his pet lambs Ferrari goes to the copious broidery on the Gospel, and his Angels predicting the Birth of Maria is really a study in sheep on the background of a domed and towered Italian city. Giotto too had attempted sheep, though they are more like pigs, and dogs, though they are elongated and skinny; his camel with grotesque ears and a sun-bonnet one can forgive.

The lives of the saints supplied other opportunities for "Dutch" pictures in the shape of miracles at home. Titian himself stooped to record the miracle of putting on again the foot which the man who had kicked his mother cut off in remorse. And in the same Scuola of the Confraternity of St. Antony at Padua you may see the neglectful nurse carrying safely to its parents at table the babe she had allowed to boil.

And yet despite all these manifold opportunities, no Italian seems quite to get the veracious atmosphere of the Dutch and to achieve the dignity of Art without departing from the homeliness of Nature. No Italian has brought Christ into the street so boldly as Erasmus Quellinus in that picture in the Museo Vicenza in which a girl with a basket of live hens on her head stops to watch the fat Dutch baby sleeping in its mother's arms. Despite the unreal presence of adoring saints in the crowd, there is here a true immanence of divinity in everyday reality. The sixteenth-century Italian Baroccio did indeed depict a

Dutch peasant-feast in his Last Supper in the cathedral of Urbino, with its bare-legged boy cook stooping for platters from a basket and its dog drinking at a bronze dish, but its homeliness is marred by the hovering of angels. Realism unadorned is essayed by Fogolino in his Holy Family in Vicenza, with the carpenter's shop, the rope of yarn, the hammer; with a boy Christ in a black tunic saying grace before a meal of boiled eggs, pomegranate, and grapes, washed down by a beaker of red wine; with the Madonna bending solicitously over him, her wooden spoon poised over her bowl; but, alas! the whole effect is of a cheap oleograph.

But then Fogolino was not a great painter, and it would have been interesting to see a superb craftsman like Paul Veronese try his hand at homely nature, unadorned by great space-harmonies and decorative magnificences. As it was, he had the delight of a Dutchman in dogs and cats, copper pots and jugs, and earthen pans and groaning tables and glittering glasses, and these it is which fascinate him, far more than the spiritual aspect of the Supper in the House of the Pharisee, so that even when he wishes to paint the soul of the pink-gowned Venetian Magdalen, he paints it through a little bowl which she overturns in her emotion at kissing the feet of Christ. This is why meals are the prime concern of Veronese, obsess him more than even his noble pillared rhythms and arched perspectives. How eagerly he grasps at The Marriage of Cana and The Disciples at Emmaus and The Meal in the House of Levi, with which that hold-all of the Bible supplied him! Spaces and staircases, arches and balconies and lordly buildings, all the palatial poetry of Verona, with its fair women and rich-robed men—these are his true adoration, and he paints, not Jesus, but the loaves and fishes. Nay, it may almost be said that unless there be food in the picture Veronese grows feeble, and must have pillars at least to prop him up. See, for example, his Susannah and the Elders, with no trace of food and only a wall to sustain him. When the Biblical cornucopia was wholly depleted of its food-stuffs, he had to forage for manna, especially when the need of decorating a monastic refectory was added to his own passion for provender. One of his discoveries was The Banquet of Gregory the Great, which is in the Monastery of the Madonna del Monte outside Vicenza, and which is based on the legend that Gregory invited twelve poor men to eat with him and Christ turned up as one of them. But Christ, who is removing the cover from a fowl, is less striking than Paul Veronese himself—who stands on the inevitable balcony with his own little boy—and at best a mere item in the rhythm of pillars and staircases and sky-effects. Nothing brings out the defect of Veronese as a religious painter so clearly as a comparison of his Disciples at Emmaus with Titian's. Titian too gives us fine shades of bread and fruit and wine, and even a little "Dutch" dog under the table; Titian too plays with pillars and a romantic background. But how his picture is suffused with the spirit! These things know their place, are absorbed in the luminous whole. A certain blurred softness in the modelling, a certain subdued glow in the colouring—as of St. Mark's—give mystery and atmosphere. The food is, so to speak, transubstantiated.

Even Moretto's Supper at Emmaus (in Brescia) is superior to Veronese's, though his Christ in pilgrim's cockle-hat and cloak has to the modern eye the look of an officer with a cocked hat and a gold epaulette.

But Veronese is not the only Italian who would have been happier as a lay painter. I am convinced that some of the romanticists of the Renaissance were born with the souls of Dutchmen, and these, as it happens, the very men who have not worn well; a proof that they were out of their element and gave up to romance and religion what was meant for realism. Take Guido Reni, the very synonym of a fallen star, the Aurora in Rome, perhaps his one enduring success—though even here Aurora's skirt is of too crude a blue, and there is insufficient feeling of mountain and sea below her. His portrait by Simone Cantarini da Pesaro shows him with a short grey beard, a black doublet, a lawn collar, and a rather pained look—there is nothing of the Aurora in this sedate and serious figure. And better than either his violent Caravaggio martyrology or his later mythologic poesy I find his portraits of his mother and his foster-mother; the mother in black with a black turn-down collar, a muslin coif, and grey hair thinning at the temples, and the foster-mother a peasant woman with bare and brawny arms. The St. Peter Reading in the Brera is also a strong study of an old man's head. Moroni had the good sense or the good fortune to shake himself almost free of religious subjects and to produce a Tailor who is worth tons of Madonnas, but even he did not utterly escape the church-market, and when one examines such a picture as his Madonna and Son, St. Catherine, St. Francis, and the Donor in the Brera, one rejoices even more that an overwhelming percentage of his product is pure portraiture. For the holy women in this picture are quite bad; St. Francis is rather better, but the real Moroni appears only in the smug donor who prays, his clasped hands showing his valuable ring. Here, of course, the painter had simply to reproduce his sitter. As much can be said of Garofalo and many another religious painter, whose "Donors" often constitute the sole success of their pious compositions.

Lorenzo Lotto, too, should perhaps have confined himself to portraiture, if of a fashionable clientèle. His pretty Adoration of the Infant might be any mother adoring any infant. Near it—in the Palazzo Martinengo in Brescia—Girolamo Romanino has a frightful fresco in the grand manner, and quite a good portrait of an old gentleman; which suggests that Romanino too should have avoided the classic. There is an altar-piece of his in Padua which, although by no means devoid of beauty, confirms this suggestion, for the Madonna and Child lack character and originality, and are infinitely inferior to the Dutch painting of the robes. The whole composition, indeed, glows and has depth only in its lower and more terrestrial part, including in that term the little girl angel who plays a tambourine below the throne.

Bronzino was another victim to his pious epoch, though he emancipated himself almost as largely as Moroni. His Madonna in the Brera is remarkable for the secular modernity of the Virgin's companions. On her right is an ultra-realistic old woman; on her left Bernard Shaw looks down with his sarcastic, sceptical gaze.

Even the Netherlanders who had had the fortune to be born free would, after their wander-years in Italy, come back as Italians and paint in the grand manner. Hence the religious and historic Van Dycks which compare so poorly with the portraits, hence Rembrandt's fat vrow as Madonna, hence the Lenten attempts of Rubens to bant.

AN EXCURSION INTO THE GROTESQUE: WITH A GLANCE AT OLD MAPS AND MODERN FALLACIES

Touching is that quaint theological tree in the cell of sainted Antoninus in San Marco, upon whose red oval leaves grow the biographies of the brethren. They lived, they prayed, they died—that is all. One little leaf suffices to tell the tale. This brother conversed with the greatest humility, and that excelled in silence. A third was found after his death covered with a rough hair shirt (aspro cilicio). In the holy shade of this goodly tree sits St. Dominic, separating—as though symbolically—the monks on his right from the nuns on his left.

Naïveté can no further go. And, indeed, if one were to regard the naïveté and forget the sweet simplicity, there is much in the mediæval world that one would relegate to the merely absurd. The masterpieces of Art have been sufficiently described. What a book remains to be written upon its grotesques!

The word is said to derive from the arabesques found in grottoes or excavated Roman tombs; those fantastic combinations of the vegetable and animal worlds by which the art of Islam avoided the representation of the real. But by the art of Christendom the grotesque was achieved with no such conscientious search after the unreal. Nor have I in mind its first fumblings, its crudities of the catacombs, its simplicities of the missal and the music-book, its Byzantine paintings with their wooden figures and gold embroidery. I am not even thinking of those early Masters whose defects of draughtsmanship were balanced by a delicious primitive poetry, which makes a Sienese Madonna preferable to a Raphael, and the early mosaics of St. Mark's more desirable than the sixteenth-century work that has replaced them. The grotesque lies deeper than unscientific drawing; it mingles even with the work of the most scholarly Masters, and springs from the absence of a sense of history or a sense of humour. That the Gospel incidents should be depicted in Italian landscape and with Italian costumes was perhaps not unnatural, since, as I have already pointed out, every nation remakes the Christ in its own image—psychologically when not physically. Even the Old Testament was de-Orientalised by Raphael and his fellow-illustrators. Bonifacio Veronese, for example, put Italian hills and music-books into The Finding of Moses, and his Egypt is less Eastern than the Venice he lived in. But that the fancy-dress Bible should include also Doges and Cardinals and Magnificent Families, and that a Tintoretto in everyday clothes should look on at his own Miracle of St. Mark or a Moretto come to his own Supper at Emmaus, this it is that lifts the eyebrows of a modern. One can permit Dominican friars to witness The Incredulity of St. Thomas, or Franciscans to assist—as in Marco Basaiti's picture—at The Agony in the Garden. These holy brethren are at least in the apostolic chain; and in the latter picture, which is becomingly devotional, the scene is suggested as a mystic vision to justify the presence of these anachronistic spectators. But how is it possible to tolerate proud Venetian senators at The Ascension of Christ, or to stomach the Medici at the building of the Tower of Babel? It is true sacred subjects had become a mere background for lay portraits, but what absence of perspective!

It would be an interesting excursion to trace the steps by which the objective conception of a picture—true to its own time and place—was reached, the evolution by which singleness of subject was substituted for exuberance of episodes and ideas, till at last Art could flower in a lovely simplicity like that of Simone Martini's Annunciation. You shall see St. Barbara throned at the centre of her anecdotal biography, or the Madonna della Misericordia sheltering virtues under her robe, while her history circles around her. Even when the picture itself is simple and single, the predella is often a congested commentary upon the text, if, indeed, it has any relevant relation to the text at all. What can be more charming than the little angels round the throne of the Madonna in Benaglio Francesco's picture in Verona—angels with golden vases of red and white roses, angels playing spinets and harps and pipes and lutes and little drums and strange stringed instruments that have passed away! But what can be more grotesque than the predella of this delightful picture, the Entombment and the saints with the insignia of their martyrdom (hammer and tongs and fiery braziers), and the cock that crew, and the kiss of Judas!

In a picture by Lorenzo Monaco at Florence the Virgin and St. John raise Christ out of his tomb, and above are not only a cross and the instruments of martyrdom, but a bust and floating hands, while spice vessels figure below.

To a modern the mere treatment of God the Father suffices to create a category of the grotesque, even though His head has usually the venerable appearance of the aged Ruskin and He is kept a discreet kit-kat or a half-length. But Fra Bartolommeo in Lucca paints Him at full length with His toes on a little angel and a placard in His hand bearing the letters alpha and omega. And Lorenzo Veneziano parts His hair neatly in the middle.

Our catalogue of grotesques is swollen by the explanatory scrolls and inscriptions of the early pictures; by the crude religious allegories, in which devils gnash teeth when Virtue routs Temptation; by the political cartoons at Siena—of Good and Bad Government (though these are more primitive than comic); by the literal genealogic trees—like that of Jesse in St. Mark's, or on the stone door-posts of the Baptistery of Parma; by the Tree of the Cross in Florence, which shoots out branches with round leaves containing scenes from the life of the central crucified figure, and supports a pyramid of saints and celestials; by the devices of symbolism for representing abstract ideas or identifying saints. All haloes are proleptic even from childhood, and a martyr and his passion can never be parted. Those poor martyrs, what they suffered at the hands of painters without a gleam of humour!

'Twas not till I had found out for myself that the overwhelming preponderance in Art of the Crucifixion, the Descent from the Cross, the Entombment, and the Pietà were due in no small measure to the opportunities they afforded of painting the nude figure, that I discovered why St. Sebastian was the most popular of all the saints, exploited in every other sacred picture, and—naked and unashamed—the almost inseparable attendant of the Madonna when she sits in saintly society. The superiority of his martyrdom at the hands of a troop of archers to other paintable forms of death leaps to the eye, for the arrows must be seen quivering in the target of his naked figure, though I have seen this pictorially precious nudity marred by such a plethora of arrows—as in the Opera del Duomo at Florence—that the saint is become a porcupine. The grim humour of the situation lies in the fact that St. Sebastian recovered from his arrows to be subsequently clubbed to death, but this deutero-martyrdom is hushed up by the Italian painters. To add to St. Sebastian's sufferings at their hands, he has been made a plague-saint and his invaluable nudity haled into plague-pictures and plague-churches, as by Bartolommeo Montagna, who turned his arrows into the metaphoric shafts of the Pest. Not that I can blame the Italian painters. If I had ever been inclined to underrate the artistic significance of the nude, I should have been converted by the full-dressed angelets of Borgognone's Gesù Moriente in the Pavian Certosa. These delicious little creatures were once without a fig-leaf, but at the Father Superior's protest they were clad in belted tunics and skirts, thus becoming squat little figures whose wings burst comically through their clothes. What might have been a masterpiece is thus a grotesque.

But if St. Sebastian must go sempiternally branded with arrows, like a British convict, it is St. Lawrence who has the clumsiest symbol to drag about. He and his gridiron are as inseparable as Don Quixote and Sancho Panza. Often it stands on end and seems the iron framework of a bed. Like his halo, it is with him long before his martyrdom, as it accompanies him to heaven. Only once in all Florence do I remember seeing it in its proper place—under the grilling saint—and then he is turning his other side to the flame in true culinary Christianity ("Jam versa: assatus est"). The artist has spared us nothing except the towels with which the angels wiped his face, and these may be seen at Rome in S. Giovanni in Laterano. St. Stephen is also heavily burdened with the stones that still keep falling on his head. In Bernardo Daddi's frescoes in S. Croce they stick to him like burrs. St. John, transformed to an angel, contemplates his own (haloed) head on a platter, as if thinking two heads are better than one. Lucy keeps her eyes in a dish. St. Bartholomew holds his skin. St. Nicholas—the patron of commerce and the pawnbroker—is known by his three golden balls. Even families had their symbols, and the Colonnas, the complacent Colonnas, had themselves painted as soaring heavenwards at the last trump, each with a small column rising from his shoulder—literal pillars of Church and State.

These symbols, and many others less grotesque, disappear either with the gradual obscuration of the legends or the development of purer artistic ideas. There is another kind of symbolism, which may be called the shorthand of primitive art, and which may be studied in the archaic mosaics of St. Mark's.

Egypt dwindles to a gate (as though it and not Turkey were the Porte). Alexandria is expressed by its Pharos. Trees stand for the Mount of Olives. There is much of the rebus in these primitive representations. The Byzantine symbolism of St. Mark's reaches its most curious climax in the representation of the four rivers that watered the Biblical Garden of Eden by classical river gods. The palm branch as the shorthand for martyrdom is a more congruous convention. In the mosaics of S. Vitale in Ravenna, Jerusalem and Bethlehem are expressed by towers, in Sant' Appolinare Nuovo a few Roman buildings stand for Classe. In a Venetian painting ascribed to Carpaccio, Bethlehem is spelt by palm-trees and a queer beast tied to one of them, probably meant for a camel.

A more pretentious form of symbolism lies in the allegory proper, but even when the painting avoids the grotesque, the meaning is often hopelessly obscure. Such popular pictures as Botticelli's Spring, Titian's Sacred and Profane Love, and Paris Bordone's Lovers are still unsolved puzzles, and perhaps only the more satisfactory for that. But allegories that are enigmatic without being beautiful are merely bores. Such are the two pictures of the school of Lazzaro Sebastiani in Venice, in which a company of figures holding scrolls is perched in the boughs of a tree, looking at a distance like a full orchestra. Both of these pictures come from monasteries, and are therefore to be presumed sacred. And in one of them Adam and Eve are unmistakable under the tree, with mice and lizards gambolling around them, so that the tree must be the Tree of Life or of Knowledge; but who is the youth who stands beneath the other tree in a strange city of spires and towers and plays on a golden 'cello, while a maiden offers him an apple? Such intellectually faded pictures illustrate clearly the limitations of painting as a medium for intellectual propositions. But the most lucid of allegories or symbolisms has its own peculiar pitfalls. Luca Mombella introduces into a Coronation of the Virgin a figure of "Humilitas" who is magnificently attired and wears pearls in her hair, while Montagna's Nestor Victorious over the Vices (in the Louvre) proves that most of the Vices are at least devoted mothers, for they burden their flight by snatching up their satyr-like brood.

But these confused or unintelligible allegories are far preferable to symbolisms which are perfectly decipherable yet perfectly repellent, like Giovanni da Modena's fresco in S. Petronio which shows us Christ on his cross agonising between two female figures, one bestriding a full-maned lion (the Catholic Church) and the other riding blindfold on a goat (Heresy). The lion has four different feet—a pedal man (St. Matthew), a pedal ox (St. Luke), an eagle's claw (St. John), and a real foot (St. Mark). The blood from the side of Christ flows into the chalice held by the Church, and in the middle of the stream is formed the wafer. The four ends of the cross turn into hands: the upper hand opens with a key the gate of Paradise—strangely like a church; the lower hand opens Hell with a winch; the right hand blesses the Catholic Church, the left stabs Heresy. Garofalo has a vast but still poorer fresco of this sort in Ferrara, brought from a refectory. Each arm of the cross branches into two hands engaged in much the same occupations as in the Bolognese fresco save that one hand crowns Wisdom. The foot of the cross also turns into hands, the right holding a cross towards Limbo, the function of the left fortunately faded. It is refreshing to turn from such geometrical symbolisms to the meaningless flower-patterns of F. dei Libri, in which Crucifixions, cherubs reading, satyrs blowing brass instruments, and putti playing citharas or puffing at bagpipes are interwoven with wriggling snakes, contemporary poets and ecclesiasts, and shaven monks performing service.

This, of course, is the conscious grotesque, like the borders which Girolamo dei Libri put round a serious picture of the Magi—vignettes of other scenes, hands of donors, floral patterns and scutcheons with strange ramping beasts.

To the deliberate grotesque belong, of course, the stone beasts that crouch before the old cathedrals, the griffin of Perugia, and the heraldic beasts of Tura. I should have added Raphael's dragons to the same category were it not that though deliberately drawn and though delightfully grotesque, they are mere representation of an object that happens to be grotesque in itself, and this is no more the artistic grotesque than the portrait of a beautiful woman is necessarily the artistic beautiful. There is a deal of movement, spirit, and invention in these great worms of Raphael, and every individual St. George, St. Michael, or St. Margaret is handsomely provided with an original and unique dragon, each with an elegant precision of fearsome form. But Raphael drew with equal hand and the same loving seriousness a monster or a Madonna.

Equally conscientious is the Medusa's head once ascribed to Da Vinci, with its carefully combed snaky locks and its frogs and bats and toads. Carpaccio's dragon has far more fun in him, for all his grisly litter of skulls and skeletons.

And I like Vasari's dragon in his St. George in Arezzo, with its spitting double tongue and its half-eaten man, and the gorgeous dragon on a piece of majolica in Urbino, into whose mouth St. George is driving his spear, and the fierce-clawed, winged dragon of the spirited Tintoretto in the National Gallery, and above all the dragon of Piero di Cosimo's Andromeda in Florence, with that delightful curling tail and that broad back on which Perseus can stand securely while delivering his stroke.

But the deliberate grotesque without fun—this, I confess, is a note in Italian art which I find disquieting. For into this polished and palatial world there intrudes at times a touch of something sinister, cynical and mocking, as though the artist, constricted by pompous conventions, sought relief by sticking out his tongue. Leonardo—whatever Mona Lisa's smile may mean—kept his grotesquerie for his caricatures. But other of the Masters were less discriminating. This something of enigmatic and perturbing—perhaps it is only the acute Renaissance consciousness of the skeleton at the feast—I find most of all in Crivelli— Venetian soldier, as he once signed himself—whose rich lacquer work has had more attention than this diablerie of his. Nobody else touches the grotesque so consciously, dares to give us such quaint, ill- drawn angels as those in his Madonna and Child in Verona, with that bird-pecked giardinetto of fruits over the Virgin's head, and Christ in a gold frock as in some Byzantine mosaic. The microscopic Crucifixion is perhaps no more incongruous with the subject of this picture than its landscapes seen through arches, its chivalry and pomp of horses. But one cannot help feeling that Crivelli had a grim joy in perching that vulture on the large gaunt tree. And in his Brera Madonna, in which St. Peter holds two heavy real keys, gilded and silvered, he gives the celestial doorkeeper a crafty ecclesiastical look, while his St. Dominic looks sawny. Even his baby Christ is cruelly squeezing a little bird. There is a leer in the whole picture. The accident of juxtaposition has accentuated the wilfulness of Crivelli's grimace, for in the Brera there are two Madonnas, side by side, yet at the extreme poles of his genius. In the Madonna della Candeletta we have beauty unalloyed. The tiny candle standing at the foot of the Madonna's throne strikes, indeed, a note of bizarrerie, but it is beautiful bizarrerie, and the Madonna, marvellously robed and embowered in fruit and leaves, who is offering a great pear to a charming Child, is less the Mother of God than a crowned queen of faery with an infant prince in a golden robe and a golden halo, and less a queen with a prince than a wonderful decorative pattern, a study in gold and marble and precious stones and brocaded gowns, broidered, rich-dyed, and fantastic with arabesques. And beside this poem hangs the other Crivelli, a gaunt crucifix with ugly, contorted figures of the Madonna and St. John. And it is sardonic humour, not naïveté, that has turned his St. Sebastian (in the Museo Poldi Pezzoli) into a porcupine.

But even Giovanni Bellini, with his sense of restful perfection and unity of theme, cannot resist putting in microscopic accessories that only catch the eye from anear, as into his green-throned Madonna and Child in the Brera he introduces a horseman, two men talking by a tree, a shepherd, a flock of sheep, and, strangest of all, a shadowy ape crouching on a tomb which bears his signature: "Johannes Bellinus." What is the significance of this shadowy ape? What mockery of the theme, or of humanity, or of himself, was here shadowed forth?

And that even more sinister ape in Tura's Virgin supporting the Dead Christ—what does he here? The mother, seated on the tomb, holds the poor bleeding figure as though it were again her baby. They are alone, they and the thieves and the cross; other men are moving away, bearing a ladder. The picture is complete, a grim, solemn, soul-moving unity. Why then did Tura, that master of the conscious grotesque, throw in that grinning monkey on that strange fruit-tree? Was he, who lived to see the Borgian Pope become the Vicar of Christ, suggesting sardonically what quaint sequels of orgiastic splendour, what pride and lust of life, were to spring from this tragic sacrifice?

A less perturbing monkey looks on with other creatures at The Creation of Man in a Venetian picture now in Ravenna. A red-girt, blue-mantled Deity floats over a huge recumbent Adam, whose thigh he touches, while the monkey, eating an apple, appears to follow with interest the next phase in evolution, when fruit would be forbidden.

Apes appear again in Fogolino's Adoration of the Magi in Vicenza; squatting below the castled rocky ways and mountain-bridges, over which winds the great procession with its beautifully caparisoned horses. These apes, like the ape on the elephant's back in Raphael's treatment of the same theme, might be merely designed to suggest the East, were it not for the disconcerting, mysterious, lobster-red, sprawling wings? What further note of discord do we catch here?

But it is in the unconscious grotesque that Italian art is richest. I have already shown some of the trap-doors that lead to it, but to enumerate them all is impossible. There are so many ways in which humour can be absent. Perhaps one might generalise as a source of the unconscious grotesque the convention dating from the Byzantine period which expresses souls as small swaddled dolls. See, for example, Paolo da Venezia's Death of Mary, where, by a seeming inversion of rôles, Christ flies up to heaven with his mother-doll. Perhaps, too, all pictures connected with stigmata or vernicles are foredoomed to farce. There may be a noble way of expressing this material transference, but I have never seen one. St. Veronica receiving on a handkerchief a head with neatly parted hair is prosaic if not comic, while St. Francis receiving the stigmata is simply ludicrous.

In a picture in the Museum of Vicenza the kneeling saint is apparently flying a kite by red strings passing through holes in his hands and feet. The seeming kite is really a small winged nude figure, feathered at head and feet like a cock—the six-winged seraph of the Legenda Trium Sociorum that bears the crucified figure,—red strings passing through corresponding holes in his head and feet. The treatment of the same scene by Giotto (in the Louvre) gives this kite-like appearance to Jesus himself.

Even more absurdly geometrical is Gentile da Fabriano's handling of the theme at Urbino, five strong red cords passing to the saint's breast, hands, and feet from an eight-winged figure on a cross, naked to its waist. It is a relief to find these Euclidian lines absent from the representation in the church of Assisi itself, though it is only in seventeenth-century painters like Sisto Badalocchio in Parma or Rochetti in Faenza that the stigmata are transmitted from a celestial glory or down a broad ray of golden light.

Macrino d'Alba at Turin shows the saint receiving the image of a praying Christ on a slate with a golden frame, and this image has the tonsured head of a monk!

And what can be quainter than the six-winged cherubs who hover round the Madonna in a picture of the Botticelli school at Parma? Two of their red wings are spread, the second pair crossed like legs, and the last pair crossed over the head, making a sort of pointed cap. The faces attached to these wings are mature, as of elderly, clean-shaven barristers. Another comical circle of these seraphs, a few with blue wings, tends to spoil a charming fifteenth-century Coronation of the Virgin in Florence.

Martyrdoms, too, are a rich mine of the grotesque, as witness the boiling of St. John in the National Gallery, with its accessories of the bellows and the blowpipe, and God lifting the saint bodily up to heaven.

In the exhilarating frescoes of Montagna in the church of the Eremitani at Padua, St. James's hair, which is yellowish throughout, turns black, apparently, under the horror of an impending mallet, despite that his halo seems like a protective plate of yellow armour. A very gay and pleasing picture this.

Another source of the grotesque is the angelic aeroplane. In an Adoration of the Shepherds by Francesco Zaganelli in Ravenna three wingless angels employ cherubs to bear them aloft, balancing themselves upon the winged heads. One needs a cherub for each foot, the second places both feet upon the same head, the third, expertest gymnast of all, maintains himself upon one foot. Another primitive aeroplane may be seen at Ferrara, in The Assumption of St. Mary of Egypt. St. Mary rises on a platform supported from beneath by a series of nude and clothed angels, to the amaze of a worthy signor walking in the field of strange palms amid quaint green buildings. A rabbit, a pigeon, and a bird continue absolutely indifferent to the phenomenon.

In a Carpaccio in the same town the cherubs fly, three heads together, like a celestial molecule. In Zacchia da Vezzano's Assumption of the Virgin at Lucca she rides on cherubs. There is an angelic aeroplane in a painted relief at San Frediano in Lucca, and in Guido Reni's Immaculate Conception at Forli (where the Virgin stands on a leaf on a cherub's head), and in Lippo Lippi's picture at Prato of the Madonna handing down her girdle to St. Thomas. Zuccari Taddeo in the Pitti uses the angelic aeroplane to carry up Mary Magdalen, who is further provided with a number of fussy heralds and avant-coureurs. Marco Antonio Franceschini in the Palazzo Durazzo-Pallavicini of Genoa likewise carries up the Magdalen on the backs of angels, her familiar hair streaming over her familiar breast. Raphael's Vision of Ezekiel suggests to the profane, God the Father holding up His arms as if to start a flying competition.

But when every generalisation is made, it is the individual genius for blundering that opens up the most spacious vistas of humourless humour. Byzantine art affords, of course, the most naïve illustrations. In the sarcophagi of the Christian emperors at Ravenna you may see sheep eating dates from tall palms. In the mosaics of the vestibule of St. Mark's you may see humanity unconcernedly drowning in the Deluge. Some, it is true, are whirled helplessly on their backs, but others are quite apathetic among the blue, curly waves. Noah looking out of the little folding doors of the Ark is as quaint as in the mosaics of Monreale Cathedral in Sicily. In the ancient church of S. Zeno at Verona there is an eleventh-century fresco of the Resurrection of Lazarus in which the bystanders hold their noses—a poetic touch that was repeated in later treatments of the theme.

In the Scuola of the Confraternity of St. Antony at Padua, Domenico Campagnola has a fresco, A Hungry She-Ass adores the Eucharistic Sacrament by a Miracle of the Saint, in order to convert a Heretic. In vain are heaps of green stuffs and corn spread and baskets tendered her and piles of beans; the ass, on her front knees, adores the Eucharist on a priestly table, so that even the baby lad is wrought up to adoration. One is irresistibly reminded of Goethe's landlady at Rome calling him to see her cat adore God the Father like a Christian, when it was licking the beard of the bust, probably because of the grease that had sunk into it. In the same Scuola there is a representation of the saint's preaching which liberates his hearers from an approaching rain-storm. People all around are flying to get out of the rain, not knowing that the saint's sermon is dry. There are charming figures of mothers and children in the audience which atone for the unconscious humour.

But when one considers the libraries written on Italy, it is strange that that book on her grotesques should be as yet merely an impious aspiration, and that nobody has mocked even at those horrid little waxworks that represent the plague-stricken. Meseems the blessèd word "Renaissance" has hypnotised student and pleasure-pilgrim alike, but some day an irreverent refugee from the Renaissance will gather up the threads I but indicate. In that delectable volume of his there will be a chapter on the camel.

For the advent of the camel marks the faint beginnings of an historic and geographic sense, and stands for all the fantastic wonder-world of the East. Strange that the Crusades or Venice's Eastern Empire should not have earlier awakened the comparative consciousness. But the East, with its quaintness and its barbaric colour, broke very slowly upon the culture of Europe—Victor Hugo had to rediscover it even for modern France. Despite Altichiero's pig-tailed Tartars, it was not till the Byzantine Empire was destroyed in 1453 and the Turks were firmly established in Europe that the Christian world became really aware that the East was a world of its own. That conquest of Constantinople, from which the blessèd Renaissance is popularly dated, by sending so many Italians flying home, must have provided Italy with Oriental information as well as Greek manuscripts. And the Renaissance (or re-born) camel represents the quickened sense of local colour. At first, indeed, there is little improvement on the Giotto breed. Apparently none of the fugitives rode off on camels. Such fat creatures as take part in The Reception of the Venetian Ambassador (a picture of the school of Gentile Bellini) were never seen on sand or land. The Magian kings should have come riding on camels with swart servitors, but only a rare artist like the animal-lover Gaudenzio Ferrari is bold enough to attempt this local truth. And the result belongs to comedy. But a people without circuses or zoological gardens, to which the camel was as remote as the centaur, was not keenly aware of the anatomical details of this exotic beast, grotesque enough at its truest. And in the hands of Gentile Bellini himself the creature became quite possible, if still curious, and in that great decorative picture St. Mark preaching in the Piazza of Alexandria there is a real feeling of the turbaned, shrouded and minareted East, even if the head-shawls of the women do appear to cover top-hats and the giraffe strolls about the piazza and the dromedary is led by a string.

Nor is Eusebio di San Giorgio's camel impossible in his Adoration of the Magi in San Pietro, Perugia, though immeasurably inferior to his oxen and his horses. Carpaccio, too, gets something of Eastern architecture and dress, if more of Venetian, into his St. Stephen at Jerusalem.

But after all there is more fascination in the primitive artistry which knew no differences of Space or Time, no colour but universal—id est, Italian—no place unlike home. The whole temper of these early painters seems to me summed up in a picture in the Uffizi by Pietro Lorenzetti, who lived about 1350, Gli Anacoreti nella Tebaide. A green water borders a white, curving shore, and land and sea are a chaos of trees, houses, steeples, people, skiffs, sailing-boats, all of the same size and brightness. A like absence of perspective—geometrical, spiritual, or humorous—is seen in Benaglio's fresco in Verona of Christ Preaching by the Lake of Galilee, or Giotto's fresco in Santa Croce depicting the Apocalypse of St. John. In the Lake of Galilee float two gigantic ducks and a gondola, while the audience includes mediæval falconers and pipers. Patmos is a vague turtle-shaped island, and the saint squats in the middle of it, while above hover the celestial figures. Temporal perspective is as confounded as spatial. Hence all those anachronisms which give us pause. Cimabue's Madonna consorts with the Doctors of the Church, Fra Angelico's with Dominicans, Alvise Vivarini's with Franciscans. As Dante explains, the imagination can ignore Time, just as—though his dubious comparison weakens his explanation—it can conceive two obtuse angles in one triangle. A truer simile may perhaps be drawn from the Baptistery of Pisa, where the janitor—humble link in the "nutritive chain"—chants a note to show the wonderful echo, and after its long reverberation has been sufficiently demonstrated he sounds the notes of a simple chord, one after another, so that the earlier notes remain alive and enter into harmony with the new ones, and one hears an enchanting quartet—yea, even a quintet or a sextet. Sometimes he will set an even more complex chord in vibration, and all the air is full of delicious harmony. Even so the mediæval thinkers conceived of the dead and the quick, the pioneers and the successors, all living in unison, vibrating simultaneously though they had started in sequence, all harmoniously at one in the echoing halls of Fame. And so things disparate could be pictured united—anachronism was merely man putting together what blind Time had put asunder. Everything happened in the timeless realm of ideas. And often—as we saw in Sicily—the strictly chronological aspect of things is, indeed, irrelevant. Space and Time are shifting illusions that the spirit disregards. Those who are in harmony are of the same hour and of the same place.

Nor do I know where to look for a better map of the world as it figured itself in the mediæval mind—for your atlas with its assumption that man inhabits mere mounds of earth fantastically patterned is as absurd as your school chronology—than that naïve Mappamondo which Pietro di Puccio frescoed on the walls of the Campo Santo of this same white Pisa. The universe is held in the literal hands of God, whose haloed head appears dominatingly above, not without a suggestion of a clerical band. In the centre of the cosmos—note the geocentric glorification—stands the earth, mapped out into continents by a couple of single straight lines. (If Asia lies north of Europe that is a mere turn to express its hyperborean barbarism; in Fra Mauro's map in the Doge's Palace the south has got to the top, perhaps because Venice was there.) America, of course, is not. And yet there are compensations even for the absence of America. For this old world is circumscribed by circle on circle. On the rim of the third are perched the mere figures of the zodiac, but the spaces between the remoter extra-terrestrial circles are a-swarm with cherubs, all heads and wings, and floating robed saints and endless haloed heads of the beatified. The dim spaces below the cosmos are solidly garrisoned by bishop with crozier and monk with breviary, and the predella is full of suggestions of beauty and sanctity. Thus the whole world lies serenely in the palms of God, and saints and angels girdle it with circles of holiness.

This is, indeed, the true way to make a map—for the actual shape of the world is only one of the factors of our habitation, just as the actual features of a beloved face do not constitute its total reality for us. 'Tis not eyes or nose one sees so much as those mental circles due to loving habit in which the face swims for us—the dear haloing circles of tender experience. Rivers and mountains have, indeed, an influence on life, just as the real eyes and nose, but the world we live in is always more mental than geographical, and the same rivers and mountains serve the life of successive races. The Red Man's America is not different from the White Man's on the atlas—save by the black dots which mark the ephemeral tumuli called cities—yet the America of the Trust and the America of the Tomahawk are two different continents. The same thin curve marks the Thames up which the pirate Vikings sailed and the Thames of Sunday picnics. More veraciously did the Arab geographers conceive of a country by its autochthones and not by its configuration. For our country lives in us much more than we live in our country.

And so, to-day, too, a true map would circumscribe our globe—not with the equally non-existent circles of the spatial latitude and longitude, but with those of the spiritual latitude and longitude in which we float—only, I fear, our modern Mappamondo would be girdled with dark rings marked "Survival of the Fittest," "Necessity for Navies," "The Need of Expansion," "The Divinity of the Dollar"; soldiers and syndicates would float around in lieu of cherubs, nor would any divine hands appear upbearing us amid the infinite spaces.

That old Pisan map leads me to suspect that Swift saw only half a fact when he complained that

"Geographers in Afric maps
With savage pictures fill their gaps."

True, many an old map might seem to attest the truth of the accusation. There is a map of the Dark Continent in the Museum of Venice, dated 1651, with a camel, a unicorn, a dromedary, and a lion's tail—all put in by hand. But in another map of "Apphrica" in the Arsenal of Venice there are not only lions and tigers, but tents and veiled figures, and the turrets and spires of strange buildings, and a gay sprinkling of flags. Surely the old cartographer was less concerned to fill his gaps than to express the poetry of geography. Maps were, in truth, of mediocre use in ancient times when the old Roman roads took one from town to town. What profited an aeronaut's panorama? Maps were only indispensable on the roadless seas. The first maps in the modern sense were thus pragmatic, not scientific, for it was from the mariner's map, or Portolano, that rigid cartography arose. But even these coast charts refused to be prosaic. There is one in the Venice Museum—a view of Italy lying sideways, as if its famous foot were asleep. Never have I seen a more joyous chart. It is all glorious with the gold and vermilion of compasses and crests and flying banners, while mountains stand out in red and gold. It must have belonged to a jolly mariner. In a complete Portolano of Europe each country flies its national flag, amid a whirl of crests and compasses. And the "Portolano del 1561 di Giacomo Maggiolo," which may be seen in the Palazzo Bianco of Genoa, is illuminated in gold and blue and vermilion and green, sprinkled with compasses, sown with towered cities crowned by golden flags, and a-flutter with flying angels and banners and the bellying sails of carracks, with kings seated on their thrones in the middle of the sea, under glorious canopies crowned with angels, while over the whole presides the Madonna in her golden chair. Most taking of the monarchs is the King of Tartary, wearing a large moustache and surrounded by golden scimitars.

There were no gaps to fill up in these Portolani. No, the cynical Swift has missed the inwardness of these old maps, in which Art was called in to give the touch of life and reality and to eke out, not the barrenness of knowledge in particular, but of science in general. There is in the Uffizi an old map of Italy which fills the Mediterranean with boats and compasses, draws the mountains, sketches the towered cities, and illumines the names with gold-leaf. There is an old map of Venice which perches Father Neptune dominatingly in the middle, and symbolises the winds by the curly locks of children blowing every way, and fills the canals with sailing-boats and galleys and gondolas. This is something like a map of Venice. On another, which is more of a plan of the city with its buildings named, Venice is alive with heraldic figures, and over the roofs and domes fly winged lions and Neptune and Venus and angels and warriors, while a stout-lunged angel blows two trumpets at once. And the spaces of the sea are full of brave beflagged vessels with swelling sails, and galleys with many oars. Surely all this is less false than the dead reticulation which expresses Venice in your modern map. The map of Genoa, too, shows the arms of the city floating over a sea crowded with red galleys and black merchant ships and white sailing-boats.

In these old maps the dull spaces of the world are lit up by fiery stars, trumpeting angels, and allegorical figures, while another symbolic group, upholding a titulary tablet, serves, as it were, to introduce the territory to the spectator. A wreathed lady and a male student thus combine to present Arabia. Greece is introduced and presided over by angels. "Terra nova detecta et Floridae promontorium" are presented by a man holding a tablet, which records how Henry VII of England sent out John Cabot and his son Sebastian, while the dry details are further vivified by a superdominant figure of a gallant signor in a feathered cap, hand on globe and learnèd tome at feet. Asia, as a nymph with a camel, presides over a map of her continent, while a prodigious Latin title—"Quae Asiae Regna et Provinciae Hac Tabula Continentur a Propontide usque ad Indos," &c. &c.—records how its three makers were sent to Russia in the fifteenth-century and how they ripped up (dissuerunt) much in the published itineraries. One of the trio, Ambrosius Contaremus, remained long in Russia to study the less-known portions; another, Josaphat Barbarus, devoted himself for sixteen years to the provinces round the Euxine and the Mæotian marsh. "Perlustrata commentariolo exponunt."

That old map of Frau Mauro which I have already mentioned belongs to this same century, being dated 1459; a circular map this, in a gilded frame, with little ships floating around and America away from home, perhaps enjoying itself in Paris. Here our familiar world shows upside down, which is, of course, as scientific as being downside up. It is notable how Anglia and Caledonia (or Anglia Barbara, as she is styled in Church Latin) are disguised by this simple shifting of the point of view, and how much like herself Hibernia looks, even topsy-turvy. Another pre-American map in the University of Ferrara pictures the winds personified, blowing from every quarter.

The Stones of Venice also assume the forms of maps, as in those stone reliefs on the rococo façade of S. Maria Zobenigo opposite the Traghetto of the Lily. These are town-maps—Candia, its name upborne by a flying boy angel; Roma with its twin brethren at the wolf's breast; Corfu, characterised by its castle and its beflagged galleys. The symbolic shorthand, which I have already noted in pictures, spread also to map-decoration as in a map at the Arsenal, wherein Ægyptus is figured by an elephant, Libia by giraffes, Judea by the crescent and minarets, Germany by a winged sage, and "Holy Russia" by churches.

If these old maps erred in the courses of rivers and the lines of mountains and in ratios of space, they are not so misleading as your modern atlas with its all too accurate earth-measurements. For even your most primitive map, your mediæval figment, with Paradise on the East, a gigantic Jerusalem in the centre, great spaces for Gryphons and Cynocephali, Sciapodes and Anthropophagi, and St. Brendan's Isles of the Blest marked clearly west of the Canaries, gave in its way a less distortive impression than that which we obtain from the most scientific chart on Mercator's projection. Your modern cartographer would persuade you that Canada is fifty times as large as Italy, and Canada, contemplating herself on a school globe, already pouts her breast with the illusion. In a true map, as distinguished from a geographical, dead Space would shrink to its spiritual nullity, and for its contribution to the human spirit, for its amplitude of history and poesy, Sicily—Italy's mere foot-note—would loom larger than all the provinces of the Canadian Confederation.

And this misleading potency of the map scientific engenders political as well as spiritual dangers. Tariff Reform in Britain rests on the notion of exchanging products preferentially with these great British colonies which bulk on the map like continents, but which, as yet in their infancy, only represent in all some poor ten million souls against the homeland's forty millions. Australia, beholding her unified contours from the Gulf of Carpentaria to Bass Strait, persists in the heroic delusion that, despite the torridity and drought of her Northern Territory, she is a single country, and that country a white man's— nay, a Briton's exclusively. For it is from the surplus population of the little island in the Northern Sea that all these continents into which Britain has blundered are to be filled up: a notion which lives in the same brains that fever with alarm over the exodus from her shores. And all save the spherical maps foster an infinity of fallacies of dimension: drawn to fill the like-sized page in the atlas, South America seems a twin of India; Ireland and Madagascar (which contains seven Erins) look much of a muchness; and Brazil, which is almost another Europe, bulges in the imagination less than the Balkan Peninsula. What wonder if statesmen have misguided the destinies of nations and misdirected wars by false impressions derived from atlases, with their deceptive distances and their obscurations of the real character of territories, rivers, or harbours. Seoul, the capital of Corea, Lord Curzon tells us, seems on the river, yet it is three or four miles away, and approachable only by a canal at times shallow. "Get large maps," advised the late Lord Salisbury; but I would say, beware of maps altogether. For your school map would foist upon you the delusion that Morocco is not the East at all, but actually ten degrees more westerly than London! Whereas every schoolboy knows that it is in the middle of the "Arabian Nights." With the Orient thus thrown south-west of Europe, we are as befogged by the atlas of to-day as by the old maps which put the Orient on the top. In truth, the Orient, like heaven, is not a place, but a state of mind.

To the deuce with your parallels of longitude! Fez in the West, forsooth!

In that volume on the grotesque a chapter—nay, a section—would deal with the attempts of Art to give form and colour to that after-world "from whence no traveller returns." The grotesquerie belongs more to the thought than to the picture, for in eschatological æsthetics the horrible can be reconciled to the decorative, as it is in Giotto's Last Judgment at Padua, which I suppose is the earliest treatment of the theme that counts, and which, as Giotto and Dante were in Padua together, was probably painted under the personal influence of that great authority and explorer. There is no justification in Dante's own work, however, for the Father's supersession by the Son, who—while Il Padre Eterno is relegated to the choir-arch—occupies, as so often, the judicial bench, and looms dominant in a large polychromatic oval like an incomplete spectrum, with saints at either hand on golden chairs, and golden companies of hovering angels, the Cross beneath his feet making a decorative division of Heaven from Hell, and its arms providing clinging-points for floating angels. Among the beatific company on the celestial side of the Cross are monks presenting their monastery to lady saints, and fussy nude corpses of all ages and both sexes bobbing up out of their coffins, some looking round in surprise, some instinctively begging for grace, and one looking back into his coffin, as into a cab for something forgotten. The Hell is a chaos of tortures, overdusked by the Personal Hell, the fee-fi-fo-fum ogre (with whom I came to grow very familiar) who gulps down sinners like oysters. You see their legs protruding, and others ready for his maw clutched in his greedy hands. Still other sinners stand on their heads or hang by their hair or quiver under the tortures of gorilla-like devils and strange serpentine beasts, or whirl like Paolo and Francesca. And over all the agony, with beautiful serene face, floats the angel, clinging to the Cross, and the saints sit placid on their golden chairs, perhaps, as in that ecstatic prevision of Tertullian, finding their bliss enhanced by these wails of woe, as one's enjoyment of one's warm hearth is spiced by the howling of the winds about.

The mere ardour of life was immoral to the mediæval mind, as we may see from the celebrated anonymous frescoes of Il Trionfo della Morte in the Campo Santo of Pisa—as if a cemetery needed any enforcement of Death's triumph! But the opportunity is seized of besmirching "The Triumph of Life," and by way of prelude to the tomb and its terrors a gay cavalcade of hunters rides to the chase, with hound and horn, winding through a lovely landscape. Their horses are arrested by three open coffins on the roadside, precisely of the shape of horse-troughs, but containing corpses, apparently a king's, a priest's, and a layman's. The last is a mere skeleton; the others are fully robed and serpents curl spitefully about them. A stag, a rabbit, and a partridge rest serenely upon a little plateau, as if conscious there will be no danger to-day from these disconcerted sportsmen. A cowled monk holds out a long scroll to the leader of the chase, like an official presenting an address. Other holy hermits read ostentatiously beneath the trees outside their humble cottage, and one milks a quaint goat. As if the hermit were more immune from death than the hunter! Overhead hover fearful fire-breathing demons bearing beautiful women head downwards to their doom. Towards the centre of the entire picture, of which this forms but a half, sweeps Death, a sombre flying figure with a great scythe, whom cripples and the sorrowful invoke in vain; underneath are his slain, upon whose bodies swoop demons with long pitchforks and angels with long crosses, fighting furiously for the spoil, in a game of pull devil, pull angel. In one case the angel has gripped the arms, the devil the feet, and they tug and lug with wings distended to their fullest, every muscle a-strain; even if the angel succeeds, the racked ghost will have known the Inferno. Let us pray the poor soul may recover breath in the Hesperian garden, where sit the meek sainted playing on lutes and lyres or nursing pet doves and spaniels.

A companion fresco devotes itself to The Last Judgment. To the sound of angel-trumpets the dead rise from their coffins, to be marched right or left by stern sworded archangels, as the great arbiter—again in a surmounting oval—may determine. Haloed saints occupy a safe platform on high and watch the suppliant, panic-stricken sinners in the dock. Hell in many compartments takes half the picture, Satan throned at centre, a grisly Colossus, horned and fanged, and each compartment a chamber of horrors unspeakable, or a caldron of stewing sinners, most noteworthy of whom are the three arch-heretics of the fourteenth century, Mohammed, Anti-Christ, and Averroes (the last grown much less respectable since Dante put him with Plato). This composition—the heretics apart—is obviously on the general lines of Giotto's, which may be considered the archetype of all the Judgment pictures, and the crudity of the conception is apparent. It is a mere parody of earthly tribunals. In the hands of a Signorelli—as at Orvieto—the vigour of the technique dominates and sweeps away the naïveté. It is the sublimity of terror—

"Where the bright Seraphim in burning row
Their loud uplifted angel trumpets blow."

But this conventional and crowded rendering has always impressed me far less than Maso di Bianco's in S. Croce, where a solitary soul appears for judgment in a wild gorge under the throne of Christ, while two down-sweeping angels, blowing their trumpets perpendicularly, assist the awesomeness of the design. What a pity Michelangelo did not handle the theme with this massive simplicity, and give us one naked, shivering soul with the fierce light of judgment beating upon him, instead of the stereotyped arrangement of the Judge on high, the blessed on his right, the damned on his left, the rising dead at his feet, with Hell opening underneath! His colossal fresco, with its huddle of naked saints—to which the clothes provided by later Popes lent the last touch of gloom—is, with the possible exception of Tintoretto's Paradise, the dismallest picture in the world, and it is even worse placed than Tintoretto's stupendous canvas.

The angel Michael, whose scales weigh souls, must have been hard at work ere he could find enough good people to fill this Paradise. When I last peeped into it in the Palace of the Doges, it was conveniently on the floor, having been removed from its wall for repair, and, standing thus propped up in the centre of the Sala del Maggior Consiglio, it loomed even more gigantic than my recollection of it, filling half the vast hall and extending to the ceiling. Its precise dimensions, according to a buzzing attendant, were twenty-two metres broad by seven metres high. Here surely is the prize of prizes for the American millionaire. The largest picture in the world! Think of it! But, alas! a pauperised Government arrogantly clings to its treasures, forbids exportation. How smuggle it out? What railway carriage could hold it? How get it even across the Grand Canal to the station? What gondola, what barca, what vapore even could carry it? Perhaps a bridge of boats might be built, as for the passing of an army. And an army indeed it holds.

Tintoretto's Heaven is, in fact, congested beyond any hygienic standard. 'Tis a restless, jostling place, unpleasing and muddy in colour, where you are doomed to carry for ever the emblems of your life, where Moses must eternally uphold his Tables of the Law and St. George sport his armour, and martyrs shiver in perpetual undress. As usual, God the Father is an absentee Lord, and Christ and the Madonna—in equal authority, not with the woman subordinate, as in a Veronese in the same Sala—dominate the chaos of figures, flying, whirling, praying, playing, or reading. To see this Heaven is to be reconciled with Earth. Some parts of it are already destroyed, and I look forward to the day when it shall pass away with a great noise. Smaller but far more select is Tintoretto's impressionist Paradiso in the Louvre, with its rainbow swirls or celestial vortices, its curving sweeps of figures flying on clouds, only prosaic by its platform where Christ, the Madonna, and the greater saints sit like the distinguished persons at a public meeting. His Purgatorio in Parma is equally imaginative, a whirl of figures and wild cliffs and rugged, lurid, serpent-haunted chasms, down which angels plunge to bring up souls to the Madonna, who sits alone in her gloriole. Bartolommeo Spranger's Heaven—which may be seen in Turin—is a place where saintly companies link hands as in a child's game, while grimacing demons or snakes tear at sinners.

Palma Giovane tried to cover the entrance wall of the Sala dello Scrutinio of the Doge's Palace with an emulation of Tintoretto, but the main renown of his Last Judgment seems to rest on his humorous idea of putting his wife both into Heaven and Hell. The use of Hell to pay off private scores is not unique with Palma, and of course everybody can plead the precedent of Dante.

In another Venetian Paradise—that of Jacobello del Fiore—the symmetrical groups of haloed saints in blue and red and gold recall exactly the groups in the La Scala ballet. The Paradise in Botticelli's Assumption of the Virgin in the National Gallery is also somewhat geometric, though the empty lilied court below gives beautiful relief. Fra Bartolommeo's large faded fresco of The Last Judgment, in Florence, with its sworded archangel to greet the poor souls as they rise from their graves, is inspired by the Pisan fresco, and is less interesting than that of Fra Angelico, his fellow Dominican at San Marco, in whom we breathe a serener, clearer air, though his sweetness and finish accentuate again the intellectual naïveté. His series of little panels in the Accademia of Florence has a quaint originality, the Judge sitting over a mystic red and green wheel, with the blessed on either hand. Angels welcome newcomers or lament over the rejected, while demons poke spears into the damned. More conventional in composition is his large easel-picture in the same room—a miracle of detailed loveliness, except for the Hell, which is botched, as though unsuited to his artistic temperament. Indeed we know he made his devil hideous out of sheer dislike of the theme. The sheep are divided from the goats by a curious row of open graves resembling sky-lights. The Judge is superdominant, angels and babes hovering round him, the trumpeting angels at his feet. In the Paradise of flowers walk the saints in couples and companies; the sinners—in crowns, mitres, or mere caps—are driven Hellward at the points of a pitchfork into their respective circles, where some are eaten of the horrible horned Satan, some are eating one another, and others are gnawing their own bloody hands. There are sinners seething in pots, sinners starving at a laden table, sinners hung up, sinners holding their own heads in their hands. Demons like brown bears gnash white teeth, and in the north-north-east corner of Hell a capacious big-toothed gullet—horrible in its suggestion of more behind—is gulping down two red-headed wretches. In his Christ in Hades the gentle painter, following an apocryphal gospel, incarnates Hell in a demon crushed beneath its door.

In the Strozzi Chapel of S. Maria Novella the theme is repeated by the brothers Orcagna. Andrea took Paradise and suffused it with tender beauty, fitting it with row upon row of seraphim and saintly figures, whose serried symmetrical haloes suggest, however, a marshalling of saints for inspection; while Bernardo made of Hell a chart of ugliness—a compartmental chaos of strange fading horrors—fading though the Heaven has lasted. But it is not easy to get decorative beauty into the Inferno, especially when broken up into parishes of pain and not part of a complete Last Judgment such as that by Andrea single-handed in the same Chapel. In this last, angels carrying the cross and the thorns make a variant in the composition. In the Spanish Chapel of the same church The Way to Paradise is treated as of more concern to mortals than the nature of the goal, of which we get the merest peep; and perhaps the artist's own concern was Beauty, for the central pattern of the picture is woven by a procession on richly caparisoned horses winding round and round. Tranquilly beautiful are the figures at the Passion, even apart from the tender figure of Christ, whose halo hides the form of the decorative polished cross he bears.

The Paradise is, however, a Dominican Paradise, for this noble fresco on examination turns out to be a complicated allegory in glorification of the order, even including the pictorial pun or rebus of black-and-white dogs (domini canes), guarding the faithful sheep and worrying the heretical wolves. The Dominican Heaven has always a marked preference for Dominican dogma, as the Dominican Hell is particularly hospitable to rival forms of teaching. Incidentally this great anonymous painting is a social Mappamondo of the mediæval, including every type in Church and State from Pope to pauper; the vanities and pomps, the penances and renunciations. A lovely peace broods over this picture, as over all the Chapel. Hell does not disturb its restful walls, save as the mild Limbo to which Christ descends to redeem Adam, Noah, and other figures, proleptically haloed. He hovers majestically over the vague scene, carrying a red-cross flag over his left shoulder. It is only the demons who give grotesquerie to the picture, but they are unsurpassable. One of these baffled imps falls prostrate in the void, another is tearing his goatee beard, a third stands scowling, with folded wings, the hair of a fourth stands on end, a bristle of wires. This last demon is livid in hue; his fellows are more or less fiery.

Bronzino has dealt less happily, if less grotesquely, with the same theme, for to his later vision it was a good opportunity for studying the nude and the half-nude. But to follow out the theme of Christ in Hades would carry me too far. I must, however, refer to the touching conception of Christ rushing to the rescue: as in the picture by Andrea Previtali in which Christ is seen in a whirl of drapery with a streaming flag, pulling up an old woman and a girl. A large cross occupies the centre of this Limbo, to which cling or pray rescued nude figures, while St. John stands by with a smaller cross.

The after-world was rendered not only in painting, but in other art-media. In his famous pulpit in the Baptistery of Pisa Niccolò Pisano carved it in relief, imaginatively rendering the faces of the damned almost animal with sin. Byzantine art treated it in mosaic and enamel, in stone and bronze, while on the rich-jewelled Pala d'Oro of St. Mark's, Christ in Hades has called forth the craft of the goldsmith. An exhaustive study of eschatological æsthetics would include also the innumerable apotheoses and receptions in Heaven, would involve a comparison with Teutonic and other pictorial conceptions, and would range from the pious sincerities of the primitives to the decorative compositions of the decadents.

I do not know if any scholar has yet thus treated the genesis and evolution of these pictorial images. They certainly did not derive from Dante, for Dante's poem itself contains an allusion to a Florentine calamity, which we know to have been the collapse in 1304 of a wooden bridge over the Arno, holding spectators of a popular representation of the horrors of the Inferno.

Moreover—apart from the demons and chimæras dire on the old Etruscan tombs—fumblings at the theme exist in art prior to Dante, as, for instance, those rude bronze reliefs in the Byzantine manner on the doors of S. Zeno in Verona, which mark, as it were, the Bronze Age of the concept. These, I was assured, were ninth-century, but even dating them at the eleventh or twelfth—and the church contains frescoes as early—they were in time for Dante to have seen them when enjoying Can Grande's hospitality in Verona. His denunciation of Alberto della Scala for appointing his bastard as abbot of the monastery shows his interest in S. Zeno. In these rude bronzes Dante beheld the bare elements of that Hell which he furnished so handsomely. Here is already the giant fee-fi-fo-fum figure holding—O primeval irony!—a quaking monk. Here is the sinner upside down whose legs are disappearing within a caldron. Here also, in another bronze relief, is Christ in Limbo, haling figures out. Christ's halo is novel, consisting of three tufts, one sticking out on either side of his head, the other on top. It may interest the decadent to learn that there is also a relief of Salome dancing, in which she anticipates all the modern contortionists.

To pass back from the Bronze Age of the Last Judgment to the Stone Age, that fine old Lombardic cathedral of Ferrara, whose lateral façades date from 1135, shows in a lunette over one of them a stone relief of The Day of Judgment. Flanked by saints, "God's in his Heaven," holding the saved souls in his lap in a sort of sheet, while the devil in his Hell pokes up his busy fire and an acolyte shoves a sinner down a dragon's mouth. The Baptistery of Parma, a structure less ancient, but still antecedent to Dante, shows on its left portal three dead men coming out of their tombs, to be received by the angels or the executioner, according to the dictum of the Judge on high, who is nursing a saved soul. The guilty lean anxiously out of curious stone buildings, apparently awaiting their turn to be decapitated.

With such compositions existing in Italy, it seems supererogatory of M. Didron to have counted more than fifty French illustrations of the "Divine Comedy," before Dante, painted on church windows or sculptured on church portals, or for M. Lafitte to seek for Dante's inspiration in the western portal of Notre-Dame, which he must have seen during his stay in Paris.

Giotto, then, did not altogether originate his conception of the Judgment scene. Indeed, already in the alleged discourse of Josephus to the Greeks concerning Hades, we have a word-picture of the Hebrew Day of Judgment in which the souls of the just are marshalled to the right and the souls of the sinners to the left.

Dante may equally be exonerated from the crime of having originated these grotesque notions of the after-world, if he cannot be exonerated from the crime of corroborating them. These infantile images were made in the brains of fasting monks and terror-stricken sinners—for brains make day-dreams as well as nightmares—on a confused basis of the classic Hades and Tartarus and Elysium and the Egyptian after-world and the Hebrew Gehennah, supplemented by misapplied texts and misunderstood metaphors. They drew their appeal from that conflict 'twixt good and evil which every man felt raging in his own soul, and which made plausible the externalisation of these forces as angels and demons fighting for its possession.

But though the first sketch of the Christian Hell appears in literature as early as the apocryphal "Acts of St. Thomas," Dante may be said to have systematised these chaotic conceptions, drawn the chart of the Hereafter, and determined the scientific frontiers between Hell and Limbo, Purgatory and Paradise. His are the nine concentric circles of the Inferno, though Acheron and Minos, Charon and Cerberus, are borrowed from his guide and master; he is the sole discoverer and surveyor of the island-mountain of Purgatory, so precisely antipodal to Jerusalem, with its seven parishes corresponding to the seven deadly sins; his are the nine Heavens, ascending to the Beatific Vision, that is circumscribed by the thrice three orders of the angelic hierarchies. Nevertheless, marvellous as is the sustained imaginativeness of the achievement, his contribution to the stock of eschatological ideas is comparatively small. The vulgar imagination is quite capable of bodying forth these grimacing, horned demons, these imps with prongs and lashes, those swooping fiends, that heavy head-gear,—not unlike the English high hat in August— those fiery floods, those gibbering, wailing ghosts, those wretches immersed in ordure, those ghastly sinners munching each other, those disgustful stenches and itchings. Dante would not be remembered for such nursery horrors. Happily, he enriched the theme with finer imaginings. They meet us at the very threshold of the dolorous city in those neutral souls good enough neither for Heaven nor Hell; like the abdicating Pope Celestine V, neither rebels against God nor true to Him. Yet Dante almost spoilt his own conception by adding the material pains inflicted by wasps and hornets to their eternal nullity. Kipling, in his probably unconscious approximation to the idea in "Tomlinson," had a sounder instinct, though perhaps Ibsen's idea of returning Peer Gynt to the Button-Moulder hits the truer penology. Dante's touch is more satisfying when he pictures the doom of those who were sad in sunny air, and must now continue sad in the more appropriate surroundings of slime. Yet there is here a touch of the Gilbertian grotesque; a foreshadowing of the Mikado, whose "object all sublime" was "to make the punishment fit the crime." This suggestion is even stronger in the twenty-seventh canto, where Mohammed and the arch-heretics who provoked schisms are ripped and cleft from chin to forelock. Savagery, too, is met by savage punishment, as in the Ugolino episode.

There are a few inventions, indeed, beyond the vulgar imagination: the six-footed serpent that transmutes the sinner to its own form, a passage palpitating with Æschylean genius; the monstrous-paunched coiner, consumed with a terrible hate; the shore "turreted with giants"; the tears that cannot be shed. Nor could the vulgar—pre-occupied with fire—have conceived a Hell of ice, though Dante's Arctic circle is bettered in the Gospel of Barnabas preserved in an Italian MS., which compounds a Hell of fire and ice united by the Justice of God, "so that neither tempers the other, but each gives its separate torment to the infidel," and in Vondel's "Lucifer" the archfiend is condemned to

"The eternal fire Unquenchable, with chilling frosts commingled."

But neither the Dutch poet nor his contemporary, Milton, condescended to the fee-fi-fo-fum infantility of Dante's three-headed King of Hell, that fantastic fiend who holds in each of his mouths one of the three archetypal traitors, Judas, Brutus, and Cassius. And that Dante's "Judgment" was not considered "The Last" is shown by the popularity of Brutus—as a tyrannicide—in the Florence of the Medici. The beauty of the verse and the imaginative intensity alone render Dante's "Inferno" bearable. Translated into the images of Signorelli or Michelangelo—and these more truly than Botticelli were Dante's illustrators—the grossness of his "Inferno" leaps to the eye, while his finer imaginings are not capable of interpretation by brush or pencil.

The paradox of the "Divina Commedia," indeed, is that it lives less by its supernatural visionings, sombre and splendid as these occasionally are, than by its passages of the earth, earthy, when the world the poet has left behind breaks in upon the starless gloom of Hell or upon the too ardent radiancy of Paradise. Nor need I prove my case by the familiar episodes of Paolo and Francesca, and of Ugolino, though Dante's fame rests so largely upon them. Never was poem more terrestrial, more surcharged with the beauty and grossness of earth-life. The delicious touches of natural beauty, the splendid descriptions of sunrise and moonlight, the keen observation of animal and insect life, of starlings and doves, of storks and frogs, of falcons and goshawks, the pictures of the jousts at Arezzo, or of the busy arsenal of Venice, the homely similes painting indirectly the labours of ploughmen and shepherds, warriors and sailors, even the demeanour of dicers—this last Dante's sole approach to humour—it is by these that Dante will live when his Heaven and Hell are rolled up like a scroll. The sound of the vesper bell that touches the earthly pilgrim moves us more than all the celestial music of the Purgatory; the vision of beatific goodness, beside the lovely picture of the ancient virtue of Florence in the homely ages, is an airy nothing—one is more interested even to hear the ladies of the day rebuked for their low-necked dresses. The dazzling circles of Paradise leave us lethargic compared with the irrelevant intrusion therein of the lark's rapture of song or the earthly pain of exile.

"Tu proverai sì come sa di sale
Lo pane altrui, e com'è duro calle
Lo scendere e'l salir per l'altrui scale."

To prove how salt is others' bread, how hard the passage up and down others' stairs! How impotent all the laboured strivings to shadow forth the vision celestial compared with this touch of the terrestrial concrete! In truth Dante did not go "out of his senses," even in his most transcendental moments of inspiration. His five senses were all he had wherewith to obtain the raw material of his imaginings, and out of his sensations of touch and sight, of smell and taste and hearing, he wove both his Hell and his Heaven. The stored repugnances of mankind, the shudders and horrors at beasts and serpents, at bites and wounds and loathsome diseases, the dread of fire—he himself was condemned to be burnt alive—the chill of ice, the nausea of stinks and dizzying motions—these are the factors of his Hell, as the odour of flowers and incense, the shimmer of jewels, the sound of music, and the pains and pleasures of anticipation are the factors of his Purgatory. As for his Paradise, it is merely the sublimation of the philosophic Elysium Aristotle and Cicero had conceived before Christianity; his very ecstasy of Light is anticipated by Seneca.

Restlessness is a recurring image of doom with Dante—and perhaps his own wander-years of exile lent vividness to the onward drifting of the neutral spirits, the unrepose of the learned sinners, the eternal whirl of Paolo and Francesca. Yet there are moments in which Dante rises beyond his gross scale of punishments to a more spiritual plane.

"Thou art more punished in that this thy pride
Lives yet unquenched; no torrent, save thy rage,
Were to thy fiery pain proportioned full."

In addressing this observation to Capaneus, Virgil, says Dante, spoke in a higher-raised accent than ever before. In a less literal sense, it is indeed a higher accent: it is even the note of modern thinking, from Spinoza onwards. The wages of sin is—sin! It is probably even the note of an earlier and still more misunderstood Master. But this note is only heard once and faintly. The wages of sin is physical torture. But surely such a Hell is unjustly balanced by such a Heaven—all Platonic intellection, Plotinian ecstasy, and ethereal Light. If the wages of sin is physical torture, then the wages of virtue should be physical rapture. Dante's Hell requires Mohammed's Heaven, just as Christ's Heaven requires an immaterial Hell. For if the Kingdom of God is within you, the Kingdom of the Devil cannot be without. This thought broke dimly on Milton when, despite his material Hell, he wrote of Satan:

"But the hot Hell that always in him burns,
Though in mid-heaven. . . ."

Dante's Purgatory possesses, indeed, some of the material attractions a logical Heaven needs: it has all the makings of an Earthly Paradise not inferior to Addison's in his "Vision of Mirza." There are even great set pieces of painting, and much that might well tempt the soul to linger on its upward way.

The soul of the present critic is also tempted to seek superiority by preferring the Paradise to the Inferno. Alas! a law of psychology has ordained that pleasures shall be less exciting than tortures, and hence the Purgatory is far duller than the Inferno, while the Paradise is hopelessly swamped in sweetness and light. The splendid vision of the snow-white Rose—wonderful as poetry—retains little spiritual value under analysis, though the majestic passion of the close of the great poem almost carries up the spirit with closed eyes to this dazzling infinitude of Light and Love.

Read as a poem of earth, the "Divine" Comedy has for us a value quite other than Dante—in his political and prophetic passion—designed. What we see in it is the complete Mappamondo of the mediæval, a complete vision of the world, with its ethics, its philosophy and its science, as it reflected itself in the shining if storm-tossed soul of the poet, whose epic was alike the climax and the conclusion of the Middle Ages. No wonder the Italian quotes it with the finality of a Gospel text. For this epic is less of a people than of humanity. Though the Florentine background is of the pettiest—including even Dante's apologia for breaking a font in the church of St. John—it is really world-history with which the poem is concerned; not world-history as the modern conceives it, for Dante's Mappamondo held neither America nor China, neither Russia nor Japan, but that selected conceptual world—that autocosm—in which the cultured of his day lived and had their being: a world in which classic and chivalric legend had their equal part—as they have in the poetry of Milton—so that the very "Paradiso" could open with an invocation to Apollo! And this world-history is unified by being strung together on a moral plan, precisely as in the Hebrew Bible, Judas and Brutus finding themselves equally in Lucifer's avenging fangs. The flames of righteous indignation redeem the crude brimstone, and if we bleed for the sinners, the sins under chastisement are mainly those we would wish purged from the universe in the white flame of righteousness. Indeed, this great sensuous, sinful Tuscan, who went unscathed through the dolorous city, is a soul on fire. He is taken up to Heaven, like Elijah, but in the fiery chariot of his own ardour. His passion is the stars, visible symbol of beauty and infinity. Each of his three great sections ends with the very words. "The stars" shine again in that noble letter refusing the Republic's terms of pardon. "What!" cries the exile, "shall I not everywhere enjoy the sight of the sun and the stars?" "The love that moves the sun and the other stars" is, indeed, the great doctrine of the poem—its literal last word. How this love, "this goodness celestial, whose signature is writ large on the universe," is to be reconciled with the spirit that moves the flame and the other dooms, he does not explain. Though ever and anon his own tears of pity flow, the doctrine of eternal hopeless torture does not appal him; not even though, at the Day of Judgment, worse is in store, for the sufferers shall by then have subtilised their practised nerves for the final damnation. It does not disconcert him—any more than it disconcerts his great admirer, Michelangelo—that unbaptised infants and heathens whose only crime was chronological should sigh in Limbo, and that Adam and Noah, Abraham and Moses themselves, should need for their salvation the special descent of Christ. For all his sublimity, his passionate metaphysic insight into the Godhead, he falls below the homely Rabbis of the Talmud, who taught eight or ten centuries earlier, "The righteous of all nations have a share in the World-to-Come." Yet there are broken lights of this truth here and there.

"But lo! of those Who call, 'Christ, Christ,' there shall be many found In judgment, further off from Him by far Than such to whom His name was never known."

And the fine temper of the man is shown in his struggle against the pitiful obsessions of a provincial theology; in his gratitude towards the great Teachers of Antiquity, his reverence for whom anticipated the Renaissance, albeit the Greeks among them were probably known to him only in Latin translations. A Dante of the Renaissance—if such were possible—might have placed Aristotle and Plato in Paradise by interposition of a Christ loving his Gospel tongue. Bernardo Pulci did, indeed, place Cicero and sundry Roman heroes in Heaven. But even during the Renaissance Savonarola proclaimed that Plato and Aristotle were in Hell, and the best that Dante in his rigider century could do for them was to put them in a painless Limbo, which they perambulate "with slow majestic port," acquiring from their continuous earthly reputation grace which holds them thus far advanced, and which it seems not beyond all hoping may ultimately exalt them to bliss. And with Aristotle, the "maestro di color che sanno," walk not only Homer and Euclid, but his Mohammedan commentator, Averroes, and even mythical figures like Orpheus and Hector. A Christendom that had never altogether lost touch with the classical world—were it only by way of Virgil, mediæval saint and sorcerer—a Christendom whose philosophers found ingenious inspiration in Aristotle, could not easily relegate to the flames either the classical writers or their works. Classic literature and mythology made a second Bible, as the lore of chivalry and general history a third; indeed, these were the three great circles in which swam the world of the mediæval Mappamondo, the Biblical circle outermost and nearest to Heaven. Yet it was a bold stroke of tolerance on Dante's part to make Virgil his guide, chronology giving him no chance, as it gave with Statius, of a legendary conversion to Christianity. And this penchant for the great Pagans accentuates his intolerance to the great Christian heretics. But if Virgil himself was excluded from Heaven "for no sin save lack of faith"—Virgil who could not possibly have believed—if even the merits of those who lived before the Gospel, could not profit them because they had missed baptism, it is not surprising to find the Christian heretics collected in the ninth canto in burning sepulchres of carefully graduated temperatures. One wishes that they, rather than Farinata degli Uberti, had held their heads high, with a fine disdain foreshadowing Milton's Satan. How Socrates would have smiled over the perverted morality of the Christian poet, as we smile over the constricted foot of a Chinese lady! Despite the attempt of a recent writer to moralise his scheme of salvation, the best that can be said for Dante is that he probably followed Aquinas in holding that there is no positive pain in that absence of the divine vision which St. Chrysostom made the severest part of the punishment of the damned. But in tolerance as well as humour he falls far below the Ha-Tofet weha-Eden ("Hell and Paradise") of his Jewish friend and imitator, Immanuel. It is in vain that Émile Gebhart (in "L'Italie Mystique") points to his revolutionary liberalism in placing Ripheus the Pagan and Trajan, the Roman Emperor, in Paradise. These apparent exceptions only bring out his lack of tolerance and humour more vividly. For, though the Æneid describes the fallen hero, Ripheus, as "justissimus unus" among the Trojans and "the most observant of right," yet it is not by the simple force of his own goodness but by some complex operation of grace under which he believes in the Christ that has not yet been born, and even turns missionary, that he penetrates among the "luci sante." As for the Emperor Trajan, complexity is still worse confounded, for he—despite the title he had won of Optimus—must serve his time in hell, and is only popped into Paradise after being resuscitated, converted and baptized by St. Gregory four hundred years after his first decease. Thus both Ripheus and Trajan died Christians, Dante assures us gravely, not Gentiles as the world imagines; one believing in the Crucifixion that was to be, and the other in the Crucifixion that had been.

"Cristiani, in ferma fede
Quel de' passuri, e quel de' passi piedi."

With all Dante's stippling and geometric chart-drawing, his conception of the after-world is not really clear. The sinners are able to deliver long monologues, amid all their agony; they foreknow things terrestrial, exactly like the Manes of Paganism; they quarrel with one another; there are even high jinks in Hell, which according to Burckhardt show an Aristophanic humour. (But then Burckhardt is a German.) Moreover, a certain free will reigns. The undefined powers of the demons import into Dante's excursion through their dominions a deal of breathlessness and terror from which one should be exempt who travels with a "safe-conduct" acquired by the interposition of powerful personages in Paradise.

Such are the nebulous rings hovering round Dante's Mappamondo Infernale. But the circles of his Mappamondo Terrestre are clear and resplendent. 'Twas within the illumination of these circles—unnecessarily narrowing though they were—that the Middle Ages, and even Ages later, built their sublime cathedrals, painted their lovely Madonnas, and wrote their great poems. For though doubtless much sacred art is merely splendid sensuous decoration, and some even of that which is indubitably spiritual may have been the work of free-thinking and free-living artists, it remains true that the Dark Ages had a light which electricity cannot replace.

But is our modern Mappamondo as scientific as we think it? Can we girdle it with no circles amid which to sail securely again through the infinities?

ST. GIULIA AND FEMALE SUFFRAGE

Vastly strange are the wanderings of saints and pictures. When a Magnificent One ordered for his gilded sala a Madonna—even with himself and his consort superadded—he was, for aught he knew, helping to decorate Hampton Court in Inghilterra, or the mansion of a master-butcher in undiscovered and unchristened Pennsylvania. And when a saint was born, an equal veil hid the place of his death or of his ultimate patronage. The fate of St. Francis, to live and die and be canonised in his birthplace, was of the rarest. His pendant, St. Dominic, came from Old Castile, and was buried in Bologna.

It is no surprise, therefore, to find St. Giulia, of Carthage, in possession of Brescia, though I must confess that until I stumbled upon the frescoes consecrated to her in the church of S. Maria del Solario her name and fame were unknown to me. Luini painted these frescoes, the sacristan said, though the connoisseurs omit to chronicle them and will doubtless repudiate the attribution. The date of 1520 appended to the somewhat free and easy Latin epigraph beneath does indeed bring them well within Luini's working period, but their authenticity interests me less than the story they tell.

St. Giulia, it would appear, was born in the seventh century of a noble Carthaginian family, and was endowed with holy learning and every spiritual grace.

"Stemate præsignis Carthagine nata libellos
Docta sacros, anima, corpus gestuque pudica,
Curatu patiens, humilis, jejuniaque pollens."

Such a maiden could only become an apostle to the heathen. Accordingly, we see her arrive at Corsica in a boat with neither oar nor sail, and start praying to the true God. A good-natured citizen warns her of the risks of such heresy, and the kindly ruler of Corsica himself adjures her to discretion, his monitions being emphasised by a man with an axe who stands behind him. But holding her prayer-book, and already crowned with her halo, she prays on. The next fresco shows the inevitable sequel. She is hanging by her hair to the bough of a pretty tree, while an executioner prods at her bleeding breasts with a three-pronged fork, though his head is turned away, as if he were not over-proud of his job. The kindly ruler, however, continues his remonstrances. In the distance a small, dim angel wings his way to her. Finally, she is stretched on a cross, and two ruffians batter her with massive clubs, but angels hold the palm and wreath over her head, and the Dove flies towards her. These celestial visions are a true interpretation and externalisation of the psychology of the martyr: these alone could support her. In our own day the visions of our martyrs are less concrete; they die for some far-seen ideal of Justice or Freedom, and this suffices to sustain them in Spanish prisons or under the Russian knout.

But what is peculiarly noteworthy in the story of Giulia is the status of woman in the Dark Ages and under the Catholic Church. St. Giulia appears to enjoy as great a roving licence as St. Augustine, her fellow-citizen in Carthage and "The City of God." She is not considered unsexed, nor does her teaching rank below man's, and she is canonised equally with the male. In fact, in leaving the home-nest to preach to the heathen, she is only following the model of Thekla in the Apocryphal "Acts of St. Paul," whose story, though it was forged by a pious elder, is none the less proof of woman's position in that highest of all ancient spheres, Religion. "I recommend unto you Phœbe, our sister," says the misogynous St. Paul himself (Romans xvi), "for she hath been a succourer of many and of myself also. Greet Priscilla and Aquila, my helpers in Christ Jesus; who have for my life laid down their own necks."

It is, indeed, doubtful whether Christianity would ever have been established but for the courage and companionship of women. I feel sure they tidied up the catacombs and gave a feeling of home to the crypts and caves. "It was the women who spread Christianity in the family," says Harnack. St. Augustine's father was a heathen; it was his mother, Monica, who taught him to pray. The Virgin Martyr, like Santa Reparata of Florence, or St. Catherine of Alexandria, is a stock figure of the Roman calendar. As in all great movements, differences of station were forgotten, and Blandine, the servant-girl of Lyons, played as majestic a part as the royal-blooded St. Catherine, whose wheel of martyrdom finds such quaint perpetuation as a firework.

Popular imagination added the Madonna to the Trinity as a sort of female representative. In Tintoretto's Paradise, as I have already noted, she figures as authoritatively as the Christ, and in a picture at Vicenza, attributed to Tiepolo, she stands on the world, crushing the snake with her foot.

Her companions were usually divided in sex and united in glory. Luca della Robbia, in his charming relief in the cathedral of Arezzo, scrupulously places one male and one female saint on her either hand, and even one male and female angel: doubtless had cherubs possessed sex possibilities, his cherubs too would have been impartially distributed. In the Accademia of Florence, Cimabue's Madonna is entirely surrounded by female saints, though a few males loom below her throne; Giotto's shows a female surplus; Bernardo Daddi's redresses the balance. Fra Angelico gives us Jesus carried to the Tomb by nine women to four men.

Italian art is full of symmetrical paradises of sex-equality, and if a church was decorated with male saints down one aisle, they would be scrupulously balanced by female saints along the other. An old Byzantine Basilica of Ravenna, which displays twenty-two virgins arrayed against thirty saints of the dominant sex, first set me wondering whether, since the Dark Ages, woman has not gone back in Christendom instead of forward. Here at least was the atmosphere for the legend, if not for the reality, of a Pope Joan, whereas at the period in which I first opened my eyes upon the world and woman, she appears to have become reduced to an absolute industrial dependence upon her lord like the fifteenth-century chicken in Giambattista della Porta's "Book of Natural Magic." For according to the delightful recipe (cited by Corvo) for inducing affection towards you in a chicken, you must—before it has its feathers—"break off its lower beak even to the jaw. Then, having not the wherewithal to peck up food, it must come to its master to be fed."

I might cite in proof of woman's retrogression since the Dark Ages the glorification of womanhood through "The Divine Comedy," but the Italian poet's translation of life into literature is, I fear, no more legal evidence of the real status of woman in the Middle Ages than her chivalrous deification at the hands of the Germanic or Provençal poets is a proof that she was treated even as an equal of her worshippers. Dante's unknown Beatrice sounds like a woman who was snubbed by her husband and brothers. But Matilda, who plays second fiddle to her, and who is equally drawn by Dante as a mild flower-culling "bella Donna" was in reality the warrior Countess of Tuscany, and the fact that Dante feminises and floralises her shows that he had no real respect for feminine dominance in the actual shapes it took in life, and that he was only prepared to idealise woman on condition of her conforming to his ideal.

The scholars and commentators who have always been so puzzled at the metamorphosis of Matilda have forgotten man's tendency to break off woman's beak, whether in reality or in imagination. But even if Preger be correct in identifying Dante's Matilda, not with the armoured Amazon of Tuscany, but with Mechtilde, the nun, whose mystic visions are the flowers she culls, it remains true that Dante's ideal was never the "Virago," a title of honour which was inscribed on her tomb, and which even at the epoch of the Renaissance implied nothing but praise. The word may serve to remind us that there is no sharp bisection of qualities between the sexes.

Matilda was, in fact, a sufficient refutation in herself of the notion that there is a rigid division between the qualities of men and women. Such a difference as is implied does, indeed, exist, but it is between men and men, and between women and women, as well as between men and women, and the popular nomenclature, which calls certain women mannish and certain men effeminate, recognises the possibility of deviation from the normal. Indeed, considering that both parents affect their child, the attempt to breed a special feminine psychology, immune from politics and fighting, must be perpetually thwarted by the criss-cross action of heredity, as upon the daughters of warriors and statesmen. Matilda—sired by the Magnificent Monster, Boniface—was a man in ten thousand. She led her own armies. She patronised learning and founded the law schools of Bologna. If she kept her husbands in subjection, casting off one after the other, she had none of the vices of the male despot; indeed, her second marriage-contract stipulated only a sexless union. There was nothing, indeed, except these vices in which she ranks below the Magnificent Monsters who preceded her in the lordship of Lucca or Lombardy. I must admit that the Countess of Tuscany fell under the influence of her spiritual director (as the Male Magnificent falls under the influence of his unspiritual directress), and that she used her power, and her treasure, as it is feared women will, to bolster up the Church; in fact, she, with her mother Beatrice, attended the Council of Rome in 1074, at which investiture by lay hands was declared illegal, and hers was the Castle of Canossa, to which Henry IV came to abase himself before the Pope. And that dubious temporal power of the Pope's might not have come into such solid being had she not left her possessions to the See of Rome, and thus practically founded the States of the Church. This, of course, is the secret of her high position in the earthly paradise of the Purgatory. But, after all, religious zeal is not a female monopoly, and even Bloody Mary could not hold a candle to Torquemada.

Catherine of Siena exercised an equally critical influence upon the fortunes of the Papacy and upon European history when she persuaded Gregory XI to move the Papal seat back from Avignon to Rome; a mission in which Rienzi had failed a generation earlier. Catherine, for all her ecstasies and self-scourgings, had far more common sense than the male mystics.

It was in allowing for such divergences from the normal that the Dark Ages surpassed our electric-lit era, whose logic confounds the optional with the compulsory, and the individual with the general. It was not pretended that every woman can or must be a warrior, but she who had military genius was not debarred from developing it. It was not claimed that every woman can or must be a saint, but St. Clara stood equal with St. Francis, and St. Catherine of Siena with St. Dominic. And at the Renaissance Boccaccio devotes a book to celebrated females, and Michelangelo writes most humble love-sonnets to the poetess, Vittoria Colonna (whose Rime still sell, and who unlike Matilda stood for religious reform). Vittoria's noble classic head, especially as seen helmeted in Michelangelo's design, suggests a very Minerva, and from various quarters we hear of the political woman, the learned woman, the patroness of the arts, and the female physician, while at the foot of the staircase of Padua University stands a statue of a lady Professor, a happier Hypatia. I forget if this is Lucrezia Cornaro, who was made a Doctor of this University and a member of so many learned societies throughout Europe, but no enumeration of Italian heroines should omit her brilliant ancestress, Caterina Cornaro, Queen of Cyprus, whose court at Asolo was one of the centres of the Renaissance.

"The education given to women in the upper classes," says Burckhardt, the learned historian of "The Renaissance in Italy," "was essentially the same as that given to men. . . . There was no question of 'women's rights' or female emancipation, because the thing in itself was a matter of course. The educated woman no less than the man strove naturally after a characteristic and complete individuality."

When one remembers the struggle in nineteenth century England for the higher education of women, and particularly the desperate resistance to their studying and practising medicine, one realises the fallacy of expecting melioration from the mere movement of time. There is no automatic progress. What is automatic is retrogression, so that the price even of stability is perpetual vigilance.

But what has St. Giulia, born at Carthage and crucified in Corsica, to do with Brescia? I have already pointed out the free trade in saints, by which they were liable to posthumous export. St. Giulia's body was transported from Corsica by Desiderio, a noble Brescian, who ascended the Longobardian throne in 735. She was placed in the church dedicated to St. Michael, the patron saint of the Longobardi, whom she ousted in 915, from which date the Church was known as St. Giulia's. A Nunnery of S. Giulia had existed from about 750, and remained in being for over a thousand years, till its suppression in 1797 by the inevitable Napoleon. Coryat, who visited it in 1608, describes it as having been in time past "a receptacle of many royall Ladies." It is now a Museum of Christian Art, and there I saw St. Giulia depicted in sculpture by Giovanni Carra, her figure nude to the waist and stretched on a real wooden cross with real nails in her hands and feet. Alas for Christian Art!

To-day our St. Giulias, in revolt against a social order founded on prostitution and sex-inequality, demand political rights as leverage for a nobler society, and, despite the advice of kindly Rulers, they are as ready as in the seventh century to be martyred for their faith, though they have replaced the passivity of St. Giulia by measures of aggression. Guariento foresaw the modern militant type when he drew those charming female angels with red and gold shields and long lances, and wings of green and gold, who stand on clouds—"suffragette" seraphs, they seem to me. You may see a battalion of them in the Museo Civico of Padua, filling a whole corridor, like a procession in the lobby at Westminster. One of these fair warriors trails by a cord a black demon with two quills like white horns, doubtless some literary Cabinet Minister. Another weighs two souls on scales, and Female Suffrage does indeed weigh men's souls in the balance, to find them mostly wanting. For of all forms of modern vulgarity, I deem nothing more dreadful than the scoffing callousness towards the sufferings of the "Suffragettes." They are only self-inflicted, we are told, as if this was not their supreme virtue. That in this age of blatant materialism women should still show that they possess souls is wondrous comforting to the idealist, tempted to believe that the fount of living waters had run dry, and that Giulia's only travels were now made by motor-car to smart country houses.

There is nothing which at first sight seems more puzzling than the wickedness of good people. For it has often been said that the truly devout and respectable Christians are the very ones who would crucify Christ afresh if he appeared again, as indeed Arnold of Brescia, who had a touch of his spirit, was crucified by Emperor, Pope, and Church. And St. Bernard, the inspirer of the Second Crusade to recover the dead bones of Christ, played a leading part in hounding him down, as the Franciscans played a leading part in hounding down Savonarola.

Now why was St. Bernard—that santo sene who was chosen by Dante to induct him into the last splendours of the Paradise, and whose noble hymns to Jesus still edify the faithful—so blind to the divine aspects of his victim? And why is it that the citizens of Ferrara, whose excellent statue and eloquent tribute to their illustrious townsman Savonarola faced my hotel window, could not be trusted not to stone their next prophet in a cruder sense of the words?

A converse question will conduct us to the answer. Why is the hooligan in the gallery of the theatre ever the chief friend of virtue? Why is the wife-bruiser the most fervid applauder of the domestic sentiment? Because the man in the gallery looks down on the tangle of life like the god his name implies: he sees it in as clear perspective as the aeronaut sees the network of alleys through which the pedestrian blunders; the plot is straightened out for him, the villain duly coloured, virtue in distress plainly marked by beauty and white muslin, and through no mists of prejudice or interest or passion he beholds the great outlines of right and wrong. 'Tis to the credit of human nature that, confronted with the bare elementals of ethics, and freed from egoistic bias, the human conscience, even the conscience most distorted in life, reacts accurately and returns a correct verdict with the unfailingness of a machine. This it is that preserves the self-respect of the blackest of us, this capacity of ours for seeing our neighbours' sins, which is the chief bulwark of public virtue. Wherefore, could St. Bernard have seen Arnold of Brescia as history sees him, or as a dramatist of insight would have drawn him, St. Bernard would have been the first to be horrified at St. Bernard's behaviour. But a Saint, no more than a hooligan, is free from passions, interests, and prejudices of his own, especially an ecclesiast and a theologian and a founder of monasteries. Wilful and obstinate as are all the saints of my acquaintance, the most domineering are the clerical. For all St. Bernard's genius and holiness, he could not endure a rival point of view. By him, and not by this interloping Italian monk, this pupil of the critical Abélard, must the world be turned to righteousness; nay the heresies of Abélard himself—"who raves not reasons"—must be condemned by the Council of Sens.

St. Bernard, if he lived to-day, would write the life of Arnold of Brescia with holy horror at his tragic fate, and to-morrow, when the passions and mists of to-day are cleared away, some future Asquith will find a fresh stimulus to rebellion against the Peers in the noble sufferings of some St. Giulia of the Suffrage.

ICY ITALY: WITH VENICE RISING FROM THE SEA

I

Peccavi. I have painted Italy, as others use, in sun-colour solely. My pen has been heliographic. That were worthy of the tourist who knows Italy only in her halcyon season. 'Tis the obsession of the alliterative image of the Sunny South, overriding one's historic memories—stories of the Po frozen over from November to April, of penitents standing barefoot in the snow, bitter adventures of mediæval brides brought tediously to their lords across icy, wind-swept ways in a sort of Irish honeymoon in the days before trains de luxe; nay, this Platonic concept swamps even the Aristotelian experience. For I have seen Florence in a London fog and Venice in a Siberian snowfall. I have seen St. Mark's Square turned into a steppe, without pigeons, without pleasure-pilgrims, snow-muffled, immaculate, bleak, given over to raw-knuckled scrapers and shovellers, knee-deep in crumbling hummocks, or pushing snow-heaped wheelbarrows towards the providential water-ways, the snow-crusted Campanile towering over the desolate glacial plain like the North Pole of childish fancy. Yea, and on the water-ways floated—O horror of desecration—white gondolas! Nature, like some vulgar millionaire, had defied the sumptuary edict consecrated by immemorial tradition, and, amazed as the Australian pioneer who first beheld black swans, I watched these white gondolas gliding along the swollen canals. And I recall Bologna in a blizzard—a snowfall so persistent that it closed the Pinacoteca by the curious method of solidly overlaying the skylight of the main Gallery and rendering the pictures invisible. It was a festa for the janitors, a holiday fallen from heaven. In the Piazza Nettuno the big fountain was snowed over, and the cab-drivers sat under great hoary umbrellas that had hitherto been green, their cabs looking like frosted cakes. A white hearse passed still whiter. The snow slashed its way even under the colonnades, and formed a slippery coating of ice on their pavements. Bran, scattered copiously in these arcades and at all the street-crossings, maintained a feeble colour-fight against the all-pervading white.

There is an icy Italy more boreal than Britain, inasmuch as less equipped against winter. For the native, too, partakes of the Platonic fallacy, and because his cold season is briefer than his warm, and oft infused with a quickening radiance, he shrugs it out of existence, especially when Carnival invites to al fresco conviviality. The beggar, indeed, recognises the winter, as becomes a practical professional man, and squats at the church-porch with his private pan of burning charcoal; but the more irresponsible burgher, with his stone floors, and his stoveless, chimneyless rooms, treats winter as an annual exception, calling for improvised measures. He is an æstival animal that builds for the summer, though his brigand-cloak, whose left fold is so sardonically thrown over his right shoulder, betrays to the scientific observer its prosaic origin as the throat-protector of an Arctic creature. Of late, under the pressure of foreign finance, the better hotels have veined themselves with steam-pipes. But the steam rises late, and the pipes are only hot when the guest has departed.

Never have I seen the pretence of perpetual summer carried further than at Rimini, where in a blinding snowstorm, when every narrow archaic street was bordered with four-foot mounds of dirty snow, and the traffic was limited to donkey-carts dragging snow through the Porta Aurea to pitch it into the river, the congealing cabmen sat all day on their powdered boxes cheerfully crying in competitive chorus—

every time they caught a glimpse of me—"To San Marino? To San Marino?" That little Republic—one of the last political curios left, like a fly in amber, in modern Europe—is a drive of many hours, even when "the white road to Rimini" is a shimmering sun-path, yet there was no suspicion of pleasantry in the cabmen's eagerness to crawl through the niveous morass. They seriously expected me to set forth on this summer expedition, with at most the carriage closed against the driving flakes. It sorted better with my humour to plough afoot over the muffled Boulevard to the new Rimini which has grown out of the old rotting Rimini of Cæsar and the Malatestas.

For there is a sham Rimini as well as a real Rimini—one of those toadstools of cities which flourish so rankly in our century of comfort. This is the Lido—an Italian Ostend, sacred to modern villas, mammoth hotels, bathing establishments, restaurants, the surgy shore tamed into a Parade for parasols. There is a staring, many-windowed, many-balconied Grand Hotel, crowned by two baroque domes, with busts on its façade and vases at its corners tapering up into rods. There is a little Lawn-Tennis Club-Bar and a big Casino, with a restaurant terrace back and front. There are pretentious Palazzini. There is a huddle of flaring houses, recalling the grotesque "new architecture" of Madrid, and a large uncouth hydropathic establishment in terra-cotta, and a long row of green bathing-huts.

Perhaps the profoundest observation of Dickens in Italy was that the marvellous quartette of buildings outside the life of Pisa—the Cathedral, the Campo Santo, the Baptistery, and the leaning Tower—is like the architectural essence of a rich old city, filtered from its prosaic necessities. Of the Lido of Rimini (and of its likes) it may be said that they are the architectural essence of a rich new city, filtered of all spiritual and poetical values.

But the Lido I saw was purged of all this vulgarity, buried under stainless snow, which lay deep and virgin over every street and grassy space, and shrouded every flaunting structure in primeval purity. The Parade was blotted out, restored to Nature, and deep drifts of snow defended it from re-invasion. The Casino lay forsaken, wrapped in the same soft spotless mantle, the dual stone steps leading to its twin drinking-terraces transformed into frozen cascades, its central gates uselessly guarded by blanched barbed wire. Desolate was even the great garage, with its cheap fresco of our modern goddess in the car, her flamboyant robe turned ermine. Beyond the buried Parade, the Adriatic rolled in sullenly, scarce visible save by a gleaming line of surf that lit up a narrow riband of its foreground; all but the breaking wave was hidden by a wild whirl of flakes that misted sea and sky into a grey nullity. Throughout the whole pleasure-city not a dog prowled nor a cat slunk nor a bird fluttered; not a footstep profaned the splendour of its snow. Its myriad casement-eyes were closed in heavy sleep; not a shutter open, not a blind raised. It was a city hibernating like some monstrous Polar animal. Not a few pleasure-cities thus abate their vitality in the winter, but so absolute a dormitation I have never witnessed. It seemed incredible that with the Spring it would stir in its sleep, it would shake the snow off its lubberly limbs, loose its gay swarm of butterfly-parasols. How could that frost-bound terrace ever ring again with the clink of glasses and the tinkle of laughter? How could bathers ever again lie basking on that frigid strand? No, it was a dead city I saw, a city overwhelmed by a new ice-age. And the seas and lands that radiated from this snowy centre were freezing too, as science had foretold; swiftly the deadly chill was spreading through every vein and artery of the nipped earth, curdling its springs and coagulating its vast oceans and crusting over even its petty oases of continents with thick-ribbed ice in which a rare microscopic rotifer alone preserved a germ of vitality. The Arctic and Antarctic zones expanded towards each other, like two blind walls closing in on life, and with a clash of giant icebergs in a biting equatorial blast, the last rift of green earth and blue water was blotted out. And now the globe was spinning again in a glacial void, as unconscious of the absence of its skin-parasites as it had been of their presence. Fated for fresh adventures and new cosmic combinations, the planet rolled its impassive whiteness through the dumb heavens. But mortals had put on mortality, and of all the haughty hopes and splendid dreams of man there remained zero. Earth, his cradle and his pasture, was become his frigidarium and his cemetery, and the snow fell silently over the few faint traces of his passing. His million, million tears had been frozen into a few icicles.

II

And there is an ugly Italy, an Italy veiled by the blue heaven, but revealing itself under sullen sunless skies in all its naked hideousness.

Nothing could be more unlike the popular conception of Italy than the environs of the Carthusian Monastery of Pavia in mid-February. Slushy roads about two yards wide, here and there encumbered with fragments of brick and stone, and everywhere bordered by heaps of snow. By one side of the road runs a narrow ice-bound irrigation canal, geometrically straight, across which rises the high, bare, dreary endless wall of blank brick surrounding the monastery. On the other hand stretch the vast fields with leafless thin trees. It was of this region that Jehan d'Auton wrote when Pavia was taken by the French: "Truly this is Paradise upon earth." Even allowing for the flowery meadows and running springs of the end of the fifteenth century, the worthy Benedictine could have found fairer Paradises nearer Paris. Much of Northern Italy is still monotonous marshland. Over the bald brick wall of Mantua, nine feet thick, that backs the Piazza sacred to Virgil, I gazed one morning at a dismal swampy lake, a couple of barges, a factory chimney, and spectral, leafless stumps of trees, the brownish soil of the lake showing through the dead sullen water, a ghost of sun hovering over rows of pollarded planes. Here, methought, had Virgil found a suggestion for his Stygian marsh. I would not say a word against Mantua itself, which is most lovable, with side-canals that might be Venetian, and ever-flowing taps and old arches, arcades and buildings. But from Mantua to Modena I saw naught but ugly brown grass over flat lands, with pollarded elms and vines stretched from tree to tree. Here and there a little canal relieved the dismal plain. Near Modena a few poplars appeared. A team of lovely oxen drawing a cart gave the landscape its one touch of beauty.

Rimini proper is picturesque enough, with its Porto Canale full of small barques with tall masts. But between it and Ravenna, what desolation! Outside the town the gaunt ruins of the Malatesta Castle—a bare wall and a bare squarish rock—were the prelude to the same bare snowy plains, the same little pollarded elms, varied by tall skeleton poplars. Once a copse of firs, bowed down by snow, broke the white flatness. Near Classe, famous for Sant' Appolinare, the waste became even marshier, sparse twigs of desolate shrubs alone peeping through the white blanket. Nearer Ravenna a few signs of life appeared, a dead cottage, or a living hovel, or a few spectral trees, or a brick bridge over an ice-laden river. On such a light brown marsh specked with stagnant pools the modern Italians have put up hoardings with advertisements of cognac. A little further East their remote progenitors put up Venice!

Never was there so apparently hopeless a site as those islands of the lagoons, preserved from malaria only by a faint pulse of the "tideless, dolorous midland sea." How so marvellous a city rose on the wooden piles of the refugees, how out of so dire a necessity they made so rare a beauty and so mighty a force, was always a puzzle to me till I read that these fugitives before the Lombard Conquerors were Romans! Then it all leapt into clearness. Venice is Rome in the key of water! The same indomitable racial energy that had built up Rome and the Roman Empire built up Venice and the Venetian Empire. Hunted from Padua, the Romans are able to express themselves in water as powerfully as in earth—to create a new empire in Italy and the East, and build a mighty fleet, and crush the Turks, and hold the carrying trade of the world, and for six centuries keep the Adriatic as a private lake. And in this new Empire they are touched by the shimmering spell of water to new creations of joyous colour on canvas, to fairy convolutions in marble, and a church that rises as lightly as a sea-flower. For here all that is sternly Roman

"Doth suffer a sea-change
Into something rich and strange."

But let us not forget that despite her seven hills Rome also began as a pile-village, and that the Campagna is of the same marshy character as the soil around Venice. I have more faith in Goethe's intuition that Rome was built up by herdsmen and a rabble than in the thesis, expounded by Guglielmo Ferrero at Rome's last birthday celebration, that it was the carefully chosen site of a colony from Alba, with Romulus and Remus in their traditional rôles. For though her seven hills enabled Rome to keep her head above water, they did not enable her to keep her feet dry. The Forum Augusti was anciently swamp and became a swamp again in the Middle Ages, and once some earlier form of gondola plied between the Capitol and the Palatine Hill. Thus the races who hailed from Rome had water in their blood, and the instinct to build on piles. It is a strange instinct which races have preserved and obeyed—in the foolish human fashion—even on land that was high and dry. What wonder if it survived in latency in these ex-Romans! Yes, Venice was Rome in the key of water, as Rome was Venice in the key of earth. And the Roman Church—is she not Rome in the key of heaven? Is it not always the same racial mastery that confronts us, the same instinct for dominance? Does the Church not hold the after-world as Rome held the ancient world, does she not own the lake of fire as the Doges owned the Adriatic? Drive Rome from her throne on the hills and she builds up her pedestal again on sea-soaked piles: hound her from the lagoons, and of a few acres around the piazza of St. Peter she makes the seat of a sovereignty even more boundless and majestic.

Hardly had I written this when I opened by hazard my first edition of Byron's "The Two Foscari" (1821), and was startled to read in his appendix as follows: "In Lady Morgan's fearless and excellent work upon 'Italy' I perceive the expression of 'Rome of the Ocean' applied to Venice. The same phrase occurs in 'The Two Foscari.' My publisher can vouch for me that the tragedy was written and sent to England some time before I had seen Lady Morgan's work, which I only received on the 16th of August. I hasten, however, to notice the coincidence and to yield the originality of the phrase to her who first placed it before the public." Byron goes on to explain that he is the more anxious to do this because the Grub Street hacks accuse him of plagiarism. But turning to the tragedy itself, I find that Byron has rather plagiarised me than the admirable "Gloriana," for her phrase might be a mere metaphor, whereas Marina observes explicitly:

"And yet you see how from their banishment
Before the Tartar into these salt isles,
Their antique energy of mind, all that
Remain'd of Rome for their inheritance,
Created by degrees an ocean-Rome."

But Byron's over-anxiety to disavow originality was due to the morbid state of mind induced by the aforesaid hacks, one of whom had even accused him of having "received five hundred pounds for writing advertisements for Day and Martin's patent blacking."

"That accusation," says Byron, "is the highest compliment to my literary powers which I ever received." I can only say the same of Byron's plagiarism from myself.

But Byron need not have been so apologetic to Lady Morgan, for 'twas the very boast of Venice to be "the legitimate heir of Rome," whose Empire Doge Dandolo re-established in that Nova Roma of Constantinople with whose art and architecture her own is so delectably crossed.

THE DYING CARNIVAL

Carnival! What a whirling word! What a vision of masks and gaiety, militant flowers and confetti! Not farewell to meat, but hail to merriment! Never, in sooth, does Italy show so earthly as when, bidding adieu to the flesh and the world, she enters into the contemplation of the tragic mystery of the self-sacrifice of God. And yet in this grossness of popular rejoicing lies more faith than in the frigid pieties of the established English Church. Even the brutalities and Jew-baitings that marked the old Roman carnival, even the profane parodies of the Mass, sprang from a naïve vividness of belief. Parody is merely the obverse side of reverence, and 'tis only when you do not believe in your God that you dare not make fun of Him or with Him. The gargoyled gutter is as characteristic of the cathedral as the mystic rose-window. Our revivals of miracle plays are performed in an atmosphere of glacial awe, which was by no means the atmosphere of their birth. This sort of reverence is too often faith fallen to freezing-point. We remove our sense of humour as we take off our slippers at alien mosques.

It was when faith was at its full—near the year 1000—and in connection with the Christmas season, that the Patriarch of Constantinople instituted the Feast of Fools and the Feast of the Ass, travestying the most sacred persons and offices. The Lord of Misrule is no heathen deity, but a most Christian majesty; and King Carnival is the spiritual successor of the old King of Saturnalia, whether Frazer be correct or not in attributing to him the direct succession. For the truly religious the carnival is necessary to the sanity of things. It is an expression of the breadth and complexity of the Cosmos, which would otherwise be missing from the Easter ritual. The God of the grotesque is as real as the God of Gethsemane and the Cosmos cannot be stretched on a crucifix. It bulges too oddly for that. And it is this grotesque side of life that finds quasi-religious expression in the Carnival processions, with their monsters known and unknown to Nature, with their fanciful hybrids and quaint permutations of the elements of reality. Humanity herein records its joyous satisfaction and sympathy with that freakish mood of Nature which produced the ornithorhynchus and the elephant, and shaped to uncouthness, instead of to symmetry and beauty. Alas! I fear humanity is only too acquiescent in these deviations of the great mother into the grotesque; the folk-spirit runs more fluently to gross pleasantry and comic tawdriness than to the Beautiful, and many a Carnival procession is a nightmare of concentrated ugliness.

The suspicion takes me that our St. Valentine's Day, so dominatingly devoted to grotesque caricature, and so coincident with the Carnival period, is really the Catholic Carnival in another guise and that prudish Protestantism has entertained the devil unawares.

But the Carnival—like St. Valentine's Day—is dying. It is more alive in the ex-Italian Riviera than in Italy proper. I have a memory of a Carnival at Siena which consisted mainly of one imperturbable merry-maker stumping with giant wooden boots through the stony alleys. A Carnival at Modena has left even less trace—some dim sense of more crowded streets with a rare mask. At Mantua, too, there was no set procession—children in fancy dress, with a few adult masqueraders, alone paid fealty to the season. At

Bologna the last night of Carnival was almost vivacious, and in the sleety colonnades branching off from the Via Ugo Bassi there was quite a dense crowd of promenaders defying the bitter wind, while muffled groups, with their coat-collars up, sat drinking at the little tables. There were some children, fantastically pranked, attended by prosaic mothers, there was a small percentage of masked faces, while a truly gallant cavalier (escorting a dame in a domino) paraded his white stockings, that looked icy, across the snowy roads. No confetti, and only an infrequent scream of hilarity. That the old plaster missiles, with other crudities, have disappeared, is indeed no cause for lamentation, but a Carnival without confetti is like an omelette without eggs.

Well might a writer in the local paper, Il Resto del Carlino, lament the brave days of old when a vast array of carriages and masks coursed through the Via S. Mamolo, and the last days of the Carnival were marked by jousts and tourneys, and tiltings at the quintain, with a queen of beauty in white satin and magnificent masqueraders showering flowers, fruits, and perfumes, and nymphs carrying Cupid tied hand and foot.

In Cremona I made trial of a Veglione whose allurements had been placarded for days. A Trionfo di Diana, heralded in large letters, peculiarly suggested pomp and revelry. And indeed I found a theatre almost as large as La Scala, illumined by a dazzling chandelier, with four tiers of boxes resplendent with the shoulders of women and the shirt fronts of men—tiaras, uniforms, orders, all the spectacular social sublime. I had not imagined that obscure Cremona—no longer famous, even for violins—held these glittering possibilities, and it set me to the analysis that Italian theatres—above the platea—are all shop-front, making a brave show of a shallow audience, for the encouragement of the actors and its own gratification, instead of obscuring and dissipating it over back benches.

The stage and the platea had been united by an isthmus of steps and in an enclosure sat a full orchestra. Around the musicians danced men in evening-dress and a few ladies in masks, most of whom, notwithstanding the superabundance of males, preferred to dance with their own sex. This was largely what the spectators had come out for to see, and the disproportion of the dancers to the wilderness of onlookers was the only comic feature of this Carnival Ball. True, a few clownish figures clothed in green and wearing little basket hats improvised mild romps on the stage, and occasionally from the unexpected vantage of a box shouted down some facetious remark, but there was no unction in them, nay not even when they capped the joke by clapping large baskets on their heads. However, the Trionfo di Diana still remained to account for the vast audience, and there came a moment when an electric thrill ran through the packed theatre, the dancing ceased, and the dancers ranged themselves, looking eagerly towards the doors. After a period of tense expectation, there came slowly up the platea a few huntsmen with live dogs and stuffed hawks, and one melancholy horn that gave a few spasmodic single toots, whereupon appeared Diana in a scanty white robe, recumbent on a floral car of foliage and roses, drawn by six hounds, one of which alone rose to the humour of the occasion, and by his inability to remain on his own side of the shaft achieved a rare ripple of laughter, while the applause that followed his adjustment brought quite a wave of warmth. But the chill fell afresh, as the procession, after a cheerless turn or two on the stage, made its exit as tamely as a spent squib. A paltrier spectacle was never seen in a penny show.

A runner, accompanied by a cyclist, who pumped him up with his pump, made a fresh onslaught upon our sense of fun, but when he too trailed off equally into nothingness, I quitted the dazzling midnight scene, leaving the beauty and fashion of Cremona to its Carnival dissipations.

Yes, the Italian Carnival is dying. Unregretted, adds the Anglo-French paper that serves the select circles of Rome. For it is only the Carnival of the streets that is passing, this genteel authority tells us reassuringly. "A far more glorious Carnival is replacing it. In the grand cosmopolitan hotels fête succeeds fête."

Alas, so even the Carnival has passed over to the Magnificent Ones, who not content with annexing the best things in their own lands sail under their pirate flag in quest of the spoils of every other, moving from Rome to Switzerland, from Ascot to Cairo, with the movement of Sport or the Sun. What a change from the days of the Roman Fathers, when religion circled round one's own hearth, and exile was practically excommunication! The mother-land is no longer a mother but a mistress, to be visited only for pleasure, and every other land is only another odalisque, devoid of sanctities, ministress to appetites. The Magnificent Ones of the Middle Ages and the Renaissance at least stayed at home and minded their serfs and their business: our modern Magnificent Ones go abroad, make new serfs everywhere, and mind only their pleasures. And hence it is that the festa of the Carnival whose only raison d'être was religious, whose only justification was its spontaneity, is to be annexed by the Magnificent Mob, ever in search of new pretexts for new clothes and new vulgarities. The froth of pleasure is to be skimmed off, and the cup of seriousness thrown away. The joyousness that ushers in Lent is to be torn from its context as the fine feathers are torn from a bird, to flutter on the hat of a demi-mondaine. The grand cosmopolitan hotels with the grand cosmopolitan rabble will usher in with grand cosmopolitan dances the period of prayer and fasting, and the dying Carnival will achieve resurrection.

NAPOLEON AND BYRON IN ITALY: OR LETTERS AND ACTION

I

As I creep humbly through this proud and prodigious Italy, peeping into palaces and passing yearningly before masterpieces, to the maddening chatter of concierges and sacristans, I am constantly stumbling upon the footsteps of him who made the grand tour in the high sense of the words. Not the British heir of bygone centuries with his mentor and his letters of introduction, not even his noble father with the family coach. No, these were pigmies little taller than myself. Your sublime tourist was Napoleon, who strode over the holy land of Beauty like a Brobdingnagian over Lilliput. He came, he saw, he commanded. He looked at a picture, a pillar, a statue—and despatched it to France. He gazed at Lombard's iron crown—and put it on. He beheld Milan Cathedral—and it became the scene of his coronation, with blessing of clergy and the old feudal homage. He perceived an ornate ducal bed—and slept in it, the poor duke a-cold. He rode through the ancient streets, not Baedeker but cocked hat in hand, graciously acknowledging the loyal cheers of the ancient stock. He examined the Sacro Catino in Genoa Cathedral and bore it off with its precious blood; he espied the rich treasure of Loreto, and lo! it was his; he saw Lucca that it was fair, and it became his sister Elisa's. He visited Venice—and wound up the Republic. He admired St. Mark's—and haled its bronze horses to Paris, transferring to it the Patriarchate as in compensation. The Patriarchal Palace itself he turned into barracks; superfluous monasteries and churches were shut up and their lands confiscated. He even destroyed, doubtless in the same righteous indignation, the lion's head over "the lion's mouth" in the Palace of the Doges, while the Bucentaur, their gorgeous galley, he burnt to extract the gold.

But he was not merely destructive and rapacious. The founder of the Code Napoléon repaired the amphitheatre of Verona, and resumed the neglected building of the façade of Milan Cathedral, and opened up the Simplon route to Italy, and marked its terminus by the Triumphal Arch of Milan. He surveyed the harbour of Spezia for a war-harbour and projected to drain Lake Trasimeno away—conceptions which to-day are realities. And all this and a hundred other feats of construction in the breathing-spaces of his Titanic single-handed fight against embattled Europe. Not seldom, as I passed my wood-shop in Venice, with its caligraphic placard All' Ingrosso e al Minuto, did I think of the Corsican superman, with his wholesale and retail dealings with the little breed of mankind. Perhaps to establish "the Kingdom of Italy," with twenty-four departments and his step-son as viceroy, and to turn the little district of Bassano into a duchy for his secretary were, to Napoleon, feats of the same apparent calibre. Even so we stride as carelessly over a brooklet as over a puddle. Surely there is a fascinating book to be written on Napoleon in Italy, as a change from the countless Napoleons in St. Helena or the flood of foolish volumes upon his mistresses.

And a final appraisement of Napoleon still remains to seek. The little fat man who had "the genius to be loved"—except by Joséphine and Marie Louise—and who provided for his family by distributing thrones, has long since ceased to be the ogre with whom British babes were frighted, though he has not yet become Heine's divine being done to death by British Philistinism. Carlyle classed him among his "Heroes" and credited him with insight because, when those around him proved there was no God, he looked up at the stars and asked, "Who made all that?" But this was surely no index of profundity—merely a theism of Pure Reason and an illustration of Napoleon's peculiar interest in action. "Who made all that?" Making, doing, that was his essential secret—unresting activity, rapid striking, utilisation of every moment. He was as alert the moment after victory as others after defeat. Was one combination destroyed, his nimble and exhaustless energy instantly fashioned an alternative. Mobility of brain and immobility of soul—these were his gifts in a crisis. When all was lost and himself a captive, "What is the use of grumbling?" he asked his attendants. "Nothing can be done." The tragedy of Napoleon was thus the obverse of the tragedy of Hamlet, whose burden lay precisely in there being something to be done. Imagine the great demiurge at work in these days of telegraphy and steam, motor-cars and aeroplanes. What might he not have achieved! As it was, he just missed creating the United States of Europe. Anatole France accuses him of having taken soldiers too seriously. As well accuse an engineer of taking cranes and levers too seriously. Soldiers were the indispensable instruments by which Napoleon raised himself to the level of those more commonplace rulers of Europe who had found their cradles suspended on the heights. It is the German Emperor who takes soldiers too seriously, who marshals them with the solemnity of a child playing with his wooden regiments. And the Kaiser, already in the purple, has not Napoleon's excuse. His is simply a false and reactionary view of life, as of a house-maid who adores uniforms. But Napoleon would have played his Machiavellian game equally with grocers; and, indeed, his lifelong ambition to sap British commerce was conceived in the spirit of a Titanic tradesman, who knows better than to count corpses. He was the fifteenth-century condottiere magnified many diameters, playing with countries and nations instead of with towns and tribes, and sweeping in his winnings across the green table of earth as in some game of the gods. As a Messiah of Pure Reason, an Apostle of the People, he was able, like Mohammed, to back the Word with the Sword, and, less veracious than the prophet of the desert, to combine for the making of History its two great factors of Force and Fraud. Through him, accordingly, History made a leap, proceeding by earthquake and catastrophe instead of by patient cumulation and attrition. He was a cosmic force—a force of Nature, as he truthfully claimed—a terremoto that tumbled the stagnant old order about the ears of Courts and Churches.

True, after the earthquake the old slow, stubborn forces reassert themselves; but the configuration of the land has been irrevocably changed. The Maya, the illusion of Royalty, comes slowly back, for it is a world of unreason, and even Bismarck believed in the divine right of the princes he despised. But the feudal order throughout Europe will never wholly recover from the shock of Napoleon. Unfortunately, from a Messiah he glided into a Magnificent One, and the marriage with Marie Louise, at first perhaps a mere cold-blooded chess-move to establish his dynasty, subtly reduced him into accepting Royalty at its own and the popular valuation. He had married beneath him, and Nemesis followed. The dyer's hand was subdued to that it worked in, and Napoleon sank into a snob. His true Waterloo was spiritual. The actual Waterloo was a moral victory.

Had he remained representative of the Republican or any other principle, exile would have had no power over him; on the contrary, it would have aggrandised his influence. But his exile represented nothing but the moping of a banished Magnificent, so that a generous spirit like Byron could find in his "Ode to Napoleon," no words too excoriating for this fallen meanness.

And while Napoleon pined in St. Helena, Marie Louise found promotion as Duchess of Parma, becoming her own mistress instead of the world's, and finding husbands nearer down to her own level than the Corsican ex-corporal. Quite happy she must have been, sitting on her throne under a great red baldachino, giving audience, surrounded by her suite and her soldiers—as Antonio Pock painted her—or smothered in diamonds at neck, waist, earrings and hair, smirking in a low-necked dress at her crimson and jewelled crown, as in the picture of Gian Battisti Borghesi. Parma preserves both these portraits, but they are not so quaint a deposit of the great Napoleonic wave as Canova's bust of Marie Louise as Concord!

There is in Milan a queer museum called "The Gallery of Knowledge and Study," the collection of which was begun by a "Noble Milanese," and the first catalogue of which was published in Latin in 1666. Here, amid sea-shells, miniatures, old maps, pottery, bronzes, silkworm analyses, and old round mirrors in great square frames, may now be seen a pair of yellow gloves which once covered the iron hands, together with the cobbler's measure of that foot which once stamped on the world. There is an air of coquetry about the pointed toe. A captain's brevet, signed by the "First Consul" and headed "French Republic," serves as a reminder of the earlier phase. The humour of museums has placed these relics in a case with those of other "illustrious men"—to wit, two Popes and St. Carlo, the dominant saint of the district (who is just celebrating his tercentenary).

But the Triumphal Arch remains Napoleon's chief monument at Milan, though it is become a sort of Vicar of Bray in stone. For when Napoleon fell, the Austrian Emperor replaced the chronicle of French victories by bas-reliefs of defeats, and re-christened it an Arch of Peace. And when in turn Lombardy was liberated by Victor Emmanuel, new inscriptions converted it into an Arch of Freedom. One can imagine the stone singing, like the Temple of Memnon at sunrise:

"But whatsoever king shall reign,
Still I'll be the Arch of Triumph."

And in Ferrara there is a Triumphal Column no less inconstant. Designed to support the statue of Duke Ercole I, it was annexed by Pope Alexander VII, who was deposed by Napoleon, whose statue has now been replaced by Ariosto's. Whether the ducal-papal-military-poetic pillar supports its ultimate statue, we may doubt, though a poet seems less obnoxious to political passion than the other sorts of hero.

Such mutations in the significance of monuments, however they deface and blur history, are not unnatural amid the vicissitudes of Italy: and, after all, an arch or a pillar is but an arch or a pillar.

But even a statue that keeps its place is not safe from supersession. In Rimini in 1614 the Commune, grateful to the Pope (Paolo V), commemorated him in bronze in the beautiful Piazza of the Fountain, the Fountain whose harmonious fall pleased the ear of Leonardo da Vinci. The monument is elaborate and handsome, with bas-reliefs in the seat and in the Papal mantle, showing in one place the city in perspective. But during the Cisalpine Republic, thanks again to Napoleon, no Pope could keep his place in Rimini, and as the simplest way of preserving him on this favoured site, the municipality erased his epitaph and re-christened him Saint Gaudenzo. Gaudenzo was the martyr Bishop of Rimini, the Protector of the City. This unearned increment was not the Saint's first, for the Church of S. Gaudenzo had been erected on the basis of a Temple of Jove. To annex the glories of both Jove and Pope is indeed a singular fortune, even in the ironic changes and chances we call history. But Napoleon, in the days when he ordered the Temple of Malatesta to be the Cathedral of Rimini, was annexing even the functions of both Pope and Jove. For he was also rearranging Europe after Austerlitz and giving the quietus to the Holy Roman Empire.

II

Only second to the impact of Napoleon on Europe was the impact of Byron. 'Tis Cæsar and Hamlet in contemporary antithesis, for Professor Minto has well said that Byron played Hamlet with the world for his stage. While Byron was soliloquising with his pen, Napoleon was energising with his sword, and whether the pen was really the mightier of the twain is a nice thesis for debating societies. But in Italy, and by the greatest modern Italian poet, Byron has been acclaimed as a man of action. In my hotel in Bologna the landlord had piously—or with an eye to custom—suspended a tablet, commissioned from Carducci, whereof a translation would run as follows:

"Here
In August and September 1819
Lodged And Conspired for Liberty
George Gordon, Lord Byron,
Who Gave to Greece His Life,
To Italy His Heart and Talent,
Than Who None Arose Among
The Moderns More Potent
To Accompany
Poetry With Action,
None More Piously Inclined
To Sing The Glories and Adventures
Of our People."

An epigraph, I fear, involving some poetic licence. True, of course, that no modern poet's life or work, save Browning's, is so interpenetrated with Italy. But Byron's amateur relation with the futile Italian conspirators of the generation before Garibaldi was a somewhat shadowy contact with action, however generous his impatient ardour for Italy's resurrection. Vaporous, too, was the conspiracy of "The Liberal" to pour new wine into the old British beer-bottle. But even his membership of the Greek committee or the equipment of a bellicose brig against Turkey, or his abortive appointment as

Commander-in-Chief in an expedition against Lepanto, scarcely brings Byron into the category of men of action. He had never the chance of sloughing Hamlet for Cæsar or even for the Corsair. It was not even given him to die in battle, as he so ardently desired in the last verse of his last poem. And though his Hellenic fervour redeemed his closing days from despair and degradation, still the fever which slew him at Missolonghi hardly warrants the claim that he gave his life for Greece. Had his microbe met him in marshy Ravenna instead of marshy Missolonghi, would it have been said that he died for Italy? For aught we know his sea voyage from Genoa to Greece may have lengthened his life.

Moreover it was as an ideologue that Byron plunged into affairs. For the Greeks whom he set out to deliver figured in his mind as direct, if degenerate, descendants of the great free spirits of old, the creators of Hellenic culture: the reality was a priest-ridden population debased by Slav stocks.

Byron had indeed an opulence of temperament which naturally spilt over into action. Like Sir Walter Scott, he was larger than a writing man, and he brought the Scott sanity rather than the Byronic ebullience into his three months' work at Missolonghi, holding himself aloof from factions and thus reconciling them in him, throwing his weight on the side of humanity, and even rising beyond his disappointment in the Greeks to perceive that their very failings made their regeneration only the more necessary. There was certainly in him the making of a leader of men. Nevertheless cerebral ferment and not conspiring for liberty was his essential form of activity. That cerebral ferment was never more ebullient and continuous than in those years of Italy and the Countess Guiccioli. Ravenna was his favourite town, and action is not precisely the note of Ravenna at whose town-gate I read with my own eyes a fabulous prohibition against vehicular traffic in the streets.

But did we concede Carducci's claim to the full, and even supplement it by Byron's passing eagerness to mould British politics, the Italian poet's characterisation of him as the most striking modern instance of the union of poetry and action, is a startling reminder of the poverty and vacuousness of the chronicle of singing men of affairs. If Byron be indeed Eclipse, truly the rest are nowhere. And the question arises, why the modern man should be so artificially bifurcated. Æschylus was both soldier and poet. Cæsar not only made history but wrote it. Dante was Prior of Florence.

"In rebus publicis administrans," says the inscription on the absurd tomb of Ariosto, and we know that Duke Alfonso sent him to suppress bands of robbers in lawless Garfagnana as well as on that even more formidable expedition to the Terrible Pontiff who had excommunicated the ruler of Ferrara. Chaucer was a diplomatist and Government Official. The ethereal singer of "The Faerie Queene" shared in the bloody attempt at the Pacification of Ireland. Milton, that virulent pamphleteer, barely escaped the block. Goethe administered Weimar. Victor Hugo, like Dante, achieved exile. Björnson contributed to the independence of Norway. The notion of a poet as aloof from life seems to be largely modern and peculiarly British. Shelley is probably responsible for this conception of the "beautiful and ineffectual angel," and in our own day Swinburne has helped to carry on the legend. But Swinburne's fellow-poet, the self-styled "Singer of an empty day," was precisely the poet who had the largest relations with life and whose wall-papers have spread to circles where his poetry is unknown or unread.

You may say that Virgil, who was neither modern nor British, practised the same attitude of detachment, the same exclusive self-consecration to letters as Wordsworth or Tennyson. But Virgil a people to express, and Wordsworth and Tennyson were passionate politicians, if they made no incursions into action proper. You may urge that the bards, skalds, minstrels, troubadours, ballad-mongers, jongleurs, have always been a class apart from action, but these were at least lauders of action, laureates of lords, while even the Minnesingers celebrated less their own mistresses than of the heroes. 'Tis a parasitism upon action, to which indeed the meek and prostrate Kipling would confine the rôle of letters.

But why should the power to feel and express the finer flavours of life and language paralyse the capacity for action? In the sanest souls both functions would co-exist in almost equal proportions. Sword in one hand and trowel in the other, Ezra's Jews rebuilt the Temple, and the new Jerusalem will not rise till we can hold both trowel and tablet. In that Platonic millennium poets must be kings and kings poets.

That fantastic, mutilated, myopic, and inefficient being, known as "the practical man," sniffs suspiciously at all movements that have thought or imagination, or an ideal for their inspiration. It may be conceded to this crippled soul that action can never take the rigid lines of theory, and that the forces of deflection must modify, if not indeed prevail over, the à priori pattern. But he is not truly a thinker whose thought cannot allow for these deviations in practice, which are as foreseeable (if not as exactly computable) as the retardation, acceleration or aberration of a planet by the pull of every other within whose attraction it rolls. Action is not pure thought but applied thinking—a species of engineering over, through, or around mountains, and opposing private domains. "Life caricatures our concepts," a dreamer complained to me, after he had stepped down into politics. Is it not perhaps that our concepts caricature life? Life is too fluid and asymmetric to bear these fixed forms of constructive polity, and Lord Acton tells us that in the whole course of history no such rounded scheme has ever found fulfilment. I do not wonder.

But the poet who has never acted on the stage of affairs is moving in a padded world of words, and the 〜ero who has never sung, or at least thrilled with the music in him, is only sub-human. The divorce of life 〜 letters tends to sterilise letters and to brutalise life. The British mistrust of poetry in affairs has a 〜 basis—of stupidity. Imagination, which is the essential factor in all science, is esteemed a Jack o' 〜rn to lure astray. And to tap one's way along, inch by inch, without any light at all, is held the method of progression.

〜which has known Mazzini, is, I trust, for ever saved from this Anglo-Saxon shallowness.

〜on is the passing of an idea from theory into practice," said Mazzini. And again, "Those who 〜ght and Action dismember God and deny the eternal Unity of things." Pensiero e Azione 〜cant title of the journal he founded to bring about the redemption of Italy. Garibaldi too 〜who even wrote poetry. Cavour, the most worldly of the trio of Italian saviours, owes his 〜ely to the imagination which could use all means and all men to educe the foreseen end.

〜should be drawn between those who dream with their eyes open, and those who 〜s shut. What Cavour saw was in congruity with fact and possibility. Prevision is not 〜dern watcher of the skies received the photograph of Halley's Comet upon his 〜it became visible to the eye, and months before it revealed itself to the farthest- 〜on the sensitised soul coming events cast their configurations before. This 〜ught in common with the nightmares and chimæras of sleep. "The prophetic 〜ming on things to come" admits the elect to glimpses of its dream. These be 〜ugh which the universe arrives at self-consciousness, as the heroes are the 〜ives at self-amelioration.

ad

hose

THE CONSOLATIONS OF PHLEBOTOMY: A PARADOX AT PAVIA

In a room leading to the Senate in the Ducal Palace of Venice I was looking at a picture by Contarini of the conquest of Verona by the Venetians in 1405.

'Twas a farrago of fine confused painting, horses asprawl over the dead and wounded, men in armour driving their daggers home in the prostrate huddled forms, galloping chargers viciously spurred by helmeted knights with swirling swords, in brief an orgie of wild and whirling devilry. The pity of it, I thought, Verona and Venice, those two fairy sisters, each magically enthroned on beauty, members of the same Venetia, peopled with the same stock, speaking almost the same dialect, why must they be at each other's throat? And this revelry of devilry might, I knew, equally serve for Venice's conquest of any other of her neighbours in that wonderful fighting fifteenth century of hers, when she must needs set up her winged lion in every market place.

And these rivalries of Venice and her neighbour-towns, I recalled, were only part of the universal urban warfare—Genoa against Pisa, Siena against Florence, Gubbio against Perugia; these again breaking into smaller circles of contention, or intersected with larger, party against party, faction against faction, guild against guild, Guelph against Ghibelline, Montague against Capulet, Oddi against Baglioni, popolani against grandi, provinces against invaders, blood-feuds horrific, innumerable, the Guelph-Ghibelline contest alone involving 7200 revolutions and 700 massacres in its three centuries! And yet there is a reverse to the shield, and a jewelled scabbard to the sword.

I stood later in the Palazzo Malaspina of Pavia where, tradition says, the imprisoned Boëthius composed "The Consolations of Philosophy," and here in a vestibule my eye was caught by a fragment of gilded gate hung aloft, and running to read the explanatory inscription, I found it—in translation—as follows:

"These Remnants of the Old Gates of Pavia
Thrice Trophies in Civil Wars
By a Magnanimous Thought Restored by Ravenna
Are To-day an Occasion for Rejoicing
Betwixt the Two Cities Desirous
Of Changing the Vestiges of the Old Discords
Into Pledges of Union & Patriotic Love
The XIII day of September MDCCCLXXVIII"

Un magnanimo pensiero, indeed! And—like the chains of Pisa's ancient harbour restored by Genoa—a pleasant sequel to the noble common struggle for Italian independence. And yet—the advocatus diaboli whispered me, or was it the shade of Boëthius in quest of "The Consolations of Phlebotomy"?—"What has become of Pavia, what of Ravenna, since they ceased to let each other's blood? Where is the Pavia of a hundred towers, where is the Castello reared and enriched by generations of Visconti Dukes, and its University, once the finest in Italy, at which Petrarch held a chair; where is the opulence of life that flowed over into the Certosa, now arid in its mausolean magnificence? Where is the Ravenna whose lawyers were as proverbial in the eleventh century as Philadelphia's are to-day, where is that hotbed of heresy which nourished the great anti-Pope Guibert? Where is even the Ravenna of Guido da Polenta, protector of Dante? Apt indeed to hold only Dante's tomb. And its young men who bawl out choruses of a Sunday night till the small hours—do they even deserve the shrine of the poet of Christendom? And Venice? And Verona? And the Rimini of the sixty galleys? What have they gained from their colourless absorption into a United Italy, compared with what they have lost—had indeed already lost—of peculiar and passionate existence? Are there two gentlemen of Verona now in whom we take a scintilla of interest? Is there a merchant of Venice whose ventures concern us a jot? Is there a single Antonio with argosies bound for Tripolis and the Indies?" "Your Ben Jonson," and by his wide posthumous reading I knew 'twas Boëthius speaking now, "said 'in short measures life may perfect be.' He should have said 'in small circles' and, perhaps, 'only in small circles.' All America—with its vasty breadths—stands to-day without a single man of the first order."

"'Tis not even"—put in the advocatus diaboli, betrayed by his unphilosophic chuckle—"as if the destruction of small patriotisms meant the destruction of war. Pavia and Ravenna," he pointed out mischievously, "must continue to fight—as part of the totality, Italy. And behold," quoth he, drawing my eyes towards the Piazza Castello, "the significance of that old castle's metamorphosis into a barrack—the poetry of war turned to prose, the frescoes of the old Pavian and Cremonese painters faded, perhaps even whitewashed over, and rough Government soldiers drilling where the Dukes played pall-mall. Gone is that rich concreteness of local strife, attenuated by its expansion into a national animosity; not insubstantial indeed under stress of invasion, but shadowy and unreal when the casus belli is remote, and by the manœuvres of my friends, the international diplomatists, the Pavian or Ravennese finds himself fighting on behalf of peoples with whom alliance is transitory and artificial."

"But he will not find himself fighting so often," I rejoined. "Countries do not join battle as recklessly as cities. The larger the bulk the slower the turning to bite." "And meantime," interposed the philosophic shade, "the war-tax in peace is heavier than anciently in war. And neither in war nor in peace can there be the joy of fighting that comes from personal keenness in the issue. The wars of town with town, of sect with sect, of neighbour with neighbour, so far from being fratricidal and unnatural, are the only human forms of war. 'Tis only neighbours that can feel what they are fighting for, 'tis only brothers that can fight with unction. The very likeness of brothers, their intimate acquaintance with the points of community, gives them an acute sense of the points of difference, and provides their combat with a solid standing-ground at the bar of reason. Least irrational of all internecion were the fratricide of twins. Save the war of self-defence, civil war is the only legitimate form of war. Military war—how monstrous the sound, what a clanking of mailed battalions! Your Bacon betrays but a shallow and conventional sense of 'The True Greatness of Kingdoms,' when he compares civil war to the heat of a fever, and foreign war to the heat of exercise which serves to keep the body in health. For what is foreign war but an arrogance of evil life, an inhuman sport, a fiendish trial of skill? Why should a home-born Briton ever fight a Russian? His boundaries are nowhere contiguous with the Russian's, his very notion of a Russ is mythical. 'Tis a cold-blooded war-game into which he is thrust from above. What's Hecuba to him or he to Hecuba? Other is it with warfare that is personal, profoundly felt. Civil war—how sacred, how close to men's bosoms! When Greek meets Greek, then comes the tug of war."

"In religious wars, too," eagerly interrupted the advocatus diaboli, "'tis nearness that is the justification—Homoousian versus Homoiousian. Why in heaven's name," he added with a spice of malice, "should a Mussulman cry haro against a Parsee, or a Shintoist against a Mormon? Here, too, the boundaries are not contiguous; 'twere the duel of whale and elephant. 'Tis the Christian sects that must naturally torture and murder one another," he wound up triumphantly.

"Ay indeed," serenely assented the shade of Boëthius. "If fighting is to be done at all, let it be between brothers and not between strangers. Where 'a hair perhaps divides the False and True' 'tis of paramount importance to determine on which side of the hair we should stand. This rigid accuracy is the glory of Science—why should not our decimal be correct to nine places even in Religion? Why wave aside these sharp differences for which the men of my day were willing to pay with their lives? When your Alfred the Great translated my magnum opus, or even as late as when your Chaucer honoured me with a modern version, these questions could vie in holy intensity, almost with your latter-day questions of Free Trade and Tariff Reform."

"Ah, the palmy days of martyrdom," sighed the advocatus diaboli, "when men were literally aflame for filioque or Immaculate Conception. O for the fiery Arians, Gnostics, Marcionites, Valentinians, Socinians, Montanists, Donatists, Iconoclasts, Arnoldites, Pelagians, Monophysites, Calixtines, Paulicians, Hussites, Cathari, Albigenses, Waldenses, Bogomilians, Calvinists, Mennonites, Baptists, Anabaptists—"

"Surely you would not call Baptists fiery?" I interjected feebly. He had apparently no sense of humour, this advocatus, for he went on coldly: "How tame and disappointing these latter-day sectarians: these Methodists, Plymouth Brethren, Christian Scientists, Irvingites, Christadelphians, 'et hoc genus omne.' I did have a flash of hope when your Methodists began to split up into Wesleyans, Protestant Methodists, Reformers, Primitives, Bryanites and the like, whose bitter brotherly differences seemed to show the old sacrosanct concern for the minutiæ of Truth and Practice. But no! no one believes nowadays, for nobody burns his fellow-Christian. Even the burning words of your King's Declaration—!"

"August shade," I interrupted, pointedly addressing myself to the last of the Roman philosophers, "I concede that when Christianity founded itself on texts, an infinite perspective of homicidal homiletics lay open to the ingenuous and the ingenious. And so long as Heaven and Hell turned on dogma and ritual, an infinite significance attached to the difference between the theological tweedledum and the theological tweedledee, so that it is just dimly conceivable one might murder one's neighbour for his own good or the greater glory of God. But do not tell me that to-day, too, the test of belief is bloodshed."

"Immo vero," cried the Roman shade emphatically. "Was I not clubbed to death because I believed in Justice and combated the extortions of the Goths? A belief for which we would not die or kill, what is it?"

"A bloodless belief," chuckled the advocatus diaboli, who, I suddenly remembered, was more legitimately entitled the defensor fidei.

RISORGIMENTO: WITH SOME REMARKS ON SAN MARINO AND THE MILLENNIUM

"Il Calavrese abate Giovacchino
Di spirito profetico dotato."
DANTE: Paradiso, Canto xii.

"Pater imposuit laborem legis, qui timor est; filius imposuit laborem disciplinæ, qui sapientia est; spiritus sanctus exhibet libertatem, quæ amor est."
JOACHIM OF FLORA: Liber Concordiæ, ii.

I

"Italy is too long," said the Italian. We were coming into Turin in the dawn, amid burning mountains of rosy snow, and the train was moving slowly, in hesitation, with pauses for reflection. "The line is single in places," he explained. "Italy is too narrow, too cramped by mountain-chains, and above all too long. It is the trouble behind all our politics. There are three Italies, three horizontal strata, that do not interfuse—the industrial and intelligent North, the stagnant and superstitious South, and the centre with Rome which is betwixt and between."

"But there is far more clericalism in the North than the South," I said. "The Church party is a political force."

"Precisely what proves my case. In the North everything is more efficient, even to the forces of reaction. The clericals are better organised, and are, moreover, supported by the propertied atheists in the interests of order. But the North is Europe—Germany, if you will—the South is already Africa." The train stopped again. He groaned. "No unity possible."

"No unity?" I exclaimed. "And what about Garibaldi and Mazzini and United Italy?"

"It is a phrase. Italy is too long."

I pondered over his words, and in imagination I saw again all the Risorgimento museums, all the tablets in all the loggias and town halls recording those who had died for the Union of Italy, all the statues of all the heroes, all the streets and piazzas dedicated to them, while in my ears resounded all the artillery of applause booming at that very moment throughout the length and narrowness of Italy in celebration of the Jubilee of the Departure of the Thousand from Quarto.

II

Any one who goes to Italy for the Renaissance will find the Risorgimento a discordant obsession; flaunting itself as it does in brand new statues and monuments whose incongruity of colour or form destroys the mellow unity of old Cathedral-Piazzas or Castello-courtyards. Florence has managed to hush up the Risorgimento in back streets or unobtrusive tablets, and Venice with her abundance of Campi has stowed it out of sight, though Victor Emmanuel ramps on horseback not far from the Bridge of Sighs, and "three youths who died for their country" intrude among the tombs of the Doges. The essence of Pisa is preserved by its isolation from life, leaving Mazzini to dominate the city of his death. But the majority of the old towns are devastated by the new national heroes—admirable and vigorous as the sculpture sometimes is—even as the old historic landmarks are obliterated by the new street names. And in addition to the pervasive quartette—Garibaldi, Cavour, Victor Emmanuel, Mazzini—local heroes aggravate the ruin of antiquity. Daniele Manin thrones in Venice over a winged lion sprawling beneath a triton; Ricasoli, "the iron Baron," rules in Tuscany; Pavia is sacred to the Cairoli; Minghetti runs through the Romagna; Crispi through the South; Genoa devotes a street, a square, and a bronze statue to Bixio, the Boanerges of the epic; Viareggio has just put up a tablet to Rosolino Pilo and Giovanni Corrao, the daring precursors of the Thousand; even Rubattino—patriot in his own despite—has his statue in Genoa harbour, on the false ground that he put his shipping line at Garibaldi's disposal. 'Tis a very shower of stones, falling on the just and the unjust alike. And sometimes—as at Asti—all the Heroes are United beneath a riot of granite monoliths and marble lions.

And even the ubiquitous heroes have peculiar glory in their peculiar haunts. Cavour is gigantic at Ancona (probably because the town was freed by Piedmontese troops); he stands in the castle of Verona, overbrooded by snow mountains: at Turin, his birthplace, Fame wildly clasps him to her breast in a mammoth monument, crying, "Audace, prudente, libero Italia."

A Vanity Fair without a hero I have never chanced on. Little Chiavari has its grandiose angel-strewn monument to Victor Emmanuel, whom Parma likewise exhibits flourishing his sword; Pesaro breaks out in tablets to those who died fighting "the hirelings of the Theocracy"; Rimini has a Piazza Cavour; priest-ridden Vicenza shelters a statue of Mazzini; Assisi itself, waking from its saintly slumber, consecrates a Piazzetta to Garibaldi, and a street to the Twentieth of September on which Italian troops broke into Rome!

Ah, Garibaldi, Garibaldi, how thou didst weigh on my wanderings! From Mantua to Ferrara, from Spoleto to Perugia, Garibaldi, always Garibaldi. I fled to dead Ravenna, lo! thou didst tower in the very Piazza of Byron; to Parma, and rugged, imposing, in thy legendary cap, leaning on thy sword, thou didst obsess the Piazza Garibaldi; to Rome itself, and twenty feet high, thou impendedst in bronze, with battle pieces and allegories around thee; I retreated to the extremest point of the Peninsula, and found myself in the Corso Garibaldi of Reggio; I crossed to Sicily, only to stumble against thy great horse in Palermo and the monument to thy valour in Calatafimi. For of the statesman, the monarch, the prophet and the soldier who combined to redeem Italy, it is naturally the soldier that is stamped most vividly on the popular imagination, the noble freelance whom the mob deemed divine even before his death, whose memory the people has rescued from the anti-climax of his end, selecting away his follies and mistakes and idealising his virtues, under the artistic law of mythopoiesis, till, shaped and perfected for eternal service, the national hero shines immaculate in his sacred niche.

And yet, as the streets show, even the popular imagination has realised that the soldier would not have sufficed. Thrice blessed, indeed, was Italy to possess Cavour and Mazzini at the same hour as Garibaldi. It is a fallacy to suppose that the hour always finds the man, or the man the hour, or that "il n'y a pas d'homme indispensable." Many an hour passes away without its man, as many a man without his hour. Great men perish, wasted, because there are no forces for them to synthetise: great forces remain inarticulate, unorganised and ineffective, because they have found no leader to be their conduit. All the more marvellous that Italy should have produced simultaneously three indispensable men, Mazzini, Cavour, and Garibaldi, each of whom had something of the other two, yet something unique of his own. None of the three quite understood the others, and Mazzini, who was much like Ibsen's Brand, was even more intolerant than Garibaldi of the Machiavellian policies of Cavour, and had to be swept aside as a visionary. For one heroic, impossible moment, indeed, the spirit triumphed, the Republic of Rome was born, and idealism enjoyed perhaps its sole run of power in human history. But with the disappearance of the Republic, Mazzini might have disappeared too, for all his influence upon the political Risorgimento; did indeed practically disappear by acquiescing in the battle-flag of Monarchy. Garibaldi and Cavour sufficed to create the combination of Force and Fraud by which political history is made. For though, if any sword might ever bear the words I saw on a sword graven by Donatello—"Valore e Giustitia"—that sword was Garibaldi's, and if ever passion was patriotic it was Cavour's, nevertheless the liberation of Italy did not escape being achieved by the usual factors of Force and Fraud.

III

And, in addition to all these busts, statues, allegories, tablets, pillars, cairns, lions, bas-reliefs, wreaths, lists of heroes, records of plébiscites anent annexations, loggias whence Garibaldi orated; in addition to all the Piazze Garibaldi and Victor Emmanuel, all the Corsi Cavour and Mazzini, all the streets of the

Twentieth of September and other heroic dates, there is the specific Museum of the Risorgimento from which no tiniest town is immune. To see one is practically to see all. With the same piety with which their ancestors collected the relics of the saints, the modern Italians have collected the relics of their heroes and the war—swords, sticks, photographs, crude paintings and engravings, old hats, letters, tricolour scarves, medals, pictures, patriotic money, helmets, epaulettes, broken bombs, cannon-balls, cartoons, caricatures, faded wreaths, autographs, sculptures, crosses, proclamations, prayer-books, pictures of steamers conveying insurgents! And Garibaldi! What town has not some shred of the "Genius of Liberty," as the tablet in the old castle of Ferrara styles him—his flask, his sword, his shirt, his gun, his letters, his telegrams! Peculiarly sacred is the red shirt which he wore at Aspromonte, though it recalls the ironic fact that when the charmed, invincible hero was at last wounded and captured, it was by soldiers of the king he had created and of the Italy whose triumph he was seeking to consummate. Something Miltonic seems to emanate from that red shirt:

"That flaming shirt which Garibaldi wore
At Aspromonte."

But for the rest, all these relics are as ugly as the relics of the saints. Beautiful and exalting as are the Museums in reality, with their record of sacrifice and patriotism in one of the most wonderful chapters of history, infinitely touching as is every yellow letter or worn glove, when imagination has transfused it, these glass cases are outwardly depressing to the last degree—a warning to the Realist, and a proof that Art in expressing the soul of a phenomenon is infinitely truer in its beauty than Nature unselected and unadorned. The wooden-legged curator of Bologna, who lost his leg at Solferino, is a mere stumping old bore; the little photograph of twenty-four Garibaldians minus arms or with crutches is simply discomforting. Even the story of the modern mother of the Gracchi, Adelaide Cairoli, who gave four sons to her country, exhales but tepidly from the picture at Pavia of a middle-aged lady in a bonnet surrounded by young soldiers in variegated costumes.

"Leonessa d'Italia," cried Carducci to Brescia, and the one word of the poet wipes out all the crude photographs and grandiose inscriptions by which that seemingly prosaic town asserts its heroism; one ceases even to smile at the tablet at the foot of the castle hill, veiling a defeat in the guise of ferocious Austrian charges, "frequently" repulsed. From a mock passport of Radetsky in the Vicenza Museum I got a more vivid sense of the racial hatred than from all the relics and tablets: "Birth: Bastard of the seven deadly sins. Age: Eighty-two, sixty-five of which have been passed in robbing Austria of the money she stole. Eyes: Of a bird of prey. Nose: Of a Jew. Mouth: Open for the swallowing of divorce! Beard: Nothing. Hair: Enough. Visage: Not human. Occupation: Projector of Conquests. On the field of battle always at the tail; in the destruction of unarmed cities always at the head. Country: No country will own him. Signature: The last five days of his stay in Milan have paralysed him and he cannot sign. Visé: Good for nowhere." And my most lively realisation of the transformation wrought in Europe since 1820 came, not from a Risorgimento museum nor from an official history, but from a black-and-white engraving of Raphael's Sposalizio "dedicated humbly" by Giuseppe Longhi in 1820 "to the Imperial Royal Apostolical Majesty of Francesco I, Emperor of Austria, King of Jerusalem, Hungary, Bohemia, Lombardy, Venice, Dalmatia, Sclavonia, Galicia, Laodomiria, Illyria, &c. &c."

IV

Even those streets or buildings that are free from the Risorgimento are pitted with records or statues. Padua records with equal pride how Dante had his exile sweetened by the hospitality of Carrara da

Giotto, and how Giovanni Prati, the singer of to-day, lived in the Via del Santo. Verona celebrates impartially Catullus and some minor poet whose name I forget, if I ever knew it, "who by making sweet verses obtained a fame more than Italian." Ferrara has a positive leprosy of white plaques. Bassano is not a great city, but "there is enough celebrity in Bassano," writes Mr. Howells, "to supply the whole world." Things were apparently not always thus; for when Childe Harold went on his pilgrimage he demanded to know where Dante, Petrarch, and Boccaccio were buried.

"Are they resolved to dust,
And have their country's marbles naught to say?
Could not her quarries furnish forth one bust?"

Could her quarries possibly furnish forth one more bust, was the question that came to me on my later pilgrimage. Too much to say have their country's marbles. No poet could lodge a night at a house but for all time his visit must be graven; every local lawyer or engineer is become a world-wonder; it is recorded where "the inventor of the perpetual electric motor" died; even an assassination must be eternalised in a tablet. As for a room in which conspirators met to smoke and plot, it is for ever glorified and sanctified.

I was relieved, when I did go to Carrara,

"Nei monti di Luni, dove ronca
Lo Carrarese,"

to find the supply of marble from its fabular mountains still held out, but the chief occupation of the town seemed to consist in cutting it into slabs with great many-bladed machines. Slowly the grim knives descended, slicing the stone, while a spray moved to and fro to prevent its overheating by friction. And as I watched these plaques gradually grinding into separate existence, I heard them beginning to babble their lapidary language, bursting into eloquent inscriptions to unknown celebrities—chemists, town councillors, hydrographers, economists—nay, commemorating the Risorgimento itself in some village yet ungrown. "Rome or Death," they cried stonily, and "Italy to her Sons,"and "Ci siamo e ci resteremo." And the knives sank lower and lower, and the glories rose higher and higher, and the spray, hissing, continued to throw cold water on the enthusiasm, like some cynic observing it was easier to celebrate the old heroism than under its continuous inspiration to create the new. Carrara itself—though one would think it took marbles as a confectioner takes tarts—has its memorials of Garibaldi and Mazzini, besides that more ancient monument to Maria Beatrice overbrooded by the magic mountains.

To what cause shall we ascribe this hypertrophy of self-consciousness since Childe Harold's day? Is it due to the Risorgimento, or the pleasure-pilgrims, or is some of it inspired by William Walton, canny British Guglielmo, to whom the municipality of Carrara has erected one of his own tablets for his services in stimulating the industry? Is it William Walton who forces all this glory upon Italy? Is it he who creates all this hero-worship? Perugino is no new discovery, yet not till 1865—341 years after his death—did the Commune of Perugia put up a tablet on that steep street which leads to his modest one-storied house, while Carducci, though not even a native, already looks out from the Carducci Gardens towards the rolling snow-mountains on the horizon. To this same 1865 belongs the imposing Dante Monument in the Piazza Santa Croce of Florence. But the six-hundredth anniversary of a poet is a trifle late for his appearance in his native city. True, it had taken him only two hundred years to force his way into Florence Cathedral, but that was merely as a painting on wood. The statue of Correggio in Parma (of course in the Piazza Garibaldi) was not erected till 1870. Tasso has been "the great unhappy poet" for three centuries. Yet not till 1895 did Urbino think it necessary to record his visit to the city as the guest of Federigo Bonaventura. As for Raphael, Urbino's own wonder-child, that thirty-six foot monument to him dates only from 1897! All these testimonials to Art would be a little more convincing if the straight iron bridges with which Venice and Verona have insulted their fairy waters, did not prove—like the flamboyant technique of the modern Italian painter—that Italy has left her art period irrevocably behind.

And the great knives of Carrara go grinding on, "ohne Hast, ohne Rast," inexorably supplying celebrity. Like the Greece of the decadence, Italy has reached its stone age, an age which seems the symptom of spent vigour, the petrifaction of what once was vital. Nor is it easy to recognise Mazzini's soldiers of humanity in a nation whose prophet is d'Annunzio, whose "smart set" repeats the morals of the Renaissance without its genius, whose masses appear to spend their lives in lounging about the streets smoking long black slow-lighting cigars, or patronising the innumerable pastrycooks. It seems a slight return for all the heroic agony of the Risorgimento that Europe should be supplied with an efficient type of restaurant, and a vividly gesturing waiter, who dissects himself in discussing the carving of the joint.

"Scuola di magnanimi Sensi,
 Auspicata promessa dell' Avvenire"

cries a memorial tablet at Brescia, but the ennoblement and the promise of the future are less obvious than the orgy of nationalistic sentiment. And when I read how at the recent meeting in North Italy between their King and the Czar, Italian citizens submitted to being treated like Russians during a royal progress; herded outside the town while within it every door was bolted and every blind drawn, as though 'twas indeed the funeral of freedom, I felt how justified was Mazzini's unwillingness to resurrect under a monarchy. And when I think of the great equestrian monument to Victor Emmanuel II which is to commemorate in 1911 the jubilee of the dynasty's sovereignty over United Italy—the monument that will cost a hundred million lire, and in the belly of whose horse a lunch d'onore was recently offered by the proprietor of the foundry to the engineers and artisans, "twenty-six persons in all"—I see how wise was Mazzini's protest against the narrowing down of a great spiritual movement to the acquisition of more territory by a reigning house. It was a commercial traveller who proudly directed my attention to this equine lunch, and this standard of greatness just suits a commercial nation. In this Gargantuan horse the whole millennial dream of Mazzini may end, and those young heroes of freedom, whose deaths lay so heavy on his conscience in his black moments, may have died but to add another to the family party of monarchs who regard the rest of humanity as a subject-race, transferable from one to the other by conquest or treaty.

However valuable a King may be to Italy as a symbol of Unity, Mazzini was historically accurate when he pointed out that the conception of kingship has no roots in Italy, the one epoch of imperial sway being a mere degeneration of the Roman Republic. It was a fine stroke of tactics to celebrate Mazzini's centenary in 1905 as a national festival, in which the King himself took part. But these centennial tablets and statues were Italy's way of stoning its prophet; this festival was Mazzini's real funeral, burying his aspirations out of sight so effectively that the man in the street has forgotten that for Mazzini the goal of Garibaldi and Cavour was only a starting-point; and a popular British Encyclopædia assures us that Mazzini "lived to see all his dreams realised."

Not that there is a word to be said against the charming and intelligent young man who presides over Italy, and who has signalised himself among his peers by founding an International Agricultural Institute. But what a climax to the long struggle against tyranny, this meeting of King and Czar! To be sure Italy had already made friends with Austria in the very year after Garibaldi's death—"in the interests of the peace of Europe."

Poor Europe. They make a spiritual desert and call it peace.

"Songs before Sunrise"—yes, but where is the sun?

V

More instinct with vitality than the most eloquent tablets to the Risorgimento are the mural inscriptions of hatred to Austria rudely chalked up by anonymous hands, especially on the Adriatic side. "Down with Austria!" "Death to Austria!" "Death to Trent and Trieste!" is the general tenor, varied by the name of Francis Joseph scrawled between skulls and crossbones. 'Tis a strange comment on the Triple Alliance, and the authorities do not seem hurried to remove this glaring contradiction. Even "Death to the Czar" survives the royal meeting.

But the Irredenta is not to be taken seriously. Not along political lines does the Risorgimento proceed, any more than along the moral lines for which Mazzini worked. The second phase, the second Risorgimento it may indeed be called, is the Industrial Resurrection. Resurrection—because Italy, whose Merchant of Venice reminds us that the Italian nobleman was always a trader, and whose leading Florentines were Magnificent Moneylenders, can hardly be regarded as an Arcadia transformed by the cult of the dollar. Even Mazzini demanded revival of "the old commercial greatness"; perhaps he might have been content to wait patiently through this materialistic epoch, if he were sure it would lead to a third Risorgimento.

Hygiene has yet to penetrate and suffuse the new prosperity. But if even Perugia still stinks in places and Foligno everywhere, the country is getting perceptibly cleaner, and perhaps godliness is next to cleanliness. But the severest moralist cannot grudge Italy her rise in wealth and happiness: the poverty of the peasantry, accentuated by the extravagant ambition of Italy to be a Great Power in the smallest of senses, has been terrible. At what a cost has Italy achieved her first Dreadnought, so perversely christened Dante Alighieri!

Beggars abound—blind, crippled, or with hideous growths—especially in the South. Doubtless the influx of the pleasure-pilgrim has increased the deformity of the population, and the Italian beggar pushes forward his monstrosity as though it were for sale, but there is real physical degeneration all the same. The discovery of New York and South America by the Italian has fortunately co-operated with the discovery of Italy by the pleasure-pilgrim and the foreign investor, and some 600,000 Italians in the South of Brazil provide the makings of a Trans-atlantic Italy. Even the semi-savage villages of Sicily are sown with steamer advertisements, and batches going and returning for jobs or harvests make an ever-weaving shuttle across the Atlantic.

And if the monuments of the First Risorgimento clash with the old historic background of Italy, still more is the Second Risorgimento in discord with it. One almost sees a new Italy, infinitely less beautiful but not devoid of backbone, struggling out of the old architectural shell which does not in the least express it. The old ducal and seignorial cities, the old republics, are developing suburbs, sometimes prosperous if prosaic, like the new quarters of Florence and Parma; sometimes grotesque, like Pesaro's sea-side resort, with its "new" architecture—lobster-red and mustard-green lattices, and sham golden doors, carved with busts; sometimes hideous, like the outskirts of Verona, where under the blue, brooding mountains rises a quarter of electrical workshops and chemical factories. Ancient towered Asti grows sparkling with its new brick Banca d'Italia, and its blued and gilded capitals in the Church of S. Secondo Martire. Look down on Genoa, with its fantasia of spires, campaniles, roof-gardens, green lattices, marble balconies, chimneys decorated with figures of doges and opening out like flowers, and see how the old narrow alleys are almost roofed with telegraph and telephone wires. Go down to the widened harbour and see the warehouses, the American sky-scrapers, the smoking chimneys, the great steamers sailing out for Buenos Ayres and New York, the emigrants with their bundles. The blue bird sings here no more; you hear only the bang of the hammer, which Young Italy declares is the voice of the century.

I look out of my window at Forli (in the Via Garibaldi!) and see a white minaret and a white campanile gleaming fantastically in the moonlight over a panorama of russet roofs. There is a stone floor in my bedroom and no chimney. In the Piazza all is heavy and mediæval: dull stone colonnades and a rough cobbled road. In a church a grotesque griffin ramps over a pavement tomb. Yet through these cumbersome stone forms I feel the new Italy struggling. The Ginnasio Communale of the town shelters with equal pomp and spaciousness the picture-gallery and the chemical laboratory. These colonnades and cobbles have no more congruity with the new spirit than the old seignorial and episcopal Palazzi with the poor "tenement families" whom they house to-day. Presently life will slough off these forms altogether. Where an old castle like that of Ferrara or an old palace like that of Lucca or Pistoja can be tamed to civic uses, it becomes a town-hall; where no old building is available, an adequate modern form is created, as in the handsome post-offices with their almost military sense of the dignity of the common life.

At Pesaro I lodged in a Bishop's Palace with "steam-heat, telephone, electric light in all the chambers, garage for automobiles, motor omnibus to all the trains!" Palatial was it indeed, so absurdly spacious that the dining-room was only accessible through vast, empty, domed and frescoed halls, and I could have held a political meeting in my bedroom, where I slept with a sense of camping out under the infinities. I had no notion that provincial churchmen were thus magnificent, and I do not wonder that the Lord Cardinal of Ostia, when he saw how the Franciscans of the Portiuncula slept on ragged mattresses and straw, without pillows or bedsteads, burst into tears, exclaiming: "We wretches use so many unnecessary things!" And yet the Cardinal did not use a single thing advertised by the ex-Palace of Pesaro.

Nowhere do new and old clash or combine more disagreeably than in Modena, where crumbling marble-pillared colonnades are painted red, and meet continuations in new brick. The Cathedral, begun in 1099, guarded and flanked by quaint stone lions, bears on its ancient campanile a tablet to Victor Emmanuel. In the great Piazza, church, picture-gallery and war-monument swear at one another. The Ducal Palace is a military school, the moat round the old rampart—where once resounded that archaic song of the war-sentinels—is a public laundry.

And the statues, tablets, monuments, of the Second Risorgimento begin to vie with those of the first. Pro Nervi, painted on the benches on that desolate cactus-grown shore, among the Leonardesque sea-sprayed rocks by the old Gropallo tower, attests the activity of a society created to boom the summer resort, while a tablet celebrates the Marchese who, foreseeing the future of Nervi, put up the first hotel and died with the name of the municipality on his lips. I do not think the Marchese himself foresaw how far Nervi would go. I know I walked miles along its tramway amid monotonous streets, with no sign of an end. Indeed the tram-line reaches Genoa.

Nor is the Marchese the only hero of the Second Risorgimento. Trust Carrara for that—Carrara and Guglielmo Walton!

And the creations of this Risorgimento rival those of the Renaissance in costliness. Where in all Europe will you find a street as luxurious as Genoa's Via XX Settembre—the long colonnade, the granite pillars, the gilded and frescoed roof, the mosaic pavement where the poorest may tread more magnificently than Agamemnon.

And the great Gallery of Victor Emmanuel in Milan, what is it but a secular parody of the Cathedral it faces—nave, transept, dome, complete even to the invisible frescoes, a Cathédrale de luxe? Very sad and solemn looked the old Cathedral at night, for all its fairy fretwork, as Life passed it by for its glittering counterpart.

VI

I went to San Marino to get away from Garibaldi. For here—I said to myself—is the one spot in Italy that is not Italy, that has kept its pristine Republicanism. Here on the Titan Mount is the one spot that cannot possibly acclaim the Union. At most I may encounter a memorial to Mazzini.

I left Rimini by the Gate of the Via Garibaldi which leads straight to San Marino, and trudging for the better part of a day I saw it impending horribly some two thousand five hundred feet above me, and after dragging myself through the Borgo or lower suburb, I toiled in the darkness up a narrow, steep, slippery, jagged path, on the brink of a sheer precipice, into—the Via Garibaldi! And in a bedroom looking down on it—for the only hotel is in a Piazzetta abutting on it—I passed the night.

In the morning I found a Garibaldi garden and a Caffè Garibaldi and a Piazza Garibaldi and a Garibaldi bust and a Garibaldi bas-relief and two Garibaldi tablets; item, a tablet to Victor Emmanuel and a centennial tablet and street to Mazzini, even a Via of Giosuè Carducci, the laureate of the Risorgimento.

Part of the explanation is that Garibaldi sought refuge here in 1849, escaping from "the Roman Republic" to the Ravenna pine-wood where poor Anita died, and his order for the day—"Soldiers, we are on a Soil of Refuge," and his letter of thanks from Caprera—"I go away proud to be a citizen of so virtuous a Republic"—are reproduced on the tablets. But the deeper cause of this sympathy is that San Marino is Italian through and through, and its hoary independence, real enough in the days of the city states, is become a farce solemnly played with separate postage stamps and currency, Regents, Councils, militia, peers, commons, Home and Foreign Secretaries, ribbons, orders, treaties, extradition treaties and a diplomatic corps in England, Austria-Hungary, Spain, France and Italy, all to cover its budget of £11,000 and its population of 10,422 souls, enumerated from week to week in the toy press and decreasing by dozens. 'Tis a game into which all Europe has entered in high good humour, the grand farçeur, Napoleon, even proposing to extend the Republic's boundaries, which comprise only thirty-three square miles. But the Sammarinese had sense enough to see that a greater realm would be treated more seriously. Mount Titan, as the seat not of a toy capital but of something answering less humorously to its name, would cease to be a joke, whereas a State less than one-fourth of the Isle of Wight might remain for Europe a blessed land of diversion from the eternal earnestness of the sword, might even save Europe's self-respect as a region of civilisation, regardful of treaties and ancient rights. So serious in fact did the Sammarinese consider the danger of being taken seriously, that Antonio Onofri who advised against this Napoleonic inflation stands immortalised as Pater Patriæ.

No doubt the inaccessibility of Mount Titan must have been the origin of San Marino's existence in those dim days of the Diocletian persecution, when the Roman Matron, Felicita, whom the stone-cutter Marinus had converted to Christianity, "made him a present of the mountain." And the same inaccessibility which suited it for a Christian colony contributed later to the success of its traditional policy of balancing between the Rimini Malatestas and the Dukes of Urbino. But what prevented Austria from following Garibaldi into San Marino? What but its enjoyment of the game, or its desperate clinging to that shred of self-respect? To-day when the cycle of history has brought us round again to the period of Ezzelino, when the intellectual or religious concepts, which anciently veiled usurpations, are contemptuously thrown aside, and the iron hand crushes in mockery of the combined Jurists of Europe, what stands between San Marino and extinction? Only the environing Italy. And Italy plays with the tiny Republic as a father plays with a child. San Marino has two mortars in the fortress of La Rocca—for what is a State without artillery to fire on solemn occasions?—and these mortars were presented by Victor Emmanuel III. Italy also receives the more desperate criminals, who are boarded out in its prisons, as it supplies the police from its reserve soldiers, and the Judge from its lawyers. Italy has provided its only distinguished citizens—they are honorary,—its national hymn was taken from Guido of Arezzo, the inventor of the musical scale, and when the beautiful if mimetic Palazzo Pubblico for the Regents and the Council was opened in 1894, it was with a speech of Carducci.

Yet "Liberty," I found, was the keynote of San Marino. Liberty was the motto of its arms, with their three mountains and plumed towers. Liberty waved in the white and blue flag and was painted on the shields of the palace corridors. S. Marino, the author of Liberty, was commemorated in the cathedral façade with its flourish of Sen. P. Q., and Liberty cried from the scroll his statue flourished. "In tuenda Libertate vigilis" warned the inscription over the court room; "animus in consulendo Liber" counselled the medallion near the tribune, and in choice Latin epigraphs the transient tyrant, Cæsar Borgia, impugner of Liberty, was denounced and derided. Sublime it was to stand before the Gothic Palace of the Regents, on this dizzy Piazza della Libertà with its gigantic statue of Liberty (her hand on her bannered spear), and to behold the sheer abyss below, and as from an aeroplane the marvellous panorama of sea and mountain around, Liberty written in every rugged convolution and glacial peak, and shimmering in every masterless wave. And yet my imagination refused to play the game; refused to take with becoming reverence the crowned and gilded pew of the Regents, the historic frescoes and friezes, the blue and orange of the "Guarda Nobile," the képis and bayonets of the militia, the red facings of the police. All this parade of "Libertas" was in inverse proportion to the substance, or even to the power of securing it. The Republic appeared like a banknote without gold behind it, and an Italian banknote at that; never so essentially Italian as in the lapidary literature asserting its separateness. This grand Palace, this costly Cathedral, both built only within the last few years simultaneously with the motor road that has destroyed the last semblance of isolation, seemed like that spasm of self-assertiveness which so often precedes extinction. And I thought that conquering nations might well mark how easily love can melt what hate would only harden. Imagine if Italy had brought her mortars against San Marino instead of presenting them to it, or if she had made a road for her mortars instead of for her motors!

But as an antique curio San Marino is delightful. I love to muse on the pomp of its Regents who are elected—like the Doges of Venice—by a mixture of choice and chance, and go in state to celebrate mass, clothed in satin breeches and velvet mantle, in doublet and sword and ermined cap, accompanied by the Noble Guard and the high officers of State, and then from the Cathedral, still to the clashing of church bells and the strains of military music, to their semestral thrones in the Palazzo Pubblico; there to hear a speech from the Government Orator—whose fee is four shillings—and to take the Latin oath not to tamper with the Libertas of the Constitution, and to receive the State seals and keys and the insignia of Grand Masters of the Order of San Marino, perhaps even the first instalment of the royal budget of a pound a month.

No autocrats are these Regents, despite their regal salary. They are mere constitutional monarchs, official headpieces to the Arringo or sovereign Council in which the real power resides. But though Republican, San Marino is not Democratic, for the Arringo fills up its vacancies by option. Liberty is not flouted however, for may not every head of a family—after the half-yearly elections—give the Arringo a piece of his mind? Time was when the citizen could stroll into its sittings and tender it the benefit of his advice, but this form of Liberty seems to have been found too excessive and cumbersome even for the land of Libertas.

Happy are the nations that have no history, and San Marino seems to have escaped almost without an anecdote. In 1461 Pope Pius II invited it to make war with the Magnificent Monster, Sigismondo Malatesta of Rimini, and rewarded its aid with four castles. Cæsar Borgia came and went in 1503, a nocturnal attack by Fabiano del Monte was repulsed in 1543, and after that nothing appears to have happened till 1739, when the Cardinal Legate, Giulio Alberoni, occupied the Republic. But the Republic having appealed to the Pope was left free again, Clement XII thus becoming a national hero with his bust in the Palazzo. But national heroes of its own it has none. It has adopted the cult of Garibaldi, though he preaches Italian Unity, and made honorary citizens of Canova, Rossini and Verdi, and it has almost appropriated the famous numismatist, Bartolommeo Borghesi, who did at least live here, if he omitted to be born here, and who dominates one of the wonderful mountain-terraces, holding a book and gazing carefully at the only point where there is no view. But as to the "Viri Clarissimi et Illustres Castri Sancti Marini" blazoned on the Palazzo staircase, between shields of "Libertas," I fear their celebrity had not reached me. Doctors, artists, counts, dignitaries of the Church—I was impartially ignorant of them all.

What is to account for this paucity of personalities? Had a great saint or a great poet arisen here, we should have explained it glibly by the pious isolation among the eternal mountains, looking down upon the eternal sea, under the everlasting stars. Had a new Acropolis or a new Parthenon risen on this hill of the Titan, we should not have lacked proofs of the inevitability of the new Athens. But nothing has arisen. Giambittisti Belluzzi, the military architect of its walls and of the Imperial Castle at Pesaro, is San Marino's highest name in art, while in literature its chroniclers point to Canon Ignazio Belzoppi, "letterato di molta fama," born in 1762, author of the heroi-comic poem, "Il Bertuccino" (The Little Monkey)—unpublished!

For life to be perfect then, small circles are not enough, pace my friend Boëthius. They must tingle with life, perhaps even with death. Can it be that the advocatus diaboli was right, and that the snug security of a diplomatic mountain-fastness has bred mediocrity? I tell him angrily that the place is a Paradise and he answers calmly that it is only a Parish. Can it be that the only Paradise possible is a Fools' Paradise?

But a serpent has entered Eden, crawling probably by the motor-car road. He has insinuated doubt of holy authority and the Sammarinese begin to eat of the Tree of Knowledge. Il Titano is the organ of the Socialists—a Titan in revolt—and the Somarino serves the Clericals—with the accent on the Santo. "Preti!!!" is the ejaculatory title of an article in the number of Il Titano that came into my hands (April 24, 1910). "We might say impostors, falsifiers, canaille," it begins pleasantly, "but we say instead 'Priests,' which is a substantive that comprises all the others."

And thus across its precipices San Marino joins hands with "Young Italy," whose programme according to the organ of that name embraces the exiling of the Vatican beyond the frontiers of Italy, the sweeping away of the bankrupt remains of Christianity, and the abandonment of Imperialism and the African adventure. I will engage there are even Futurists in San Marino.

VII

I must confess to a smiling sympathy with this "Youngest Italy" party—if the little half-baked literary and artistic clique of Futurists can be called a party. I can understand the oppression of all the glorious Italian past, all those massive buildings and masterpieces, and stereotyped forms of thought. Like the son of a genius, modern Italy is cramped and overshadowed. Hence the rabid yearning for some new form of energising, this glorification of the moment and perpetual change. In a fantastic fury of iconoclasm the Futurists demand even the destruction of the creations of ancient genius that overhang their lives—they would make an art-pyre as fervently as Savonarola. Climbing the Clock Tower of St. Mark's Square, they threw down coloured handbills repudiating the vulgar voluptuous Venice of the tourist. "Hasten to fill its fetid little canals with the ruins of its tumbling and leprous palaces. Burn the gondolas, those see-saws for fools!" So far so good. But mark the beatific vision that is to replace this putrefying beauty. "Raise to the sky the rigid geometry of large metallic bridges, and manufactories with waving hair of smoke. Abolish everywhere the languishing curves of the old architectures." How characteristic of the Second Risorgimento! It must be by an oversight that the smoke is still permitted to be "waving." I imagine that the resurrection of the old Campanile of Venice must have been the last straw. For ten hundred and fourteen years this gloomy old tower had impended, and when it did at last fall of its own sheer decrepitude, lo! it must be stood up again, exact to the last massy inch, and even with the same inscription—Verbum caro factum est—on its bells. As if a bell could have no new message after a millennium! Let the historian, at any rate, mark that the Futurists did not rise till the Campanile was not allowed to fall. The police, taking the Futurists seriously, prohibit their meetings, which will end in making them take themselves seriously. But they are a useful counteractive to the Zealots of the Zona Monumentale, who, in their passion for the ruins of Rome, forget the claims of life. When the Present says, "I must live," the artist and the archæologist too often reply: "Je n'en vois pas la nécessité." Carducci even called on Fever to guard the Appian Way. But cities exist for citizens, not for spectators, and when the telephone bell of the Present rings, we should reply like the Italian waiter: "Pronto! Desidera?" We cannot do in Rome as the Romans do, for they have to live, not look at Ruins. And let us not expect the Romans to do in Rome as we do. If tramways must run along the Via Appia, at least Fever will retire before them. How long is it our duty to guard the ruins of the Past? Suppose the tombs and temples of the Appian Way should threaten to collapse altogether, have we to keep them in a state of artificial ruin? Augustus boasted that he found Rome brick and made it marble. If the industrial Risorgimento found Rome marble and made it brick, I suppose there are compensations for Augustus. Imperial Rome never thought of dedicating a slab of that marble to the nameless pauper dead, worn out in the obscure service of their country, as Industrial Rome has done in a touching inscription. And should Rome extend the tale of its bricks to house the homeless troglodytes who pig in the remains of that ancient marble, I will throw up my cap with the Futurists.

Pisa is to me a dream-city, but to the Pisans it is a centre of the glass industry and the cloth industry, with municipalised gas. They have done handsomely in leaving me my dream-city outside the town life. If topographical obstacles prevent other ancient cities from thus surviving themselves, let me be thankful for small mercies. There was one old inn at Perugia which had escaped the electric light and the pleasure-pilgrims, and where the porter peeled the potatoes, but as I sat this very Spring, dining in the quaint courtyard, lo! to my chagrin the light of modernity flooded it for the first time. But there chanced too that night so joyous a band of University students, on gymnastic business bent, the old courtyard resounded with such pranks, and songs, and cheers, such fulness of young new life, that I felt Perugia could not for ever live on griffins and Peruginos and Baglioni horrors. In that moment even the joyous madness of the Futurists appeared to me saner than the gloom of a Gissing concluding his Italian journeys "By the Ionian Sea" with the wish that he could live for ever in the Past, the Present and its interests blotted out.

It is a cheap æsthetic to retire to the Past, too blind to see beauty in the Present, and too anæmic to build it for the Future. But humanity is not a museum-curator; the cult of ancestors, once the backbone of Hindu-Aryan civilisation, survives only in China. The cult of descendants has taken its place, the Golden Age is before, not behind, and the debt we owe to our fathers we pay to our sons, not necessarily in the same currency. No doubt the Past is ivy-clad, the Present raw and the Future dim. But as happiness does not come from the search for happiness, neither does beauty come from the search for beauty. "Rather seek ye the Kingdom of God and all these things shall be added unto you."

VIII

So despite the slow black cigar, the ubiquitous farmacia and pasticceria, despite the pervasive petrifaction of past glory, I feel that a vigorous breeze of young thought moves through Italy, and that Mazzini is not entirely swallowed up in the belly of the Great Horse. "Il nullismo" was an Asti election-poster's shrewd summary of the programme of the Clerical Moderates, "lo star quieti—forma ipocrita di reazione." If Italy escapes the reaction involved in standing still, we may yet see a Third Risorgimento that will resurrect Mazzini. Even a Republican Congress has met freely, if with closed doors.

The popular Italian newspapers, like the windows of the bookshops, are far more intellectual than our own, and there is a healthy readiness to try social experiments under the popular referendum. If the nationalisation of the railways does not yet pay, on account of the multiplicity of officials, it has at least provided a more punctual service than of yore, and the third-class passenger is treated as a human being. A Jew as Premier and another as Syndic of Rome constitute an amende honorable for the Italy which established the Ghetto and, cramping a prolific race, produced in Venice the first specimen of the American sky-scraper. Capital punishment is abolished—the apostle, Beccaria, duly petrified at Milan— and despite the legend of the stiletto and the vendetta nobody demands its restoration. Phlebotomy prevails alarmingly, through the habit of using a knife as if it were the mere point of the fist, but it is a peaceable and polite people. The niente with which the veriest vagabond deprecates your thanks, the prego of the courtlier defence against gratitude, are the outer and audible sign of an inner gentleness. Irritatingly vague as regards time and space and money, a foe to definite agreements, a lover of the horizon and the buona mano, running restaurants with unpriced menus, and shops with unmarked goods, the Italian has always the saving grace of respect for things of the mind. Who ever saw a picture of Tennyson labelled—like the photographs of Carducci—"Mighty Master, Sublime Poet, Refulgent National Glory!" There are moods in which I could applaud even the stones.

But it is the revolt against Rome which stirs most furiously the intelligenza of Italy—as of all the Latin world. While in England the fight against Christianity is confined to a few guerilla papers in low esteem, in Italy it is a pitched battle. And the modern Anti-Pope is far more formidable to the Vatican than the mediæval, being a rival idea, not a rival man. The Vatican handicaps itself superfluously by sneering at the Risorgimento—though I am told its haughty refusal to recognise the Unity of Italy brings in shekels from Mexico, Colombia, and other strongholds of the spirit. Instead of joining in the recent Garibaldi jubilation, it asked through its organ whether the prosperity of the South had not been sacrificed to the interests of the North. And so far from making concessions to Modernism, it is sitting tighter than ever, issuing lamentable Syllabuses and Encyclicals, accumulating lists of suspects. It censured Minocchi for allegorising the first three chapters of Genesis, and excommunicated Murri for saying the Pope ought not to play at politics. The freethinkers complain uneasily of its aggressiveness, lamenting—with unconscious humour—that it makes propaganda! The army itself—ay, even the old Garibaldians—are not safe from its guiles! As if the Congregation of the Propaganda were of to-day!

But the confiscation of monasteries and churches to military and civil uses—to barracks, agricultural colleges, gymnasia, hospitals, what-not—the transformation of elaborate historic shrines into State Monuments, are indications of the ground lost to the Church in its own peculiar land. Strange was it to see squads of half-nude lads at gymnastics in the old Renaissance church of St. Mary Magdalen at Pesaro. Still more surprising to see a carpenter sawing away in the lofty, well-preserved Church of the Jesuits in Pavia, his wood stacked in the forsaken frescoed chapels, as in a strange return of Christendom to its origins, or an illustration of the new Logion, "Cleave the wood and ye shall find me." I bought coal at a still more decayed church, taking off my hat involuntarily.

The journalism of the street-nomenclature keeps pace with the progress of anti-Clericalism. "Sons of an age which you foresaw," the epitaph on Giordano Bruno's tomb assures that victim of the Inquisition, and many a Via or Piazza Giordano Bruno in places apparently remote from the currents of thought—Pesaro, Perugia, Foligno, Urbino on its isolated rock—testifies that even a tombstone may speak the truth, provided that it is only posthumous enough. Urbino, indeed, lonely rugged Urbino, is compelled to put up in the Church of S. Francesco the significant warning: "The law punishes disturbers of religious functions." And even more illuminating than the Giordano Bruno streets or the Giordano Bruno societies is the mushroom rapidity with which streets of Francesco Ferrer have sprung up all over Italy. Florence, with biting sarcasm, has made its Via Francesco Ferrer out of its Archbishop Street. Tiny San Gimignano of the many towers has inserted a tablet to Ferrer in the wall of an open loggia of a theatre, "in order that Thought should be fruitful and survive Death." . . . "Victim," it cries, "of the sacerdotal tyranny, inaugurating the not distant time when there shall be neither oppressed nor oppressors!"

Such millennial dreams in such mediæval cities prove that Mazzini was no sport of nature, but a true son of Italy; seed-plot of all the mysticisms and aspirations from St. Francis and Dante to Gioberti and David Lazzaretti.

IX

"ROME OF THE CÆSARS gave the Unity of Civilisation that force imposed on Europe. ROME OF THE POPES gave a Unity of Civilisation that Authority imposed on a great part of the human race. ROME OF THE PEOPLE will give, when you Italians are nobler than you are now, a Unity of civilisation accepted by the free consent of the nations for Humanity." In this magnificent synthesis, written in 1844, Mazzini proclaimed the mission of Rome to the world. His mental outlook was infinitely broader than Lazzaretti's, whose story is one of Life's many plagiarisms of the Palestinian original, complete even to martyrdom and an awaited Resurrection. Yet Mazzini shared with the peasant-prophet of Monte Amiata the assurance of a not distant Millennium to be inaugurated by his followers. 'Twas a blindness due to standing in his own white light. The simplest observation of the facts reveals that humanity is only at its alphabet, that we are living in the mere infancy of our planet's human history, in a Dark Age to which the millennial century will look back with incredulity, though a few Gissings will be anxious to live in it. The overwhelming majority of mankind to-day abides religiously in primitive autocosms, which have little resemblance to the cosmos as it is, and every variety of savagery from African cannibalism to European rubber-hunting and American negro-lynching is still in vogue. Half the land of the globe is still in undisturbed possession of our animal and insect inferiors. Canada, Australia and South America show a few human figures dotting the endless spaces—in Matto Grosso in Brazil a hundred thousand people occupy half a million square miles, in Patagonia each man may have a San Marino Republic to himself, in Alaska the population of a small English country town is spread over six hundred thousand square miles. Even the United States, which are sixty times as large as England, have only double its population. In Asia, the cradle of so-called civilisation, there are still nomad populations, and large tracts, as of Arabia and Tibet, have never been penetrated by the foot of an explorer. The bulk of Africa as of Russia—which is half Europe plus half Asia—is still given over to barbarism. One third of the whole human race is packed into China, a land where torture is still legal. Decidedly there is plenty of scope for "the mission of Rome," nor need the lover of the picturesque yet apprehend the monotony of the Millennium, as, girdled by stars and infinities, crossed by the tails of comets, rent and seamed by earthquakes, our planet continues its amazing adventure.

X

But if spiritual Imperialism has made little progress in the land of Mazzini, Rome does not lack its party of material Imperialism, ever egging on Italy to deeds of derringdo and to the fulfilment of its "manifest destiny" in Tripoli and Cyrenaica, whose arid deserts flow with milk and honey under the imperialistic pen. More in sorrow than in anger a writer in the Tribuna rebukes these hotheads as merely literary: conquistadors by fury of metaphor and prosopopœia, whereas real Imperialism—Francesco Coppola perceives with envy—is the irresistible instinct of an imperial race, whose expansion is unconscious or even anti-conscious, and which is rich in strong silent Kiplingesque heroes. Italy, a young nation, whose bones are not yet set, whose teeth are not yet sprouted, is falling, he laments, into the senile decay of socialistic rhetoric, and pacifical and humanitarian doctrine. The degenerate Italians have pulled up the railway lines to prevent the soldiers going off to the wars of expansion, have made a pother about "slavery," and have diverted the world by setting Civil and Military Governors cock-fighting before Commissions of Inquiry. "And then we call ourselves the heirs of Rome!"

But, prithee, good Signor Coppola, is it not enough to be the heirs of Italy? Is it not enough to inhabit the most beautiful land in the world, the richest-dyed in historic tints, the greatest breeder of great men, the garden of the arts, the temple of religion? Is there no such thing as Intensive Imperialism? To produce the highest life per square mile is surely infinitely more Imperial than to multiply Saharas of mediocrity, to follow Stock Exchange adventures in Abyssinia or to decimate the dervishes of Benadir? In the village of my home there is only a single shop, and it writes over its windows the proud legend: "To lead in every department is our ambition." But Italy, in open competition with the world, achieved the hegemony of civilisation in every department. What, beside this, is the military heirship of Rome?

And has England, the heir of Rome, so enviable a position? Far from it, alas! That unconscious or anti-conscious instinct of hers has landed her in the gravest situation of which consciousness was ever called upon to take stock. Holding nearly a quarter of the globe with a white population—outside these islands—of only ten millions; with a heterogeneous empire of Colonies, Crown Colonies, and Possessions, incapable of being brought under a single constitution or concept but that of force and tending to destroy such constitutions or ethical concepts as survive at home; with manifold subject races which she is too proud to make freemen of the Empire as Rome did; threatened and troubled in Europe by Germany, in Asia by India, in Africa by Egypt, in America by the States, in Australia by the Chinese and Japanese, the heir of Rome has seen her palmy days. The equilibrium is too unstable, and the part that came with the sword must perish with the sword. The Russo-Japanese war—the most important event in history since the fall of Rome—by destroying the glamour of the white man and showing that Christianity is not essential to success in slaughter—has shaken the foundations of her Indian and Egyptian Empire. The old apprehension that Russia was the menace to India is justifying itself, but it is Russia's weakness, not her strength, that has provided the menace. Britain's only future—no mean one indeed—lies in Canada, Australia and South Africa, and even here it is impossible for her to fill these great continents or sub-continents with the emigrating surplus of her decaying population, especially as her emigrants prefer the United States and are often excluded from her own Colonies. Her utmost hope is to keep these colonies British in constitution. They cannot be British in language—French Canada and Dutch South Africa forbid that; they cannot even be predominantly white, for North Australia is tropical and South Africa is not a white man's country but a whited sepulchre—an aristocracy exploiting the coloured labour it despises, a society poised perilously on its apex. How unwieldy such an Empire at its best beside the United States—one continuous area, one language, one constitution, and but for the hereditary curse of the negro problem, one free and equal brotherhood! But how cumbrous even the United States, only kept from breaking into separate States with separate dialects by the modern network of railways, telegraphs and newspapers! How much more favourable to intensive and exalted living, a compact little country like Italy, rich in all the essentials of greatness and happiness!

There was the epic sweep of a statesman in Chamberlain's vision of a true British Empire of federated freemen, but even with him Ireland was incongruously excluded, and the first fine prophetic rapture has chilled into commercialism under the British incapacity for imaginative synthesis. What was originally a consummation devoutly to be desired, and to be achieved only by sacrifice, is now presented as a policy that will pay, and even pay immediately. In the same breath we have an heroic trumpet-call and an estimate of the profits. It would, indeed, be strange if the good coincided so closely with the lucrative. But that is the trickery of all forms of Protectionist teaching, to dazzle with two alternative advantages simultaneously. Matilda is the heiress and Madge is beautiful—who would remain a bachelor when wealth and beauty are to be had for the asking?

Meantime the British Empire—so envied of the Italian Imperialist—is fast being conquered by Germany. For what is the mere absence of the German flag from our shores to our Germanisation in ideas, our transformation to German notions of conscription, our permeation by the doctrine of blood and iron? Already a pamphleteer calls for Lord Kitchener to "take away that bauble." Whether the new German province which is replacing the old land of freedom continues to be called British or not, is a secondary matter. The formal consummation of the conquest would even relieve England of nightmares of unmanly terror and mountains of taxation. I like to think that it was this German province, and not the England of Edward VII which, ensuing Peace before Honour, made a compact with the Power of Darkness and put back the clock of Europe. It could not surely be the old Colossus of Freedom, whose untold millions fertilise every soil on earth and whose ships outnumber overwhelmingly the united vessels of the world—it could not surely be "the England of our dreams" which grasped the hand of Russia and sent Finland and Persia to their dooms, and now trembles to stir a finger for any cause, however forlorn, and any ideal, however British.

Let the nation of Mazzini take heed before it loses its own soul to gain the world.

XI

No, it was a road of quagmires and quicksands into which Depretis and Crispi led Italy. The less she knows and thinks of Empire the better for her and for mankind. Latin self-consciousness, if it has its faults of rhetoric, at least enables Young Italy to see that Empire is not to be bought without an ethic of blood and iron, which is foreign to the home ethic. Imperialism is only for races strong or stupid enough to run a double standard. Italy has given her blood prodigally enough for the right to be Italy, but she has given it of her own free will. And volunteer armies, self-inspired, are the only sort that a true civilisation can tolerate. Despicable is the nation which sends mercenaries to do its fighting. The soldier like the priest—whose black robe makes the eternal ground-bass of Italy—is one of the unfortunate differentiations of humanity—a type that should never have been evolved. Specialisation—division of labour—is all very well when it gives us doctors, carpenters, engineers, lawyers, but every man must do his own praying and his own fighting. It is comforting to find Young Italy as set against soldiers as against priests.

Though United Italy has followed the normal path of nationhood—large army, large navy, large taxes, and my country right or wrong—there is still a saving remnant to justify Mazzini's prophetic faith in his people. And, indeed, one does not know where else to look for "the saviours of the world." The French—once the favourites in the rôle—have too hobbledehoyish a devotion to the sex-joke, the Germans are too tamed, the Americans too untamed, the Spaniards and Russians too brutalised by bull-fights or pogroms, the English too inconsequent. Possibly the New Zealanders may be the first to build the model State, possibly some people of Latin America, that land of sociology and secular education. But these are too remote for their results to leaven the Old World, and on the whole the Italians with their ancient civilisation and their renewed youth appear least unfitted to lead humanity onwards.

But the notion that the Millennium can be reached through a people with a mission, inspiring as it may yet prove to Italy, is a notion not without its limitations and drawbacks. It may easily degenerate into aggression as with the English or into inactive vanity as with the Jews.

True that the Jews—the original missionary people, in whom the families of the earth were to be blessed—have made the Millennium possible by their creation of the Bourse. In their Bank of Amsterdam, founded in 1609 by the refugees from Spain and Portugal, the infinitely complex system of international finance took its rise. Professor Sombart, the German professor of economics, credits the Jews with the entire invention of the apparatus of the Stock Exchange. And the Stock Exchange, in criss-crossing with threads of gold all these noisy nationalities, is turning war into a ridiculous destruction of one's own wealth. In the security necessary for international investments lies the prime hope of the world's peace. But it was an evolution whose form was not foreseen by the Hebrew prophets. Isaiah predicted that the peoples would beat their swords into ploughshares; he should have said shares in ploughs.

The success of Esperanto—likewise invented by a Jew—the spread of World Congresses, and even of World Sports, constitute, like Science and Art, a valuable corrective to the excesses of Nationalism, which has been sadly overdone in the reaction against the cosmopolitanism of the eighteenth century. Nationality, born as it is of historical, biological, and geographical differences, is a natural division of human groups, though a division devoid of the rigidity which patriots pretend, inasmuch as all nationalities are constantly intermarrying both physically and spiritually. But Nationalism—as Bernard Shaw has pointed out—is a disease. It is a morbid state due to defect of the organs of Nationality—to wit, territory and liberty. In health we are not conscious of our organs, it is dyspepsia not digestion that forces itself upon our attention. Nationalism rages in Poland or in Ireland as it once raged in Italy. But for Italy, which has won back territory and liberty, to continue at fever heat would be sickness, not health. Even too much self-admonition to do noble things for national reasons rather than for their own sakes is a morbid self-consciousness. To make history too consciously is to make histrionics.

XII

Neither the reformed Vatican of Gioberti nor the kingless Quirinal of Mazzini can provide the next phase in human evolution. Profound was that teaching of Jesus—you cannot put the new wine in the old bottles. It was not unnatural that an Italian should look to Rome for the third mission. Rome of the Cæsars, Rome of the Popes, Rome of the People! What a fascinating trinity! The conception of a Rome that having lived twice as a world-force must live again, seized Mazzini in his youth, enthralled his maturity, and was the key-note of his speech to the Roman Assembly in the brief hour of his glory. "After the Rome of conquering soldiers, after the Rome of the triumphant Word, the Rome of virtue and of example." And he repeated it, not yet disillusioned, in the very last years of his life; founding a journal to bring Roma del Popolo into being. And yet he had in the interim published "From the Council to God," that wonderful sketch of the new religion for which the world is thirsting, had added one of the grandest pages to the unclosed Bible of humanity. That page, indeed, is perhaps still theology rather than theonomy, still too saturated with the old optimism—humanity may have to part even with the assurance of personal immortality, and go, starred with sorrows and sacrifices, to its obscure doom. But this optimism, this burning conviction of a new heaven and a new earth, is the very stuff of which great religions are made, and Mazzini appears like the mighty prophet of the next phase of the spirit, the divine iconoclast whose fuller faith was to give the death-blow to the old theology. And the real miscarriage of Mazzini's career is not that he laboured for a Republic and begot a Monarchy, not that he sowed for a new social order and reaped stones and statues, but that he spent himself on the doubtful means instead of the certain end, on the creation of a United Italy which was to be the organon of the new spirit, but which is only a nation like the others. The great soul that might have kindled the new faith wore itself out in futile political conspiracies and vain exiles. How much grander, how much worthier of his genius and saintliness, might have been Mazzini's achievement, had he not been obsessed, like the Middle Ages, by the figment of the Holy Roman Empire; had he, instead of working through Nationalism, gone straight for the foundation of a new international Church. Moses, a greater than Mazzini, had failed in this dream of a prophet-people, nor is there any more assurance that the Law will go forth from Rome than from Zion. Mazzini himself protested against the notion that the French continued to be the chosen people; after 1814 their initiative ended, he urged. He protested, too, against the notion that an instrument created for one purpose can be used for another. Why, then, did he, whose organising powers might have found supreme scope in establishing the religion of the future, throw away his life for Nationalism? Valuable instrument of world-progress as nationality within sane limits may be, alluring as is the idea of working through one's own nation, perfecting a model people, in whom all the families of the earth shall be blessed, the instruments of the new order exist insufficiently in any one people, if indeed they exist sufficiently in the whole population of the globe. More insistently even than nationalities the world needs a new Church. By giving up to Italy what was meant for mankind, Mazzini missed creating what he prophesied, missed fulfilling and purging of its monastic and mediæval limitations that earlier prophecy of the twelfth-century Calabrian abbot whom Dante placed in Paradise. "The Kingdom of the Father has passed, the Kingdom of the Son is passing," taught Joachim of Flora. "The Third Kingdom will be the Kingdom of the Holy Ghost."

Israel Zangwill was born in London on 21st January 1864, to a family of Jewish immigrants from the Russian Empire. His father, Moses, was from modern-day Latvia, and his mother, Ellen Hannah Marks Zangwill, from modern-day Poland.

Zangwill was initially educated in Plymouth and Bristol. At age 9 he was enrolled into the Jews' Free School in Spitalfields in east London. The school was for the children of Jewish immigrants and added to its teaching, of both secular and religious matters, with supplies of clothing, food, and health care. Zangwill excelled here. He began to teach part-time at the school and eventually full time. Whilst teaching he also studied with the University of London and by 1884 had earned his BA with triple honours in philosophy, history, and the sciences.

He had already co-written a tale entitled 'The Premier and the Painter' when he resigned as a teacher owing to differences with the managers of the school. Zangwill now turned to journalism for his new career path, initiating Ariel, The London Puck, as well as working in various capacities for the London press.

His writing earned him the sobriquet "the Dickens of the Ghetto" primarily based on his much lauded novel 'Children of the Ghetto: A Study of a Peculiar People' in 1892 and its glimpse of the poverty-stricken life in London's Jewish quarter.

As a writer he was keen to reflect on his political and social outlooks. His simulation of Yiddish sentence structure in English aroused great interest. His mystery work, 'The Big Bow Mystery' (1892) was the first locked room mystery novel. Social satire flowed with 'The King of Schnorrers' (1894). A follow up to 'Children of the Ghetto' was 'Ghetto Tragedies' in 1894 and 'Dreamers of the Ghetto' in 1898 which included essays on famous Jews such as Baruch Spinoza, Heinrich Heine and Ferdinand Lassalle.

Zangwill was also involved with narrowly focused Jewish issues as an assimilationist, an early Zionist, and later a territorialist. In the early 1890s he had joined the Lovers of Zion movement in England. A few years later, in 1897, he took part in the "pilgrimage" of English Jews to Palestine. That same year he also joined Theodor Herzl (considered the father of modern political Zionism) in founding the World Zionist Organization and would take part in the first seven Zionist congresses. Zangwill was much admired as an orator and spoke movingly and eloquently on the issues he was passionate on.

In 1901 he had written that "Palestine is a country without a people; the Jews are a people without a country". On Herzl's visits to London, they worked closely together. In a debate at the Article Club in November 1901 however Zangwill was still mis-using the facts: "Palestine has but a small population of Arabs and fellahin and wandering, lawless, blackmailing Bedouin tribes." And made a direct plea to "restore the country without a people to the people without a country. For we have something to give as well as to get. We can sweep away the blackmailer—be he Pasha or Bedouin—we can make the wilderness blossom as the rose, and build up in the heart of the world a civilisation that may be a mediator and interpreter between the East and the West."

In 1902, Zangwill wrote that Palestine "remains at this moment an almost uninhabited, forsaken and ruined Turkish territory". But from this point on Zangwill began to see things differently which would, in 1905, result in his breakaway from Zionism.

Zangwill quit the established philosophy of Zionism when his plan for a homeland in Uganda was rejected and instead founded his own organisation; the Jewish Territorialist Organization. Its stated goal was to create a Jewish homeland in whatever territory in the world could be found for them. At that point in time suggestions were as varied as Canada, Australia, Mesopotamia, Argentina, Uganda and Cyrenaica.

Amongst the challenges in his life he found time to write poetry. He had translated a medieval Jewish poet in 1903 and his own volume 'Blind Children' in 1908 shows his promise in this new endeavour.

In 1908, Zangwill told a London court that he had been naive when he made his 1901 speech and had since recognised that the Arab population was twice that of the United States.

Zangwill was a supporter of both feminism and pacifism, but his greatest effect was as a writer who gained a wide audience with the idea of combining ethnicities into a single, American nation. The hero of 'The Melting Pot', proclaims: "America is God's Crucible, the great Melting-Pot where all the races of Europe are melting and reforming... Germans and Frenchmen, Irishmen and Englishmen, Jews and Russians – into the Crucible with you all! God is making the American."'

'The Melting Pot' made Zangwill's name as an admired playwright. The title itself was popularised as the phrase to use to describe American absorption of immigrants when it ran in the United States.

When the play opened in Washington D.C. on 5th October 1909, former President Theodore Roosevelt leaned over the edge of his box and shouted, "That's a great play, Mr. Zangwill, that's a great play." In a later letter in 1912 Roosevelt went further "That particular play I shall always count among the very strong and real influences upon my thought and my life."

'The Melting Pot' shone a spotlight on America's growth through the input of its new waves of immigrants. Zangwill was writing as "a Jew who no longer wanted to be a Jew. His real hope was for a world in which the entire lexicon of racial and religious difference is thrown away."

According to Ze'ev Jabotinsky, Zangwill told him in 1916 that, "If you wish to give a country to a people without a country, it is utter foolishness to allow it to be the country of two peoples. This can only cause trouble. The Jews will suffer and so will their neighbours. One of the two: a different place must be found either for the Jews or for their neighbours".

In 1917 he wrote "'Give the country without a people,' magnanimously pleaded Lord Shaftesbury, 'to the people without a country.' Alas, it was a misleading mistake. The country holds 600,000 Arabs."

With the end of World War I, and a more clearly defined idea of a Jewish settlement in Palestine, Zangwill once more returned to the Zionist effort and made efforts on behalf of the Balfour Declaration, proclaiming the right of a Jewish homeland in Palestine

In 1921 Zangwill wrote "If Lord Shaftesbury was literally inexact in describing Palestine as a country without a people, he was essentially correct, for there is no Arab people living in intimate fusion with the country, utilizing its resources and stamping it with a characteristic impress: there is at best an Arab encampment, the break-up of which would throw upon the Jews the actual manual labor of regeneration and prevent them from exploiting the fellahin, whose numbers and lower wages are moreover a considerable obstacle to the proposed immigration from Poland and other suffering centers".

Despite his advocacy on Jewish matters he would be disappointed to know that despite Israel now being established the quarrels of the Middle East continue to divide.

Israel Zangwill died on 1st August 1926 in Midhurst, West Sussex.

Israel Zangwill – A Concise Bibliography

The Bachelors' Club (1891)
The Old Maid's Club (1892)
Children of the Ghetto: A Study of a Peculiar People (1892)
Grandchildren of the Ghetto (1892)
The Big Bow Mystery (1892)
Merely Mary Ann (1893)
The King of Schnorrers (1894)
The Master (1895) (based on the life of George Wylie Hutchinson)
Without Prejudices (1896)
Dreamers of the Ghetto (1898)
Ghetto Tragedies, (1899)
"The Return to Palestine", New Liberal Review, (Dec. 1901)
Children of the Ghetto (1902)
"Providence, Palestine and the Rothschilds", The Speaker, vol. 4, no. 125 (22 February 1902)
Selected Religious Poems (1903) Translation of the Jewish Medieval Poet Solomon in Cabirol.
The Grey Wig: Stories and Novelettes (1903)
The Serio-Comic Governess (1904)
Merely Mary Ann (1904)
Ghetto Comedies, (1907)
Blind Children (1908) Poetry
The Melting Pot (1909)
Italian Fantasies (1910) Travel
Chosen Peoples, (1919)
The War For The World (1916)
The Principle of Nationalities (1917)
Chosen Peoples (1918)
Hands Off Russia: Speech by Mr. Israel Zangwill at the Albert Hall, February 8th, 1919. London: Workers' Socialist Federation, n.d. (1919)
The Voice of Jerusalem. (1921)

Filmography

Children of the Ghetto (1915, based on the play Children of the Ghetto)
The Melting Pot (1915, based on the play The Melting Pot)
Merely Mary Ann (1916, based on the play Merely Mary Ann)

The Moment Before (1916, based on the play The Moment of Death)
Mary Ann (1918, based on the play Merely Mary Ann)
Nurse Marjorie (1920, based on the play Nurse Marjorie)
Merely Mary Ann (1920, based on the play Merely Mary Ann)
The Bachelor's Club (1921, based on the novel We Moderns)
We Moderns (1925, based on the play We Moderns)
Too Much Money (1926, based on the play Too Much Money)
Perfect Crime (1928, based on the novel The Big Bow Mystery)
Merely Mary Ann (1931, based on the play Merely Mary Ann)
The Crime Doctor (1934, based on the novel The Big Bow Mystery)
The Verdict (1946, based on the novel The Big Bow Mystery)

www.ingramcontent.com/pod-product-compliance
Lightning Source LLC
Chambersburg PA
CBHW072112170626
46813CB00004B/1516